"Caitlín R. Kiernan is [barcode obscures text]

"Caitlín R. Kiernan draw[barcode obscures text] honorable of sources, a pas[barcode obscures text] for the act of writing."
—Peter Straub

"Caitlín R. Kiernan writes like a Gothic cathedral on fire."—Poppy Z. Brite

Murder of Angels

"I love a book like this that happily blends genres, highlighting the best from each, but delivering them in new configurations.... In *Murder of Angels*, the darkness is poetic, the fantasy is gritty, and the real-world sections are rooted in deep and true emotions." —Charles de Lint

"Stylish.... The novel's unusual blend of otherworldly and supernatural horror gives it a uniquely weird cast. Kiernan's true achievement, however, is the careful crafting of her mellifluous prose to sustain an intense atmosphere of dread. Dream and nightmare, hallucination and reality, private fantasy and objective experience all merge seamlessly, making this one of the more relentless horror reads of the year." — *Publishers Weekly*

"[Kiernan] paints her pages in feverish, chiaroscuro shades." —*Kirkus Reviews*

"Kiernan is devising something of an antifantasy—or perhaps a mythic antiheroic journey—with *Murder of Angels*.... [The novel] adds a heretofore missing cosmology and further depth to the now rapidly expanding Kiernanian universe while displaying pronounced authorial confidence." —Dark Echo

"A cutting-edge tale of worlds on the brink with an interesting champion . . . Caitlín R. Kiernan provides a dark, foreboding, and surreal novel." —*Midwest Book Review*

"There are a handful of writers whose technical and storytelling abilities attain such a lofty pinnacle that the end result leaves you in awe of their talent. Caitlín R. Kiernan is such a writer. She weaves multilayered and substantial narratives with threads of delicate, poetic prose. It is a pleasure to read her work, not just for the story but also for an appreciation of her writing skills." —Horror Reader

continued . . .

Daughter of Hounds

"The plot springs abundant surprises ... an effective mix of atmosphere and action." —*Publishers Weekly*

"Kiernan's storytelling is stellar, and the misunderstandings and lies of stories within the main story evoke a satisfying tension in the characters." —*Booklist*

"Caitlín R. Kiernan pays homage to Lovecraft in the very scary *Daughter of Hounds*. There is a sense of the foreboding Gothic that creeps out the audience, and the antagonists who set much of the pace seem freaky and deadly. Reminiscent of Poppy Z. Brite's darkest thrillers, Ms. Kiernan provides Goth horror fans with a suspense-laden tale that keeps readers' attention." —Alternate Worlds

"Kiernan's writing is what really makes the book special. . . .[It's] best described as 'What if John Bellairs had written *Pulp Fiction*?' Erudite discussions and entrancing descriptions intertwine with snappy, punchy dialogue that is as often as not laced with Tarantinoesque rhythmic profanity. All of this adds up to a pretty explosive and captivating read. . . . Highly recommended."
—The Green Man Review

Low Red Moon

"Kiernan only grows in versatility, and readers should continue to expect great things from her." —*Locus*

"The familiar caveat 'not for the faint of heart' is appropriate here—the novel is one of sustained dread punctuated by explosions of unmitigated terror."
—*Irish Literary Review*

"Effective evocations of the supernatural ... a memorable expansion of the author's unique fictional universe."
—*Publishers Weekly*

Threshold
Winner of the International Horror Guild Award for Best Novel

"*Threshold* is a bonfire proclaiming Caitlín R. Kiernan's elevated position in the annals of contemporary literature. It is an exceptional novel you mustn't miss. Highly recommended."
—*Cemetery Dance*

"A distinctively modern tale that invokes cosmic terrors redolent of past masters H. P. Lovecraft and Algernon Blackwood. . . . A finale that veers unexpectedly from a seemingly inevitable display of supernatural fireworks to a subtly disarming denouement only underscores the intelligence behind this carefully crafted tale of awe-inspired nightmare." —*Publishers Weekly*

"Kiernan's prose is tough and characterized by nightmarish description. Her brand of horror is subtle, the kind that is hidden in the earth's ancient strata and never stays where it can be clearly seen." —*Booklist*

"*Threshold* confirms Kiernan's reputation as one of dark fiction's premier stylists. Her poetic descriptions ring true and evoke a sense of cosmic dread to rival Lovecraft. Her writing envelopes the reader in a fog concealing barely glimpsed horrors that frighten all the more for being just out of sight." —*Gauntlet Magazine*

Praise for *Silk*
Winner of the International Horror Guild Award
for Best First Novel
Finalist for the Bram Stoker Award for Best First Novel
Nominated for the British Fantasy Award

"A wonderful book." —Peter Straub

"Caitlín R. Kiernan is the poet and bard of the wasted and the lost." —Neil Gaiman

"If the title alone doesn't make you want to read *Silk*, the first page will do the trick. Kiernan's work is populated with the physically freaky, mentally unstable, sexually marginalized characters who have caused so much consternation in conventional circles—but Caitlín R. Kiernan is headed in an entirely different direction. Her unfolding of strange events evokes not horror, but a far larger sense of awe." —Poppy Z. Brite

"[Kiernan] has what it takes to excite me as a reader. . . . I just loved this book and can't wait to see what she writes next." —Charles de Lint

NOVELS BY CAITLÍN R. KIERNAN

Silk
Threshold
Low Red Moon
Murder of Angels
Daughter of Hounds

Murder of Angels

CAITLÍN R. KIERNAN

A ROC BOOK

ROC
Published by New American Library, a division of
Penguin Group (USA) Inc., 375 Hudson Street,
New York, New York 10014, USA
Penguin Group (Canada), 90 Eglinton Avenue East, Suite 700, Toronto,
Ontario M4P 2Y3, Canada (a division of Pearson Penguin Canada Inc.)
Penguin Books Ltd., 80 Strand, London WC2R 0RL, England
Penguin Ireland, 25 St. Stephen's Green, Dublin 2,
Ireland (a division of Penguin Books Ltd.)
Penguin Group (Australia), 250 Camberwell Road, Camberwell, Victoria 3124,
Australia (a division of Pearson Australia Group Pty. Ltd.)
Penguin Books India Pvt. Ltd., 11 Community Centre, Panchsheel Park,
New Delhi - 110 017, India
Penguin Group (NZ), 67 Apollo Drive, Rosedale, North Shore 0632,
New Zealand (a division of Pearson New Zealand Ltd.)
Penguin Books (South Africa) (Pty.) Ltd., 24 Sturdee Avenue,
Rosebank, Johannesburg 2196, South Africa

Penguin Books Ltd., Registered Offices:
80 Strand, London WC2R 0RL, England

Published by Roc, an imprint of New American Library, a division of Penguin
Group (USA) Inc. Previously published in a Roc trade paperback edition.

First Roc Mass Market Printing, April 2008
10 9 8 7 6 5 4 3 2 1

For the Green Fairy, who surely got me through this one.

And for Spooky, who gets me through everything else.

In memory of Elizabeth Tillman Aldridge (1970–1995)

I will hold you to the light,
that's what forever means.

—Bruderschaft, "Forever"

AUTHOR'S NOTE

Upon completing Chapter Six of *Murder of Angels,* I realized that I'd unconsciously borrowed the refrain "These things happen" from Paul Thomas Anderson's superb (and notably Fortean) film *Magnolia* (1999). For the next several months I debated whether to leave it in or take it out. In the end, I made the decision to keep the phrase, but to acknowledge its origins. As with all things, serendipity is critical to writing, and it seemed to me as though omitting it would lessen the force and significance of the chapter. To varying degrees, this novel owes similar debts to Matthew Arnold, John Milton, Lewis Carroll, The Cure, Brian Eno, The Crüxshadows, L. Frank Baum, The Sisters of Mercy, Carl Jung, VNV Nation, Joseph Campbell, and the works of two Vietnamese poets, Van Hanh (d. 1018) and Vien Chieu (988–1050). Also, three songs played an important role in the conception of this novel: "All Along the Watchtower" and "Changing of the Guards" by Bob Dylan, and "The Queen and the Soldier" by Suzanne Vega.

Murder of Angels was begun in July 2000, then shelved while I wrote *Low Red Moon* and begun again in January 2003. Of all my novels, it was the most difficult, and I'd likely never have finished without the help of a number of people. My grateful thanks to Darren McKeeman and Sherilyn Connely, who were my eyes in San Francisco; to Kathryn Pollnac, who acted as tireless first reader, proofreader, and sounding board; to Rogue and Jessica, for being there when I needed to talk; to Jim and Jennifer, Byron, Sissy and Kat, Jean-Paul, Jada and Katharine, for their friendship; to Derek cf. Pegritz and Nyarlathotep: The Crawling Chaos, for sharing their music with my writing; to Poppy Z. Brite, Neil Gaiman, and Peter Straub, for listening; to Jack Morgan, who read an early draft and offered many helpful comments; to William K. Schafer for Subterranean Press, where books are still books; to my agents, Merrilee Heifetz and Julien Thuan, and my editor, John Morgan; to everyone on the phorum (my social life), all those who have followed the writing of this book via my blog, and to all the other "greys" at Nebari.net. This novel was written on a Macintosh iBook.

The abyss becomes me, I wear this chaos well . . .

> —VNV Nation, "Genesis" (2002)

Dark revolving in silent activity:
Unseen in tormenting passions;
An activity unknown and horrible;
A self-contemplating shadow,
In enormous labours occupied.

—William Blake, *The Book of Urizen* (1794)

PROLOGUE

The Beginning of the End of Time

1

On past the scurry and endless, breaking dreams of Manhattan, north and east past all the sour rivers and the industrial tatters of Greenwich and Bridgeport, and as the miles and towns slip by, there are still hints of the world before. Dulled and brittle hints left unshattered by The Fall, The Fall before The Fall, but *he* can see them, sure, the tall, pale man that the dark children haven't found a name for, or they know all his names but are too afraid to ever say them aloud. Past New Haven, New London, following the Connecticut coastline because the sight of the ocean is still a small comfort to him, something so vast and alive out there, and if it isn't pure at least it hasn't rotted like the damned and zombified cities, like the faces of the people trapped and not-quite-dying inside their casket walls.

And some nights, the children find him in smoky, music-bruised clubs, or cemeteries, or walking alone on rocky beaches. He leaves them rumors strewn like stale bread crumbs, and the ones who need to hear what he has to say can find him, and all the others don't really matter, anyway. The others are content with their lies or half-truths, and their eyes give them away every time, the fact of their fear and their contentment with shadows. The things that he says, his shining steel and red molten words, his face, the sound of his breath, all of it only an intrusion into the faithless peace they've fashioned from shreds of night and mystery.

Yesterday, Mystic, with all its high, maritime streets and tourist-haunted seaport scenery, and hardly anything or anyone waiting for him there; suspicious glances from policemen and shopkeepers, old women selling shells and wooden sailing ships built inside tiny bottles, and so he slipped away sometime after midnight. Only a few miles more to Stonington Village, long and time-crooked finger of land pointing towards a cold Atlantic heart, and it's a better place for him to be. He knows that they will find him here, a handful or less, perhaps, but the ones who do come will sit still and listen.

So another night and the big, ugly Lincoln Continental that he's driven since Chicago is parked in the sand and gravel cul-de-sac at the end of Water Street. The old, old town crouched sleepy at his back, aged and unwary town, colonial walls and whitewashed fences, and there's a granite marker at the water's edge to commemorate an unredeemable summer day in 1814 when the HMS *Ramillies* burned and sank somewhere just offshore and the townspeople held back a British landing party.

"Did you hear that?" the nervous woman who calls herself Archer Day whispers in his ear, and he waits a moment before answering her, strains to hear whatever might be hiding behind or beneath the waves lapping against the worn schist boulders and seaweed concrete. Foghorns calling out to one another across the sound and the rheumy chug of a fishing boat traversing the harbor, the chill wind and nothing else.

"You're just scaring yourself again," he says finally, and she nods her head slowly, because she wants to believe him, every single word he says, because she *always* wants to believe him. "It's nothing but the sea," he says.

"I thought it was music," she whispers. "I thought I heard music in the sky."

And so he looks up then, because it will make her feel better if he does, stares defiantly up at the July moon one night past full, baleful white-orange eye to make the water shimmer or shiver, the cold and pinprick stars, and he takes a deep breath, filling his lungs with the moist and salty night.

"No, I don't hear it."

"It sounded almost like trumpets," Archer Day says, and he turns and looks at her, her anxious brown eyes gone black in the night, the moonlight caught in her ginger hair that's grown so long and shaggy, tangled by the breeze. He brushes a hand gently across her cheek and then kisses her on the forehead.

"Not yet," he says. "You know how it will be."

"I know what you tell me," and she isn't looking at him anymore, is staring out to sea instead, watching a buoy bobbing up and down in the waves, the distant, vigilant beams of the lighthouses far out on Lords Point and Fishers Island. Her eyes almost as secret as his soul, and he wants to hold her. Would hold her close to him and tell her not to be afraid, if he remembered how. If he didn't know all the things she knows and tenfold more, so he only brushes the windblown hair away from her face instead.

"She was in my dreams again last night," she says. "She said something about the sky—"

"It's getting late," he tells her, as if he hasn't heard, and glances back towards the town. "They'll be waiting. Some of them will have come a long way."

"Yeah. They're always waiting," Archer whispers, and she pulls away from him and walks back to the car without saying another word, just her boots crunching gravel and broken bits of mussel shell. He watches her go, waits until she's safe inside the Lincoln and he can hear music blaring from the tape deck before he turns to look out across the sound again. The deep and deathless sea to give him courage, to keep him moving night after inevitable night, but the moon's out there, too. A moon that shines the fevery color of an infection, and the ocean not so very vast, not so eternal, that the moon doesn't drag it back and forth at will, and "tide" is just another pretty word for coercion, after all, another unnecessary reminder that gravity always wins.

But there are no trumpets in the sky, and the only wings are the wings of hungry night birds skimming low above the waves.

2

This plot of land a boneyard since sometime in 1849, Stonington Cemetery secure behind thick rock and mortar walls, behind wrought-iron pickets crowned with rusted fleur-de-lis. Tidy city of the dead, garden of the dead, marble headstone rows and manicured lawns, ancient maples and the sugar scent of rhododendrons, the great drooping hemlocks, and this is where they've come to wait for him. And ask any one of them why here, why *this* place in particular, and they would only shrug or look anxiously at the toes of their shoes. Where else would he ever find them? Where else would he ever know to look? Where else would ever be *right*?

They've all heard things, or read cryptic posts to Internet newsgroups, or dreamed these gray memorials carved with dates and names and Bible passages. All these and none of the above, if the question were ever asked aloud. But it only matters that they've come, all of them, a dozen if there were just one more, and they sit together and apart, uneasy in one another's company, suspicious and resentful and confused, because they all thought for certain they would be the *only* one, his message meant for them and them alone. Most have met before tonight, have shared sex or pain or hesitant snatches of conversation, a cigarette or suicidal love notes, stingy or extravagant fragments of themselves, even if they pretend now that they're strangers. Velvet and torn fishnet, fingernails polished black or wounded shades of red, gaudy rings like vampire bats and ankhs and the delicate skulls of birds cast in silver.

"Well, I don't think he's coming," a girl in a raveling summer sweater and long skirt says, thrift-store crinoline skirt that rustles like dead leaves every time she moves. "I don't think *anyone's* coming."

"You don't know that," someone else replies, a boy hiding himself in shadows and long bangs that cover the left side of his face like a caul. "You *can't* know that," and he's starting to sound angry or scared or something that's just a little bit of both.

"It's a *joke*," the pale boy sitting at his feet says. "Like Linus Van Pelt and the Great fucking Pumpkin," and then no one says anything because now they've all heard the low, mechanical-animal growl of a car turning off Elm Road, tires rolling slowly through the open cemetery gates, and no one says another word. Eleven faces filled suddenly with expectation and dread, with furious desperation, and even breathing might be too much, a single sigh to shatter this crystal moment and wake whichever one is having this dream. This exquisite nightmare, Hell and Heaven caught in the twin will-o'-the-wisp brilliance of those headlights moving towards them between the trees and graves, parting the darkness as they come.

"Jesus," the girl in the sweater whispers, and all of them stand very still and wait for the car. It might only be the caretaker, or the cops, or a high school couple looking for someplace dark to make out.

"It's still not too late, is it? Not too late to run, I mean?" a girl in a black Rasputina T-shirt asks apprehensively, hopefully, asking loudly enough that they can all hear her. But it is, and she knows it. They all know it. It's been too late for a long, long time, all their short lives or the moment their parents met, everything forever leading inescapably to *now*. And in a few more seconds the purple and rust-colored Lincoln comes to a stop and the driver's-side door opens. The motor idling like a dying clockwork tiger and all the summer garden graveyard smells suddenly shoved aside to make room for its hot metal stink, burning oil and exhaust fumes. Their eyes shielded against the blinding headlights, twenty-two eyes squinting painfully through the glare. And when the tall man finally climbs out and stands beside his noisy car, he's nothing that any of them expected. Something more and less, expectation turned cruelly back upon itself, and they have never imagined such an ordinary monster.

"Which of you is Theda?" he asks, and the girl in the raveling sweater takes one small step towards him.

"Then you called me," he says to her.

A restless murmur trickles through the group, then bright flecks of fear and jealousy like a sparking electrical current, and for a moment none of them notices the milk-skinned woman who has slipped out of the passenger side of the car and stands there watching him watching them all.

"She's the one," the woman says. "*She* has the mark," but the tall man doesn't look at her, doesn't take his eyes off the girl named Theda.

"I didn't think you would come," she says, starting to cry and speaking so quietly that he has to move nearer to hear what she's saying. "I swear to God, I thought it was all bullshit. I *never* thought you would really ever come."

"I never thought we'd find you," he replies, his voice like a drowning man washed unexpectedly ashore, and his fingertips gently touch the space between her eyebrows, linger there a moment as though her skin were Braille-dimpled pages.

"No," the woman from the car says impatiently. "Not there. Look at her *wrists*," and Theda is already pushing up the sleeves of her baggy sweater, raising both her arms so he can see the symbols carved into her flesh, the small, irregular crosses of pink-white scar tissue drawn against a pulsing canvas of veins and arteries.

"The dreams—" she whispers, but he shakes his head and the expression on his face is more than enough to silence her.

"I know. I've seen it all. I've seen everything," he says, and that only makes her cry harder. "I stood at the edge of the pit and she brought me back. She led me across the outskirts of Hell, through the fire and back up to the World again."

Theda's eyes are bright and wide, irises the color of unfinished emeralds to glimmer wet in the headlights, and she's begun to tremble now; her hands so small in his, his calloused thumbs pressed tightly against her scars, the razor-blade tattoos, and "She was the most . . . the most beautiful thing . . ." he says, but then she's sobbing too hard to say anything more. He smiles down at her, the faintest, guarded smile that is neither kind nor cruel.

"Hush," he says. "She doesn't want us to cry. She hasn't ever wanted us to cry."

"Well, what *does* she want, then?" a boy in silver-gray velvet and lips like city smog asks, and the man turns and stares at him for a moment without saying anything.

"You just come across too goddamn much like a preacher to me, that's all," the boy mumbles, trying hard to sound like no one who's ever needed a savior, someone who's been kicked around enough he doesn't dare rely on dreams or visions or pretty stories, nothing out there but himself so he'll never be hurt or disappointed again. "You sound like you're selling something," he says, but takes a cautious step or two backwards, towards the sheltering night waiting just beyond the reach of the Lincoln's headlights.

And Theda and all the others hold their breath when the tall man raises his right hand, opens it so they can see the soft place where his palm should be, the impossible gyre of colors they've never seen before, the colors there are not even names for. It's Archer's trick, of course, Archer's magic flowing through him, but it's also what he needs them to see.

"The only part of the treasure left was a stone," he says, his thunder-and-firestorm voice spilling out loud across the cemetery, words he wishes were true seeping out of him hot and wild, and now the woman from the car is standing next to the man, an arm around his waist and one hand resting on the top of Theda's head. Her white fingers twine themselves in the girl's jet-black hair and the man hasn't stopped talking, hasn't taken his eyes off the boy in smoggy lipstick.

"A stone full of God's most beautiful and most terrible secrets. And they knew that they had been wrong and they couldn't hide themselves or the stone forever. So they found a way to take it apart and put it back together again, *inside* themselves. But that still wasn't enough, was it, child? Just ask Theda here. She's *seen* them, His jackals, waiting for us in the dead of night, waiting in the shadows behind shadows."

The old wounds on Theda's wrists have begun to bleed again, and the warm blood drips unnoticed onto the grass at her feet.

"I am her fist and her tongue, child. She left me alive to remember what I've seen, to find all the whining, ungrateful little shits like you while there's still time."

From the center of his palm, dead-heart center of the kaleidoscope gyre, one shining thread and the small white spider spinning silk from light and hurt and the tinfoil shreds of the man's discarded soul. They all see it, this final proof against the rehearsed sneers and skepticism of their fallen, unbelieving age. The boy sinks to his knees, and in another moment the only thing left in the whole, wide world is the man's booming voice, the swirl of color in his hand, the white spider dangling above Theda's upturned face. And in the long, cicada-whisper hours left before dawn, he weaves them charms against the hungry day.

3

And three thousand miles away, the girl named Niki opens her eyes on darkness, blinking back shreds of nightmare mist, gradually remembering that there's no one in the bed but her, slowly remembering why. She lies very still and stares at the high bedroom ceiling, letting what's left of the dream seep through her like rainwater percolating down and down and down through pure and cleansing sands, settling finally in forgetful, merciful aquifers; "Daria?" she whispers once, even though she knows that no one will answer.

She won't be home for another two weeks, Niki. You know that. You know that perfectly well.

In the dream, she was still so young and there was so much time that had yet to be lost to her, and Niki lay in the big bed in Spyder Baxter's room and stared at the pale thing dangling, head down, from the ceiling.

Way back there, way back *then,* Niki whispers in her lover's ear, *I want you to get help. I want you to tell your doctor what you told me. I want you to tell her about the body you hid in the fucking basement.*

Time to burn, to toss aside like candy-wrapper discards, time to slip between her fingers while she looked the other way. And Spyder Baxter, sad and crazy, fucked-up *Lila* Baxter with her bleached white hair and blue eyes and the cross carved into her forehead like damnation's mark. Spyder to stand for all the past, every single failure, every single sacrifice, Spyder to take her sins away and drown in them.

"Spyder?" Niki whispers, and the dark room in the big house on Steiner Street whispers nothing much back. Nothing much at all. A passing car. Muted city sounds leaking in. The clock on the bedside table clicking to itself like an insect metronome.

The alarm clock is digital, Niki thinks, and the ticking abruptly stops. She shuts her eyes again, trying to remember the things her psychologist has taught her, all the telltale differences between dreams and reality, but all she can hear is Spyder and the sound of drywall straining beneath the weight of the pale, dangling thing, the thing that Spyder *became.*

To save you, she said. *To save you all.*

The chrysalis, its shining skin like a clot of iridescent cream, a whiteness washed with shifting, indecisive colors. The shape beneath its skin, familiar and entirely alien, breathing in and out, in and out, and Spyder mumbles something in her ear that Niki doesn't understand.

"What?" she asks. "What did you say?" but the chrysalis only swings and creaks and breathes.

Niki opens her eyes again and not enough time has passed that the room is any lighter, still hours until dawn, sunrise that really makes no difference because her demons have never been shy about the sun. The clock is ticking again, and this time she doesn't argue with it. There's another sound, too, like thunder far off, or waves against a rocky beach, and she sits up and listens.

"Schizophrenia *can* be managed," her psychologist says, whispering from some secret nook or shadow. "You can live a normal life, Niki, if you'll *let* me help you."

"You don't know," Spyder says, way back then, and the ticking clock, the thunder and the waves; Niki tries to hear her memories of Dr. Dalby's voice instead, but he's the least substantial phantom in the room.

"I know *now*," she whispers. "I do, Spyder. I know now."

Niki pushes back the blanket, the sheets, exposing her bare legs, and ten years earlier, she does the same thing, in that other bed, that other room. The chrysalis swings almost imperceptibly from its fleshy vinculum, making the ceiling sag with its weight. She knows that Daria's somewhere in the house looking for her, not this house now, but that house then, the tumbledown house at the dead end of Cullom Street. Not San Francisco, but Birmingham, and in another moment the bedroom door will open and Daria will try to save her again.

"You can't help me," Spyder mumbles in her ear. "Not here. Not now."

"That these . . . these *events* you've described left such a deep and horrifying impression upon you is completely understandable, Niki. You were only a kid, weren't you? All those things you *thought* you saw—"

"The whole world," Spyder says, "the entire fucking *universe,* is held together with strings. I read that in a physics book. Strings in space and time, Niki, strings of energy and matter, light and darkness. And what I need to know, what I have to learn, is who the hell's *pulling* those strings."

In a moment, the chrysalis, ripe and swollen, will begin to split and spill its wriggling contents across the floor.

"Let me go," Niki says, her voice sounding very loud in the empty bedroom in the big house that Daria Parker bought for her. "Let me forget and just be me again."

"You will not believe the things that you will see," Spyder murmurs. "The things I will show you."

"I believe it already," she replies, not taking her eyes off the chrysalis, Spyder wrapped up tight in that impossible, transforming second skin, and Daria's calling Niki's name now.

Spyder kisses her cheek, and then she smiles her lost and secret smile, that smile that Niki fell in love with once upon a time. "The things that pull the strings," she says. "You'll see."

"I don't want to see any more," Niki replies. "I've seen enough already."

"We've barely scratched the surface," Dr. Dalby assures her from the chair behind his wide desk.

"I've seen all I ever *want* to see."

And then the bedroom door opens, here, not there, so it isn't Daria, her hands and face streaked with burns from the air clogged with acid threads. Just Marvin in his purple paisley bathrobe, Marvin Gale who watches over her because Daria can't afford real angels.

"Are you okay, Niki?" he asks. "I thought I heard you talking—"

"Just a nightmare," she answers quickly, and she knows the look on his face, the doubtful scowl, even though it's too dark to see his eyes.

"You sure about that?"

"A bad dream," she says. "That's all. I'm fine."

"Yeah, all right. You need anything before I go back to bed?" and she shakes her head no. "I'm fine," she says again.

"You're sure about that?"

"*Yes,* Marvin," and he shrugs and rubs at his eyes with hands the color of roasted coffee beans. His black skin so dark that he's little more than a silhouette against the light from the hall, and somehow his always being there for her only makes Niki miss Daria that much more.

"I'm going back to sleep," Niki says and lies down.

"Sounds like a good idea," Marvin mutters and stops rubbing his eyes. "You call me if you need me," and then he's gone. And she's alone again. Alone *still.*

Listening to the thunder.

And the waves.

The ticking clock and the ceiling beginning to crack under the weight of the twitching, dangling thing.

Her heart and an airplane passing overhead.

It's almost daybreak before she's finally asleep again, and if there are dreams this time, she won't remember them.

PART ONE

Disintegration

*Buy the sky and sell the sky and lift your arms up to the sky
And ask the sky and ask the sky . . .*

—R.E.M., "Fall on Me" (1986)

Usually, in mythology, the hero wins his battle against the monster. But there are other hero myths in which the hero gives in to the monster. A familiar type is that of Jonah and the whale, in which the hero is swallowed by a sea monster that carries him on a night sea journey from west to east, thus symbolizing the supposed transit of the sun from sunset to dawn. The hero goes into darkness, which represents a kind of death.

—Joseph L. Henderson, "Ancient Myths
and Modern Man" (1968)

CHAPTER ONE

Dark in Day

"**W**ell, then what *were* you doing, Marvin?" Daria Parker asks and jabs him in the chest with an index finger. "I mean, Christ, what the fuck am I paying you for? You're supposed to *watch* her."

"I have to sleep sometime," he says, and that makes her want to hit him, slap his face and never mind how hard it will be to get a replacement, someone else to keep an eye on Niki for what Daria can afford to pay. But his exhausted, bloodshot eyes and the stubble on his gaunt cheeks are enough to stop her.

"Can you get me a fucking drink? Can you at *least* do that much for me?" she growls, tamed and broken lion growl, burying the violence deep in words and not taking her eyes off Niki curled up small and naked on their bed, fetal Niki with her bandaged hand asleep beneath a framed print of John Everett Millais' *Ophelia*. Beautiful, lost Ophelia, floating along with her bouquet and her face turned towards unmerciful Heaven. Her skirts filled with air and buoying her up, but she'll sink soon enough, the very next moment after the artist is done with her. And right now irony is the last thing Daria needs.

"It's not even ten thirty," Marvin says. "How about I get you some coffee, instead? Or there's juice—"

"Marvin, are you my goddamn mother now? Did I fucking *ask* you for coffee or juice? *Please,* okay, just get me the damn drink?"

The little room is bright, morning sun off eggshell walls, a blue vase of Peruvian lilies on the table beside the bed. Daria turns away from Niki and Ophelia and stares out the second-story window of her big, apricot and cream–colored Victorian house at the busy morning traffic down on Steiner Street and the neatly mown green swatch of Alamo Square laid out beyond. This too-big house she bought for her and Niki right after *Skin Like Glass* went platinum and *Rolling Stone* was calling her the next Patti Smith. The next Angry Voice of Misunderstood Women Everywhere, and then the world spins three hundred sixty degrees, and she imagines someone else out there somewhere, staring across the square at this bedroom window, at *her,* so scared and angry and completely insignificant. Forget the rock-star shtick and she's nobody at all, a frightened, hungover refugee from another world, the girl who fell to earth or San Francisco, and yesterday her lover tried to kill herself with a handful of pills.

"I'm sorry, Marvin," she says, blinking at the sunlight, blinking because she's trying not to cry. "I think my brain's still back in Little Rock," but Marvin's gone to get her drink, or maybe he's finally had enough of this shit and walked out on them, halfway back to anywhere sane by now.

"Fuck me," she whispers and sits down on the edge of the bed. There's still a pack of cigarettes in the inside pocket of her leather jacket, the pack she bought from a newsstand at the airport, and she takes one out and lights it, blowing the smoke away from Niki.

"If the band doesn't string me up for this one, baby, the promoters will, or Jarod or the fucking label. I already told Alex he might as well get in line with the rest," she says and touches Niki's forehead with the calloused fingertips of her right hand, brushes tangled black hair from Niki's face, and she makes a tiny, uneasy sound in her sleep. Her almond skin feels cool as stone, as smooth and incomprehensible as marble. And at this moment, in this clean Pacific light, she might almost be the same girl that Daria Parker saw for the first time nearly ten years ago, ten years plus a lifetime or two; the same rumpled, carelessly beautiful Vietnamese girl on the run from herself and New Orleans and a head full of ghosts, stranded and alone in downtown Birmingham.

Daria glances back up at Ophelia hanging on the wall, and Jesus, she never liked that painting to begin with. Despair like something sacred, something virtuous.

"You're scaring the holy shit out of me, Niki. Do you know that? I can't keep doing this," and then Marvin's back with her drink, Bombay and tonic and fresh lime in a tall, plastic tumbler, ice cubes that are round, and she thanks him for it. Daria raises the glass to her lips, and it's half empty when she sets it down on the table next to the blue vase, the cold gin warm and familiar in her belly, burning its way quickly towards her dizzy head, and she tries not to notice that Marvin's staring at her.

"You still haven't told me what happened," she says to him, and Marvin shakes his head, sits down on the hardwood floor beneath the window, makes a steeple with his fingers and thumbs and rests his chin on it.

"What makes you think I know? I woke up yesterday morning and she was gone."

"And she didn't say anything or do anything Friday night?" Daria asks, then takes another long drag from her cigarette and reaches for the rest of her drink.

"I ordered take-out. We watched a movie, and then she listened to some old CDs until she took her meds and got sleepy and went upstairs to bed."

Daria exhales, and the smoke hangs thick and gray in the space between them. "And that's all?" she asks. "You're not leaving anything out?" and Marvin glares at her and frowns.

"It was Thai take-out," he says.

"Fuck you, Marvin," and Daria closes her eyes and rubs hard at her left temple.

"You're doing it again."

"Doing what? What is *it* that I'm doing again?"

He watches her silently for a moment, the stern and gentle press of his gaze against her tender, jet-lagged skin and the feather-iron weight of his silence. She knows he's choosing his words more carefully now, and Daria lets herself wish she'd stayed in Little Rock. She can feel guilty about it later, when the headache's gone and Marvin's gone.

"You know what I mean," he says. "Thinking maybe if you just try hard enough you can be Sherlock Holmes and Sigmund Freud and Florence Nightingale all rolled into one."

"Is that what you think I'm doing?" she whispers and opens her eyes, is dimly disappointed that nothing's changed, still the same bright San Francisco morning filling up the bedroom and wounded, sleeping Niki still right there in front of her. The room smells like cigarette smoke and clean linen, no trace whatsoever of the lilies on the table and she wonders if they even have a scent.

"Yeah. Something like that."

"I'm losing her, Marvin. She's slipping away from me a little bit at a time, and sooner or later she's gonna get it right. Maybe next time, or maybe the time after that—"

"Unless she doesn't really want to die," Marvin says and produces a pale green ceramic ashtray, seemingly out of thin air, and hands it to Daria. "It's not that hard to die. And we both know Niki's not a stupid lady."

Daria taps her cigarette once against the rim of the ashtray and doesn't look at Marvin. Doesn't look at anything but the tiny heap of powder-gray ash marring the clean ashtray, the glazed finish, and she knows that Marvin washed it by hand. He washes and dries everything by hand because he says that dishwashers are too rough on dishes.

"You might as well know I never bought into that whole 'cry for help' thing," she says. "If somebody needs my help, if *Niki* needs my help, she knows how to ask for it without putting me through this shit."

Marvin nods his head once, noncommittal nod, and then he goes to the bedroom window, stands there with his back to her and Niki, staring down at the traffic on Alamo Square. Daria crushes the butt of her cigarette out in the ashtray and sets it on the table.

"You think I don't know how much Niki needs me here?" she asks, but he doesn't answer, and Daria sighs loudly and reaches for her pack of cigarettes, her old Zippo lighter.

"You're smoking too much again," he says very quietly.

"Yeah? Well, it's a goddamn miracle I'm not doing a hell of a lot worse than that," and Daria has to flick her thumb across the striker wheel four times before the Zippo gives up an unsteady inch of blue-orange flame.

"She was playing your music," Marvin says. "Friday night, before she went up to bed. She plays your music all the time these days. I finally had to ask her to use the headphones because she'd put one song on repeat and it was driving me crazy."

The Zippo's flame sputters and dies before Daria can light the cigarette hanging limply from her lips. She curses and flips the cover shut again, turns to face Marvin and the Sunday morning sunshine streaming in around him.

"Look, I don't need you laying some kind of fucking guilt trip on me, okay? Jesus," and she takes the cigarette from her mouth and puts it back in the pack.

"You said you wanted to know everything."

"Then why didn't you tell me before now? If you thought it was important that she was listening to my music Friday night, why didn't you tell me that to begin with?"

"Take her with you, Dar," Marvin says, and he glances at Niki; she's rolled over onto her left side now, and her face is buried deep in the white cotton folds of sheets and pillowcases. "That's what she needs. Just to be near you for a little while. Just a few days—"

"No," and something in the way she says it, spitting that one word out at him, so emphatic, so final, something cold and ugly in her voice—but nothing she can take back, no matter how it makes her feel. "You weren't with us when she freaked out on me in Boston. I can't work and watch after her at the same time."

Marvin rubs nervously at his stubbly chin, his dark cheeks specked with darker whiskers when he's never anything but clean shaven.

"Then take me with you, too," he says. "*I'll* watch her when you can't."

"I said *no,* Marvin, so don't ask again. Does she even look like she's in any shape to be on the road?" and Daria pauses, knows he isn't going to answer her, but leaves space for an answer anyway. "Now, if you don't think you can do your job, I can look for someone else."

"I'm *trying* to do my job," he says, the angry smudge at the edges of his voice. "I'm trying to keep her alive."

"Well, you sure could've fooled me."

And then neither of them says anything else, only one or two heated words away from something that can't be taken back, apologized for, excused. Daria sits in the chair by the bed, running strong fingers through her spiky blond hair, staring at Niki's bare shoulders as though there might be answers printed on her skin like tattoos or scars. The answers she needs to hold the world together around her, around them both, some secret talisman or incantation against all her fears and failures.

She was playing your music. She plays your music all the time these days.

"Will you leave us alone for a while?" Daria says. "I need to get my head together, that's all. I have to figure out what the hell I'm going to do next."

"Yeah, Dar, sure," he replies, the reluctance plain to hear, but at least he doesn't sound pissed off anymore. "If you need me, I'll be in the kitchen."

"And take this damned thing with you," and she reaches into her jacket, removes her cell phone from a pocket and hands it to Marvin. "If anyone calls, *especially* that prick—"

"You're busy."

"Whatever. You can tell them I'm off screwing a herd of sheep for all I care."

Marvin turns the phone over in his hand a couple of times, as if preparing to pass judgment on its molded plastic faceplate, plastic the indecent color of ripe cranberries. "It does have an off switch, you know?" he says and points to a tiny black button on one side.

"Then turn it off and take it with you."

Marvin nods his head and walks past her to the bedroom door, has already started pulling it shut behind him when he stops and looks back at Daria.

"Hey. Who was Spider?" he asks her, and she stares at him like someone struck dumb, struck stupid, someone too far gone to ever be surprised by anything ever again but this one thing.

"What?"

"*Spider.* Last night, at the hospital, when Niki started coming back around, she asked for someone named Spider a couple of times. I'd almost forgotten—"

"I don't know," Daria lies, answering the question much too quickly, and she can see from his expression, the mix of confusion and concern, that Marvin knows perfectly well that she's lying.

"I'm sorry," he says. "I thought it might be important," and he closes the door, leaving Daria Parker alone with Niki and Ophelia and the sun-bright walls.

"She wrote this song when we lived in Boulder," Niki said, and Marvin frowned at her, at Niki Ky sitting in the center of about a hundred jewel cases, the scatter of CDs like tiny space-age Frisbees. Niki in a gray-green cardigan at least two sizes too large and a black T-shirt underneath, faded black cotton and a big white letter Z with a question mark behind it—Z? inside a white silk-screened square—and then the song started again.

"When we still lived with Mort and Theo on Arapahoe," she said.

"Yeah," Marvin replied and he turned a page in the book he was trying to read. "You told me."

"She used to play it on Pearl Street, for spare change, you know, and I'd sit on top of the big bronze beaver and listen. Sometimes Mort would tap along on his snare drum, if he didn't have to work that day."

"You told me that, too, dear," and Marvin stared at her over the top of his paperback Somerset Maugham novel. "But haven't you played it enough for one night?"

"You had to have a license, but there were lots of street performers on Pearl. No cars allowed. We knew a girl who juggled wineglasses, and a guy named Silence who played the hammer dulcimer."

Marvin made a face like a cat trapped in a small child's lap, sighed and glanced back down at his book.

"I'm sorry," Niki said, not entirely certain what she was apologizing for and feeling more annoyed at Marvin than sorry for playing "Dark in Day" twelve times in a row.

"No," he said, but no change at all in his expression, the strained patience, his good-nurse face that she hated so much. "It's not your fault. I think I'm getting a headache."

Niki picked up one of the CDs, turned it over and stared at her reflection in the iridescent plastic. Her face too round, too fat because the Elavil made her gain weight and hold water. Dark circles beneath her eyes and the disc's center hole where her nose ought to be. She held the CD at an angle so it caught the lamplight, sliced it up into spectrum wedges, violet to blue to green, yellow to red, and she hummed quietly with the song. Daria's bass thumping out the rhythm like an erratic heartbeat, breathless fingertip dance across steel strings to draw music from nothing, and Niki murmured the last part of the chorus just loud enough that Marvin would hear.

" 'Dark in day, I'd always say, that's not the way to know,' " her voice and Daria's, pretending they were together because Daria was still on tour, out singing for other people in Nashville or Louisville or Memphis, some distant Southern city that Niki had never seen and never wanted to see. And her reflection in the CD wavered then, as if the plastic were water now and someone had just dipped their hand into it, concentric ripples racing themselves towards the edge of the disc, and Niki dropped it.

"Is something wrong?" Marvin asked, and no, Niki said, didn't *say* the word aloud but shook her head, not taking her eyes off the CD lying on the floor. It had stopped rippling and she stared back up at herself from the mercury-smooth underbelly of the disc.

"You're *sure*, Niki?" and she looked up at Marvin, hoping he wouldn't see that she was frightened, because then he'd try to get her to tell him why, to explain another one of the things that no one ever believed she really saw or heard. The things they gave her pills for, so that she wouldn't really see or hear them, either.

"I dropped it," she said. "Sorry," and then she smiled for him, and Marvin smiled back and stopped looking so concerned.

"It's almost midnight," he said. "Don't forget your medicine. And will you please use the headphones if you're going to keep playing that same song over and over?"

Niki glanced nervously back at the CD, but it was still just a CD again. Nothing that shimmered or rippled like ice water, and she reached for the headphones lying in their place on the shelf beside the stereo as "Dark in Day" ended and began again.

Lady lost in all your pain and thunder, all your shattered wonder . . .

She reached down and used one finger to gently flip the disc over so she wouldn't have to see the mirrored side anymore. The safer, printed-on side instead, Tom Waits' *Bone Machine,* and hardly any of the silver showing through.

Walking where the spinning world grows brittle, and I can't find you there . . .

She plugged the black headphones into the stereo, and Daria's voice shrank to a whisper, a small, faraway sound until Niki pulled the phones down over her head so that the music swelled suddenly around her again, wrapped her tight in electric piano and drums and the constant, comforting thump, thump, thump of the bass guitar.

You never look over your shoulder anymore, Daria sang, her gravel-and-whiskey voice suspended somewhere indefinable between Niki's ears, somewhere inside her head. *I'm afraid what you would see.* And Niki began singing again, never mind if it annoyed Marvin, because everything she did annoyed Marvin, and singing made her feel a little closer to Daria.

" 'Dark in day, I'd always say, dark in day, that's not so far to fall.' "

The three prescription bottles were lined up neatly for her on one of the big speakers, the pills sealed inside like flies and ants and moths in polished chunks of amber. All her crazy medicine, her psychoactive trinity: Elavil and Xanax and the powder-blue Klonopin tablets. It made her feel better to have the bottles nearby, especially when Daria wasn't. Niki reached for the Xanax, first station of that pharmaceutical cross, calming palindrome, and the glass of water that Marvin had brought her almost half an hour before.

Lady lost where night can't reach you anymore, tripping softly 'round the edges you endure ...

She popped the top off the plastic bottle and tipped it carefully so that only two or three of the pills would spill out into her open palm. Always careful, because she hated it when she poured out a whole handful by accident, that sudden rush like candy from a vending machine, and always a few that slipped, inevitably, between her fingers, bounced or rolled away across the floor, and she'd have to scramble about to find them. She tapped the mouth of the bottle once against her hand, but nothing happened. Niki checked to be sure the bottle wasn't empty, saw there were at least two weeks' worth of tablets left inside and tried again. And that time a single white pill came rolling out and lay glistening like a droplet of milk on her skin. It certainly wasn't Xanax, whatever it was, wasn't anything she was supposed to be taking and nothing she remembered ever having taken before, that tiny, glistening sphere like a ripe mistletoe berry, and *Those are poisonous, aren't they?* she thought, holding the strange pill closer to her face.

Dark in day, Daria sang inside her head, *I'd always say, dark in day, that's not so far to fall.*

And then a very faint, rubbery *pop,* and the white pill extended eight long and jointed legs, raised itself up, and she could see that there were eyes, too, shiny eyes so pale they were almost transparent, a half-circle dewdrop crown of eyes staring up at her. Niki squeezed her hand shut around the thing, the impossible spider pill, and glanced quickly towards Marvin. He was still sitting on the sofa, his nose buried in *The Moon and Sixpence.* So he hadn't seen, had not seen anything at all and he wouldn't, even if she walked across the room and showed it to him.

Pain then, little pain like someone pricking at her skin with a sharp sewing needle, and so she opened her hand again. But the spider was gone and there were only three pink Xanax, instead; Niki put the extra pill back into the bottle, set the bottle down on the floor beside her. She exhaled slowly and then took a deep, hitching breath. Her heart was racing, adrenaline-dizzy rush and beads of cold sweat, a faintly metallic taste like aluminum in her mouth.

You hold it all inside, you hold it all in, you hold it all inside you . . .

Niki chewed her lower lip and concentrated on breathing more slowly, breathing evenly, knew from experience she'd only wind up hyperventilating if she didn't. She stared at her palm like a fortune-teller trying to divine the future from two Xanax; but there *was* something else there, something other than the pills, so small she hadn't noticed it at first. A pinpoint welt, raised skin gone a slightly brighter shade of pink than her medication, and she closed her hand again, making a fist so tight her short nails dug painfully into her flesh.

The song ended, and this time Niki pulled the headphones off, let them fall to the floor among the CDs. The noise drew Marvin's attention, but only for a moment. She forced a smile for him, something false but credible enough to pass for a smile, a strained charm against his questions, and he smiled back, relieved, and let his eyes drift once more to his book.

Not real, she whispered, not aloud but safe inside her head, the way that Dr. Dalby had taught her. *Not real at all. Even if it meant something, even if I needed to see it and pay attention and remember I saw it, nothing real.*

Like a memory or a ghost. Nothing that can hurt me.

But when she opened her hand again the welt was still there, the swelling a little more pronounced than before, and her palm had begun to throb slightly. The patient, faithful Xanax, as well, and four half-moon dimples left by her fingernails; any harder and she might have drawn blood, and that would have freaked Marvin out for sure.

Don't you lock up. Keep moving, and so she pressed her lips to her hand; the small welt felt hot when the tip of her tongue brushed over it, and Niki dry-swallowed the pills. She snapped the cap back on the Xanax bottle, took the Elavil next, then the Klonopin last of all, this routine methodical as counting rosary beads, and she drank all the water Marvin had brought her, even though it was warm and tasted faintly of dishwashing liquid. If she hadn't he might have asked why, and one question could have led to another, and another. She set the prescription bottles back on the speaker, pressed the OFF button on the CD player, and "I think I'll go to bed now," she said. "I'll see you in the morning, Marvin."

"Good night, dear," Marvin replied, not bothering to look up at her. "Sweet dreams."

"Yeah. You too," she whispered, and then Niki took a deep breath and climbed the stairs alone.

Awaking from a dream of something she should have done differently, something lost, and Niki Ky stared up at the ceiling for a few minutes before she rolled over and looked at the alarm clock. LED numbers and letters that glowed the same murky yellow-green as cartoon toxic waste, 6:07 A.M., and the darkness outside the bedroom window in case she needed a second opinion. Niki watched the window, wondering what woke her so suddenly, so completely, and if she was going to be able to get to sleep again. Her dreams, especially the very bad ones, usually left her disoriented for hours, uncertain if this world was real or if the other might have been. She'd once argued with Dr. Dalby for an hour over whether or not anyone could ever know the difference, could ever be sure.

And then Niki realized that her right hand was still hurting, so maybe that was what had pulled her out of the dream place; she held it up and examined her palm in the darkness, the pale, reflected glow of the city coming in through the curtains, and so she could make out the welt, swollen as fat and dark as a red-wasp sting. Something she'd hoped had only been part of the dream, the white spider pill and her injured hand; she touched it gently, tentatively, with the fingers of her left hand, pressed the soft pad of her index finger against the swelling, and it felt hard and feverish. Niki winced and sat up, switched on the lamp beside the bed, a Tiffany-shaded reading lamp Daria had given her as a gift on her twenty-sixth birthday, blue and green and violet kaleidoscope glass and the bronze mermaid rising graceful from the base, the whole sea caught in her outstretched arms.

Niki leaned back against the tall oak headboard and squinted at her hand; the lamplight hurt her eyes and she closed them for a second or two, opened them and blinked as her stubborn pupils began to adjust. The swelling was almost as big around as a quarter now, a purple-red hill disrupting the familiar topography of her hand, an ugly new obstacle for her troubled lifeline, and Niki touched it again. The solid center of the bump seemed to roll very slightly, as though a steel bead had been inserted just underneath the skin. She pushed at it a little harder, stopped when the pain made her eyes begin to water, tried to close her hand so she wouldn't have to look at it anymore, but the muscles ached too much to make a fist.

"Shit," she whispered, thinking that she should go to the

bathroom down the hall and put something on the swelling, Bactine or Neosporin cream, maybe a Band-Aid, too. That she should probably show it to Marvin in the morning; no need to tell him about the tiny white spider, but surely this was real enough that even he could see it.

"Maybe you should *cut* it out," said the boy standing at the foot of the bed, and when she looked up at him he smiled and his teeth were the color of polished hematite. He must have been there all along, watching her, waiting; his thin, solemn face was dirty, dirty face and dirtier hands, black grime beneath his nails. He held his head at an odd angle, like it was too heavy or his neck too weak to support it properly, and there was a ring of bruises circling his throat. The boy was dead.

"It might start to fester," he said. "You should find a razor and cut it out before it does."

"Maybe. I'll ask Marvin about it in the morning," Niki said, talking to a dead boy with a crooked neck, a dead boy standing there in her bedroom, and she knew she wasn't *that* crazy, so she was still dreaming, same act, different scene, that's all.

"You shouldn't wait that long, Niki. It might be too late by then. It might eat in too deep and you'll never get it back out."

"How do you know my name?" she asked him, and the boy smiled at her again, a cold, secretive kind of smile, she thought. A smile because she didn't understand and *he* did, that sort of a smile.

"You take too many pills," he said, his dark, iron-ore teeth moving up and down, something nestled at the corner of his mouth that might have been a scab or an insect. "You don't remember things you should. You don't remember me."

And then she does, and Niki closes her eyes, lies down hoping that she can force the dream to change again, some less tangible nightmare, some lesser regret or failure looking to settle the score with her.

"You never even told that fucking shrink of yours about

me, Nicolan," Danny Boudreaux said. "Daria pays someone a hundred and fifty dollars an hour just to listen to you whine, and you don't even have the guts to start at the beginning."

"Go away," Niki whispered. "Leave me alone," and she reached for Daria's pillow and put it over her head, dim hope that he would go away if he couldn't see her face anymore.

"You're never going to be able to run *that* fast," he sneered, and Niki felt all the sheets and blankets yanked suddenly away, the violent flutter of cloth like a fleeing ghost, and a damp gust of air washed over her. Heavy, smothering air too dank even for a San Francisco autumn morning, the stench of mold and mushrooms, stagnant water and vegetable rot, and she would drown in half the time it took to scream.

"Yeah, you should definitely cut it out now," the dead boy said, and when she opened her eyes, Niki was standing at the center of the bed, naked and shivering, staring down at the discarded bedclothes strewn across the floor; polished hardwood and clean white sheets, the purple wool blanket they'd had since Colorado lying in a rumpled wad near the closet door, and there was no one in the room but her.

"Wake up," she said, but nothing changed, not the shadows or the cloying, mildew stink that still hung thick around her, the frigid, syrup-thick air that seemed to cling to her bare arms and legs, her exposed belly and breasts, and she couldn't even remember taking off her T-shirt. But there it was on the floor, tangled up with the sheets, and her panties almost all the way over by the bedroom door.

Her hand throbbed, and when she called for Marvin her breath fogged in the freezing air.

He can't hear me, she thought. *Marvin isn't anywhere in this dream and he can't hear me and he'll never come to wake me up.*

There was a high, scraping noise at the window, then, and Niki turned too slowly, caught only the very briefest glimpse between and through the curtains, mercifully brief sight of whatever had been looking in at her, whatever had seen her scared and naked and talking to herself or Danny Boudreaux. A lingering, animate pool of night mashing itself flat against the glass, and then it was gone, and she could see the sloping rooftops and the predawn sky again.

Nothing that can hurt me. Nothing real.

Niki had begun to shiver, and she stepped down off the bed, stepped past the purple blanket and opened the closet door. There were small, murmuring things hiding in there, back behind the coat hangers and her dresses, behind old shoe boxes, things that bristled like hedgehogs and watched her with painted, porcelain eyes. But she was pretty sure they wouldn't bother her, not if she left them alone, that they were almost as afraid of dead boys and the fleeting, voyeur shape at the window as she was. They let her have what she needed, a gray sweatshirt and a pair of jeans, so she ignored them. Niki pulled the jeans on, wrestled the sweatshirt over her head, not bothering with underwear, no time, and it probably didn't matter anyway.

Where you going now, Nicolan? someone whispered, someone hiding under the bed; at least it wasn't Danny's voice, wasn't anyone else she recognized. *What will we say, if they come looking for you again? They have the keys, you know?*

Niki finished buttoning the fly of her jeans, and by then her hand was hurting so badly, raw and pulsing ache like a rotting tooth, like cancer, and she had to stop and lean against the wall for a moment. Violet-white swirls of living light behind her eyes, inside her head, brilliant, twitching worms that would devour her if she let them.

The Lady of Situations, the dusty voice beneath the bed purled, except now Niki was pretty sure it was two voices, or three, speaking in almost-perfect unison. *She wanted the keys, but they stole them from her and locked them all away in gray towers of fire and barbed wire, didn't they?*

The heart keys, the soul keys, the Diamond Key to the Third Day of June and Lost Faith.

She opened the Pit, Nicolan, and now He counts all the nights of your life on the fingers of dead whores.

She didn't tell them to shut the fuck up, wanted to but she didn't, because perhaps those were all things that she needed to know, or maybe it would be worse if they *stopped* talking and came out from under the bed. Niki Ky stood still, sweating, giddy sick, her stomach gone as bitter as arsenic, and she listened to the voices while the pain ebbed and faded slowly down to something that couldn't pull her apart if that's what it decided she was there for.

Do you even know *the way down to her? The road beyond the whistling dogs, Niki, and never mind the bricks. Those bricks aren't gold, no, they're only yellow so you'll* think *they're gold.*

Yellow is the color of decay and duplicity, the color of broken promises.

Yellow is the man with your heart.

And when they were finally done, when she was sure that she'd heard every single word, Niki crossed the bedroom to the telephone sitting on the dresser. "Wake up," she said, hopeless, but she said it one last time anyway, just in case, and then she picked up the receiver.

A rainy, cool summer afternoon, four months before that night of ghosts or memories gone as dry and tangible as ghosts, and Dr. Dalby watched her and fiddled patiently with one end of his meticulously groomed salt-and-pepper mustache, stared out at Niki through the glasses that made his eyes look much too big for his wrinkled face.

"You take your time," he said, smiled his storybook grandfather smile, and glanced at the clock on his desk.

She nodded and watched the low, gauzy clouds drifting above the city. The psychologist's office had one big window and a view of the bay, a stingy glimpse of Alcatraz if Niki stood on the couch. Nothing like a real doctor's office, velvet wallpaper the bottomless color of evergreen forests, hemlock green walls and Edwardian antiques, old books and the cherry-sweet smell of his pipe that always reminded Niki of her parents' tobacco shop in New Orleans. There was a small brocade pillow on the sofa, woven anemones and silver-leafed geraniums, and she hugged the pillow while she talked.

"Spyder hung herself," Niki said, finally. "While I was asleep, she hung herself."

Dr. Dalby took a very deep breath and chewed thoughtfully at the stem of his pipe; she didn't have to take her eyes off the window, the slate gray bay and the clouds, to know that he was watching her with that expression of his, trademark therapist face that was part concern and part curiosity, part studied courtesy for crazy girls. Waiting quietly to see if she was done (he'd never interrupted her, not even once) and then, "That's not what you told me before," he said.

"I was confused before. What I told you before was a dream. But I know the difference now."

"What did she *use* to hang herself, Nicolan?"

"She used an extension cord," Niki replied. "An orange extension cord from the kitchen," and she hugged the brocade pillow a little bit tighter, hugged it the way a drowning woman might cling to a life preserver.

"Look at me, please," and she did, looked into his pale blue eyes behind those thick bifocal lenses, forced herself not to turn away again when he leaned towards her.

"You won't ever get better by lying to me," he said.

"But I'm not lying."

"You're not telling the truth, so what would you call it? If Spyder hung herself, why didn't the police find her body? Why did you and Daria and your friends run away, if she only hung herself?"

"We were scared," Niki said, trying hard to sound convincing, like she, at least, believed what she was saying. "They were afraid that I'd get in trouble."

Dr. Dalby chewed his pipe for a moment, glanced at the clock again, then back at Niki. He was frowning, and she wasn't sure if she'd ever seen him do that before.

"The first time I saw you and Daria, I said that I would

listen to whatever either of you needed to tell me," he said. "And that I would always be open to the possibility that you were telling me the truth, no matter how bizarre or unlikely that truth might seem, as long as I thought *you* believed it yourselves."

"I don't know *why* the police didn't find her," Niki said intently, almost whispering. "I don't know," and she did turn away from him, then; better to watch the formless, shifting clouds than the doubt gathering on his face.

"I want to be well and I *can't* if I believe the things I told you. I don't think I can even be *alive* if I have to keep believing in the things I told you."

"You're frightened," he said.

"Yes, I am. I'm afraid," and Niki bit down on the tip of her tongue, pain to fight back tears she didn't want to cry, didn't want him to see; too much like surrender, her sitting there sobbing while he reached for tissue from the big box of Kleenex on his desk.

"What happened to Spyder that night, don't you think that it's over?"

"No . . . I don't."

"But if she hung herself, Nicolan, like you say, like you just told me, if that's all that happened, then there's nothing in the world for you to be afraid of now, is there?"

"You don't *know*," Niki growled at him. "You don't know shit, old man. Maybe, when I'm *dead*—" and a trickle of blood and saliva leaked out with the words, slipped between her lips and dribbled slowly down her chin. Her whole mouth filling up with the salty, warm taste of blood, but if Dr. Dalby noticed he didn't say anything. Didn't move, didn't even reach for a Kleenex; Niki wiped her chin with the back of her hand.

"I'm sorry," she said, forcing anger and fear into something shaped more like calm. She stared back at him and swallowed blood. "I was confused, that's all. I'm not going to talk anymore today, Dr. Dalby. I bit my tongue and my mouth hurts. I'm not going to talk anymore."

He nodded, leaned back in his chair, but didn't take his

eyes off her, didn't turn away or let her go early, and Niki sat silently on the couch and watched the rain until her hour was up.

Niki waited on top of the low, concrete wall surrounding Alamo Square, bundled warm in blue fake fur and hiking boots, waiting for the taxi she'd called before leaving the house. She faced dawn, and behind her the last violet and charcoal scraps of night still bruised the western horizon as the world rolled slow and infallible towards the sun, towards the next compulsory day; firelight orange already flashing off the glass and steel husk of downtown, and *Daria's out there somewhere,* she thought. Someplace beyond the white church spires and skyscraper slabs, the gaudy monolith of the Transamerica Pyramid, past the bay and the distant, fog-bound Oakland hills. In some other place, a thousand or two thousand miles away, another world filled up with other people, and Niki wondered if she could find her if she tried, if she told the driver to take her straight to the airport, if she could be half that brave, would she even be able to find Daria, then?

But that's not where you're going, not today, and Niki turned quickly, startled and heart racing, because the voice sounded so close, almost right on top of her. The same voice she'd heard speaking to her from under her bed only an hour before, or someone imitating that voice perfectly. But there was nothing there now except the park, the lanes leading into the tall and shadowy trees set farther back from Steiner, towards the wooded center of the square. A few blackbirds and sparrows pecking determinedly at the dew-beaded grass, but no sign of the speaker; a deep puddle of night still hanging on beneath those old trees, though, and Niki stared at it, at the gloom between the trunks and limbs. *It sees me, too,* she thought.

A breeze rustled loudly through the branches, ocean-raw breath to set leaf and twig tongues wagging, and maybe that was all she'd heard. The wind in the trees, not a voice, and she was sure that was probably what Marvin or

Daria would tell her if they were there, what Dr. Dalby would say.

Then the shadows moved, or something stitched into the shadows, something huge that slipped ink smooth on long and jointed legs from the cover of a great oak, and for a moment she might have seen it clearly as it crossed the path. And then it was gone again. *Just a dog,* Daria would say if she were there, reassuring, certain. *Only a stray dog, Niki, out looking for its breakfast.*

A dingy yellow cab pulled up close to the curb, and the driver honked his horn at her; Niki Ky stared at the trees a moment longer, at the oblivious blackbirds and sparrows, and then she turned her head and stared at the cabby.

Wouldn't a dog have scared the birds away? she thought. *Wouldn't* anything *have scared the birds away?*

The cabby was an old black man wearing a mostly orange Giants baseball cap, and he stared back at her, motioned for her to hurry up, impatient come-on-if-you're-coming motion, and Niki slipped down off the concrete wall, trying to forget about the trees and stray dogs, and crossed the sidewalk to the taxi. The old man rolled down his window, and "You called for a cab?" he asked her.

"Yes," she said. "Yes sir, I did," and she put her hands into the pockets of her coat to be sure she had the things that she needed, her billfold and pills, her house keys. She resisted an impulse to look over her shoulder before getting into the cab. Inside it was warm, stuffy warm, and smelled like worn Naugahyde and cinnamon-scented air freshener. There was tinny jazz playing on the radio, much too early for jazz, she thought, but there it was anyway. The driver watched Niki in the rearview mirror, waiting for her to give him directions, and when she didn't he frowned.

"Where you goin'?" he asked.

"Oh," she said, like the necessity for any particular destination hadn't occurred to her, more the need to escape Marvin and the house on Steiner Street than the desire to actually be somewhere else.

"I want coffee," she told him, "*Good* coffee," which was

true, she did. But the driver grunted and rolled his eyes at her, so Niki added, "Cafe Alhazred, on Fulton," though it wasn't her favorite, just the first thing that popped into her head.

"Ma'am, are you high or somethin'?" he asked. "I know it ain't exactly none of my concern, and it don't make me much difference if you are. I ain't gonna put you out. I just want to know, in case somethin' happens."

Niki nodded her head, thinking that she should feel more offended at his question than she did, and then she remembered the three prescription bottles in her pocket and took one of them out to show the driver. She held the Xanax bottle up so he could see it.

"I'm on prescription medication," she said, wishing that he'd just drive and stop glaring at her in the mirror. "Sometimes it makes me a little groggy in the morning."

"You don't say?"

"I don't think it's any of your business."

"Yeah, you're probably right," the driver said. "Sorry," and he pushed the lever that started the cab's meter running and pulled away from the curb. "Say, exactly what kind of animal you gotta skin to get a fur coat that color, anyhow?"

"It's not real fur," Niki replied absentmindedly and glanced at the house as they passed it, all the tall windows dark, the curtains drawn. *So Marvin must still be asleep, and I got away,* she thought.

"That's sorta reassurin'," the driver said and turned west onto Fulton Street.

"I think you must talk more than any cab driver I've ever met," Niki said to him and put her boots up on the back of the seat, the brown suede boots with bright, canary-yellow laces that made her feet look huge and blocky, Frankenstein feet, and she slid far enough down that she didn't have to look at the square anymore.

"Well, I don't intend to drive this ol' hack *all* my life. I plan on writin' a novel one day, a best seller, after I retire, and so I gotta pay close attention and talk to folks. I figure my book's gonna have real people, not a bunch'a made-up phonies."

"Someone will just sue you," Niki said. She realized that she hadn't put the pill bottle back in her pocket, and she shook it a couple of times. The pills made a dry, pleasant sound against the plastic, a comforting noise like a baby's rattle or a very small maraca.

"Oh, I ain't gonna use nobody's real name. I'll come up with brand-new ones that fit people *better* than their real names."

"Doesn't matter," Niki said. "They'll figure out what you did and sue you, anyway."

"Damn, you sure got a cynical streak, girl," the driver mumbled and then honked his horn at a UPS truck that had pulled out in front of him. "Someone go and piss in your cornflakes this mornin' or what?"

"I hope you don't have your heart set on a tip," she said and opened the bottle, shook one of the Xanax out into her hand. The swelling on her palm was worse, but the welt had almost stopped hurting, had begun to feel a little numb, in fact. The bump had turned the color of a raisin.

"Now, see? That is *exactly* what I mean. I'll probably be naming you somethin' awful, like . . ." and then he paused to honk at a rusty red Toyota and call the driver a blind hippie son of a bitch. He tugged once at the frayed brim of his Giants cap, and "Well, somethin' disagreeable," he said. "Eudora Bittlesnipe, maybe, or maybe Miss Suzy Sourmilk."

"No one's going to read a book full of names like that," Niki said and popped the pill into her mouth. "It'll be a big flop, and you'll wind up living on the street."

"Well, though it's been an inspirin' pleasure making your acquaintance, Miss Bittlesnipe, and I hate to see you go, I think this is your stop," and he pulled over at the corner of Fulton and Divisadero.

Niki sat up, quickly swapped the pill bottle for her billfold, plain black leather with her initials in silver thread, and she took out five dollars and told the driver to keep the thirty cents she had coming in change.

"Hell's bells. Guess I'll be able to retire a lot sooner than I thought," he said, pulled a pencil stub from behind his left ear, licked the tip and jotted something down on a clipboard. His two-way radio crackled to life, momentarily drowning the jazz station in a sudden burst of static and angry, unintelligible voices speaking in Spanish.

"Thanks for the ride," Niki said, climbing out of the backseat, and "Hey, wait a sec," the driver called out to her over the sputtering racket from the radio. But the door of the cab was already swinging shut and, besides, she wasn't in the mood for any more witty conversation. She crossed the street to Cafe Alhazred and went inside.

The interior of the coffee shop was a fanciful, mismatched fusion of Middle Eastern kitsch, someone trying hard to invoke the markets of Cairo or Baghdad and getting *I Dream of Jeannie* instead; sand brown plaster walls decorated with an incongruous assortment of Egyptian hieroglyphs and Arabic graffiti, lancet archways and beaded curtains, a few dusty hookahs scattered about here and there like a lazy afterthought, framed and faded photographs of desert places. A pretend Casablanca for the punks and hippies, the goths and less classifiable misfits that had long ago claimed Cafe Alhazred as their own.

Niki ordered a tall double latte, paid at the register, and took an empty table near the front of the cafe, sipped at the scalding mix of steamed milk and espresso and inspected the people filing hurriedly past the windows. Men and women on their way to work or somewhere else, two purposeful and intertwining trails like strange insects caught in a forced march, northeast or southwest, and she closed her eyes for a moment. Nothing but the warm coffee smells, the commingled conversations of other customers, and an old Brian Eno song playing softly in the background.

I really got away, she thought again, oddly satisfied by

the simple fact of it, but not quite believing it was true, either, and not quite sure why. Marvin had never actually stopped her from going out without him, but since he'd come to live with them, to watch over her, she'd never *tried* to venture farther than Alamo Square park alone.

But I did it, didn't I? I got away from him and that house. Now I can go anywhere. Anywhere at all.

Niki opened her eyes, half expecting to be back in her bedroom, but nothing had changed, and she was still sitting there in the wobbly wooden chair at the little table, the Friday morning stream of pedestrians marching past. Only now there was someone standing out there looking in, an ashen-skinned child no more than five or six, seven at the most, gazing straight at her. The girl's long hair was black, and she stood with her face pressed against the window, her breath fogging up a small patch of the plate glass. Her blue eyes so pale they made Niki think of ice, and the child wasn't wearing a coat, not even long sleeves, just a T-shirt and grimy-looking jeans.

Niki smiled at her, and the girl blinked her cold blue eyes and smiled back, a hesitant, uneasy smile as though she wasn't precisely sure what smiles meant or how to make one, and then she pointed one finger towards the sky. Niki looked up and saw nothing over her head but the ceiling of Cafe Alhazred, and when she looked back down again the child was gone, just a snotty smear on the glass to prove that she'd ever been there.

We dream of a ship that sails away, Brian Eno sang above and between the murmuring voices crowding the cafe. . . . *a thousand miles away.*

Niki raised the big mug of coffee, both hands and the cup already halfway between the Formica tabletop and her lips when she noticed the mark the child had traced on the windowpane, the simple cruciform design, and she stopped, caught in the disorienting blur of recognition and unwanted memories, the déjà vu freeze-frame collision of then and now and the singer's insinuating, dulcet-gentle voice.

We dream of a ship that sails away . . .

It isn't real, Nicolan. It isn't anything that can ever hurt you.

. . . a thousand miles away.

And a flash of pain through her right hand, spike-steel sharp and electric bright across her stiff and swollen palm, dividing fivefold and racing itself swiftly towards the tips of her cramping fingers. Niki cried out and dropped the mug. It bounced off the table, dumping hot coffee in her lap before it hit the floor and shattered. She tried to stand, but a fresh wave of pain clenched her hand into a tight fist, and she almost slipped on the wet floor, ceramic shards of the broken cup crunching beneath her boots, and she sat right back down again.

"Hey, what's wrong?" someone asked. "Are you sick or something?" Someone male who sounded scared and confused, and Niki peered out through her watering eyes at a skinny boy with a shaved head and a ring in his lower lip.

. . . we dream of a ship that sails away . . .

"My *hand*," she gasped, but her voice too small, breathless, lost in the white fire searing its way greedily up her arm, and the stupid, baffled expression on his face all she needed to know that the boy didn't understand. Wasting her time because he would never possibly understand any of it, and so she got to her feet again, shoved roughly past him, past other tables and other people. All of them looking at her now, sly and knowing glances from beady, dark eyes, suspicious scowls, and Niki tried desperately to think through the alternating waves of pain and nausea, lightheaded and sick and only trying to remember where the hell the restroom was hidden.

And someone pointed the way, finally, though she didn't remember asking them, and she stumbled past the counter and down the long hallway, past cardboard boxes of to-go cups and plastic spoons. *What if someone's in there,* she thought, but the door was open, the doorknob loose and jiggly in her hand, and she locked it behind her.

. . . a thousand miles away.

The restroom was hardly even as large as a closet and smelled like disinfectant and mildew, shit and drying urine, and everything too stark in the green-white fluorescent light, too perfectly defined. Niki leaned over the tiny rust-stained sink and twisted the handle marked H, but cold water gushed from the faucet, and there wasn't time to wait for it to decide to get warm someday. She gritted her teeth, held her hand under the icy water, and stared back at herself from the scratched and streaky mirror hung above the sink.

Her own face in there but almost unrecognizable, pale and sweat-slick junky's face, puffy, bloodshot eyes and black hair tangled like a rat's matted nest, and she couldn't remember if she'd brushed it before leaving the house. That face could belong to almost anyone, anyone lost and insane, anyone damned. Her hand throbbed, and Niki shut off the tap.

"You should have listened to me," the dead boy behind her admonished, Danny watching her in the mirror. "It's probably too late now. It's probably in your blood by now."

"It's killing me," she said, whimpered, and the center of the welt had gone the color of vanilla custard, the fat pustule surrounded by skin so dark it looked as if it had already begun to decay.

"No," he said. "It won't kill you. If you're dead, you're no good to anyone. This will be worse than dying, Niki."

Then something seemed to move inside the welt, something larval coiling and uncoiling in its amniotic rot, and the pain doubled and she screamed.

"Shhhhh," the dead boy hissed and held one cautious finger to his lips. "Hold it down or they'll *hear* you, Niki. And then they'll come to find out what's wrong in here, and they'll all see what's happening to you."

"Fuck," she grunted, and spittle flew from her lips and speckled the brown walls, the lower half of the dirty mirror. "You're *dead,*" she said. "You got *out.* You ran the fuck away and left me alone."

"You think it's some kind of party over here?" he asked

her and smiled or sneered, black teeth and his eyes almost twinkled the way they did when he was still alive. "Well it ain't, sugardoll. It isn't even Hell. It isn't anything you can begin to imagine."

"You left me," she said again, and he shook his head, the ruined ghost of his pretty, drag queen's face twisting into an angry snarl.

"No, Niki. *You left me.* You ran out on me. I told you the truth because I loved you, and you fucking *ran.*"

"Oh," she whispered, "oh, God," gasped, consciousness thin and brittle as onionskin now, black at the narrowing edges of her vision, and the thing beneath her flesh wriggled, worming its way in deeper.

"You wanted her," Danny Boudreaux said. "You wanted her and now she has you, forever and fucking ever."

He laughed at her, empty, soulless laugh like the end of time making fun of the beginning, and Niki screamed again and squeezed the welt between her left thumb and index finger. For a moment the shiny surface of the blister held, a second that might have lasted for hours, days, while she screamed and the dead boy with the crooked neck laughed his apocalypse laugh for her. And then it burst, popped loud, and Niki grabbed at one end of the squirming thing trying to burrow quickly away from her and the dim restroom light.

"*No,*" she said. "No, you *don't.* I won't let you in," and Niki held on to it tightly, her wet fingers slippery with pus and blood, its transparent body like a strand of water, living tissue that insubstantial, jellyfish siphonophore tendril or some deep-sea worm. It grew taut, then went limp, shimmered like a pearl before slipping effortlessly from her grasp and vanishing into the seeping red hole in the palm of her hand.

"Sorry," the dead boy said, sounding almost as though he might have meant it. "I thought for a minute there you might win after all."

Niki's legs folded, and she fell to the floor, landed in a heap on the filthy, piss-damp tile and sat there sobbing and cradling her aching hand. Her treacherous right hand become the ragged passage into her body, her heart, her soul if that's where the thing meant to go. Bright, clean blood flowed freely from the hole, and she let it bleed. Danny was gone, and someone was banging on the restroom door. She wasn't sure if the lock worked or not, so she leaned on the door and braced one of her boots against the toilet bowl.

"What's going on in there?" a man with a Middle Eastern accent shouted at her from the other side. "Don't make me call the police."

"I'm sick," she shouted back at him. "I'm just sick."

"But you were screaming," the man said. "I heard you," and she could tell that he didn't believe her.

"So I'm *very* sick, okay? But I'm getting better. I'll be out in a minute. I'm sorry."

"I *will* call the police if you scream again," he said, and then she listened as his angry footsteps retreated down the hallway. Niki shut her eyes, wondering if there was anything in the restroom she could use for a bandage, and waited hopelessly for whatever was going to happen next.

Another taxi ride down Fulton to the evergreen sanctuary of Golden Gate Park, and this time a driver who didn't try to talk her ear off. He dropped Niki in front of the California Academy of Sciences, and she stood on the museum steps for a while, watched as noisy groups of schoolchildren were herded about by their teachers. She'd torn away a strip of the sweatshirt she was wearing under the blue fur coat and wrapped it tightly around her hand, not so tight that she'd cut off the circulation, but tight enough that it would stop the bleeding and stay put.

She was there because this was where the thing that had crawled inside her said to come. This drab Eisenhower-era edifice of gray stone blocks and concrete columns, an austere and secular church for modern stargazers and alchemists. In a few minutes, she would go inside and see whatever it was she was supposed to see, but for the moment, better to stand out here beneath the wide blue sky and smell the clean ocean air, the mild autumn breeze, the flowers and grass, and Niki imagined that she could smell nasturtiums and roses growing somewhere nearby.

Some of the older kids noticed her, and a few pointed rude fingers and stared, laughter for the frowzy Vietnamese woman in her coat that looked like maybe someone had skinned Grover the Muppet and sewn the pieces back together for her to wear. Her messy hair and the sloppy, bloodstained bandage on her hand, and *I bet I look like a homeless person,* she thought. *A street lunatic, a damn crack whore,* which made her sad, sad and tired, but made her smile, too, thinking about Daria's money, Daria's big house on Alamo Square.

"You don't look so good, lady," one of the boys said, bolder than the rest, sixth- or seventh-grader in a Sponge-Bob T-shirt and his red hair shaved almost down to his scalp.

"I don't feel so hot, either," she said and wiped sweat from her forehead, held out her rag-swaddled hand so the boy could get a better look.

"What's the matter with you, anyway?" he asked. "You got AIDS or something?"

And then his teacher noticed, and she rushed over to reclaim the boy, a strained, unapologetic smile for Niki, and she pulled the boy away, tucked him into line with his restless classmates. But he glanced back at Niki over his shoulder and stuck his tongue out at her.

What you waiting for now, Niki? Too afraid of what you're going to see in there?

"Leave me alone," she said, talking to no one at all, or herself, to the boy or the muttering, colorless thing nestled somewhere inside her. "Just leave me the hell alone," and she walked past the children, up the stairs, into the museum.

Eight dollars and fifty cents to get through the door, past guards and docents and into the *Tyrannosaurus*-haunted atrium. The skeleton loomed above her like a sentinel outside the ebony gates of Hades or Mordor or Midian, something that might lunge from its pedestal, loud clatter of bones and steel rods, to snap her apart in those petrified jaws, those long stone-dagger teeth.

"I'm not afraid of you," she whispered confidently to the dinosaur, not even a real fossil, remembering the first time she'd come here with Daria, and the *Tyrannosaurus* was only a clever replica, nothing but molded fiberglass and plaster and paint. Damnation's scarecrow wired together to impress the gullible, and Niki glared defiantly up at its empty eye sockets, and the skeleton stayed right where it was.

"Can I help you find something, miss?" a girl asked her, a very polite girl wearing a plastic name tag with the museum logo printed on it, and Niki turned her back to the phony *Tyrannosaurus*. The girl's name was Linda, and she had a smile that reminded Niki of an airline stewardess.

"Do you have spiders?" Niki asked her. "I need to see the spiders, if there are any."

"Yes, ma'am," the girl said and pointed at the other side of the atrium, behind the tyrannosaur. "They're located in the Hall of Insects," and she smiled again and handed Niki a colorful, glossy pamphlet with a map of the museum.

"Thank you," she said, but the girl was already busy asking if she could help someone else.

Niki Ky sat alone in the Hall of Insects, sat on a long wooden bench in front of a big display case of spiders and scorpions, mites and ticks and less familiar creepy crawlies; a hundred minuscule corpses, minute crucifixions for the curious to gawk at, sideshow for the squeamish or a nightmare for arachnophobes. Beneath the sweatshirt rag her hand had begun to itch, and she concentrated on the display, trying not to scratch at it or mess with the bandage.

Niki had read all the labels before she sat down, read them three times through because she was afraid of missing the one thing that was most important. But none of it seeming any more or less significant than the rest. Now she just sat there, waiting and thinking about the tiny bodies, about the spiders, mostly, the spiders the reason that she'd come here, after all. As if she'd ever need so obvious a reminder, about as tactful as Dickens' Christmas ghosts or a lead pipe across her skull. She reached into the pocket of her coat and took out the first bottle that her fingertips encountered, the Klonopin, and she opened it.

"Of course, they aren't insects, you know," Dr. Dalby said, and she hadn't even noticed him standing there in front of her, leaning on his silver-handled walking stick and peering at the exhibit through his bifocals. "They're actually members of the Class Arachnida."

"I *know* that," Niki said, interrupting him, and she put two of the pills in her mouth. They tasted faintly sweet and made her tongue tingle, faint and not unpleasant numbness as they started to dissolve. "Spyder told me that."

"Yes," the old man said. "She would have, wouldn't she?"

"I guess no one wants a Hall of Arachnids," she mumbled, and Dr. Dalby nodded his head.

"No, I don't suppose they do. But it does seem a shame, don't you think? Says here there are more than . . ." and he paused, reading one of the labels again. "More than thirty-eight thousand species of spiders, and only about four thousand species of mammals. And, it says, arachnids were the first terrestrial animals, with scorpions dating back to the Silurian, over four hundred million years ago."

"I read it already, Dr. Dalby," and Niki dry swallowed the two half-dissolved pills, put three more in her mouth. "I read it *all,* three times."

"But that little lady there, *she's* a gem, isn't she?" and he pointed at a dead black widow. "Family Theridiidae, genus *Latrodectus,* species *mactans.* I wish I remembered more of my Latin. I'd tell you what the heck all that means."

"Spyder knew," Niki said. "But I don't. She told me once, but I can't remember anymore. There are five species in North America," and then Niki shut her eyes and recited them for the psychologist: "*Latrodectus mactans, Latrodec-*

tus variolus, Latrodectus geometricus, Latrodectus hesperus, and *Latrodectus bishopi,*" and he smiled at her.

"That's impressive, Nicolan."

She opened her eyes, and "You're not really Dr. Dalby, are you?" she asked the old man. "You don't smell like him."

"Right now, I'm who you need me to be."

Niki laughed, louder than she'd intended to laugh, and several people in the Hall of Insects turned to stare at her.

"Sorry about that," she said, though she wasn't, and took two more Klonopin.

"This isn't what you think it is," the man who wasn't really Dr. Dalby said and he sat down on the bench next to her and touched her gently on the shoulder. "It's not just phantoms and hallucinations. It's so much more than that."

Niki didn't look up, stayed focused on the prescription bottle because she didn't want to see the things in his eyes and certainly didn't want him to see the things in hers.

"I don't care," she said. "I've had enough of everything for one fucked-up lifetime."

"You know, Niki," and then she was sure it wasn't Dr. Dalby because he'd never once called her Niki. "Some people say spiders connect the world of the living with the world of the dead. They guard the underworld, and sometimes they even spin webs that connect the earth and Heaven."

"Oh, is *that* why you're here? To take me to Heaven?"

He didn't say anything for a moment, rubbed at his mustache like it itched and arched his eyebrows.

"No," he said, finally. "I can't do that."

"Then fuck off," and she shook four more pills out into her bandaged palm.

"There's no way to ever finish the story without you," he said, but not his voice now, a woman's voice instead, and the air around Niki grew suddenly cold and smelled like dust and Old Spice aftershave, sweat and a skunky hint of marijuana smoke. Niki watched the Klonopin bottle slip from her fingers and the blue pills spill out and bounce away across the museum floor.

"You put this goddamn thing inside me," she said and swallowed. Anger rising slow, swimming against and through the honey-thick tide of benzodiazepines clouding her brain, and she wouldn't turn to see if it was *really* Spyder or if it was only another ghost, something pretending to be Spyder so Niki would have to pay attention. "That's a cheap trick," she said. "That's a really cheap fucking trick."

A thirsty sound like wind in dry autumn leaves then, or thunder very far away, and Niki knew that whoever had been sitting there beside her was gone. She glanced up at the spider display one more time, Plexiglas coffin for widows and tarantulas and granddaddy longlegs, and then she bent down and started picking up the scattered pills.

CHAPTER TWO

The Wolves We All Can See

Almost noon, and Daria has lost count of how many cups of strong black coffee, how many cigarettes, since she and Marvin came downstairs, leaving Niki alone to sleep and dream beneath the painting of Ophelia. They're sitting together in the big kitchen, and the air smells like tobacco smoke and coffee. There's a sandwich in front of her that she hasn't even touched, the sandwich she let Marvin make for her even though eating was the very last thing on her mind. Sprouts and low-fat gouda cheese, thick slices of ripe avocado on whole wheat, a perfect, healthy sandwich on a cobal blue glass saucer. And it's times like these Daria wishes she'd never become a fucking vegetarian; something else that she did for Niki, indulging Niki's guilt, and the sandwich looks about as appetizing as a field of grass.

"You might have told me these things just a little bit sooner," Marvin says, and Daria pushes the unwanted sandwich a few inches farther away from her. "It's hard enough without everything being on some sort of top secret, need-to-know basis."

"I figured if Niki wanted you to know about Spyder and Danny, she'd tell you herself. Frankly, it didn't seem like any of your business. You're not her shrink."

Marvin rubs his eyes and reaches for Daria's sandwich.

"You're not even going to eat this, are you?" he asks, and she shakes her head, glad to see the sandwich find a better home so she won't have to sit staring at the damned thing any longer.

"I can't stand to see food go to waste," Marvin says, and he sniffs at it.

"I didn't mean that the way it probably sounded, about Danny and Spyder not being any of your business. Maybe I should have told you."

Marvin glances at her, a brief and wounded glance, then back to the sandwich, and he sniffs it again. And God, it annoys her the way he's always sniffing at his food, sniffing like a stray dog, so she looks down at her empty coffee cup, instead.

"Hey, it's your call, Dar," he says. "You're the boss. You set the terms. But I think the fact that Niki had two lovers commit suicide within five months of each other is pretty significant to anyone who wants to help her."

"Jesus, Marvin. I'm trying to say I was wrong, if you'll shut the hell up and listen." And Daria picks up her coffee cup, chipped milk white mug with Edward Gorey art printed on it, pushes her chair back and stands up. She looks at the empty pot in the coffee machine and briefly considers brewing another, then thinks better of it; her stomach hurts enough already, sour and aching, faintly nauseous, and so she walks to the sink and rinses out her mug. The water is cold, clean, and she splashes some of it on her face.

"And they both *hung* themselves." Marvin's speaking more softly now, as if he's afraid Niki might hear them, as if she might be listening. "That's a hell of a thing to have to carry around for ten years."

"Yeah," and Daria shuts off the tap, dries her face on an orange dish towel and wipes rough terry cloth across her tingling skin, wrinkles her nose at the perfume smell of fabric softener. "She was just a kid. I don't think she was even eighteen yet. Hell, we were *all* just kids."

"Do you guys ever talk about it?" he asks, and when

Daria turns around Marvin's chewing a mouthful of the sandwich and watching her intently, his dark eyes so curious and concerned, and she wishes she could send him home, get through the next few hours on her own somehow.

"Not really."

Marvin nods his head slowly and takes a sip from his coffee cup, swallows and sets the sandwich back down on the blue saucer.

"Not ever?"

"I spent the last decade trying to forget all about Birmingham. Most times it seems like all that crazy shit happened to somebody else."

"And I suppose you've just been hoping it seems that way to Niki, too?"

"You know, Marvin, you're starting to get me pissed. Maybe you better back off a little."

So neither of them says anything for a few minutes. Daria sits back down at the kitchen table and lights another cigarette, smokes it silently while she stares at the cover of an old issue of *Bassics* magazine, Benny Rietveld glowering back at her from the glossy paper. Marvin finishes the sandwich, misses nothing but a few crumbs, one stray sprout like a huge white-green sperm; he carries the saucer to the sink and washes it, then sets it in the rack on the counter to dry.

"We're going to be *fine*," Daria says, to herself or Marvin or no one at all. "We're going to make it," and she closes her eyes and watches the indistinct blobs of not-quite-orange and not-quite-purple light floating about behind her eyelids. *As long as I don't start crying,* she thinks and chews hard at her lower lip. Reminding herself it could have gone so much worse, the terrible thoughts that haunted her on the long flight home from Arkansas to San Francisco—finding Niki dead or a comatose vegetable for the rest of her life—and she wants to feel grateful. Wants to feel relieved, but there's nothing left inside her but lingering shreds of fear and the familiar and smothering dread that has dogged her almost as long as Niki Ky has had to live with the memory of her dead lovers.

"Anytime you need someone to listen, all you got to do is ask," Marvin says. "You know that you and Niki are more than just another job to me," and she can feel his hands resting heavy as stone on her shoulders, the unwelcome, unconditional weight of his sympathy. Something she can neither accept nor return, and she squeezes her eyes shut even tighter, wants to slap his hands away, wants to tell him to take his compassion and fuck the hell off.

"There's nothing you could say that would change that," he says.

Daria sighs and takes a deep breath, another drag off her cigarette, and she opens her eyes as the smoke leaks from her nostrils and hangs suspended like a spent ghost disintegrating above the table.

"No, Marvin, you are definitely wrong about that," she says. "There are things I could tell that you can't even *imagine* . . . but, if I did, you'd never want to see me or Niki again—" and then Daria shakes her head, interrupting herself, because she knows that if she ever got started she wouldn't be able to stop, and the ice is thin enough already. Her silence as much the key to sanity as her strength; not denial, not lies, but the right to keep impossible things to herself and she's never lied to herself, or anyone else about the things she saw and heard the night that Spyder Baxter died. That terrible December night in the old house on Cullom Street, and that should have been the end of it, the moment when they all woke up and went back to living lives without suicides and secrets and regret so bottomless she'll never stop falling.

"With all due respect, I think you're full of it, Daria," and Marvin takes his big hands off her shoulders and sits down again.

But that's something, at least, a small and comfortless re-lief, not to have him pressing down on her, one more thing to bear, and she shrugs her shoulders and stubs out her cigarette in a pewter ashtray already overflowing with Marlboro butts.

"That's your prerogative," she says, trying not to sound angry or exasperated, trying not to sound anything but tired.

"I guess so."

"What are you guys talking about?" Niki asks, and Daria turns to see her standing in the doorway, disheveled and frowzy in her tattered bathrobe and bare feet, rubbing at her eyes like a sleepy child. Her sickly, pale face and bandaged hand, the purple-red half circles beneath her eyes, and she looks small and breakable, a china-doll changeling slipped in when no one was looking.

"I really don't think you should be out of bed yet, honey," Daria says and Niki stops rubbing her eyes and squints at them both.

"I'm hungry. I woke up hungry," she says and those six words better than any of Marvin's reassurances, better than any mantra or self-talk bullshit Daria will ever come up with. Niki yawns and asks Marvin to make her toast, please, toast with Marmite and butter, toast and a glass of ice water, and he's already busy slicing fresh bread when Daria gets up and leads Niki to a chair at the kitchen table.

She looks so tired, Niki thinks, and finishes her toast, asks for something else, and Marvin peels a blood orange for her, pulls it apart into fleshy, seedless wedges.

"You need to get some sleep," she says to Daria. "You're smoking too much again."

"I feel fine," Daria says, but Niki knows she's lying, always knows when Daria's lying and not about to let her off that easily. "You *look* almost as bad as I feel," she says, and Daria frowns at her.

"I slept on the plane."

Marvin goes back to his chair. "Even if that were true," he says, "which I doubt, it wouldn't hurt you to lie down for a little while."

"It's okay now," Niki says. "*I'm* okay," and she manages

a weak smile for Daria, trying to look the least bit reassuring. "Marvin's right here, and all I'm gonna do is sit and eat my orange."

"Do you know how many cups of coffee I've had? I probably couldn't sleep now if my life depended on it."

"Then just lie down for a little while," and Niki wipes her sticky fingers through her snarled black hair. "I'll come back upstairs when I'm done and lie down beside you."

"I have to leave tonight," Daria says, and for a moment Niki doesn't reply, selects another wedge of the orange and nips through the thin skin with her front teeth, sucks at the pulpy, tart insides.

"I'm sorry, Niki. There's no way we can afford to cancel another show."

Niki wipes citrus juice the color of rose petals from her lips with the back of her good hand and swallows. "It's all right," she says, smiling again, pretending she means it so maybe Daria will believe her. "I'm better now. I know you have responsibilities."

"I wouldn't go if I didn't have to."

And because she doesn't know anything else to say, because her head hurts again and she's tired of trying to remember the *right* things to say, because she doesn't want to think about Daria leaving again, she looks away, holds the last slice of blood orange a few inches from her left eye and begins to sing "Strange Fruit" very quietly. Singing to herself and no one else except maybe the orange, singing to it the way that Siouxsie Sioux sang "Strange Fruit" more than the way Billie Holiday did.

"Maybe I'll go lie down in the living room," Daria says and stands up from the table. "I'll just lie down on the couch, and maybe we can talk about it later."

Niki stops singing and glances up at her. "I'm okay," she says, in case Daria didn't hear her the first time. "I'll stay in here with Marvin. I'll be here if you need me."

"We'll both be fine," Marvin adds, and Daria nods once, yeah, whatever sort of nod, takes her pack of cigarettes and her lighter and leaves the kitchen without another word.

Niki pops the last wedge into her mouth and licks the drops of juice from the tips of her fingers. When she notices that Marvin's watching her from his end of the table, she points at the overflowing ashtray, and he gets up, dumps it in the garbage, then sprays the smoky air with a can of Glade.

"So what did she tell you?" Niki asks him, recalling their murmuring voices as she came down the stairs, the almost-whispers, almost-anger, and Marvin sets the can of air freshener on the table and takes his seat again.

"She told me about Spyder and Danny. She told me how they died," and for a moment Niki's head is too full of adrenaline and her heart races, skips a beat or two, maybe, and she doesn't look at him until it's beating normally again and the dizzy, panicked feeling is starting to fade.

"Well, it's not a secret, is it? I would have told you, if you'd ever asked me."

"I didn't know to ask, Niki. I didn't have any idea."

"Did she tell you *all* of it?" Niki asks him, and now there's a bright and razor-edged flutter deep in her belly, something wicked coiled down there that's scary, but it's better than the panic. Marvin stares back at her from his end of the table, and she can see that he's trying hard to figure out what to say next, whether yes or no is the wrong answer this time. Tick-tock, clockwork gears behind his eyes, and she takes a tiny sip from her glass of water. "I didn't think so," she says. "No, she wouldn't ever have done that."

"I'm not sure what you mean. She told me . . ." and he pauses, hesitates, looks towards the doorway like he's hoping that Daria will reappear and get him out of this mess.

"She told me Danny was a transsexual and that Spyder was schizophrenic. And she told me about Spyder's father."

And the scary thing in the pit of Niki's stomach coils itself a little tighter, the adrenaline and fear egging her on, pulling her back, leaving her to her own devices; she takes another drink of water, a big mouthful this time, watching

Marvin over the rim of the glass as she drinks. When she's done, the glass is almost empty, just a couple of melting ice cubes trapped at the bottom.

"Did she tell you about the dead boy we left in Spyder's basement? Or the thing that attacked Mort's van? Did she tell you about the cocoon?"

"No," Marvin says calmly. "She didn't," and his eyes are fixed on hers, grade-school game, test of wills, and *Who's going to blink first?* Niki asks herself. *Who the hell's going to blink first?*

"Did she tell you *why* she's afraid to sleep with the lights off? Or why she's afraid to sleep with them on?"

Marvin shakes his head, folds his hands on the tabletop in front of him, and "Niki, if you want to talk to me," he says, "I'll listen to whatever you want to say. But you might as well stop trying to freak me out."

And the thing in her guts dissolves, undone by his patience, by the constant, undaunted tone of his voice, and she's the one who blinks first, after all.

"I wasn't," she says, and her mouth has gone so dry, wishing there were more ice water in her glass. "I wasn't trying to freak you out."

The sound of sirens then, an ambulance racing along Steiner Street, leaving or approaching an emergency, a death or something close enough, and Niki stares at Marvin and listens until the sirens are too far away for her to hear anymore.

"Somebody's done for," she whispers, softest, acid smile to bend the corners of her mouth, and Marvin puts both elbows on the table and rests his chin on his hands.

"They didn't want to let you come home this time, you know," he says. "But Daria threatened to call your lawyer. They made her sign a release."

"That's stupid. She should have let them keep me. Crazy people belong in hospitals, not running around loose in the real world, fucking up everyone else's lives."

"Do you really think that, or are you just angry?"

"I really think that *and* I'm angry," Niki says, spitting the words at him, cobra-toothed girl spitting venom so maybe he'll leave her alone. But he doesn't.

"Sometimes people have to find their own ways to get well, outside of hospitals."

"Yeah, well, *fuck* that, Marvin. Fuck that. If they'd kept Spyder—" but the cautious glimmer in his eyes makes her stop, triumphant glimmer so she knows he thinks he's only helping, imagines he's found some clever new trick to pry his way inside her. Just like Dr. Dalby, digging at all the soft places, and she tugs at the white gauze wrapped tightly around her hand until it hurts.

"What were you going to say, Niki? If they'd kept Spyder, what?"

"She didn't have insurance," Niki says, and pulls at the bandage again, pain so she won't have to cry, pain to make her angrier. "She didn't have a rich rock-star girlfriend to pay her therapy bills and hire some nosy asshole like you to keep his eye on her. All she had was me, Marvin. At the end, that's all she had. Just *me*."

"And you screwed it up, right? Whatever happened, Spyder dying, that was all your fault."

"I think it's none of your goddamned business."

"Then why are you telling me?"

Niki grabs the water glass with her injured right hand, pulls it back over her shoulder, a fine and deadly missile aimed straight at Marvin's head, but he doesn't move, doesn't even flinch. And so she's sitting there like an idiot, steady trickle of cold water running down her arm and into the sleeve of her bathrobe; she drops the glass, lets it slip, useless, from her aching fingers, and it shatters loudly on the kitchen floor.

From the living room, Daria shouting, Daria sounding confused and alarmed; "What was that? Is something wrong?" and "No," Marvin shouts back. "I dropped a glass, that's all."

And then, lowering his voice, "Why are you telling me, Niki, if it's none of my goddamned business?" and she doesn't answer, glances down at the slicing, crystal shards scattered across the tile floor, waiting there for her bare feet.

"I'm sorry, Marvin."

"You don't have to be sorry. You didn't hurt anyone. It was just a glass."

"Yeah," she says, even though she knows better, knows what it means when she comes that close to letting go, turning loose and making a hole for the violence and scalding red fury to spill through into the world. She nudges a piece of glass with one big toe, pushes it an inch or two across the floor, and then she looks up at Marvin again.

"I grew up in New Orleans," she says, and he nods his head because he knows that already, and she nods back at him. "Anne Rice and Marie Laveau, Dr. John, voodoo queens, all that spooky shit. We used to get stoned and sneak into the cemeteries, hang out in Lafayette and St. Louis *praying* we'd see a ghost or a vampire. Just a *glimpse* would have been enough. We held séances and left flowers and bottles of wine. I even knew this one sick fuck used to sacrifice pigeons and rats to the Elder Gods and the Great Old Ones."

"So, did you?"

"Did I what? Sacrifice rats to Cthulhu?"

Marvin rolls his eyes, and for an instant, half an instant, there's the slimmest, fleeting fissure in his calm, a glint of impatience, and that makes her feel a little bit better.

"No. Did you ever see a ghost?"

"We never saw bupkes, Marvin, unless we were tripping and so fucked up we imagined we were seeing things. But we all wanted it so bad, just that one tiny peek at something bigger and more terrible than our lives. Just a fucking peek, just so we'd *know*.

"But we were wrong. *That's* what I learned in Birmingham, what Spyder showed me—that it's better not to look, not to see, better to believe that it's all just a bunch of fairy stories and silly lies to scare children and there aren't any ghosts at all or magic or monsters or nothing."

"What did you see, Niki?" Marvin asks her, not prying

now, no nursemaid tricks, only asking because he wants to know. She gazes into his eyes for a moment and doesn't say anything at all. His deep eyes so brown they may as well be black, her reflection looking back out from them, and she can tell he's never seen anything he wasn't meant to see.

"Listen," she says, whispering now, whispering so Daria won't hear, and he leans towards her. "I have to go back. Back to Birmingham. We started something, and it isn't over, so I have to go back and finish it. If I don't, it's going to destroy me, and then it's going to destroy Daria."

"Oh," he says and slumps back in his chair, rubs the palms of his hands together and glances nervously towards the clock hung on the wall above the refrigerator. And Niki doesn't say anything else, sits silently, watching him watch the clock, and thinking about the last time she saw Spyder Baxter.

Daria didn't even decorate the house herself; a friend from another band's boyfriend spending her money for her while she was off touring Europe and recording in LA, filling up the place with an incongruous heap of Victorian antiques and the sort of crap Douglas Coupland called "Japanese Minimalism." So these rooms no more her than that painting above the bed, and she lies on a brocade-upholstered love seat in the living room and stares at a Robert Mapplethorpe photograph hanging on the wall across from her. Vulgarity for vulgarity's sake, for the shallow sake of hipness, and she thinks about tossing the hideous thing out the window, and screw the chunk it must have taken out of her bank account.

She closes her eyes, trying to relax, but her head's buzzing from all the coffee and nicotine, a wasp nest built somewhere inside her skull, squirming red wasps and yellow jackets burrowing deep between honeycombed cerebral hemispheres. Her sour stomach is starting to cramp and she thinks about getting up, climbing the stairs, and in her overnight bag there's a bottle of the pills her doctor gives her for what he promises her isn't an ulcer. Daria's still thinking about the pills, about how they don't work as well as they used to, when she falls asleep to the sound of Niki and Marvin whispering to each other in the next room.

And somewhere later, the simple, colorless nothing of unconsciousness bleeds imperceptibly into the ragged edges of an old, neglected dream, and she's standing in the weedy yard in front of Spyder Baxter's dilapidated house on the side of Red Mountain. The day after it snowed all night long, snow up to her ankles, and the lead-flat sky peeking down at her through barren pecan and oak branches. The day they found a dead and frozen girl lying in the middle of Cullom Street, the witchy little goth girl named Robin who'd slept with Spyder before Niki came along, and Daria wishes she'd thought to wear a warm hat because the wind is already making her ears ache.

There isn't time for this shit, she thinks, and if she doesn't hurry she'll miss her flight back east, will miss the Atlanta show, but the wind laughs at her, whips the fallen snow into swirling, pixie-drunk cyclones.

All the time is here, the wind whispers, *all the time you'll ever need,* and Daria looks up at the sky again, the clouds skimming low above the city like the glacier belly of Heaven coming down to grind the earth to dust. Absinthe lightning and thunder and the brittle sound of sunless, frozen worlds; the limbs above her head are trimmed with red icicles, guitar strings and loops of something that looks like wet white yarn, but isn't.

"She was afraid I would spin a web as pretty as hers," the naked, green-haired girl standing on the front porch says, and Daria can see her skeleton outlined beneath withered, frostbite skin, blue and gray, gangrene black; a raw constellation of crimson and violet welts across her Auschwitz arms and face, running sores that weep pus and saccharine tears, and the girl looks over her shoulder, past all the junk crowding Spyder's porch, and she points at an open window.

"You saw, didn't you?" she asks Daria, her voice hard and crack-shear fractured as the sky. "You saw her mercy."

And then a small, staccato sound like a dry twig snapping, wet bone breaking, *snap,* and she turns, but there are only the tall, sleeping trees and the snow-covered path leading back to the street. The air smells like cinnamon and ammonia now, and there are tracks, and Daria would rather not think about what could possibly leave tracks like that.

"The rebel Watchers, exiled fathers of the Nephilim," the girl says. "They have another name, but the sky would bleed if I ever said it aloud."

"I'm cold," Daria says, because she is, shivers and hugs herself; around her, the trees are waking up, have begun to sway and creak and shake the nuisance snow from their bare branches.

"You should have *left* her here," the girl growls, and when Daria turns around again she isn't on the porch anymore, is standing only a few feet away, instead, and tiny, milky, translucent spiders have begun to spill in wriggling clots from the empty sockets where her eyes should be. They gather on her hatchet cheeks, burrow into her hair, drip to the ground at her feet.

"It doesn't matter, though. He'll have her anyway, sooner or later," the dead girl says. "No one gets away. She has His mark and He guards all the passages, all the exits. Spyder knew that, even if she was too afraid to tell us. Even if she lied."

"You stay away from Niki," Daria says, and she knows that it isn't thunder she's hearing at all, no, the drumbeat rustle of vast and spiteful wings above the trees, and she doesn't look away from the grinning, spider-covered face. "Do you hear me? Stay the fuck away from her," and the girl grins wider and holds out her hands. There's a syringe and a small plastic bag of white powder in her palms, a rusted spoon, a guitar pick, and a length of rubber tubing.

"I know your hell, too, Daria," she says.

The house laughs, coughs up sulfur dust and bad memories, and now someone's calling Daria from someplace safe and very, very far away.

"He loved you," the dead girl says. "He would have died for you. He did, I think."

Then the wind rushes by and pulls the girl apart, steals her away in a spinning cloud of rot and baby spiders, and now Daria can see what's waiting for her past the open window. The white, unfinished thing hanging head down from the bedroom ceiling, and when she opens her eyes, Niki is kneeling next to the love seat, tears streaking her cheeks and the bandage on her hand starting to unravel.

"I'm so sorry," she says. "I tried. I tried to die and make it be over. I tried to keep them from finding you, too," and part of Daria Parker's head is still lost in the dream of snow and angel wings and smiling, zombie ghosts. She sits up slowly, dizzy, disoriented, and the nausea and pain in her stomach are worse than before she fell asleep.

"No . . . it's okay," she says, mouth gone as dry as cracker crumbs, tongue like something she doesn't quite remember how to use. "I was having a nightmare, that's all, Niki. Just a stupid, goddamn nightmare." And she puts an arm around Niki's waist, pulls her close and holds her while the dream begins to fade, and Niki sobs, and long, late-afternoon shadows fill the room.

"No, it's absolutely out of the question," Daria says, and then her cell phone starts ringing again, and this time she turns it off instead of answering it. "Jesus, Niki, stop and *think* about this a minute. It's crazy."

"Then it ought to be right up my alley." Niki's curled into the window seat, knees pulled up beneath her chin, and she pretends to watch Alamo Square while Daria fusses about with the tangle of clean and dirty clothes stuffed into her bulging overnight bag sitting at the foot of the bed.

"That's not what I meant and you fucking well know it."

"I know that's why you never listen to me anymore. Anything you don't want to hear, all you have to do is re-mind me I'm crazy, and that's the end of it."

"Bullshit," Daria mutters and bends over to pick up a

pair of pale yellow panties that have escaped the bag and fallen to the floor. "But you're not about to guilt-trip me into thinking that you going back to Birmingham is any kind of good idea, so you may as well stop trying."

Niki pushes her bangs out of her eyes and stares down at the park. There's a child playing Frisbee with a big black dog and for a moment she thinks the dog has noticed her, that it's staring up at her, and she looks away.

"If I'm crazy, Daria, then what difference does it make? If it's all in my head, I'm just as safe there as I am here."

"I said *no*, Niki, so how about let's just drop it," and somehow the yellow panties have gotten pushed under the edge of the bed, and Daria has to get down on her knees to retrieve them. Niki watches her instead of the dog and tries to think of something to say to get Daria's attention, get her mind off the airplane and the band and Atlanta, because it's already three o'clock and she's running out of time.

"I know the things you dream about," she says. "I know you see things too, even when you're awake."

Daria stands up, stands staring at Niki, the panties in one hand and she rubs at her forehead with the other.

"What the hell is that supposed to mean?"

"You know what it means," Niki says and turns back to the child and his dog because it's easier than the bright flecks of anger and resentment in Daria's eyes. The dog is definitely looking at her, stealing glances at the high bedroom window whenever it knows for certain that its boy won't notice.

"No, Niki, I don't. That's probably why I asked you."

"You try to be just like everyone else, like you don't know better. You want me to believe you don't know better."

Daria sighs loudly and clicks her tongue once against the roof of her mouth, but Niki doesn't turn around. The child throws the Frisbee, and it sails twenty or thirty feet before the dog leaps into the air and catches it.

"I know you feel alone," Daria says, and Niki can hear

how hard she's trying not to get pissed off, the fraying calm in her voice. "I understand that it would probably make you feel better if you were right and I did see these . . . these *things*. But I don't, Niki, and I'm not going to lie to you and say that I do."

"You have dreams," Niki says, sounding defensive and wishing that she didn't.

"Yes, I have dreams. I have nightmares, and sometimes they're really fucking awful, but what the hell do you expect?"

"You were *there*," Niki whispers, close to tears again, and she's sick of crying, doesn't want to start crying again because Daria will only think it's a trick to get her to listen, to get her to stay. "You were there, and you saw what happened in Spyder's house."

"She hung herself, Niki. That's what I saw that night. That's all I saw."

"I know you're lying to me, Dar," and now she is crying, and Niki smacks the window once with her bandaged hand. The glass quivers in its frame, but doesn't break, and the noise makes the dog and the child pause and look up at her. "You're scared to death and so you pretend it never happened, that you never saw anything you can't explain away or—"

"That's not true, Niki."

"Yes, goddamn it, it *is* true," and Niki turns to face Daria, speaking through clenched teeth, and both her hands are balled into small, hard fists. "It's true and you know it's true. And no matter how many therapists you send me to or how many pills I take, it's *still* going to be true. Spyder didn't kill herself, and you know that as well as I do."

"I've heard enough of this, Niki. I have a plane to catch," and Daria stuffs the panties back into the overnight bag and zips it shut. "Some of us have to live in the real world."

"Fuck you, Daria," and Niki wipes her nose with the back of her bandaged hand. There's a small, dark splotch of blood seeping through the gauze where it covers her palm, so she knows she's ripped the stitches loose.

"You can't stop me from going back," she says. "Not if I mean to."

Daria picks up the bag and glances at the clock beside the bed, the clock and the vase of lilies, then back at Niki.

"No, you're wrong about that, too. I *could* stop you. You're not well, and if I thought it was the right thing to do, I could stop you. You'd still be in that fucking hospital, if I'd let them keep you. But I couldn't stand that, knowing you were locked up in there like some kind of a lab animal."

"I *have* to go back," Niki says, and she knows she's fucked it all up again, too late to even hope that Daria will listen to anything else she says, too late to stop her from walking away. Walking out, and now she's pleading, the fury drained from her as quickly as it came, and she wishes that her hand didn't hurt so damn much and then maybe she could think more clearly. "I don't want to, but I have to. I don't ever want to see that place again, I swear to god."

"You're a grown woman, Niki. You have to make your own decisions. I love you, but I can't play these games with you, and I can't spend the rest of my life trying to be sure you never hurt yourself again."

"I don't want to go," Niki says, and when Daria turns away from her, heading for the bedroom door, for the stairs and the airport, she jumps to her feet, and "Please," she begs. "Please, Daria. I don't want to have to go back there alone. I don't think I can face it alone."

"Then stay here. I'll be back in two weeks, and I'll call you when I get to the hotel." Then she takes her bag and leaves Niki standing by herself in the bedroom.

"I don't want to," she says, after Daria and Marvin have stopped talking downstairs, after the sound of the front door opening and slamming closed again, whispering the words for herself because there's no one to hear her now except the ghost of Danny Boudreaux smirking from a corner. A few drops of blood have leaked through the gauze and dripped from her hand to the hardwood floor; in a little while she goes back to the window seat, and the boy with the Frisbee and the dog have gone, if they were ever there at all.

And later, two hours, two and a half, and by now, she thinks, Daria's plane is probably in the air, somewhere high above the clouds over Arizona or New Mexico, winging its way far from Niki and everything she represents. And in the big house on Steiner Street, Niki has finished packing her own suitcase, has only left the bedroom once on a quick trip down the hall for the stuff that she needed from the bathroom—toothpaste and her toothbrush, maxi pads and deodorant, a bottle of shampoo—and she's trying to remember anything she might have forgotten, anything she might possibly need, when Marvin finally comes upstairs to check on her.

"Hey there," he says. "I would have looked in on you sooner, but Daria said to give you some time alone." And then his eyes are on the open suitcase instead of her. "You're really serious about this, aren't you."

"I already called the airport. I couldn't get a flight out until almost nine tonight."

"She told me not to stop you, Niki."

"I don't think she gives a shit what I do, as long as I stay out of her way while I'm doing it."

"You don't believe that. I know you don't believe that," and he comes in, sits down on the bed beside the suitcase. Niki closes it and the zipper sticks twice before she gets it to work right.

"Whatever. It doesn't matter."

Marvin scratches at his chin, and "Jesus," he sighs. "Can we please just talk about this for a minute. Maybe Daria has decided it's a good idea to let you go wandering off alone—"

"I'm not 'wandering off' anywhere. I know exactly where I'm going. When I'm finished, I'll try to come back."

"What do you mean, you'll *try*?"

"I mean I'll try, that's all," she says, then wrestles the heavy suitcase to the floor between them and sits down on the edge of the bed next to Marvin. "In the kitchen, I told you everything I could, everything I know for sure." But the way Marvin's looking at her makes her feel like she hasn't tried to tell him anything, like she's holding back, even though she isn't, and she wishes he would stop.

"This is so totally fucked up. You know that, right? I mean, yesterday you almost *died* on us, Niki."

"I feel better now."

"You look like Death with a hangover. Daria must have been thinking with her ass, taking you out of the hospital like that."

"Look, I asked you to help me, and you said that you couldn't, so the least you can do is lay off. I know what I did, Marvin, and I know what I look like. All I said was I *feel* better."

Marvin kicks once at the suitcase, halfhearted kick with the toe of his right sneaker and the bag rocks back on two of its small plastic wheels, but doesn't fall over.

"I'll be okay," Niki says. "I'll let you know when I get into Denver."

Fresh confusion on Marvin's face to make her flinch and "Denver?" he asks. "I thought you said you had to get to Birmingham."

"I have to go to Colorado first. I have to see Mort and Theo, and I have to look for something I left there."

Marvin glances up at the ceiling, white paint and plaster and a jagged, hairline crack from an earthquake last spring that no one's gotten around to having repaired. He closes his eyes and Niki wonders what he's been taking to stay awake.

"I want to believe you," he says. "I'm sure you probably think that's a load, but it isn't. I want to think this isn't all some twisted fantasy bullshit your brain's spitting up because it isn't wired the right way or it's not getting enough dopamine or whatever. I'm trying so hard, Niki—"

"Don't, Marvin. You can't force yourself into belief. I never should have told you. I should have kept my mouth shut. None of this even has anything to do with you."

He opens his eyes, clears his throat and turns towards her. "Before, the girl I was taking care of before you . . ." and he pauses, standing here at the brink of some confidence because he thinks he owes her one, tit-for-tat, reciprocal confession, and *I should stop him,* she thinks. *I should stop him now before this goes any further and it's too late to go back.* But he's already talking again, and she doesn't have the courage to do anything but sit on the bed and listen.

"The girl before you, I lost her. She was only fifteen, and she'd already tried to kill herself four times. She said she saw wolves whenever she was left alone—not real wolves, but that's what she always called them because she said there wasn't a word for what they were. She told me they'd come after her because she was really one of them, but she'd been born wrong. That's exactly the way she put it. 'I was born wrong.'

"I hadn't been with her a month when she broke a mirror and slashed her throat. Her parents were both at work, and I couldn't keep pressure on the wound *and* reach the fucking telephone. So this fifteen-year-old girl bleeds to death right there in my arms. And the whole time, I could see how scared she was. I knew, I fucking *knew* she thought the wolves were coming, that she could *see* them coming, and this time it didn't matter if I was there or not."

He stops, breathless, his Adam's apple and a spot beneath his left eye twitching, and Niki realizes that he's holding her hands now; Marvin holding both her hands in his like he's about to kiss her or get down on one knee and propose marriage. Like he's afraid of losing her, too, the same way he lost the girl who saw wolves, the same way she lost Spyder and Danny, and maybe if he can just hold on to her long enough it doesn't have to happen.

"I've never seen wolves," Niki says uncertainly, all she can think of, and the silence between them so absolute it's starting to hurt, starting to embarrass, and now there are tears leaking from Marvin's eyes and winding slowly down his stubbled cheeks.

"I know that, and maybe that other girl, maybe she never saw any wolves either, but that's not the point. She *believed* she saw wolves, Niki, and in the end that's all that mattered."

"Yeah, I know," Niki says, thinking of the things Spyder thought she saw, not wanting to see him cry, and he squeezes her hands tighter. It hurts, but she doesn't say so; she squeezes back instead, gazes past Marvin at Danny Boudreaux staring at them from his corner. Some wild expression stretched like a latex Halloween mask across his cold and irrefutable ghost's face, jealousy or hope or a wicked, secretive smile, no way for her to be sure, and then he's gone and there's nothing but a smudgy bit of shadow left behind.

"I can't believe what you told me, Niki, so I'm just gonna have to take your word for it. If I can't see what you see, then I can at least trust you. I'm not going to let you do this alone."

And when he finally lets go of her hands, releasing them slowly like he's afraid she's going to run, all the dark blood that's leaked through Niki's torn stitches and raveling bandages spills out between their fingers and trickles onto the bed. Marvin's face goes slack, then taut and sick, realizing what he's done to her, horror vying with apology for control, and he opens his mouth to say something, but "No," she says, places her good hand over his lips and smiles a smile she doesn't have to fake. "I'm okay. It doesn't hurt all that bad. I think I'm going to be okay now."

While Marvin packs and calls the airline, Niki goes back to the upstairs bathroom to look at her hand. Down the hall, past the room where Daria keeps her record collection and her guitars, and the bathroom is big and white and smells faintly of Dow Scrubbing Bubbles and strongly of the bowl of lavender potpourri on the back of the commode. Clean smells, and Niki wonders how the bathroom would smell if Daria hadn't hired Marvin. The lion-footed, cast-iron tub and all those little hexagonal tiles on the floor, a narrow, stained-glass window above the tub so she can see the last of the day, and she sits down on the toilet seat and begins unwrapping the gauze. Marvin wanted to do it, but she refused, so he fussed with the bloody bed-clothes instead, carting them off to the laundry hamper and apologizing over and over even though she asked him not to; the stitches torn before he squeezed her hand, any-way, and it's something she wants to do herself.

The entire palm side of the dressing is stained, some of the blood already gone dry and stiff, and she unwinds it slowly, winces when she gets near the end and some of the gauze has stuck to her skin, stuck to the crusty edges of the hole in her hand. Niki lets the bandage fall to the floor, a sloppy pile of crimson and maroon and white at her feet. The stitches have come loose, all eight of them, and she knows that Marvin's probably going to insist she see a doc-tor again before they leave town. Niki stares at her hand, trying to remember exactly what did and didn't happen in the restroom at Cafe Alhazred: the swelling and whatever grew inside it, the thing that had burrowed into her flesh, Danny, and then someone shouting and pounding angrily on the door.

Niki reaches for a coral pink washcloth hanging on a rack near the tub and wraps it around her hand, squeezes it and grits her teeth against the pain.

Was any of it real, the squirming, transparent child of her infection, something she saw or only something that she thought she saw?

Do you really think there's any difference? and she hopes that voice is only hers, her own voice from her own sick head, because she honestly isn't in the mood for Danny Boudreaux right now. No time for anything that might slow her down, no hope but movement, and she stands up and goes to the sink, twists one of the brass knobs, and in a mo-ment hot water is gurgling into the porcelain basin.

"You wanted her, and now she has you, forever," exactly what Danny said at Alhazred, and that's what the face in the mirror says when she looks up from the sink. But it isn't her face in the glass, and it isn't Danny's either, this haggard young man with eyes like stolen fire, eyes like the last breath rattling out of a dying man's chest, but then he's gone, and she's staring into her own dark and frightened eyes.

Niki raises her left hand and cautiously places her fingertips against the mirror, half expecting her hand to pass straight through, nothing solid there to stop her. But it's just a mirror, and the silvered glass is smooth and cold and reflects nothing but the lost girl she's become, the lost woman, and she looks back down at the water filling the sink.

"All I have do is make it to the airport," she says, wishing she were already in Boulder, and so many opportunities to back out had come and passed her by; over the Rocky Mountains and safe for a while with Mort and Theo before she has to see this shit through to the end. Niki shuts off the tap and lowers her right hand slowly into the clear, steaming water; it doesn't hurt half so much as she expected, and she wonders whether that's good or bad, watches with more curiosity than concern as her blood starts to turn the water red. *Just like Moses,* she thinks, and it annoys her that she can't remember which number plague that was.

"How are you doing in here?" Marvin asks, and she turns her head towards the bathroom door, making sure he's really there and really him before she answers.

"I think I'll live," and he comes closer, then, scowls down at her hand, and by now the water looks more like cherry Kool-Aid.

"Damn. You realize we're going to have to get that stitched closed again before we leave."

"That's what I thought you'd say," and she lifts her hand out of the water so he can look at it more closely.

"Yeah, well, bleeding to death would probably be a lot more inconvenient. God, Niki, how did you even *do* this?"

"I already told you that," and she did, but Marvin shakes his head anyway.

"Well, at least it doesn't look as if there's any infection setting in," and he opens the medicine cabinet, his own little ER stashed away in there, and takes out a sterile gauze pad and a roll of surgical tape, a plastic bottle of hydrogen peroxide. "This will probably do until we can get you to a doctor, if you'll go easy on this hand."

"The flight's at nine," she reminds him.

"We're not going to miss the flight, and if we do, we'll get another one."

"I want to ask you something," but then he pours the peroxide over her hand and it stings, foams the ugly color of funeral-parlor carnations. "Shit, Marvin," she hisses and tries to pull her hand away.

"Don't be a pussy. What do you want to ask me?"

Niki waits until the stinging starts to fade, until he's rinsed her hand and dabbed it dry with a fresh washcloth and has started bandaging it again.

"It's kind of personal," but he only shrugs.

"Sex, drugs, or politics?" he asks, and "Neither," she says, and he glances up at her.

"Then it has to be religion, right?" and Niki nods. "I was Catholic," he continues, "once upon a time. Ancient history."

"So you don't believe in God anymore?"

"I believe we'll find out when the time comes," he says and takes a small pair of scissors from the medicine cabinet to snip the sticky white surgical tape. "Whether we want to or not."

She doesn't say anything for a moment, watches him working on her hand while she weighs words in her head, words and their consequences, and she can tell it makes Marvin feel better that there's finally something he can do for her.

"What if you're wrong, and we never get to find out? It's kind of presumptuous, isn't it, assuming that dead people get all the answers? Maybe they don't know any more than we do."

"My, but we're in an existential mood today, aren't we?"

"It's just something I was thinking about yesterday morning, that's all. How terrible it would be to be dead, to be a ghost and know that you're dead, and still not know if there's a God."

"Is that how you think it works?"

"I don't know what I think anymore," Niki says, and then Marvin's finished, has started putting everything back into the medicine cabinet, and the bloody water is swirling away down the drain. "But I've seen ghosts, and they don't seem very happy about it. Being dead, I mean."

"Are you afraid of them?" he asks, not exactly changing the subject, and he closes the medicine cabinet; Niki looks at the mirror, but the only reflections she can see there are hers and Marvin's.

"There are worse things than ghosts," she replies.

"Like wolves?" he asks her, and Niki doesn't answer, glances down at the floor, instead. There's a single red drop of her blood spattering the tiles.

"We should hurry," she says, and Marvin doesn't reply, and she waits impatiently while he takes time to wipe the floor clean again.

Thirty-five thousand feet above the mesas and buttes of Monument Valley and Daria stares through the tiny window in the 767's fuselage, watching the sunset turning the tops of the clouds all the brilliant colors of the desert below. Flying into night, deep indigo sky ahead and fire behind them, and soon there will be stars. A cramped seat in coach because she's too worried about money these days to spring for first-class tickets when this will get her to Atlanta just as fast. She has her headphones on, an old Belly album in her Discman, Tanya Donelly singing "Untogether" to simple acoustic guitar, and it makes her miss Niki that much worse. Music from the year they met, though not exactly the sort of thing she would have listened to back then. Too busy trying to keep up with the boys to suffer anything so pretty or vulnerable, too busy learning to be harder than she already was, and for a moment Daria thinks about digging a different CD out of the backpack at her feet. But the song ends, and the next track is faster and edgier and a little easier to take.

She closes her eyes, so far beyond sleepy, but it's a nice thought, anyway, dozing off to the soothing thrum of jet engines, and then the man sitting in the seat next to her touches her lightly on the shoulder.

"You're Daria Parker, aren't you? The singer," he asks, only a very faint hint of hesitation in his voice, and she almost says *No, I'm not. No, but people are always telling me how much I look like her.* She's done it plenty enough times before, and it usually works.

Instead, she opens her eyes, the sky outside the window a shade or two darker than before, and "Yeah," she says, and the man shakes her hand. Nothing remarkable about him, but nothing unremarkable, either, and she wonders how anyone could look that perfectly average. He introduces himself, perfectly average name she'll forget as soon as he stops bothering her and goes back to the computer magazine lying open in his lap.

"Wow. I *knew* it was you," he says. "I never would have recognized you, but my daughter has a poster of your band on her bedroom door. She'll die when I tell her about this."

Daria slips her headphones off and tries to remember all the polite things to say to an inquisitive stranger on an airplane, the careful, practiced words and phrases that neither insult nor encourage, but she's drawing a blank, and he still hasn't stopped shaking her hand.

"What's her name?"

"Alma. It's a family name. Well, my mother's middle name, anyway," and he finally lets go of her hand, has to so he can dig out his wallet to show her a picture of his daughter.

"How old is she?" Daria asks as the man flips hastily past his driver's license, a library card, and at least a dozen credit cards.

"Fourteen. Fifteen next month," and then he passes the wallet to Daria and the girl in the photograph stares back at her through the not-quite-transparent plastic of a protective sleeve. The sort of picture they take once a year at school, yearbook-bland sort of photograph your parents have to buy, and aside from one very large pimple, Alma looks almost as average as her father.

"She has every one of your records. Even an old cassette tape she bought off eBay, from when you were in that other band, the Dead Kittens."

"Stiff Kitten," Daria says, correcting him even though she probably shouldn't, probably rude, but he just nods his head agreeably and takes the wallet when Daria hands it back to him.

"Right, yeah. Stiff Kitten. Anyway, she paid seventy-three dollars for that old tape, if you can believe it."

"I don't even have a copy of that myself," which is true, her last copy of the demo she recorded with Mort and Keith lost before she and Niki moved to San Francisco. "I haven't heard it in years."

"Well, let me tell you, I sure have. She plays it constantly. I keep telling her she's going to wear it out. Personally, I prefer your newer stuff."

"Me, too," she says, and the man laughs.

"Would you mind signing something for her? I hate to bother you, but she'd kill me—"

"No, it's okay, really," relieved that they've gotten around to the inevitable and he'll probably stop talking soon, hoping that she doesn't *look* relieved, but running out of chit-chat and patience. Just wanting to shut her eyes again, put the headphones back on, and with any luck she can sleep the rest of the way to Atlanta.

The man tears a subscription card out of the computer magazine and Daria signs one side of it with a ballpoint pen from his shirt pocket. "To Alma, be true," and "That's nice," the man says when he reads it. "That's very nice. Thank you. She'll be tickled pink."

Daria almost laughs, the very last thing in the world she would have expected him to say, *tickled pink,* and then she sees the tattoo on the back of his right hand. Fading blue-black-green ink scar worked deep into his skin, concentric and radial lines connecting to form a spider's web, and he sees that she's staring at it.

"Stupid, isn't it? Had that done when I was in college. My wife says I should have it removed, but I don't know. It reminds me of things I might forget, otherwise."

And Daria doesn't reply, gives the man's pen back to him, and he asks her a couple more questions—what's it like, all the travel, the fans, has she ever met one of the Beatles—and she answers each question with the first thing that comes into her head. Forcing herself not to look at the tattoo again, and then the stewardess comes trundling down the narrow aisle with the beverage cart. The man asks for a beer, a lite beer, and Daria takes the opportunity to turn away and put the headphones over her ears again. Outside, it's almost dark, a handful of stars twinkling high and cold and white, and she stares at them through her ghost-dim reflection until she falls asleep.

CHAPTER THREE

Ghosts and Angels

Niki wanted to call a taxi, but they took Marvin's car, instead. A very small concession, she thought, give and take, only something to make her seem a little more reasonable. On the outside, the old VW Beetle looks like someone's been at it with a sledgehammer and a crowbar; inside, it smells like mold and the ancient, duct-taped upholstery, the fainter, sweeter scents of his cologne and something she thinks might be peppermint Altoids. A puttering, noisy punch line of a car and "How much *does* Daria pay you?" she asks him, though *How much* doesn't *she pay you?* seems more to the point.

"Enough," he says, turning off Steiner onto Fell, the streetlights much, much brighter than his wavering low beams.

"Obviously not enough to buy a new car," she mutters, thinking that Marvin won't hear her over the Volkswagen's clattering engine, but he does.

"Yes. Enough to buy a new car, if I *wanted* a new car. I've had Mariah here since I started college. She gets me everywhere I need to go. How's the hand feeling?"

"It hurts."

"More or less than before?" and Niki thinks about that for a few seconds before answering, staring down at the bandage, thinking about Cafe Alhazred and the old man at the museum who wasn't Dr. Dalby.

"Just about the same," she says, finally.

"Well, then. It could be worse."

"I *don't* need to see a doctor," she whispers emphatically.

"Yes, Niki, you do," he says, and she wonders how he can hear anything at all over the racket the car's making. "You do, and you will. We're not going to argue about this."

She sighs and holds her aching hand up, rests it against the cool, streaky glass of the passenger's side window. And wonders again if maybe this whole thing isn't just a trick to get her to the hospital, a trick to keep her in San Francisco. Maybe Marvin didn't really call the airport at all. Maybe he called Dr. Dalby, instead.

Maybe they're already waiting for her at the hospital.

You just get her here, and we'll take it from there.

Thorazine and restraining straps, needles and pills and perhaps it wasn't even Marvin. Maybe Daria set the whole thing in motion before she left the house.

"We're going to do this," Marvin says resolutely. "But we're going to do it *right*. I'm not sure you understand how serious that cut could be if it gets infected. Hell, for all I know it's *already* infected."

"It doesn't feel infected. It just hurts some, that's all."

"Trust me," Marvin says, squinting at the street through the Volkswagen's dirty windshield. "We'll be in and out and on our way in no time."

He's lying, Danny Boudreaux whispers from the backseat, his ghost's voice like venom and sugar. *You know he's lying, Niki. I can see it in your eyes.*

She glances reluctantly at the side-view mirror, and there's nothing in the backseat but their luggage, half hidden in the darkness behind her.

"I never said that I didn't trust you, Marvin," and so he smiles a nervous smile for her, then wrestles the stick into third.

"It was just a figure of speech, you know that. Don't start getting paranoid on me, Niki."

"I've always trusted you. You and Daria both. The two

of you, you're the only people I have left in the world now, aren't you?"

There's a red light up ahead, and Marvin shifts down again, grimacing at the noises coming from the transmission. "Easy, girl," he says, and Niki isn't sure if he's talking to the car or to her.

Listen to me, Danny whispers urgently from the backseat. *Listen to me while there's still time. You know damn well what's going to happen when he gets you to the hospital. You know they'll lock you up again.*

"You don't have to whisper," she says, glancing back to the mirror and the pile of luggage. "He can't hear you."

You don't know what he can hear, Niki.

"Who are you talking to?" Marvin asks, flipping a lever for the right turn signal, and the car comes to a stop at the intersection of Fell and Divisadero. A teenage girl on inline skates and a homeless man in a baggy pink sweatshirt and cowboy hat cross the street in front of them.

"Myself," Niki tells Marvin. "I'm talking to myself," but she can see he doesn't believe her, the look in his eyes, his hesitant frown.

"If you're hearing voices again, you need to say so. You know keeping them a secret only makes things worse."

Lying nigger fag, Danny Boudreaux sneers, but she's pretty sure it's not Danny's voice anymore; some other voice back there, words ground against words like metal grinding metal, like the Volkswagen's worn-out transmission. *You know better, Niki. I fucking know you know better than to trust this faggot son of a bitch.*

"I don't hear *anything*," she insists, biting at her lower lip and turning away from the mirror, staring up at the traffic light, instead. "I don't hear anything at all."

"You know you can tell me the truth," Marvin says, and he steals a nervous peek at the rearview mirror, so maybe he *can* hear the voices.

This time they won't stop with the drugs, Niki. This time you'll get electroshock. This time—this time they'll plug you in and fill your head so full of lightning you'll never think

*of anything else ever again. Just white fire and crackling
sparks trapped inside your skull with no way out until it
burns you to a cinder.*

"Is that really what you think?" she replies, replying to
the crankshaft, gear-rust voice in the backseat, not Marvin,
but he nods his head, anyway.

I can smell the smoke already.

"Yeah, Niki. That's really what I think. I think you know
that you can trust me."

The stoplight like a crimson eye blazing in the chilly November night, a single dragon's eye peering into this world
from someplace else, peering in and finding her trapped inside the ugly little car with Marvin and the ghosts in the
backseat. She's cornered, rat in a cage, rabbit with no place
left to run, and in another second or two, it'll tear its way
through, shredding the space between worlds in its steel
and ivory claws.

*He has more eyes than you could ever count. If you had
three eternities, you'd never count them all.*

"We're going to the airport," Niki says quietly, shutting
her eyes so she doesn't have to see the dragon seeing her.
"You're taking me to the doctor, and then we're going to
the airport."

"Yes. That's exactly what we're doing."

"You wouldn't lie to me, Marvin? Not ever? Not even if
you thought it was for my own good?"

"No, I wouldn't lie to you, Niki."

They've prepared a special place for you, the voice from
the backseat purls. *You should know that. Here and there. A
place where no one will ever find you, not even Spyder.*

"I *need* to believe that, Marvin. I fucking *want* to believe
that," but she's reaching for the door, her hand around the
handle before her eyes are even open, and he sees her and
grabs her shoulder.

"What are you doing, Niki. I told you—"

"I can't take any chances. You don't know what's at
stake. You don't know—"

"I *can't* know what you won't *tell* me." And now he

sounds frightened, more frightened than angry. The light changes, crimson eye blinking itself to emerald green, and he looks at it and then quickly back to Niki.

"Please, Niki. I need you to let go of the door handle. The light's changed."

"Yeah, but it's not looking for *you,* Marvin, is it? It's not fucking looking for you," and it scares her how small and far away her voice sounds now, like she's watching a movie or television and the volume's been turned almost all the way down; her heart so much louder than her voice, her heart grown as wide and endless as the black California night spread out overhead.

Claws to tear through time and space and anything in between, anything in its way. Claws to tear the sky, to tear your heart apart—

"You can't even *hear* it."

"I'm going to pull over now, okay? And I need you to be still, just long enough for me to pull over, and then we'll get out of the car if that's what you need to do."

Liar, the voice growls softly, unbelieving, and now it only sounds like Danny Boudreaux again. Only sounds like the strangled voice of a dead boy, not the vulcanized rubber tongues of damned and scorched machineries. *He's just trying to save himself. He's made deals, and if you get away, if he* lets *you get away—*

Behind the Volkswagen, someone begins honking their horn, and Niki looks up at the green light again.

"I fucking swear to God, Niki, I am not lying to you," and Marvin cuts the wheel, nowhere to park but the crosswalk, and for a moment, the still point between breathing in and breathing out, she can't look away from the light, from the eye. Red means stop, green means go, go Niki, go *now,* while there's still somewhere left to run.

"I'm sorry, Marvin," she says and opens the door, jerking free of his grip and almost tumbling out onto the pavement, catching herself at the last and stepping quickly away from the car.

"Niki, don't *do* this! Please, *listen* to me," but she's already turned her back on him and his musty car and all the other cars trapped there behind the sputtering Volkswagen. She's not running yet, because none of this feels real enough to let herself start running, not just yet, but she is walking very fast, the soles of her boots loud against the sidewalk.

You better *run, babe,* Danny says, and she realizes that he's following her. *You better run fast, because you can bet he's going to be coming after you any minute now.*

Niki looks back over her shoulder; Marvin's pulling over to the curb, and she starts walking faster. Her head's grown so full that she can't think—the drivers still blowing their horns because Marvin can't get out of their way quickly enough, Danny and all the other voices, the ruby fire and green ice of the dragon's eye. Everything getting in through her ears and her eyes, flooding her, and there's no way she can shut it all out, no inch of silence left anywhere in her deafened soul.

Where you going, Niki? Danny asks her. *Where you headed in such a goddamned hurry?*

"You leave me alone," she spits back, wishing there were flesh and blood left of him, something solid for her to dig her nails and teeth into, something that could bleed. "You're dead. You're fucking dead because you were too afraid to live anymore. You're dead, so leave me the hell alone and *be* fucking dead!"

That morning you left me, that was the end of the world for me, Nicolan. That morning I trusted you, and you left me alone. I knew you'd never ever be coming back for me.

"Where am I going? Where the hell am I supposed to go now?" she asks, not asking *him,* not asking anyone, just repeating questions over and over and over because she needs the answers more than she's ever needed anything in her life.

That's not true, Niki. Not more than you needed me, not more than you needed Spyder—

"I said leave me the fuck alone! Get out of my head!" and she spins around, swinging at empty air, at the insubstantial, unresisting night draped so thick about her.

You'll find the way. She believes in you, so I know that you'll find the way.

Her own scalding tears to blind her, to blur the softening edges of brick walls and blacktop rivers, Divisadero Street become a smeared tableau, oil on canvas, and she thinks if she can only stand still long enough Marvin will find her and take her back home again.

You'll follow the road that Orc took, and Esau. You'll follow the road beneath the lake, the Serpent's Road, because He's watching all the other ways.

And this voice she'll know when she's forgotten every other sound in the universe, when even the stars have burned themselves away to nothing and the earth has finally ceased to spin. This voice seared into her mind so deeply, so raw, its touch can never heal, can never even scar; Niki screams and falls, and there's nothing but the sidewalk concrete there to catch her.

They have set themselves against us, Niki, and they will stop at nothing, not until we're all dead. Not until we are all held forever within the borders of fire and slag and—

"Spyder?" Niki sobs, one hand held up high, held out, and someone's pulling her off the ground, pulling her back up into the world, into the light, into herself. "Oh God, Spyder, please help me make them understand."

There are still two of you to stand against them. Bring him to me, Niki, by the Serpent's Road, the road beneath the lake that burns.

Bring him down to me.

"Spyder! Wait—" but the voice has gone, and the night snaps suddenly back upon itself like a broken rubber band, something wound once too often. She's standing on the sidewalk, and Marvin's holding her so tightly she can hardly breathe. He's crying, too, and she hangs on to him, hanging on for whatever life she has left that might be worth saving.

"Don't you dare do that to me again," he says and hugs her tighter. "Don't you dare."

And she doesn't tell him that she won't, and she doesn't

tell him that she will, and in a few minutes he leads her back down Divisadero to the Volkswagen waiting at the corner.

Niki was born two years after the fall of Saigon, twenty-three years after Eisenhower had agreed to fund and train South Vietnamese soldiers to fight the communists. Her parents were among the lucky few, the handful of South Vietnamese evacuated along with American citizens. John and Nancy Ky had become Americans and immigrated to New Orleans, traded in tradition and their Vietnamese names, the horrors of their lives in Tay Ninh and Saigon for citizenship and a small tobacco shop on Magazine Street. They had named their only child Nicolan Jeane, and would have named the son her father had wished for Nicolas. But Niki's birth left her mother bedridden for more than a month, and the doctors warned that another pregnancy would very likely kill her.

Neither of Niki's parents ever made a habit of talking about their lives before New Orleans, and they kept themselves apart from the city's tight-knit Vietnamese community. They seemed always to struggle to answer any questions Niki asked about their lives before America in as few words as possible, as if bad memories and bad days had ears and could be summoned like demons. Occasionally, there were letters, exotic stamps and picture postcards from halfway around the world, messages from faceless relatives written in the mysterious alphabet that she never learned to read. Her mother kept these in some secret place, or maybe she simply threw them away. Niki treasured her rare glimpses of this correspondence, would sometimes hold an envelope to her nose and lips, hoping for some whiff or faint taste of a world that must have been so much more marvelous than their boxy white and avocado green house in the Metairie suburbs.

And when she was ten years old, just a few days past her tenth birthday, there was a terrible Gulf storm. The ghost of a hurricane that had died at sea, slinging its spirit landward, and she awoke in the night or in the morning before dawn, and her mother was sitting at the foot of her bed. Niki lay very still, listening to the rain battering the roof, the wind dragging itself across and through everything. The room smelled like the menthol cigarettes her mother had smoked for as long as Niki could remember, and she watched the glowing orange tip of the Salem, a silent marker for her mother's dim silhouette.

"Do you hear that, Niki?" her mother asked. "The sky is falling."

Niki listened, hearing nothing but the storm and a garbage can rattling about noisily somewhere behind the house.

"No, mother. It's just a storm. It's only rain and wind."

"Yes," her mother replied. "Yes. Of course, Niki."

The cigarette glowed more intensely in the darkness, but she didn't hear her mother exhale over the roar and wail of the storm.

"When I was a girl," her mother said, "when I was only a little older than you, Niki, I saw, with my own eyes, the sky fall down to earth. I saw the stars fall down and burn the world. I saw *children*—"

And then lightning flashed so bright and violent, and her mother seemed to wither in the electric-white glare, hardly alive in her flannel housecoat and the lines on her face drawn deep as wounds. Off towards the river, the thunder rumbled contentedly to itself, and Niki realized how tightly her mother was squeezing her leg through the covers.

"It's okay, Mother," Niki whispered, trying to sound like she believed what she was saying, but for the first time she could remember, she was frightened of the night and one of its wild delta storms.

Her mother said nothing else, didn't move from where she sat at the foot of the bed, and Niki eventually drifted back into uneasy dreams, sleep so shallow that the sound of the thunder and the rain came right through. The next morning, her mother said nothing, never brought it up, that night, the things she'd said, and Niki knew better than to ever mention it. But afterwards, on very stormy nights, she would lie awake, and sometimes she heard her mother moving around in the kitchen, restless utensil sounds, or the dry scuff of her slippers on the hallway floor outside Niki's door.

And years later, not long before she finally dropped out of high school, she heard a song by R.E.M. on the radio—"Fall on Me"—bought the album even though she'd never particularly liked the band, and played that one track over and over again, thinking of her mother and that night and the storm. By that time, she'd read and seen enough to guess at her mother's nightmares, had understood enough of jellied gasoline and mortars and hauntings to glimpse the bright edges of that insomnia. Finally, twenty or thirty times through, having picked most of the lyrics from the tangled weave of voice and music, singer and song, she put the record away and never listened to it again.

If New Orleans taught Niki Ky nothing else, it taught her the respect due to ghosts, proper respect for pain so deep it transcended flesh and blood, and scarred time.

If her father had bad dreams, they'd never shown.

"Is that the way it was, Nicolan? Are you certain?" and Dr. Dalby watched her, watches her, is always watching her. Looking for the careless expression to expose a lie, the unguarded turn of a hand, flutter of eyelids, her teeth closing tightly on her lower lip. Every uncalculated act become her traitor, all unconscious Judases to give away the things she wants no one else to ever see.

"That's what I remember."

"But you understand, those may not be the same thing, what you remember and what actually happened. We've talked about that—"

"I just said it's what I remember."

"The night of the storm," he says, not quite changing the subject. "Did you ever tell Spyder about that night? What your mother said to you about the sky falling? The way that song affected you?"

"Spyder hated R.E.M."

A pause while he scribbles something in his notes, then the psychologist stares at her across the rims of his spectacles.

"Do you realize what you just said, Nicolan?"

"Spyder hated R.E.M.?"

"Yes. Her nightmares, her insomnia, the medication she took so she could sleep—"

"I'm not in the mood for word games today, Dr. Dalby. Can we table that one for next week?" and then she stares at her feet, wondering what meaning he'll read into the invisible dashed line between her eyes and the tips of her shoes.

"I don't think of it as a game. There's meaning in every word we use, whether we choose to acknowledge that meaning, whether or not we intend it, whether or not we're even aware of it."

"When I use a word," Niki said, trying not to sound as angry as she was beginning to feel, "it means just what I choose it to mean—neither more nor less."

And Dr. Dalby sits silently a moment, chewing at the eraser tip of his pencil and staring at her, staring at Niki staring at her shoes, the purple paisley Docs that Daria brought her all the way from London.

"Yes, well, the question is," he said at last, "whether you can make words mean so many different things."

Niki looks up at him, glaring, wishing her eyes could bleed fire, and "They've a temper, some of them," she says, and then stops herself, because she realizes these aren't her words, that they aren't even Dr. Dalby's words—Alice and Humpty Dumpty, something she read ages ago, lines from a little girl's nonsense book she thought she'd forgotten.

"There is *always* sense in a thing," the psychologist says, "whether or not we choose to acknowledge it."

"Yeah," Niki replies, looking back down at the toes of her purple boots. "I've figured that much out."

"That puts you well ahead of the curve, Nicolan."

And she opens her eyes, pulling free of the dream as eas-

ily as she slipped into it, slipping away from the pipe-
smoke and old-book smells of Dr. Dalby's office, and the
world stinks like Marvin's musty old Volkswagen again.

"Hey, you okay?" he asks, and she nods her head
sleepily.

"I just dozed off. Are we almost there?"

"Yeah, we're almost there. Kaiser's just up ahead," and
so Niki shuts her eyes and decides she'll wait until they're
all the way there to open them again.

Niki Ky met Danny Boudreaux their freshman year of
high school, but they didn't start sleeping together until
years later; one summer night after a rave, sweaty ware-
house district chaos and both of them fucked up on ecstasy
and, finally, there were no inhibitions left to stand in the
way. It wasn't an embarrassment the next morning, but had
seemed natural, something that should have happened,
even though Danny had always gone mainly for boys. He
worked drag at a couple of bars in the Quarter, was good
enough that sometimes he talked about going to Vegas and
making real money. A tall and pretty boy with only the
barest trace of a Cajun accent, and he used a lot of foam
rubber padding for his shows so no one would see the way
his hip bones jutted beneath the sequins.

And then, late July and she met Danny for a beer at
Coop's after work, early Saturday morning and it was after
work for both of them, the bar crammed full of punks and
tourists. They went back to his place on the Ursulines because it was closer, raced sunrise together across the cobblestones, racing the stifling heat of morning, running
drunk and sleepy, laughing like a couple of tardy vampires.
Before bed, they had cold cereal and cartoons. And Danny
started talking.

The frail, pretty boy dropped the bomb he'd carried all
his life, waiting for the right moment or the right ear, or
simply the day he couldn't carry it any longer. More than
drag, a *lot* more than that, and she sat still and listened,
stared silently down at the Trix going soggy in her bowl

while *Scooby Doo* blared from Danny's little black-and-white television.

"I've been seeing a doctor," he said. "I started taking hormones a couple of months ago, Niki."

And when he was done there was still nothing for her to say, nothing to make it real enough to answer, and finally he broke the silence for her and asked, "Niki? Are you all right? I'm sorry—"

"No, I'm fine," she said, not even looking at him, speaking to the safety of the TV instead, its senseless phosphor security, and she smiled and shrugged like it was no big shit, like he'd just asked if she wanted to go to a movie tonight or if she wanted another cup of coffee.

"I'm fucking wasted, Danny," she said. "We'll talk about it after I get some sleep, okay?"

"Yeah," he replied and then offered another apology that she hadn't asked for before they crawled off to bed.

She lay awake beside him, staring out at the summer day blazing away behind the curtains, only one bright slice getting into the apartment. Concentrating on the clunking, rheumy noises coming from his old air conditioner, the uneven rhythm of his breath, until she was sure he was asleep, and Danny Boudreaux always slept like the dead. She got dressed and wrote a note to leave beside the bed— *Danny, I have to figure this out. I just don't know. Love, Niki*—before she walked back across the Quarter to her own apartment, sweat-drenched and sun-dazed by the time she reached the other end of Decatur Street.

They've been waiting for almost two hours, and Marvin's throwing angry words at a male nurse with a clipboard and a shaved head; but it's too late already, too late to make the airport and the nine P.M. flight, so she really doesn't think it matters much whether or not they sit here the rest of the fucking night. Except that her hand has started bleeding again, and the pain is worse, and no one seems to care but Marvin. And the stark fluorescent lights shining down on her from the ceiling are making her nervous, light so empty, so bleak, that she can hardly imagine anything that could seem more unhealthy. Bleached and antiseptic light to forbid even the barest rind of a shadow, to gradually pick her apart, molecule by molecule.

"Do you even know how long she's been sitting there?"

"Yes sir," the nurse says, frowning, looking at his clipboard instead of Marvin. "You just told me."

"She's fucking *bleeding* all over your goddamn floor."

"We'll try to get her in with the next available—"

"You'll *try*?"

"Sir, we're doing all we can with what we have," and then Niki tunes them out again, already enough on her mind, enough to keep her busy—her confusion and the pain and the sound of her blood dripping to the floor—without their bickering.

Part of her is still stuck fast in the dream of Dr. Dalby. Niki hadn't meant to fall asleep, but she was so exhausted after Marvin led her back down Divisadero Street to the car, promising her that everything would be fine and there were no dragons hiding in the stoplights, no ghosts whispering over her shoulder. She's trying to remember what he wanted to know about Spyder, why it seems to matter so much now, but the ache in her hand is making it hard to think of anything else. Blue-white fire across her palm, something cold enough or hot enough or corrosive enough to burn straight through to the bone and keep on burning.

They've a temper, some of them.

There is always sense in a thing, whether or not we choose to acknowledge it.

The blood seeping slowly, steadily, through the gauze bandage Marvin wrapped around her hand is dark, and she wonders if that's worse than if it wasn't. Wonders what's going on beneath the dressing, what the doctors will find when they finally have time for her and one of them unwraps it. Maybe something coiled up snug inside the wound, something the watery color of jellyfish, her medusa hand, and she glances back up at Marvin and the nurse.

"I have to pee," she says to Marvin, but the nurse answers her.

"Down that hall," and he points the way. "Just past the water fountain."

"I really don't think you should go alone," Marvin says, and when he turns towards her, the bald nurse takes the opportunity to make his escape, disappearing quickly into one of the examination rooms.

"Fucker," Marvin growls under his breath. "You could be sitting here bleeding to death for all he cares."

"I think that's the problem," Niki says. "I'm not bleeding to death, and you're acting like I am."

Marvin checks his watch again, then glances at the clock hung on the wall above the nurses' station.

"You know we're going to miss the flight. We couldn't make it if we left right this minute."

"Then I guess we'll leave in the morning. Coming here was your idea, not mine. Now, I really do have to pee, Marvin," and she stands up, surprised to find she's a little dizzy, and Niki wonders if she could have possibly lost that much blood. She blinks at the fluorescent lights overhead and tries not to *act* like she's dizzy.

"I should go with you," Marvin says.

"I'm not going to have you watching me take a piss, Marvin."

"You don't look well."

"That's why you brought me to the hospital."

"I just don't think you should be alone, that's all. Not after what happened on the way over here."

And then, because she's about to wet herself and there'll be blood *and* piss on the floor, she sighs and nods her head.

"You can walk me as far the restroom door, but I'm going in *alone*," and all the resolve she has left inside her put into that last word, rolled into that last syllable; Marvin shakes his head the way he does whenever he realizes that he's lost a round.

"Don't you *dare* touch *anything* in there with your right hand," he says. "There's no telling what sort of disease-resistant, flesh-eating bugs are breeding in this place."

"That would be kind of ironic," Niki says and sets off in the direction the nurse pointed, hoping that it isn't far. She's not so crazy that she wouldn't be embarrassed as hell if she ended up pissing herself in public.

"That's not funny, Niki. I mean it. Use your *left* hand and wash it when you're done, with hot water *and* soap."

"I'm twenty-six years old, Marvin. I think I can wash my hands without step-by-step instructions," and now she can see the water fountain and the restroom door just beyond. The dizziness is a lot worse than when she first stood up, so she's walking close enough to the wall that she can catch herself if necessary.

"Do you think Daria's in Atlanta yet?" she asks Marvin, because she needs to think about something besides being dizzy and needing to piss. He checks his watch again.

"Yeah. She should be. Do you want me to call her? I didn't know if I should or—"

"No, I was just wondering, that's all. I just like to know where she is," and then they've reached the restroom door, painted matte brown like chocolate milk. "I can take it from here," she says.

"If you need me, just shout, okay? And I'll hear you."

Niki pushes at the door, opening it just enough that she gets a sudden, cloying whiff of toilet cakes and Lysol, flower-scented liquid soap, and part of her wishes Marvin would go somewhere and find another nurse to yell at, but another part wishes just as hard that she weren't too embarrassed and stubborn to let him follow her inside. She'd gone into the restroom at Cafe Alhazred alone, hadn't she? And isn't that where and when things really began to fall apart?

No, it was a long time before that.

A long, long time before that.

"I'll be fine," she says. "I'll wash my hands, just like you said."

"Just your *left* hand," Marvin reminds her quickly.

"How the hell am I supposed to wash my left hand and not touch anything with my right hand?" she asks him, and he sighs and makes a tight furrow of his eyebrows and the smooth patch of skin in between.

"Never mind," she mutters. "I'll figure it out." And Niki pushes the door the rest of the way open, steps inside, letting it swing quietly shut behind her. The restroom isn't as bright as the ER, the floor a chessboard of gray and white tiles, the wall too, as high as her chest, and then wallpaper the color of a sky before snow. Three stalls, a counter with three sinks, a big mirror, more fluorescence, but the light doesn't seem as harsh, as desolate, as it does in the waiting room. And there are no people here, either. She wonders if Marvin would let her stay until a doctor finally gets around to looking at her hand.

She chooses the stall nearest the door, for no particular reason, and slides the shiny metal bolt firmly into place, tests it by putting the weight of her left shoulder against the door to be sure it's not going to come open so anyone who happens by can see her sitting there with her pants down around her ankles.

Her urine is almost as dark as apple juice, yellow tinting towards orange, and she tries to remember how long it's been since she's had anything to drink. A sip of filtered water when she took her meds before leaving the house, but nothing since, and she realizes how dry her mouth is, her tongue like dust and ashes.

Niki wipes herself and drops the wad of paper into the toilet, is about to stand and pull her jeans up when the lights flicker and dim, and there's a faint crackling sound from somewhere on her left, from one of the other stalls, maybe. And she stops, perfectly freeze-frame still, and listens and watches the softly pulsating bulbs overhead. Another brownout, or maybe a blackout on the way, she thinks, but then the crackling sound grows louder than before and the too-clean restroom smells, and the smell of her own urine, are replaced by an odor that reminds her of burning tires; it stings her nose, and her eyes begin to tear.

"Marvin!" she calls out immediately, deciding she can worry about modesty some other time, in some other rest-room, one where the lights aren't fluttering like an epileptic's brain and the air doesn't smell like fire and melting rubber. "Marvin! Can you hear me?"

But no one answers, and she stands up slowly, reaches back and reflexively flushes the toilet; for a few seconds the swirling sound of water, the little maelstrom trapped inside its porcelain bowl, drowns out the crackling. Niki's pretty sure that her hand hurts worse than it did only a moment or two before, and the throbbing has begun to ebb and swell in time to the unsteady lights. She gets her pants up as quickly as she can using just her left hand, fumbling with the zipper and the inconvenient button at the top, as the burning-tire smell grows stronger and the fluorescents flicker.

"Marvin, if you can fucking hear me, *please* get your ass in here right this second!"

She slides back the latch, opens the door, and in the last instant before the lights flare bright as an artificial super-nova and then blink out altogether, Niki realizes that the crackling is radio static, or something very much *like* radio static. And now there's a darkness as profound as any she's ever known, as absolute and impenetrable, and she doesn't move, doesn't breathe, stands with her hand on the stall door listening as the crackling resolves itself into thin and papery voices, voices filtered through diodes and transistor tubes and years past counting.

"Angels. I can see angels now."

. . . light issues forth, and at the other door . . .

"Listen, child. Listen hard enough and you'll hear their wings, like war drums on the wind. Close your eyes and listen—"

. . . darkness enters, till her hour to veil the heaven, though darkness there might well seem twilight here.

"Blood falling from the stars, blood from stones and silence, but I can hear them now, and the sky will never be quiet for me again."

Niki takes one step forward, half out of the stall, still half in, but the floor beneath her feet has begun to list and roll like the deck of a small boat caught off guard on a stormy sea, and she almost falls. *Not a blackout,* she thinks. *Not a blackout at all. A goddamn earthquake.* She calls for Marvin again, screaming, but the radio voices have grown so loud that she can hardly hear herself over them, so there's no way that he's going to hear her all the way out in the hall. No way he'll ever come to help, to pull her back out into the ugly, safe-white hospital light.

If there is *still light left out there, if there's light left anywhere.*

Thunder that isn't thunder rumbling, rising from someplace far below, thunder and violence born from grinding, shifting rock and slipping fault-line fractures; the restroom floor heaves, and Niki is thrown, sprawling, to her knees.

. . . spread out their starry wings with dreadful shade . . .

"*I see them. I see them all tumbling down like smoldering, bleeding hailstones. And I see them crawling away, broken and lost.*"

"*Hold the line—*"

And then the thunder has grown so complete, so whole and deafening, that Niki doesn't have to listen to the crackling radio voices anymore. She slumps sobbing against the cool restroom wall, and her hands desperately probe about in the darkness for something solid that she can hold on to, anything steady, anything at all.

"Take my hand, Niki. Quick," Spyder Baxter says, and there is light now, the crimson light of an inferno to break the gloom apart and strew the shards like fallen leaves, light as hot and red as the seething blood of angels. "I can show you the way back."

Niki stares up at her, amazed, disbelieving, and she knows now that none of this can possibly be real after all. No earthquake, no phantom voices, no flickering lights, just a crazy girl running scared, locked up helpless inside her own head, and she shuts her eyes tight—the way that Dr. Dalby taught her—and "I am *here,*" she says as though she's certain. "I am here, and I am *real,* and I know the difference between what is and isn't. I know—"

"There's not much time," Spyder says urgently and takes her bandaged hand.

"This isn't real," Niki sobs. "This can't be—"

"It doesn't *matter,* Niki," Spyder replies, her soothing, velvet voice calm and clear above the thunder. "It can kill you, either way."

Niki opens her eyes again, and Spyder is still there, smiling down at her. That pale, hard face that she'd almost forgotten, her memories long since grown worn and unreliable, dulled by the fear and drugs and nightmares, almost forgotten because she left Birmingham without so much as a single photograph to keep the forgetting at bay. Spyder's tangled white dreadlocks, her heavy-lidded eyes that someone might mistake for Asian, and irises the clearest, icebound blue.

"You have to trust me," Spyder says and glances over her left shoulder, towards the source of the brightening, ruddy light. When she looks back, the cruciform scar between her eyes has begun to glow softly, light the same cold shade as her eyes, the same light seeping thick from the intricate spiderweb tattoos covering both arms from the backs of her hands to her shoulders. "You shouldn't have come here yet, Niki. It's too soon. You have to start at the beginning. And you sure as hell shouldn't have come alone."

"I don't know what's happening," Niki whispers, and the heaving world thunders an angry reply, words from cracking, splitting stone, and she would scream again, would scream for Marvin, for Daria, but Spyder is lifting her to her feet.

"That's why it's too soon," she says. "That's why you can't be here yet. That's why you can't come alone."

And Niki can see that she isn't even in the restroom anymore, that she's standing with Spyder on a black volcanic plain. The gray and white checkerboard tiles, the three stalls, the restroom walls, *all* of it replaced by cooling lava and black plumes of smoke that smell like acid and rotting eggs. There's no sun overhead, no moon, no stars, only the roiling smoke hanging low and poisonous, reflecting the crimson glow across its restless, sulfurous belly.

"We'll have to cross the Dog's Bridge," Spyder says and frowns. "There's no other way left. Not from here. Not from now. You do everything I tell you, Niki, and don't you dare look back."

"Is this Hell?" Niki asks. "Is that where we are?"

"Niki, you can't keep using someone else's stories like that," Spyder replies, her frown deepening, drawing shadowed lines across her smooth, milky skin. "You're going to have to find the truth of this for yourself."

"I don't know *anything*, Spyder."

"No. That's just what they want you to believe. That's what they *need* you to believe. That's the lie that will damn you, Niki, and you have to see past it. You have to find your own eyes down here or the crows and maggots will be picking your bones before you've even begun."

"I didn't think I would ever see you again," Niki says, squeezing Spyder's hand tighter despite the pain, crying harder even though she's trying to stop.

"Remember what I said, Niki. Once you start across the bridge, don't you dare look back. Not for anything. No matter *what* you hear. And remember to count your steps, *all* of them."

"I was trying to get to the airport," Niki says, wiping at her eyes and snotty nose with the back of her left hand. "I was trying to get back to Birmingham."

"I know. And you will. But first we have to get you out of here, and we have to do it *now*."

And Spyder starts walking, towing Niki along behind her. Niki can tell that they're moving slowly towards the place where the red glow is coming from, and she's busy trying not to stumble and fall again as Spyder picks their way over and between the broken jumbles of lava, once-liquid stone frozen sharp as razors. Here and there, fissures leak a sickly yellow steam, and Niki has to cover her nose and mouth with her free hand or it makes her gag. The stench from those fissures is almost enough to convince her that the earth here, the very land in this place, has died and is already quickly decomposing beneath her feet.

Overhead, something on ragged kite wings screeches and wheels on the thermals, gliding in and out of the low, smoky clouds. Niki only catches a glimpse of it from the corner of one eye, but that glimpse is enough that she knows she doesn't want a better look. All around them, small albino things scurry fast across and between the rocks, disturbed by their passage.

"The world is very thin here," Spyder says, having to shout now to make herself heard above the thunder still bellowing underfoot. "It never lasts long. This is only the latest scab du jour," and she motions at the glistening, uneven lava around them. "But the Dog's Bridge, it's usually in the same place."

Niki can hear the radio voices again, a barely audible murmur playing somewhere just beneath the rumbling earth, trying to distract her from the things that Spyder's saying.

Great things, and full of wonder in our ears . . .

"Mark my words, this child will be the ruin of us all. She'll have us all in the fires before she's done."

Far differing from this World, thou hast revealed . . .

"She isn't even our child, Trisha. Mark my word. Demons leave their babies in our cribs—"

Spyder stops, because this is where the land ends, for now, falling steeply away to a seemingly endless molten sea of red-orange and blue-white lava a thousand feet below. The light's grown so bright that Niki has to squint, and she can feel the heat beginning to blister her face. The rising heat bends the light, turning everything ahead of them into a vast, inconstant mirage; if there's an opposite shore, Niki can't see any sign of it.

"That way," Spyder says, *"there,"* and she points to their right. "Right there where it's supposed to be."

Niki looks away from the sea of fire, beyond the compass tip of Spyder's index finger, and the Dog's Bridge rises in a crooked, sagging arch above the inferno. Not too far away from where they're standing, over another pile of boulders, another lava flat or two. She blinks at the precarious jackstraw ford built not from stone or steel, but from countless bones bleached and wired together, a billion disassembled skeletons for its soaring piers and buttresses.

"The bridges are eternal," Spyder whispers, as though she's afraid someone might overhear. "Don't let anyone or anything tell you different. The bridges will be here when the rest of this shit's just a goddamn burnt-out memory."

The world shudders, and a geyser of fire, miles and miles away, rises up from the sea to scorch the black sky blacker.

"That's the way, Niki. Walk fast, and don't look back."

Niki turns away from the ossuary bridge and the fountain of fire, turning to Spyder, the blue cross shining between her eyes. "You're coming with me," she says.

"Not this time. This time you have to do it on your own. The path might close—"

"I can't cross that fucking thing, not *alone*."

"You can, and you will."

"I won't let you do this to me, not again."

But Spyder releases her hand, fresh blood showing wetly through the bandages, and takes a step backwards, away from Niki. The geyser falls back into the sea, and the scalded clouds scream and writhe.

"You left me once before, and you're not going to do it to me again, goddamn it!"

"I'm not leaving you, Niki. But there are rules here, and I can't cross the bridge with you. Not this time."

"Fuck that, Spyder. You come with me, or I don't go."

Spyder frowns again and looks out across the sea of fire.

"Count your steps, and don't look back," she says, and before Niki can reply, before she can tell her how far up her ass she can shove all of this, Spyder Baxter dissolves in a dust-devil swirl of sparkling cinders. And Niki stands there for a long, long time, minutes or hours or days, no way to tell in this place without day or night, waiting for

Spyder to come back. But she doesn't come back, and when Niki's hand hurts too much to wait any longer, she turns, finally, and follows the narrow trail that winds along the edge of the cliff to the foot of the Dog's Bridge.

She counts her steps, just like Spyder told her to do, and she doesn't look back.

"Do you remember what Campbell said about schizophrenia?" Dr. Dalby asks her, and Niki shrugs and stares past him out the big window behind his desk, the San Francisco skyline glittering white and silver.

"You remember, the essay that I asked you and Daria to read together last month," he says, prompting, and she shrugs again.

"Yeah," Niki says. "What about it?"

"You said you read it."

"Sure, we read it," Niki replies, nodding her head, her eyes still on the skyscrapers and a smudgy flock of pigeons lighting on a rooftop across the street. She has a vague memory of the essay, photocopied pages stapled together and sent away with her like a homework assignment. But she can't remember whether they ever read it or not.

"I want to read you a few lines from it now, if that's okay. It's something you need to remember. Is it okay if I read it to you now, Nicolan?"

"Go ahead," she tells him. "I'm listening."

And he clears his throat, takes a sip of water from the glass on his desk, and begins.

" 'The whole problem, it would seem, is somehow to go through it, even time and again, without shipwreck; the answer being *not* that one should *not* be permitted to go crazy; but that one should have been taught something already of the scenery to be entered and the powers likely to be met, given a formula of some kind by which to recognize, subdue them, and incorporate their energies.' "

He pauses a moment then, watching her, waiting in case she wants to say something. Niki stops counting the pigeons and looks at Dr. Dalby instead, because it's always easier if she at least pretends to listen.

"Are you still with me?" he asks her.

"I got nowhere else to go," she says and smiles for him, but he doesn't smile back for her.

"Good. I want to read a few more lines, skipping ahead to the end of the essay, okay?"

"We're almost out of time," Niki says, glancing at the clock. "My hour's almost up."

"There's time for this," he says and then begins reading again before she can object. " 'The trick must be to become aware of it'—and here, Campbell is talking about the visionary object or its witness, the visionary subject—'to become aware of it without becoming *lost* in it: to understand that we may all be saviors when functioning in relation to our friends and enemies—savior figures, but never *The Savior*.' "

Niki shuts her eyes a moment, just to be sure, and then opens them again.

"Spyder thought she could save us all," she says.

"Yes. I think she must have."

"I've never asked anyone to save me. The hour's up, Dr. Dalby," and he checks his wristwatch.

"So it is. Remember these things. You'll need them, I expect."

"I'll try."

"Try hard. You have to cross this bridge alone."

"Just like all the others," Niki whispers, and outside the window all the pigeons take flight at once.

"Watch your step, Nicolan," Dr. Dalby says and takes another sip of water. "And don't look down."

The Dog's Bridge rises so high above the sea of fire that its crest almost brushes the underside of the sulfur clouds before finally beginning the long descent to the opposite shore. Niki walks down the middle, because there are no guardrails, nothing to prevent a fall, and the bridge of bones sways slightly in the hot wind, shifts as the lava flows slowly by far below. But mostly, she's careful not to lose count, because then she'd have to go back to the beginning and start all over again, and Spyder said not to turn back, no matter what happened.

The deck of yellow-white and ivory creaks loudly beneath her boots, long bones and vertebrae, tooth-studded jaws and parts of broken skulls all wired together, the bones of men and animals and gigantic beasts she's glad she's never seen alive. Sweat pours from her face and drips to splotch the dry path at her feet. The heat and fumes alone almost enough to kill, she thinks, and looks at her hand again, Marvin's bandage gone now, sloughed off like some sweaty second skin, and the wound has turned an even deeper red than the sky.

The sea makes a sound like dying, and the clouds moan a low and threatful rebuttal. Something falls, screeching, burning alive, a living meteor streaking past the bridge, plummeting towards the lava. She doesn't stop walking, doesn't stop to see what it might have been.

"Watch your step, and don't look down," Niki says out loud, staring straight ahead. "And don't fucking look up, either."

Bone snaps and crunches beneath her boots, and the hot wind blows like sandpaper fingers through her tangled hair, across her blistered skin, and Niki keeps counting. In the end, she finds the other side, because all bridges, even here, eventually lead *somewhere*.

And when she opens her eyes, Marvin's kneeling there beside her, brushing hair from her face, and the checkerboard tile of the restroom floor is smooth and cool as ice beneath her. She blinks up at the fluorescent bulbs, the white light that means nothing at all, only electricity and a bit of glowing, ionized gas and nothing more to it than that. Nothing to marvel at and no riddles here to solve, nothing to have to fear.

Hold the line.

"Don't move," Marvin says, and she can hear how scared

he is, and how relieved, can see it in his eyes. "Someone's coming."

"Did you feel it? Was it an earthquake?" she asks weakly, but he only looks confused.

"You just be still now. Someone's coming to help. They'll be here in a second."

"I'm okay," she says, and Niki closes her eyes again because she doesn't want to see how worried he looks. "I was dizzy. I must have fainted. I think I fainted and fell, that's all."

"I heard you call my name," he says. "I came as quickly as I could."

"Yeah," she whispers. "You did real good, Marvin," turning her head to one side so that the cool tile presses against her right cheek, skin that still remembers the heat of a flaming sea. And Niki keeps her eyes shut until they come to check her pulse and ask her questions and take her away to one of the examination rooms.

CHAPTER FOUR

This Only Song I Know

Daria Parker is lying alone on the wide hotel bed, much too wide for just one, staring out the sliding-glass balcony doors at the glittering Atlanta skyline stretching away into the night. Dylan's playing on her laptop, *Street Legal,* and she rolls over and stares at Alex Singer, who's been staring at her back for the last fifteen or twenty minutes. He's sitting on a love seat on the other side of the room, sipping a bourbon and 7UP. His guitar case is lying at his feet. He sighs and glances towards the sliding doors.

"So, why won't you call her?" he asks. His Manchester accent gets heavier when he's exhausted or drunk, and it's heavier than she's heard it in a long time.

"No. It's easier if I don't. Marvin can take care of things. Isn't that what I pay him for?"

"Easier for who? You or Niki?"

"Easier for all of us," Daria replies and almost tells him to leave. She's too tired for Alex and his disapproval and his questions. She just wants to sleep, wants to not think about Niki or San Francisco or work for a few hours. Her sinuses are still aching from the dry, recirculated air of the plane, and her stomach is sour as old milk.

"I don't know, Dar," Alex says softly, almost whispering, and takes another sip of his drink.

"*What?* What don't you know, Alex?"

"I'm saying you gotta deal with this shit. Get it under control. We can't cancel another date."

"Niki's my problem, *not* yours."

"Right. Well, at least we agree on something then. *You're* my problem."

Daria grits her teeth and shuts her eyes, willing herself not to take the bait this time, too weary and sick and worried to get into an argument with Alex tonight. To get into the *same* old threadbare argument all over again.

"What time's the signing at Tower," she asks him.

"They want us there by three. Jarod says there are fliers up all over the city. He's expecting a crowd."

"That figures," Daria mutters to herself.

"And you've got an interview at four. Nothing major, just some local music reporter."

"I thought we had a radio spot lined up."

"They changed their minds."

Daria opens one eye and glares at the guitarist.

"*Who* changed their minds?" she asks and opens the other eye.

"Hell, Dar, I don't know. The fuckwits at the station. Try talking to Jarod every now and then if you want to know what's up with your schedule. I'm not your bloody manager."

"You're not my bloody marriage counselor, either, but that hasn't stopped you yet."

"Touché," he sighs and finishes his drink in one long gulp, then tosses the plastic cup at a garbage can near the bed. He misses, and melting ice scatters across the beige carpet like fake, glassy jewels.

"Why don't you go trash your own room," Daria growls, and he grins and reaches for the big bottle of Seagram's he brought in with him.

"That's no fun, love."

"I've got to get some sleep."

"Did you know that Arkansas cocksucker is threatening to sue us?" Alex says, twisting the plastic cap off the bottle. "Jarod's trying to talk them down, you know, but—"

"Are you fucking deaf?"

Alex takes a drink from the bottle, then stands and steps over the guitar case. Daria lies on her back, staring up at him, his soft gray eyes and rough, unshaven cheeks, his black hair pulled back in a short ponytail. He's wearing a red Pixies T-shirt that's been washed so many times it's turning pink, and the St. Christopher's medal she's never seen him without. She takes a deep breath and exhales slowly.

"They can't sue me," Daria says, trying hard to frown, but smiling a reluctant quarter smile instead, wishing he'd done a little more to piss her off. "I can't afford it."

"Yeah, I told Jarod you'd say something like that."

Daria reaches up and takes the bottle from him, tips it to her lips and shuts her eyes as the bourbon burns her mouth and throat numb. A little more and maybe her head will be numb, as well. Alex leans over and licks away a stray trickle of liquor from her chin.

"Jesus, I'm a goddamn bastard," she says and takes another drink. "I'm a fucking cunt."

"We do what we have to do," he replies, sitting down on the edge of the bed, running his sturdy fingers through her hair. "Whatever it takes to get us through the night."

"Is that what I'm doing? Whatever it takes?"

"Way I see it, that's exactly what you're doing."

Alex starts to kiss her, but she pushes him away and sits up. She turns to face the balcony and the city lights again.

"You just don't get it, do you?"

He shakes his head, then takes another long drink from the bottle before screwing the cap back on and setting it on the floor.

"Don't it get lonely, way up there on that cross all by yourself?" he asks and wipes his mouth.

"Fuck you."

"What I can never can figure out is how you managed to drive that last nail in. That must have been a bitch."

"Will you just please shut up now?"

And he does, for a few minutes, while she stares at the

night beyond the twenty-seventh floor and the Dylan CD ends and starts over again.

"I can't stop loving her, Alex. I've tried. I fucking swear, I've tried, and I *can't*."

"I never asked you to stop loving her. But you can't live like this, either. How much longer do you think you can keep going, the way things are?"

Daria reaches for her Marlboros and lighter, but the pack is empty; she crumples it into a tight ball and flings it at the balcony doors. It bounces silently off the glass and lies on the carpet near the spilled ice. Bob Dylan's voice bleeds from the speakers, as haggard and sad and urgent as her own worn-out soul, and the tears come before she can stop them.

"Fuck it," she whispers. "Fuck it all."

"You just gotta let someone else carry some of the weight," Alex says. "Just a little."

And then he puts his arms around her and holds her until dawn has begun to bruise the sky dull shades of rose and violet, and she finally stops crying and sleeps.

Excerpt from "Outside the Vicious Circle: A Conversation with Daria Parker" (*Women Who Rock*, March 2002; pp. 27–28).

WWR: So, how long did it take you to get sick of answering the lesbian question?

DP: Oh, am I a lesbian? Jesus, is that official now, you know, on record somewhere? (laughs) Yeah, I guess I got sick of it pretty damn quick. I think I was kind of naive. I figured people would have gotten enough of the whole celebrity dyke confessional thing with k.d. lang and Melissa Etheridge and Ellen Degeneres, and so on. I don't know what they expected me to add. I just write songs. I just play my fucking bass. If they want the *Well of Loneliness,* they should go to the library. I'm not the poster girl for lesbian equality in the music industry. I know it pisses people off when I say that, but after my records started selling, I felt this enormous pressure to be the next lesbian messiah or something. I'm sorry, but I just don't want any part of that.

WWR: But you're not ashamed of your sexuality? It's very evident in the songs on both *Skin Like Glass* and *Exit West*. These are songs written by a woman to a woman whom she loves, whom she has sexual feelings for.

DP: I think I should have the freedom to be honest, as an artist, as a human being, without having to become a political activist. If I was writing love songs to men, or if I was a man writing love songs to women, we wouldn't be having this conversation. I'm a songwriter, not a *lesbian* songwriter. I don't want people to think of me that way, not because I'm ashamed of being a dyke or because I'm afraid people won't buy my records or whatever. I just want people to think of me as a musician. I don't have an axe to grind. And, you know, I think that's what people are really afraid of. As long as they can hang a sign around my neck, stick that pink triangle on me, I'm not a such a big threat to anyone. I'm visible. I'm in this neat little box marked "caution—lesbian singer," and the walls of that box limit the impact of my work, or, if what I do happens to piss you off, the amount of damage I can do.

WWR: Is it true you declined interviews with both *Curve* and *The Advocate*?

DP: Yes, it is. And it's also true I got a lot of hate mail because of that. But if I'd given the damn interviews, I'd have gotten hate mail from born-again Christians and Mormons and mothers who were afraid their teenage daughters were gay. Either way, I get the reactionaries, from one side or the other. It was a lose-lose situation, and I did what I felt was right for me. I think it's a shame people are more interested in condemning me for making my own decisions than taking the time to try to understand why I made those decisions.

WWR: And the girl in Florida, Becky Silverlake, the suicide—

DP: Is not something that I talk about in interviews.

WWR: Her mother still insists that the lyrics to "Seldom Seen" were a factor in her daughter's death and that *Exit West* is, in her words, "a clear and shameless invitation to troubled teenagers to turn to suicide as a solution to their suffering and alienation."

DP: Christ, I said I don't talk about Becky fucking Silverlake. I thought that was understood?

WWR: And your lover, Nicolan Ky—

DP: Is the other thing I don't talk about in interviews. Next question.

Daria opens her eyes and squints at the dazzling slivers of sunlight leaking in around the edges of the thick hotel drapes. Alex must have drawn them. She can hear him snoring softly behind her, hogging most of the bed. And she can hear someone bumping about in the hall outside the room and tries to remember if she hung the DO NOT DISTURB sign on the door. She blinks at the light, unable to recall any details of the nightmare that woke her. She used to write her dreams in a notebook, because Dr. Dalby said there might be something that would help Niki, but she stopped doing that a long time ago.

Daria looks at the clock radio and is relieved to see it's still early, still five minutes till noon, so there's plenty of time for her to get her shit together, maybe even eat something before the Tower Records thing. If she's lucky, she might have another twenty or thirty minutes before Jarod starts calling to make sure she's up and moving, to make sure she's sober and in the same city, the same state, the same time zone, as the rest of the band.

She pushes back the blanket and sheets, the heavy down comforter, and sits up, naked and shivering, wanting a cigarette but needing to piss worse, wondering where her clothes have gone. Alex's faded Pixies shirt is tangled in the covers, so she slips it on and then goes to the bathroom without trying to wake him. Alex sleeps like the dead and wakes like a grizzly bear on crack, and she knows better than to try to get him moving before there's lots of strong black coffee on hand.

Daria flips on the bathroom light and almost manages not to see her reflection in the big mirror above the sink until she's wiped herself dry and flushed. Then she sits on the toilet, still shivering, staring back at her face, and wonders what kind of fool would want to see themselves taking a squirt first thing in the morning.

"You look like hell," she whispers. "You know that, don't you? You look like death on a bad day."

Through the bathroom wall, she can hear the barely muffled roar of a vacuum cleaner from the room across the hallway and thinks about offering the maid a fifty to find some other room to clean, another room at the other end of the hall or, better yet, on another floor altogether.

It's hardly been eighteen hours since she left the house on Alamo Square, and already it seems like another life, someone else's life, almost as unreal now as the forgotten nightmare. That house and Niki, something she keeps trying to wake up from. She thinks about Alex, asleep on the bed, Alex holding her in the night, the solid, undeniable fact of him, and the thought brings hardly any guilt at all. Ten years of her life spent watching out for Niki, and she wasn't lying when she told Alex that she still loved her. Ten years making sure Niki was safe, that she was taking her meds, that she didn't hurt herself, and there's nothing left. No more she can do. Nothing but regret that what she did was never enough, and there's no way she can ever save Niki Ky.

Need and desire are not enough. There was a time when she thought they could be, somehow, if she believed, if she gave everything she had, but that time's passed, and she knows that it'll never come again.

"Hey, you stole my fuckin' shirt," Alex says, mumbling around a cigarette, and Daria wonders how long he's been standing there in the doorway, watching her. He's naked, and she smiles at the small tattoo on his left hip—a grinning, winged cupid armed with a machine gun. He got that years before they met, the price of a bet he lost to some former girlfriend or another. Every now and then, he talks about having it removed, but she doubts he ever will.

" 'Hey' yourself. I thought you were asleep," she says.

"Yeah, well, you piss louder than any woman I've ever known."

"You're saying I woke you up taking a piss?"

"Sounded like goddamn Niagara Falls in here."

"Shut up and give me a cigarette," she says, and he takes another long drag, then gives her his.

"What are you doing in here, anyway?" he asks and then massages his bloodshot eyes.

"Niagara Falls, remember?"

"I'm gonna call room service and get some fucking coffee and shit," he says. "You want anything?"

"I should probably eat something."

"Yeah, you probably should. You're skin and bones, you know that? Want a muffin? I bet they have muffins."

"Yeah," she replies. "A muffin would be good," but her stomach roils at the thought of solid food.

"Well, if they ain't got muffins, you want some toast and jam?"

"Sure. Whatever."

Alex nods his head, scratches himself a moment, then turns around and disappears into the darkness.

"And turn on a light," she shouts after him, "before you trip over something and break your neck."

A few seconds later, she hears him pulling the drapes open, and he curses as the bright midday sun floods the room. Daria looks back at the mirror, at her pale face and matted, bleach-stripped hair. Her face that looks like it's aged ten years in the last five, and she wishes she could go back to bed, back to Alex, and forget about the signing and the show and everything else.

She stands up and turns on the tap, icy water gushing into the marble sink, and sets her cigarette down on the edge of the counter. Daria splashes her face and the back of her neck, gasping as the cold stings her skin, dragging her the rest of the way awake. She bends over and dunks her head into the basin, sloshing water out onto the floor. The gurgle from the tap is so loud that she can't hear anything else, and she holds her breath and keeps her head in the sink as long as she can stand it.

The white hotel towel smells too clean, like detergent and fabric softener, but it feels good against her face, against her scalp, and when she's done, most of her hair is standing straight up.

"They have muffins," Alex shouts. "You want blueberry or bran?"

"Blueberry," she shouts back, reaching for her cigarette. It's a little damp, but she hardly notices, the nicotine just about her best friend in the world right now.

"They say they're out of blueberry," Alex yells.

Daria frowns and drops the wet towel on the tile at her feet. "You just asked me which I wanted."

"I didn't *know* they were out. He just fuckin' told me."

"I fucking hate bran muffins. Everyone hates bran muffins."

And she hears him ordering her toast.

"You want blueberry or strawberry jam?" he shouts.

"Surprise me," she mutters, just loud enough that she won't have to repeat herself, no longer interested in trying to eat. She turns off the water and flicks the butt of her cigarette into the toilet. It drowns with a faint hiss. She steps out of the bathroom, and the sunlight through the balcony doors is disorienting and hurts her eyes.

"He didn't *tell* me they were out of blueberry," Alex says again, stepping into a pair of boxers. "I don't know why he didn't tell me that to start with."

"It doesn't matter. I'm not hungry, anyway. If I tried to eat right now I'd probably just throw it up. I need a drink."

Alex stops rummaging through a navy-blue backpack and glances at the pint of Seagram's still sitting on the floor near the foot of the bed. "Try to eat some of the toast first, Dar," he says. "Just a few bites? Maybe a cup of coffee, yeah?"

"Let's not start in with that right now, Alex. I'm not in the mood for mothering. My head hurts, and I'm cold, and my stomach's killing me, and I want a drink, not a lecture on nutrition."

"Put on some clothes if you're cold."

"Just lay off, okay?"

He sighs and goes back to digging through the backpack. "It's your funeral, love. Just don't expect me to hang around for the service, if you get my drift."

"I get your fucking drift," she says and sits down beside his guitar case. "No one's asking you to hold my hand. I need a lover, not a nursemaid."

"That, dear, is a matter of opinion."

While Alex dresses, Daria sits on the floor drinking bourbon and staring at the city and the gray-blue sky beyond the balcony doors. For a moment, she can't remember what month it is, what season, summer or spring or autumn, but the confusion passes, the way it always does. She never loses her way for very long. This is where I am, this is *when* I am.

"Maybe you better turn the ringer back on," Alex says, and she looks at the phone on the end table beside the bed. The red-orange message light is blinking urgently. "I bet your cell's off, too. I bet you had it off all night."

"As a matter of fact," she replies and watches the blinking light as she takes a drink of bourbon. It hits her empty stomach like a small grenade, and she closes her eyes until the pain passes.

"If you're gonna puke, aim *away* from the guitar."

"I'm not going to puke," Daria whispers, though she might. It's always a possibility. She opens her eyes again and stares at the phone.

"There's a message. It might be important," Alex says.

"It's always important. When was it ever not fucking important?"

"Would you rather talk to Jarod or have him pounding on the door?"

And she almost slips, then, almost says, *That's not what I'm afraid of, Alex. It might be Niki, or Marvin,* but she catches herself and doesn't say anything at all. The pain in her belly is melting as the Seagram's warms her from the inside out, and she's beginning to feel a little less lost, a little more in control. It *isn't* Niki on the phone, and it isn't Marvin. It's only Jarod Parris or someone else that she has absolutely no desire to talk to. She looks away from the phone and takes another swallow of whiskey.

"I promised you'd be sober," Alex says and zips his backpack closed.

"You shouldn't make promises I can't keep," she tells him. "That's pretty much the same thing as lying."

"You know, Dar, I bet Keith Barry used to say shit like that to you. Hell, I wouldn't be surprised if you were quoting the motherfucker."

And for a moment she's too stunned to reply, to tell him to shove it up his self-righteous, hypocritical ass, too stunned to do anything but sit there on the floor and stare at the morning light shining through the last couple of inches of amber liquid in the bottle.

"You ever let yourself think about that?" Alex asks, sitting down on a corner of the bed. "You're a smart girl. You don't need me to connect the dots for you."

Daria screws the cap back on the bottle and considers hurling it at the sliding doors, wonders if she could throw it hard enough to shatter the tall sheets of plate glass.

"That's not fair," she says very softly. "That's not fair, and you know it."

"You think? Then tell me this—just how long's it been since you went a whole day without getting wasted?"

"Keith was a junky—"

"And you're an alcoholic. Six of one, half dozen of the other, babe."

"Jesus, you've got some fucking nerve," she says and laughs a dry, dead sort of a laugh. "Where the hell do you get off saying something like that to me?"

"I *should* have said it a year ago. I should have said it after that shit you pulled in London."

"I'm not a goddamn alcoholic," and Daria wraps her right hand tightly around the neck of the Seagram's bottle, thinking again about flinging it at the balcony doors. She imagines the satisfying explosion as the glass shatters, raining whiskey and deadly razor shards to the street twenty-seven stories below. She imagines people on the sidewalk, hearing the noise, looking up—

"Hell, Dar. I don't expect nobody in this fucked-up business to stay clean twenty-four/seven. They'd have to be a bloody saint or something. But you're falling apart, and I can't stand by and watch it happen."

"What are you saying, Alex?" she asks him, not wanting to hear the answer, but not strong enough to keep the question to herself, either.

"All I'm saying is there's some heavy shit you gotta deal with, love, and you gotta do it *soon*. I'm saying I can't pretend to look the other way anymore. I've been doing that too long as it is."

"It's *your* fucking bottle, asshole," she says and holds it up. He reaches down and takes it from her.

"Yeah, it is. Maybe that's where we have to start."

Daria stares at her empty hand for a moment, the ghost of the bottle still pressed into her flesh.

"Don't fucking talk to me about Keith Barry, you understand? Not ever again. If it makes you feel better about yourself to tell me I'm a drunk, fine, whatever, but that's the last time I want to hear his name from your lips."

Alex nods, then tosses the bottle into the air, end over end, and catches it.

"You have no idea what you're talking about. You weren't there and you have no *idea*—" and she stops, her voice too unsteady to continue. Too close to tears and the last thing she's going to do now is let him see her cry.

"Bugger," he says, shrugs and tosses the bottle again, catches it again. "Fair enough. All I know is what you've told me. But the rest of this—"

"Can wait," she says and reaches for her panties lying on the carpet near the guitar case. She sniffs at them and tries to remember the last time she put on a clean pair. Not San Francisco, so it must have been Little Rock, the night Marvin called to tell her that Niki had tried to kill herself. Not even three days, but it feels like at least three weeks.

"Yes ma'am," Alex says. "You're the boss," and then there's a loud knock at the door, three sharp raps, and Daria's heart jumps. But it's only room service, just the breakfast she has no interest in, the toast and jam instead of a blueberry muffin.

"Just a second," Alex shouts, pulling on his jeans. "I'm coming."

When he goes to the door, Daria picks up the bottle of whiskey again and wonders if there's enough left to get her through the next few hours.

Excerpt from "Outside the Vicious Circle: A Conversation with Daria Parker" (*Women Who Rock*, March 2002; pp. 28-29):

WWR: Is there any chance that you'll ever record any of the songs you wrote with Stiff Kitten or, going even farther back, Yer Funeral or Ecstatic Wreck?

DP: I don't think so. Stiff Kitten is a place and a time I'd prefer not to revisit. It was important to me, that band and those songs, and the things I learned back then. I probably couldn't have gotten where I am now without them. But they're still part of the past. I'm not a very nostalgic person. I'm more interested in the songs that I haven't written yet than the songs that I wrote when I was really still just a kid. As for Yer Funeral, I think the best thing you could say about Yer Funeral is that we didn't last very long, and we were really fucking loud. Loud was important. I was determined to be as loud as the boys, all those punker assholes who acted like girls had no place in the scene. It was a big deal to me back then, standing my ground. And I think it was even worse, being stuck in a place like Birmingham. I was literally the only woman doing what I was doing, and so I got a lot of resentment for that. It was a boy's club, you know, and I think I definitely threw a wrench into their dick-measuring contests.

WWR: In the piece that *Rolling Stone* did last year, they describe the death of Keith Barry (guitarist for Stiff Kitten) as a turning point in your career. Do you think that's true?

DP: Yeah, well, *Rolling Stone* was talking out their ass, which is nothing new. I didn't even *have* a career back then. All I had was my bass and a crappy job at a coffee shop and a junky boyfriend. After Keith died, I didn't even have that anymore. I mean, he died and that was the end of Stiff Kitten and it was almost the end of me. It's the sort of thing I look back on now and I don't even begin to understand how I lived through it, or why I bothered. I think, mostly, I was too pissed at him to give up. He was really good—fucking *genius* good—and he just pissed it away that night in Atlanta. So yeah, I guess it was a turning point in the sense that it tore everything in the world down and forced me to start over from scratch. It forced me to find ways to stay alive when all I wanted to do was lie down and die. But I don't like calling it a "turning point" in my career. That seems to trivialize Keith's death, somehow. It's what happened, and we are who we are, all of us, because of the things that happen to us.

WWR: It's pretty obvious that some of the songs on *Exit West* were an attempt to express your feelings about his death and its effect on you, and maybe your feelings on suicide in general. I'm thinking, of course, of "Seldom Seen," but also "Bleeding Day" and "Standing Near Heaven."

DP: You don't live through a suicide, no matter who you are, whether it's accidental or intentional, without it leaving a profound mark on what you do. If you're an artist, it comes out in your work, sooner or later, at least if you're any sort of *honest* artist. If you're a writer, how do you not write about it? Even years later, you still find yourself thinking about it, having bad dreams about it, writing about it, wondering what you didn't do that might have prevented it, or what you *did* do that might have caused it. It colors the whole world. It turns everything into guilt and confusion and bitterness. When Keith died, I think my first reaction, after the shock, was anger. I was furious because I knew—I fucking *knew*— that he'd changed everything forever, and no matter what I did, I could never, ever make it the way it was before. Even if I somehow made it better someday, he'd taken a choice away from me and forced me into this other place for the rest of my life. He'd punched this big fucking hole in me, and there was no way it would ever go away completely. That probably sounds selfish, but so was what he did to me, and to the band, to himself. So, yeah, a lot of that anger's in "Bleeding Day" and "Seldom Seen." I had to put it somewhere. It's not the sort of thing you can carry around inside you forever. It starts to eat your soul.

WWR: You recently played a show in Birmingham, didn't you? That must have been pretty bizarre.

DP: No, it was just another show. I stayed focused and didn't let it freak me out. I just went to Birmingham and did the show. It wasn't like going home or reliving my wild punk-rock past or any of that crap. It was just a show, that's all. We had a great turnout that night.

WWR: So you didn't check out any of the old haunts?

DP: Hell, no. Most of those places are long gone now, anyway. Dr. Jekyll's and everything. Gentrification took care of that, which is really just as well. Dr. Jekyll's was pretty much Birmingham's one and only punk and hardcore club. Back then, of course, we all thought it was the shit, like we were headlining the Cathay or fucking CBGB's or something. It was just this tiny hole in the wall, but we could play our music there, and most of the time no one bothered us. I think the biggest thing that ever happened was a Black Flag show, but that must have been almost a decade before I even started playing with Stiff Kitten. Mostly, though, it was all these bands that came and went, and nobody will ever know or care who they were. Someone told me that there's a parking lot now where Dr. Jekyll's used to be, and I was like, hell yeah and thank God.

And this is the night that Daria Parker met Keith Barry, this muggy summer weeknight in 1993, before Dr. Jekyll's was even Dr. Jekyll's. It was still called the Cave back then, an all too accurate name for the dark and smoky little dive on the east end of Morris Avenue. Just past the train tracks that cut the city into north and south, tucked in snug among the empty warehouses and cobblestones, the gaslights that had long since been converted to mere electricity. A decade earlier, Morris had been littered with nightclubs and restaurants, the place to be seen until it wasn't anymore and the parties had moved on. This night, *that* night, the marquee read EC-STATIC WRECK in red plastic letters; the band Daria fronted after Yer Funeral had finally disintegrated, trading grinding hardcore for something only slightly less violent, but something that gave her melodies and words enough breathing room that she didn't suffocate in the roar of her own music.

Through the glare of the lights, she caught glimpses of him sitting out there alone, sipping beer from a plastic cup and watching her. He was the only person in the club besides the albino kid who tended bar, and the guy at the door, and a booth full of goths who all seemed more interested in trying to hear each other above the music than listening to the band. An audience of one, and in those days, that wasn't so unusual. It hadn't mattered to her, one or a hundred. As long as she could play, and as long as there was someone, anyone, to listen, that was all she needed. They played their set, all the songs they had. Sometimes Daria was singing to him, because he was there, and sometimes she was only singing for herself, only slapping the strings of her black Fender bass for her own satisfaction. Back then, the music was better than sex, better than any drug she'd ever tried, almost heaven, the words and chords and toothache, heartbeat throb of the drums behind her.

Keith Barry clapped and wolf-whistled between the songs. She smiled and squinted through sweat and her tangled hair and the lights, trying to put a name with the hard, almost-familiar face. When the set was finished, he hooted for more, and she mumbled a thank you into the microphone. They didn't play an encore, because they didn't have anything else to play. As they left the stage, she realized that three of the fingers on her right hand, her thumb and index and middle finger, were bleeding. But it was nothing she couldn't patch up with a few drops of Krazy Glue and some Band-Aids, nothing that wouldn't heal. Three bloody fingers were a very small price to pay for the rush that would probably keep her going until the next show, whenever and wherever that might be.

Daria followed the others down the short, smelly hallway leading back to the ten-by-four closet that passed itself off as a dressing room. She wiped the blood from her injured hand onto the front of her T-shirt, three dark smears on yellow cotton, three more stains, and she could point to them in days to come and say, "See that shit there? *That* was a damn good night."

"Pretty sweet, Dar," Sherman James said, and then he slapped her hard on the back. Sherman wasn't bad, but she knew he was a lot more interested in his engineering classes at UAB than his guitar. "Too bad only half a dozen people heard it."

"Hey, fuck 'em," she said. "They don't know what they're missing, right?" and Daria put her bass down on the tattered old sofa taking up one wall of the room. She found a spot on the concrete floor where she could sit cross-legged and have a closer look at her fingers. Sherman made a dumb joke about playing to ghosts and roaches, and Donny White, who had known Sherman since high school, clacked his drumsticks loudly against the graffitied, swimming-pool-blue wall and laughed like it was actually funny.

"Yeah, man," Donny snickered and tapped out three quarter time on the plaster. "Audiences are for pussies. We don't need no steenkin' audience—"

"Speak for yourself," Daria muttered, wrapping a Band-Aid tightly around the pad of her thumb. "A few more warm bodies sure as hell wouldn't break my heart."

"You know what I meant."

"I know what you *think* you meant."

And when she looked up, the almost-familiar face was staring sheepishly back at her from the doorway. The man wearing the face was tall and scarecrow thin, dressed like a bum, and his name finally came to her—Keith Barry—the name and what it meant. He'd played guitar for a local punk band called Stiff Kitten, the best thing Birmingham had going for it until their vocalist had died a few months earlier. Her death was the stuff of local legend. She'd gotten wasted on vodka and speed and driven her car under the wheels of a moving freight train.

"Hi," he said.

"Hi," she replied. Daria smiled for him, and he almost smiled back.

"You're Keith Barry, aren't you?" she asked. "You used to play with Stiff Kitten."

He looked confused for a second, like an actor who's forgotten his lines or missed a cue, then slowly nodded his head.

"Yeah. That's me."

"Damn," Sherman said. He stood up too quickly, almost knocking over the rusty folding chair where he'd been sitting. He held one hand out expectantly. "Dude, you guys were absolutely fucking killer."

"Thanks," Keith Barry said uncertainly, looking down at his shoes or the floor, not shaking Sherman's hand.

"No, dude, I mean it. You guys fuckin' rocked," Sherman burbled recklessly on. "That really sucked, though, Sarah dying like that and all. She was fuckin' hot."

"Yeah," Keith Barry murmured, and now there was hardly a trace of emotion in his voice. He nodded again and raised his head, staring directly into Sherman's eyes. "It did. Do you always talk so goddamn much?"

"Jesus, Sherman," Daria groaned. "Will you sit down and shut up for one minute?" Sherman's smile faded, and he sat back down in the rusty chair.

"Listen, can I, uhm, can I talk to you a sec?" Keith Barry asked her then, tugging nervously at his shirt collar.

"Sure," and she wrapped the last Band-Aid around her index finger, then stood and dusted off the seat of her jeans. He led her back down the hallway and stopped at the stairs leading up to the stage. Daria leaned against the wall, both thumbs hooked into her belt loops.

"I'm sorry about Sherman," she said and looked back the way they'd come. "He isn't a dork on purpose, not usually."

"Oh hell, don't worry about it. You guys have a name?"

"You got a cigarette?" she asked, and he fumbled at his shirt pocket, but turned up only an empty pack and a few dry crumbs of tobacco.

"Thanks anyway," Daria said, wishing she'd thought to buy a pack before the show. "Right now we're Ecstatic Wreck, but that's just until we think of something better."

"Ecstatic Wreck, hunh? Hey, that's not so bad. I've heard worse," and she could tell how hard he was trying not to show the jitters, but his hands shook, anyway, and there were beads of sweat standing out on his forehead and cheeks. Keith Barry's heroin addiction was almost as famous as Sarah Milligan's run-in with the train.

"Yeah, well, I played with some other guys for a while, but they all joined the army, if you can believe that shit. Anyway, tonight was our first show."

"No kidding? Wow," and he rubbed nervously at the stubble on his chin. "Anyway, I just wanted to tell you you're good. Hell, you're better than good."

"Thanks," she said, a little embarrassed for both of them and trying not to show it. "That means a lot, coming from you. I used to go to all your shows."

"You want to maybe get a beer or go for a walk or something?"

She thought about it a moment, then shook her head.

"Sorry," she said. "That'd be cool, but I have plans already." She didn't, unless load out and the drive home alone counted as plans. She didn't have anything until work the next day, but the fevery sheen in Keith Barry's eyes made her nervous, warned her to keep her distance, here be tygers and plenty worse things than tygers.

"Maybe another time then," he said, sounding disappointed, but he smiled and ran his long fingers through his dirty, mouse-brown hair.

"Definitely. Absolutely."

They shook hands, his palm cool and slick with sweat, and she left him standing there. She turned and walked quickly towards the dressing room, walking fast before she changed her mind.

"Hey," he called after her. "What's your name?"

"Daria," she called back, without even turning around.

Two weeks later, Ecstatic Wreck played the Cave again, another Wednesday night, and this time there were a few more people. The stingy reward for a couple hundred fliers and word-of-mouth.

Keith Barry came back, too.

They played all the same songs in a different order, and added a jangling cover of David Bowie's "Starman." When the show was over, Keith was waiting at the edge of the stage.

"There's someone I want you to meet," he said and handed her a cold bottle of beer. She looked at the beer, then at Keith Barry. He was dressed a little better than before, and his hair was combed; his hands weren't shaking, and there was a confidence in his voice that told her he'd fixed before the show. She took a sip of the beer, promised the boys that she'd only be a minute, and let him lead her to a booth near the very back of the club. He said the sound was better back there, as good as the sound could ever get in a dump like the Cave. Then he introduced her to a skinny guy in a baseball cap and a blue mechanic's shirt with the name MORT stitched on the pocket.

"My man Mortimer here, he was our drummer," Keith said and sat down next to Mort, motioning for Daria to take the seat across from them. Mort looked uncomfortable, but said hi and smiled. Daria looked over her shoulder at the stage, Sherman and Donny already breaking everything down, and then she looked back at Keith.

"I really should help them," she said.

"C'mon. They're doin' just fine on their own," Keith replied and pointed at the empty seat again. "There's something we got to talk to you about. It's something important."

"Something important," she mumbled and sighed, but sat down. She took another swallow of beer, and it soothed her dry, exhausted throat.

"We want to put the band back together," Keith Barry

said. "We've been talking about it, me and Mort, and we think it's time we got off our lazy asses and went back to work. Sarah's gone, sure, but there's no reason we have to bury Stiff Kitten with her."

Daria stared at him a minute, then glanced at Mort, and he must have seen the growing impatience, the suspicion, in her eyes, because he just shrugged and began picking apart a soggy napkin.

"That's really great," she said, turning back to Keith. "But what's it got to do with me?"

"What's it got to do with you?" he repeated, as if he wasn't exactly sure what she was asking. "See, that's what I was just getting to."

"He wants you to dump your band," Mort said without looking at her, still busy dissecting the napkin. "He wants you to play with us."

"Oh," she whispered. "You've gotta be kidding."

"No," Keith said, glaring at Mort, glaring like he could kill a man with those eyes alone. "I'm not fucking kidding. We need a singer and a bass player, and we're never gonna find anyone better than you."

"I'd be a shit," Daria said, "if I walked out on them like that. We're just getting started."

Keith frowned, then sighed and slumped back into the booth. "They're not the ones you should be worrying about," he said, and lit a cigarette.

"They're my friends—"

"Sure, they're your friends. And I'm sure they're sweet guys. But you *know* that they're nowhere near as good as you are, right? You know they never *will* be."

"Jesus," she whispered, and stared hard at Keith Barry through the veil of smoke hanging in the air between them. "Yeah, I know that," she said, finally. "But I also know that your arm's got a bad habit."

Keith took another drag and shook his head. "I guess that must make you Sherlock fucking Holmes."

"All I'm saying is, I want to know if it's something you got a handle on, or if it's got you. You're sitting there ask-

ing me to ditch some really good guys. I think I have a right
to ask."

"You some kind of fucking saint?" he asked angrily, and
she knew that was her cue to thank them both for the beer
and the compliments and walk away. But she chewed at
her lower lip, instead, and waited for him to answer her
question.

"You're about to blow this thing," Mort said, scattering
bits of shredded napkin across the table in front of him.
"The lady asked you a question."

Keith smoked his cigarette and stared past Daria, towards the stage.

"You gonna answer her or not?"

"Yeah," he said, finally. "It's under control. I just fucking
need to get back to work, that's all. It's not a problem."

She nodded her head and finished her beer. It was even
hotter back here in the shadows than it had been on stage
and she was starting to feel a little dizzy, a little sick to her
stomach.

Walk away, she thought. *Tell him thanks and walk away
and just keep walking.*

"Look," she said, all the false cool she'd ever have rolled
up in that one word. "I'm gonna have to think about this
for a couple of days." And then she set the empty beer bottle down onto the table in front of her.

"No problem," Keith said. "I'm not asking you to make
a decision right this minute. I know you need some time."

"I just gotta think about it, that's all."

"This is my number at work," Mort said, and he slid a
business card from a northside machine shop across the
table to her. "Just ask for me. And whatever you decide,
thanks for thinking about it."

"You won't be sorry," Keith said, like it was already a
done deal, and stubbed his cigarette out in the overflowing
ashtray. "You won't regret it. I swear. Me, you, and Mort,
we'll wake all these motherfuckers up."

"Yeah, well, we'll see," she said. "I'm not making any

promises," and Daria slipped Mort's card into a pocket and walked back to the stage alone.

After the signing—two interminable hours of autographs and smiles for flashing cameras, the pretense that it's all about the fans, about the music, instead of the mortgage and the credit cards and Niki's doctor bills—and after the interview, Alex leads her to the waiting car and tells the driver to take them back to the hotel. She lights a cigarette and watches the streetlights, the ugly parade of strip malls and apartment buildings and fast-food restaurants along Peachtree Street. The stark white blaze of mercury vapor and halogen and fluorescence set against the last few moments of November dusk, and when she shivers Alex puts an arm around her.

"You were great," he says. "You're a trooper."

I'm a phony, she starts to tell him, but it's an old argument, an old confession, and she doesn't feel like having it again right now. "I need a drink," she says instead.

"We'll be back at the hotel soon."

"Great, but I need a drink now, not soon."

Alex frowns and pulls the silver flask out of his leather jacket. She gave it to him for his thirty-fifth birthday, almost three years ago now, back when the money was still something new, and it still felt good to give people expensive things. She screws the cap off, and there's rum inside; she hates rum and Alex knows it. Daria tips the mouth of the flask to her lips and tries to ignore the sugary taste. Who really gives a shit what it tastes like, anyway, as long as it makes her numb.

"I didn't think you liked rum."

"Fuck you," she says, and takes another drink.

"I don't think there's time before the show," Alex says and smiles, but she doesn't laugh.

"I have a headache. I've had a splitting headache all goddamn day long."

"Do you have your pills?" he asks.

"They make me sick to my stomach."

"I think that's why you're only supposed to take them with food, love."

She screws the cap back on the flask and tries to remember the last time she ate—a bite or two of the dry room-service toast Alex ordered her for breakfast, and a handful of salted almonds on the plane from San Francisco. There was Marvin's avocado and cheese sandwich, but she didn't even touch that.

"How long does it take to starve to death?"

"Don't know," Alex replies. "I've never tried."

"I think it takes a really long time. At least a month."

"Are you hungry, Dar?" he asks hopefully. "You want to pick something up? I could tell the driver to—"

"No," she says. "I was just wondering, that's all. I'll eat something after the show. I promise."

"I'm gonna hold you to that," he replies and slips the silver flask back into his jacket. "Don't you start thinking that I won't."

Daria rests her head against the window and takes another drag off her cigarette.

"This is where it happened," she says.

"This is where what happened?"

"Where Keith killed himself. It was down here somewhere. I don't remember the street name. Hell, I'm not sure if I ever knew the street name."

"Oh," Alex says and holds her tighter. His arms feel good around her, safe as houses, and she closes her eyes because she knows there's no danger of falling asleep, no danger of dreams. Her head hurts too much for sleep, her head and her stomach, and, besides, in another five or ten minutes they'll be back at the hotel.

"All I can remember is it was in some alley near Peachtree. He used his pocketknife."

"I know how it happened," Alex says, and she feels him pull away an inch or two, his embrace not as certain as it was a moment before.

"He was still alive when the cops found him. Just barely,

but he was still breathing. They said he might have lived, if he hadn't taken the pills."

And he releases her then, slides across the leather upholstery to his side of the wide backseat, and Daria opens her eyes. Her cigarette has burned down almost to the filter, and she puts it out in the little ashtray set into the back of the driver's seat, then lights another. Alex isn't looking at her, is busy pretending to watch the traffic, instead. The car crosses a short bridge, and a reflective green sign reads PEACHTREE CREEK. If there's actually a creek down there, Daria can't see it, nothing but impenetrable shadows pooled thick beneath glaring billboard lights.

"Jesus," she hisses. "Is everything in this city named after a fucking peach tree?"

"I couldn't tell you."

Daria turns and stares at Alex for a minute, a full minute at least, waiting for him to turn towards her, waiting for some sort of explanation for this sudden shift in his mood, but he keeps his eyes on all the other cars rushing past outside.

"Are you pissed at me about something?" she asks, and he shakes his head, but still doesn't look at her.

"No, I'm not pissed at you, Dar. I'll just never understand the irresistible gravity of assholes."

"What are you talking about now?"

"Assholes. They suck you in, and you never get away again."

"You mean Keith?"

"Yeah, I mean Keith. I mean the way he's all you can think about, when the junky son of a bitch has been dead for more than a decade. How many times did you think about Niki today? How many times did you think maybe you should pick up the phone and see if she's okay?"

Daria presses a button, and her window opens silently, letting in the chilly night air; it feels good against her face, feels clean even though it stinks of carbon monoxide and diesel fumes. The wind whips at her hair, invisible fingers to scrub away the filth that seems to cling to her no matter how often she bathes. She flicks the cigarette out the open window, and the wind snatches it.

"That means a whole hell of lot," she says, "coming from the man who screws her wife every chance he gets."

Alex grins and laughs softly and drums the fingers of his right hand impatiently on his knee.

"One day I'm gonna learn to keep me mouth shut," he says. "One day, I'm gonna learn not to butt heads with you."

"One day," she whispers and presses the button on the door, closing the window again, shutting out the cold wind and the oily, mechanical smells of the autumn night.

WWR: As an artist, what would you say scares you most?

DP: Waking up in the morning. Because I *know* that one morning, sooner or later, I'm going to open my eyes and all this will have been a dream, and I'll be back there in Birmingham, or maybe Boulder, if I'm lucky, playing for pennies and working in coffeehouses. It'll all be gone, just like *that* (snaps fingers). And I'll be a failure again. That's what scares me the most.

Back in the hotel room, Daria sits cross-legged in the middle of the bed and listens to the messages that have backed up on her cell phone. A call from Jarod, asking if she'd like to make an appearance at a local nightclub after the show; a message from Lyle, her piano player, saying he was going to have a few drinks with an old friend before the show, but not to worry, he'll make soundcheck on time; a last minute request for an interview; another call from Jarod, to say maybe that particular nightclub wasn't such a good idea after all and he'd get back to her. All the usual crap, the sizzling white noise before the storm, and she listens to each in its turn, then presses delete, watching the city through the wide glass balcony doors, the dizzying maze of buildings and streets glittering red and green and gold, arctic white and glacier blue.

Alex comes out of the bathroom and sits down on the love seat across from the bed. He yawns once, burps into his hand, then begins flipping through an Atlanta phone book.

"You think we can get some sushi delivered?" he asks, and she shrugs, but doesn't answer.

"I could fucking kill for spicy tuna rolls and *unagi* right about now."

"Call the concierge," Daria says and deletes a third message from Jarod Parris, telling her he's just learned that Michael Stipe's going to be at the show, and would she rather meet him before or afterwards.

"Those stupid fuckers never know where to get good sushi," Alex mutters. "They never even know where to get good pizza."

"Hey, Jarod says Michael Stipe's going to make the show tonight."

"No shit," Alex says and goes back to flipping through the *Yellow Pages*. "Do I bow or do I curtsy?"

The cell phone beeps twice, then informs her that the final message was left at 5:17 P.M. There's a sudden, painful burst of static through the speaker, and Daria curses and holds the phone an inch or two farther away from her ear. A moment later, a man begins to speak in a low and gravelly voice she doesn't recognize, a voice that's neither old nor young, a voice like cold fingers pressed against the back of her neck.

"You'll remember me," he says, "later on. You'll remember the night I tried to warn you about Spyder, the night in Birmingham when I told you Niki was in danger."

"What about Thai?" Alex asks. "Here's a Thai place that delivers—"

"Shut up a second," Daria hisses, and he does, sits staring at her, the phone book lying open in his lap.

"It's finally coming to an end," the man on the phone says, and there's more static before he continues. "She's calling us all back to the start. She's already found Niki. I think she's shown her the way past the fire, across the Dog's Bridge."

"Who the hell is it?" Alex asks, and she shakes her head and shushes him again.

"Listen to me, Daria Parker. It really doesn't matter if you don't believe or understand what I'm saying. You *will*. Niki's on her way back to Cullom Street. She's received the mark. You've seen it, on her hand. Niki Ky is becoming the Hierophant, and she'll open the gates. She'll unleash the Dragon."

Alex closes the phone book and sets it aside.

"We have to be there to stop her. *All* of us have to be there to stop her. All the worlds are winding down. All the worlds are spinning to a stop. Find her, Daria, before the jackals do. Before *I* do. If I find her first, I have to kill her, and I've killed too many people already."

There's a last wave of static before the computerized recording asks whether she wants to press 7 to delete the message or 9 to save it.

"Christ, Dar, what's happening? Who is it?"

But she doesn't answer him; she shakes her head and presses 9. "Message saved," the computer says in its measured, androgynous voice. "You have no new messages."

If I find her first, I have to kill her . . .

Daria's unsteady fingers linger a moment above the keypad, then she enters her home number, the ten digits that are all that stand between her and Niki, and waits for Marvin to answer the phone.

. . . I've killed too many people already.

On the fourth ring, the answering machine picks up, and a recording of Marvin's voice repeats the number she's just dialed, then asks that she please leave her name and number, the date and time. "Wait for the tone," Marvin says, "then speak your mind."

Daria hangs up and enters five digits, then a sixth, then presses cancel.

"God*damn* it!" she growls and almost throws her Nokia

at the hotel wall. "Alex, I can't even remember her number. I can't fucking remember the number for Niki's cell."

"Just hold on," he says, reaching for Daria's purse on the table beside the love seat. "You've got it in your PDA, right? So just calm down and tell me what the hell's going on before you give me a heart attack."

"I don't *know*," she replies, crying now, and she wipes furiously at her eyes with the back of her hand. "I think something's happened to Niki. I think something terrible's happened to Niki."

And there's a sound like the battered silence after thunder, or the moment before a train whistle blows, and she looks up at the balcony beyond the open drapes. A dead man wearing Keith Barry's face is standing on the other side of the glass, watching her. She can see that both his wrists are slashed, and he turns away and points at the sky. Above the city lights, a falling star streaks across the darkness and is gone, a single white shard of Heaven torn loose and hurled burning to earth.

And Daria Parker shuts her eyes, and she falls, too.

CHAPTER FIVE

Pillars of Fire

Almost twenty-four hours now since the hospital, and Niki isn't on a plane to Colorado, or Birmingham, or anywhere else. She's sitting in a hotel room—because she wouldn't go back to the house on Alamo Square—staring at the lights on the Bay Bridge, the glittering lights of Oakland laid out across the black water. Like stars come down to earth, like grounded, fallen things, and that's how she feels, sitting at the big window looking out, the television talking to itself so she won't feel so alone. It isn't working, because she is alone, even though Marvin's lying there on one of the twin beds behind her, pretending to watch a Jimmy Stewart movie on TV. She knows he's really watching her, can feel his eyes, his exhausted, nervous attention.

"Well, it's definitely infected," the doctor said and frowned, the doctor who finally saw her after Marvin found her unconscious on the restroom floor, after she'd crossed the sea of fire and lava on a bridge made of bones, after she'd talked to Spyder and then had to come back *here,* as if here and now could ever possibly matter again.

"You should have been more careful with those sutures," the doctor said. "You fool around with something like this and you can wind up losing a hand. I've seen it happen."

Marvin glared at her, his sharpest, most merciless I-told-you-so glare, but he didn't say anything. He took a deep breath, instead, and let it out very slowly, the air whistling softly between his front teeth.

"So I'll live?" Niki asked, and the doctor nodded his head and reached for a syringe.

"You're very lucky, Ms. Ky," he said. "You don't seem to understand that. This could have been a lot worse."

Oh, don't you worry, she thought. *It will be. It'll be a whole lot worse, and there's not anything you or anyone else can do.*

Under the bright lights of the examination room, the hole in her right palm was the too-ripe color of strawberry preserves, and she didn't bother asking the doctor if he could see the tranparent bit of something wriggling about at the center. He'd have said so if he could.

"A few more hours and there's no telling how bad this might have been."

Marvin made a disgusted sort of noise and laughed.

"Do you know how long we sat in the waiting room?" he asked. "Did anyone tell you we were sitting out there two hours?"

The doctor apologized and mumbled something about staff shortages and working double shifts; Niki could tell from the tone in his voice that he spent a lot of time apologizing. He cleaned the wound and sewed it shut again, sewing shut the door to her soul, the door that the wriggling thing had opened, then gave her a stronger antibiotic and wrapped her hand in fresh white gauze.

It itches and aches, and she pretends not to think about it.

"I should try to reach her again," Marvin says.

"She doesn't want to talk to you, Marvin. Why do you think she's keeping her phone turned off?"

"She's got to turn it back on sometime. She's got to check her messages sooner or later."

Niki taps at the glass with the middle finger of her left hand and shakes her head. "She said that she'd call when she got to Atlanta. She promised me she'd call."

"Daria's under a lot of stress, Niki. I don't know how she keeps going the way she does."

Niki taps the glass and watches the lights. There's a boat passing beneath the bridge, something small, and she imagines that it might be a tugboat. She thinks about standing on the listing deck, the cold and salty wind stinging her face, tangling her hair, blowing her soul clean again. And if she looked up, the steel-girder belly of the bridge would be there high above her, a wide black stripe to hide the brilliant sky. In a moment, the boat will be clear of the bridge, chugging north past Treasure Island. She closes her eyes and tries not to hear the television.

After the Dog's Bridge, there was no sense in airplanes, no sense left in any of her plans, and when the doctor was finished, she told Marvin to find them a hotel with a view of the bay. After that yawning abyss of flame and smoke, she needed to see water, the cold comfort of the Pacific lapping patiently at the ragged edge of the continent.

"I know she's fucking Alex," Niki says.

"What?" Marvin asks, and she can tell how hard he's trying to sound surprised, like that's the very last thing in the whole world he ever expected her to say. "Niki, what the hell are you talking about? That's not true."

"Yes, it is. I've known for a long time."

"You're just angry—"

"No. I'm not angry, Marvin. I'm not angry at all," and that's the truth. She might have been angry about Daria and the Brit guitar player, a long time back, months ago, when she thought there was still hope for her and Daria. But now it only makes her a little sad, and she's tired of pretending she doesn't know what's going on.

She opens her eyes, and the little boat's just a speck in the darkness.

"She loves you, Niki," Marvin says, and she stops tapping at the glass.

"Yeah. I know she does. That's the worst part of it, I think. It would be easier if she didn't."

"But you still love her."

"Do I?" Niki asks, asking herself more than she's asking him. "I thought I did. Just a few hours ago, I was pretty sure I did. But now—"

"Now you're tired and confused and need to get some sleep."

Niki turns around in her chair and stares at Marvin for a moment. His eyes are bloodshot, and there's stubble on his cheeks. He probably hasn't slept since Saturday morning, and now it's Monday night, and he's still trying to stay awake because someone has to watch her.

"I'm *not* confused," she says. "I'm very tired, and my hand hurts, but I'm not confused. I'm crazy, Marvin, but I'm not a child. And I'm not stupid, either."

Marvin sighs and rubs his eyes.

"Let's both get some sleep, and then we'll talk about this, okay? I can't even think straight anymore."

Niki glances back at the window, but there's no sign of the little boat now. For all she knows, the bay has opened up and swallowed it whole.

"I'm sorry I've been such a bitch to you," Niki says.

"Come lie down," he says, and switches off the television with the remote control, so there's only the restless sound of the traffic outside, the murmur of people on the street, the wind pressing itself against the walls of the hotel. "Lie down, and we'll talk about it in the morning. Your meds are on the bathroom counter by the sink."

"That girl who saw the wolves, that wasn't your fault, what happened to her."

"No," he says, then sighs and switches the TV on again. "Of course not. I know that," and the box springs squeak, like a handful of captured mice, so she knows without having to look that he's sitting up.

"You did everything you could," she whispers, then begins tapping her finger against the window again. "Everything anyone could have done."

"Niki, what are you trying to say?" he asks, but then his cell phone starts ringing, and she doesn't have to think of a way not to answer the question.

* * *

When Niki finally reached the far side of the Dog's Bridge, there was someone waiting for her, the same someone who waits for anyone who crosses the span. He sat on his haunches, crouched at the base of one of the great stone piers, where the intricate weave of bone and wire was anchored forever to the inconstant, volcanic earth. When he saw her coming, the creature stood up, joints popping loudly, stretching his long arms and legs like he must have been sitting in that same spot for a very long time. Standing up straight, he was at least a couple of feet taller than Niki. The creature yawned once, showing off sharp eye-teeth the color of clotted milk, scratched his chin, then blinked his crimson eyes at her. In the dim, shifting light from the soot and ash sky, his smooth skin glistened black as coal; he was naked, save for a battered derby perched crookedly on his narrow skull.

"You certainly took your own sweet time," he growled and licked his thin lips.

"It was a long way," Niki said, wishing there'd been no one at all on this side of the bridge, except maybe Spyder, but certainly not this scowling, ribsy creature with its red, pupilless eyes. "I came as fast as I could."

"Are you kidding? No one *ever* crosses that bridge as fast as they can," he replied. "They *pick* their way across, inch by goddamned inch, as though their lives depend on every single step. They dawdle, and they gawk, and—"

"I didn't dawdle," Niki protested.

"Oh, yes, you did, sweetheart. I watched you. I listened. You're no different than all the rest of them."

"I never said I was."

"You didn't have to," the black thing grunted and sat down again. "By now, every thistle and scorpion and grubworm on the hub knows your name. Round these parts, you're the new It girl and the black guard has your number. But personally," he sneered, "I don't see what all the fuss is about. You wouldn't make a decent mouthful for a starving rat."

"I don't know what you're talking about. I was at the hospital, and I went to take a piss—"

"Yeah. Sure, sure, sure. I read the papers, child. I got the skinny. But the only thing matters to me is how you're mucking everything up by starting at the end, when you haven't the foggiest where the beginning's at. Do you have any idea the sort of ripples that causes?"

Niki turned and looked back at the bridge, the tops of its high, misshapen towers lost in the low clouds.

"Spyder sent me across," she said and swallowed, her mouth as dry as sand, dry as dust, and thought how good a glass of Marvin's limeade would be.

"Of course she did. That one, she does whatever the hell she likes and protocol be damned. But, you mark my word, the black guard's gonna catch up with her ass one day, too. Way things are headed, maybe one day real soon."

"What's the black guard?" Niki asked, not really wanting to know and starting to wonder if maybe she should have stayed on the other side, and she sat down on the rocky ground in front of the tall thing.

"Oh, you'll find out soon enough. Those cheeky, conniving fuckers. They come skulking round here, making *me* promises, offering—" and he paused and sniffed at the sulfurous air a moment. Behind them, the sea of fire belched and heaved and bubbled, and the Dog's Bridge creaked in the scorched and parching furnace wind.

"—offering me *things*," he continued. "Sweet things. Things I haven't tasted in centuries, mind you. And all *I* have to do is hand them your pretty head on a pike."

"Is that what happens next?" Niki asked. "Are you going to kill me and cut off my head?"

The tall thing looked offended, rolled its red eyes and snorted. "This is still *my* bridge, Hierophant. My fucking bridge, and my rules, and as long as you know how many steps it took you to get across, I got no beef with you. I'm a bridge keeper, not a merchant. I don't make *deals*."

"Your bridge?"

"Damn straight, girlie. My bridge, for as long as it's been

standing, and it'll *be* my bridge until those fires finally burn themselves out, or I get bored with it, whichever comes first."

"Then you're the dog?"

"Do I *look* like a goddamn dog?"

"You don't look much like anything I've ever seen," Niki replied, and the creature rolled its eyes again.

"I didn't name the stinking bridge," he said, and licked his lips. "And I'll wager there's a whole lot of things you ain't seen yet. Way I hear it, though, that's all gonna change, moppet. Way I hear it—"

"I don't care. My hand hurts, and I'm tired of listening to you." She got up and dusted off the seat of her jeans with her good hand.

"Then give me the number, and fuck off to wherever it is you're bound," the creature snarled and leaned back against the pier. "You think I don't have better things to do than sit here yacking with rabble like you all day long?"

"The number?" Niki asked, and the bridge keeper leaned forward, perking his ears, grinned wide and smiled an eager, hungry smile.

"How many steps, girlie. That side to this side. The number. Else I get something sweet, after all. Surely, she must have *told* you—"

"Yeah, she told me," Niki said quickly and took a couple of steps back from the black and grinning thing, caught one heel on a piece of slate and almost tripped. "My hand hurts, and I'm thirsty, that's all. I just forgot for a second. I didn't know what you meant."

"So stop wasting my time," the bridge keeper said. "Stop getting my hopes up. Spit it out."

"What happens then? Do you send me back?"

"I don't send nobody nowhere, lady. I watch this here bridge. That's all. Do you have the number or not?"

Niki opened her mouth to tell him, "Four thous—" but then he sprang to his feet, faster than she would have guessed, and one hand clamped tight across her mouth. His skin tasted as bad as the air smelled.

"Geekus crow!" he growled and glanced anxiously over his shoulder. "You don't go saying it out *loud*, you little ninny. Anything at all might be listening. The number's mine, and nobody hears it but me."

He looked back at her, then, stared deep inside her with those blazing crimson eyes, his gaze to push apart the most secret convolutions of her mind, her spirit, her heart, and in an instant, the bridge keeper had snatched the number from her head.

"Now get out of here," he snarled and sat back down. "I'm sick of your ugly face."

And worlds parted for her, and time, and the space between worlds and time and the things that aren't quite either, and she felt the cold restroom tiles beneath her. "Don't move," Marvin said. "Someone's coming."

"I'm sorry," Daria says again, the third or fourth or fifth time since Marvin handed the phone to Niki. The words so easy from her lips, and Niki thinks it might be easier to believe had she said it only once. "I should have called. I promised you I would, and I should have called. Things have been crazy ever since the plane landed."

"It's okay," Niki tells her, and she knows those words come too easily, as well. "I know you're busy."

"I'm not too busy to keep my promises."

Marvin is sitting on one corner of his bed, watching Niki expectantly, his eyes asking urgent questions that will have to wait. She turns her back on him, facing the window and the bay again.

"What are you doing in a hotel?" Daria asks. "Why aren't you at home?"

"I didn't want to be at home anymore. It's creepy there alone."

"But you're not alone, baby. Marvin's there. That's why he's there, so you won't be alone."

"I like hotels," Niki says, and takes a step nearer the window. "I like those little bottles of shampoo."

There's a moment or two of nothing but static over the

line then, not silence, but no one saying anything, either, and Niki wonders if she has the courage to pass the phone back to Marvin or, better yet, the courage to just hang up. *I don't want to talk to you,* she says inside her head. *I don't want to talk to you and I don't want to hear you. I don't think we matter anymore.*

"So, why *did* you decide to call?" she asks instead, and that almost seems bold enough, a halfway decent compromise, if she doesn't have the balls to go all the way.

"I was worried about you—"

"I'm fine," Niki replies quickly, cutting Daria off. "Me and Marvin are just sitting here watching television. It's *Harvey,* you know, with Jimmy Stewart and the pooka."

"I got a strange phone call," Daria says. "It scared me, that's all. I needed to hear your voice. I needed to know that you're all right."

"The *hospital,*" Marvin whispers behind her. "You have to tell her, Niki."

Niki ignores him. "What kind of phone call?"

"I don't know," Daria says and coughs. "It was probably just some asshole who got my number somehow, someone trying to mess with my head. I guess I shouldn't have let it get to me. It freaked me out."

"You shouldn't smoke so much," Niki says. "It makes you cough. It's bad for your voice."

"If you *don't* tell her, Niki, I will. I'll have to. It would be better if you did."

"Was that Marvin?" Daria asks. "Did he say something?"

"No," Niki says. "It was just the television. The volume's turned up too loud. Marvin, turn the TV down. I can't hear Daria."

Marvin shakes his head, makes his exasperated-with-Niki face, and lies down on the bed.

"What kind of phone call was it, Dar? What did they say?"

More static, the sound of Daria looking for the right words, filtering, deciding what is fit for Niki to hear and what isn't; Niki sits down in the chair beside the window and waits for Daria to figure it out. She's learned better than to push, that pushing usually only leads to Daria telling her less, or nothing at all.

"I'm thinking about coming home," Daria says, finally. "I shouldn't have left you there."

"You have a show tonight."

"I could come right after the show. I could go straight from the show to the airport. I could be there by morning, Niki."

"Tomorrow night's Miami," Niki reminds her. "Miami and then Orlando on Wednesday, and then—"

"Why can't you just be quiet and *listen* for five seconds?"

"You can't miss any more shows."

"Niki, we're more important than the shows."

Niki touches the window, the cold plate glass, the invisible barrier keeping out the night, holding back the wind.

"We need the money. There's the mortgage."

"We're more important than the money or the goddamned house," and Niki can hear the frayed edge in Daria's voice beginning to unravel completely. In a moment, she'll be shouting or crying or both.

"What did he say?" Niki asks.

"Who?"

"The asshole, the guy who got your number. It must have been something pretty awful, the way you sound, the things you're saying."

"Yeah, well, we can talk about it when I get there, okay? I really don't want to get into what he said, not on the phone."

"Where's Alex going to sleep?" and that last bit out quick, before Niki can consider the consequences, before she can weigh the damage her words will do. The way they'll cut, the blood they'll draw, how she can never take them back. Daria doesn't answer her, doesn't say anything, and the connection crackles faintly in Niki's ear.

"The bay is very pretty tonight, Dar. It's so pretty it doesn't even look real. It looks like a painting."

Through the phone, she can hear the familiar sounds of Daria lighting a cigarette—the crinkle of cellophane, her thumb on the strike wheel of her lighter, the sudden rush of smoke from Daria's lips and nostrils. Behind Niki, Marvin asks for the phone.

"I'm trying to do the right thing," Daria says, her voice shaking, and Niki knows she's struggling to hold it steady. "I'm tired, and I'm sick, and I'm scared, but I'm fucking trying to do the right thing."

"I think it's too late for that," Niki replies. Down on the bay, beneath the bridge, there's a sudden flash of light, and she stands up.

"Niki, please, don't say that. When I get back home, we'll talk. I mean *really* tal—"

"We should have talked a long time ago, Daria."

"I *know* that. I know that now."

"I don't think there's any time left for talking. Something's happening."

"No," Daria says. "Please, Niki. Listen to me. I can be there for breakfast. We can go to that place on the waterfront you like so much."

Beneath the bridge, the light ebbs, flickers, and almost winks out. And then it explodes, a perfect circle of blue-white waves radiating across the black water, rushing soundlessly towards shore. Light so bright that Niki squints, then turns her head away. She lets the phone slip from her fingers and fall to the carpet, opens her mouth to warn Marvin, but then the blast wave hits and the hotel window comes apart in a storm of jagged, melting glass.

The light fills her eyes, burning them to wisps of steam. Her skin turns black and curls like frying bacon, exposing flesh and bone and blood that boils away in an instant. The air stinks of cinders and ozone, and the California night has become a hurricane of fire.

The Dragon is awake and insatiable after its sleep. In a moment more, it will have devoured the city and moved on. Before sunrise, the whole world will burn inside its bottomless cauldron belly.

"No," Niki Ky whispers. "Not yet."

The Dragon hears her and pulls back in on itself, a blazing serpent vanishing down its own gullet.

And there is no fire.

There is only the night, filled with possibility, with things that can be avoided and things that are inevitable.

Niki stands at the window, staring down at the dark waters of the bay. She can still hear Daria's voice, but now it's too small and quiet and far off for her to make out any of the words. Niki glances down at the cell phone, still right there in her good hand, and she sets it carefully on the windowsill. The bedsprings squeak, and then Marvin's holding her, asking her questions that she's too tired to understand.

"I'm sorry," she says to him. "Please, tell her I said that I'm sorry," and then oblivion opens itself wide, swelling to fill the space between the hotel room walls, between horizons, and gives her a place to hide for a while.

For a long time, or a time that only seems long because there's no sun or moon, and no clocks nor anyone to remind her that time is passing, Niki is nowhere, nowhen, and her thoughts are not important. There's no sorrow for Daria, no anger, no pain, no loneliness, no fear of her own insanity. Her hand doesn't hurt, and she doesn't remember the terrible things that no one else can see. And then somebody's talking, and the perfect nothingness is ruined, and she opens her eyes.

Or some other, more primal, part of herself.

She unfolds.

And she's standing in the front yard of Spyder's old house in Birmingham. There's a cool wind blowing through the pecan trees, rustling the limbs, the dry autumn leaves. The night air smells like cinnamon and musty, windowless rooms where no one ever goes, and she looks up at the sky above the mountain. The stars are much brighter than they should be, or closer to earth, and they seem to writhe in the indigo heavens.

"Things happened here," Spyder says, speaking softly

from somewhere directly behind Niki. "Things that never should have happened. Things that violated and broke you. The things that are killing you."

"I know," Niki says. "I've known that all along."

"Don't turn around," Spyder says. "You can't see me here. It isn't allowed."

"I wasn't going to turn around," Niki replies and takes a step towards the house. All the windows are dark, no lights in there, not an electric bulb or a candle, only the night choking every inch of wall and floor and ceiling.

"Why am I here, Spyder?" Niki asks. "I know this is where it started, but I don't know why I'm here. I feel like I'm going in circles."

"Yes," Spyder replies, "you are. Circles, and circles within circles."

"Then I'm never going to get anywhere, am I?"

The ground shudders beneath her feet; all the moldering leaves, the soil, the earthworms, and black, scurrying beetles, all the decaying, living matter, everything shudders, and Niki looks at the sky again.

"We're making this up as we go along," Spyder says.

"Why?"

"Because that's the way it has to be. Because that's the only way to keep it secret."

"From the black guard?" Niki asks her.

"From the black guard, and the priests who watch the Dragon, and the angels who are still out there looking for the stone."

"The angels," Niki whispers. "You made that story up, Spyder. That was just something you told them so they wouldn't leave you alone. There *aren't* any angels, not here."

Niki takes another step nearer the abandoned house.

"You can't go in there," Spyder says and grabs her shoulder before she can get any closer. "It's not what you see. It's not what it wants you to think it is."

"I don't believe there's anything there at all. I think I hallucinated, and then I fainted, and I'm back in the hotel room. I think Marvin's wiping my face with a damp wash-cloth. I think *Harvey*'s playing on the television."

The ground shudders again, more violently than before, and Spyder takes her hand off Niki's shoulder.

"I think I'm just a crazy girl. There are no bridges over lakes of fire, or dragons, or ghosts."

"I thought they would keep to *this* place," Spyder mutters to herself, as if she isn't listening and hasn't heard anything Niki's said, as though none of it matters. "I thought they'd have to keep to this place."

"No ghosts," Niki says again. "Not yours or Danny's. I make it all up because I'm sick. But I'm going to wake up now, and in the morning Daria will be home and everything will be right again."

"When was anything ever *right*, Niki?"

Niki takes another step towards the house, if only because the thing behind her, the thing from her head pretending to be Spyder, doesn't want her to, so maybe, she thinks, that's the way back.

"Don't," Spyder warns her. "You don't know, Niki. You can't begin to imagine what's waiting in there for you."

"It's just an old house, that's all. The house where you killed yourself. The house where your father went insane and raped you, and where your mother died. Just an old house, Spyder, full of bad memories. I've been there before. It didn't kill me then."

"I didn't let it. I protected you. I won't be able to this time."

"Then I'll protect myself. I'm a big girl now."

Behind her, there's a noise like rusted hinges and tearing cloth, and suddenly the air reeks of something lying dead and swollen beneath a summer sun.

"The bridge keeper should have killed you," Spyder snarls, and Niki hears her take a step, the fallen leaves crunching loudly beneath her shoes. "He should have saved us the trouble."

And—

Spyder Baxter is standing on the porch of the house,

starlight dripping from her dreadlocks, the scar between her eyes glowing softly in the gloom.

"Don't turn around," she says. "Get down, and don't look behind you."

But Niki does turn and look, because if none of it's real, if it's all only bad memories and delusion, then there's nothing back there that can hurt her, and if Spyder's standing on the porch—

The shadow thing beneath the trees smiles, and its yellow eyes roll back to show her the void held inside its skull.

"Get *down*," Spyder says again, and this time Niki does as she's told. She falls to the ground, unable to take her eyes off the smiling thing, scrambling backwards towards the porch and Spyder.

"Too late," the shadow smirks, and it reaches for Niki with one ebony scarecrow arm. "She's *seen* me. She's seen me, and you know the rules."

"Fuck you," Spyder growls, and the night air shimmers and sparks and sizzles around them. Overhead, the stars waver, then vanish as the ground shudders so violently that the trunks of the trees sway and creak. The shadow thing begins to scream a second or two before it bursts into flame, fire the immaculate color of the light from Spyder's cruciform scar. Niki stops crawling and covers her ears, but the screams slip between her fingers, through flesh and bone, and she can only shut her eyes and wait for it to end.

"Don't look at it, Niki. Keep your eyes closed as tight as you can and don't see it."

And when she's certain that the screaming will go on forever, when the force of the sound has become a weight pressing in on the frail boundaries of her body and soul and in only another instant she'll be crushed to jelly, Niki screams, too. Opens her mouth wide and screams until the night collapses, comes down in crumbling slabs and splintered moments, vomiting her back into the nowhere.

Niki Ky folds herself shut again, creasing herself as easily as tissue-thin sheets of origami paper.

Doors open, and doors close.

And before the voices from the television and the gentle, incandescent light of the hotel room, before Marvin and the certainty of what has to happen next, what she has to *do* next, Niki looks over her shoulder, and even in this place that is no place, with the gulf of an eternity yawning between her and it, she can see the shadow burning.

One day in April, almost a year ago. A day when Daria was supposed to go with her to see Dr. Dalby, but then something came up at the last minute, the band or an interview or something else that couldn't wait, and so Niki went alone. It wasn't raining that day, but there was no sun, and the fog outside his office window was so thick there might have been nothing beyond it, the entire universe shrunk down to that one room and the old man watching her while he fidgeted with his mustache.

"You had to be there, I guess," Niki said. "It's complicated, what happened to Spyder."

"There's no rush," the psychologist said. "You can take all the time you need. You don't have to try to tell the whole story in one session."

Niki laughed and shook her head. "I couldn't tell the whole story in a *hundred* sessions," she replied and hugged the needlepoint anemones and geraniums.

"Then don't tell me the whole story. Just tell me the important parts, the parts that you think matter."

"Yeah, the parts that matter," she said and took a deep breath. Outside, the fog made gray, floating shapes, phantoms of water vapor and pollution to match the phantoms in her head. "That'll be a breeze."

"No, it won't. But it might be worth the effort."

"And it might not."

"That's right, Nicolan. It might not. It might be a dead end. A complete waste of time. That's just the chance you have to take."

And she drew another deep breath, a sip of water from the bottle on the floor beside her feet, and started talking, letting the past drain like infection. How she came to Birmingham, still running from Danny's suicide, how she met Daria and Spyder, the first night she heard Daria sing, the first time she saw the house on Cullom Street.

"There were all these goth kids who hung around with Spyder," she said and took another sip of water, swished it around in her mouth a few seconds before swallowing. "They thought she was the coolest thing in the world, you know? They practically worshipped her. I suppose she gave them meaning, or purpose, or something."

"Did they resent you?" Dr. Dalby asked. "Did they see you as an intruder?"

"You're jumping ahead," she replied, and he apologized and told her to continue.

"There were these two guys, Byron and Walter, and a girl named Robin. She was Spyder's lover. She's the one who performed the peyote ceremony in Spyder's basement."

"And Spyder tried to stop her?"

"Yeah, she was afraid. But Robin went ahead and did it anyway. I don't know exactly what happened. Spyder would never tell me. But it was something bad. They all freaked out, and she had to go down there after them, down there where her father had raped her when she was just a little kid."

"That would have been very traumatic for her."

Niki stared at him a second and then laughed again. "You think so?" she asked, and shook her head.

"I'm sorry. It's a professional hazard, I suppose, stating the obvious. Go on."

Her hands were trembling, even though she'd hardly gotten started, all the worst of it still unspoken, and she hugged the brocade pillow tighter. *If Daria had come,* she told herself, *it wouldn't be so hard, and I wouldn't be so scared.* But she knew that was a lie.

"Spyder said Robin was into all sorts of occult crap. Wicca and séances and tarot cards. Peyote. Just about anything that came along, I think."

"Isn't that a bit like what you told me about New Orleans, you and your friends and all the things you did in the old cemeteries? Your ceremonies to raise ghosts?"

Niki shrugged. "No, I think Robin must have been a lot worse than we ever were. At least, that's the way Spyder made her sound."

"When our myths fail us," Dr. Dalby said thoughtfully, "or when we're never given myths to start with—"

"—we're forced to invent them," Niki finished for him.

The old man nodded his head and smiled. "That's what you were doing in New Orleans, and it sounds like that's what Robin was doing in Spyder's basement. But it can be very dangerous, creating myths. That's one of the things that children should learn, but rarely ever do."

"I don't know what happened down there," Niki said again. "But afterwards, they started seeing things, awful things, or maybe they only thought they were seeing things. And then, what Spyder did to try to help, I'm pretty sure she only made it worse. She told them a story, just something she made up so they wouldn't be so afraid of whatever was happening to them. She was scared she was going to lose them, and they were everything in the world to her. Her story was supposed to make them less afraid, but I think it also made them need her more."

"You think she did that on purpose? You think she was manipulating them, trying to control them?"

Niki thought about that for a moment, and watched the fog outside the office window.

"You don't have to answer, if you'd rather not."

"I know," she said, and then "Spyder was so afraid of being alone. I think that scared her more than anything."

"You've already told me she had no family, that her friends were all she had. And in a place like Alabama, someone like Spyder must have had a hard time finding friends. So that would have made it even more difficult for her, I'd imagine."

"Yeah. Anyway, she told them all this fucked-up story about how they were descended from angels. That there'd been a war in Heaven and there'd been some angels that had refused to take a side in the war. Instead, they'd stolen a stone from God, because they thought he couldn't be trusted with it, and they hid it on the earth somewhere."

"Spyder didn't make that story up, Nicolan," Dr. Dalby said, and his eyes sparkled in the light from the lamp on his desk. "That's quite an old story. The stone's part of the tradition surrounding the Holy Grail. It's been called the *lapis exilis,* and *lapis lapsus ex illis stellis,* the stone that came from the stars. Sometimes it's actually considered a part of the grail."

"Spyder read a lot," Niki said, still watching the fog.

"What else did Spyder tell them?" he asked.

"She said God sent other angels to find the ones who'd stolen the stone, to kill them and bring it back to him. And because they knew they'd be found sooner or later, the angels came up with a way to take the stone apart and put the pieces inside themselves. Then they mated with mortal men and women, and the stone was passed along, hidden inside the babies that were born. They thought God would never hurt innocent children to get it back."

"That's the story of the Nephilim. At least, it's based on the story of the Nephilim."

"That's a goth band."

"Is it?" the psychologist asked her, and smiled. "Let me read you something," and he got up and selected a black leather Bible from the tall bookshelf near his desk. He flipped through the onionskin pages for a moment, and "Here it is," he said. "Genesis 6:4. 'The Nephilim were on the earth in those days—and also afterwards—when the sons of God went to the daughters of men and had children by them. They were the heroes of old, men of renown.' "

"Oh," Niki sighed and reached for her water bottle. "I didn't know Spyder ever read the Bible."

"There are many names for the Nephilim," Dr. Dalby said and sat down again. "They turn up in both the Bible and the Dead Sea Scrolls. They're called the Emim, the Rephaim, the Gibborim, the Awwim. They're supposed to have been giants. They were corrupt and corrupted mankind, and eventually God sent Gabriel to start a civil war to destroy them all."

"So, you think Spyder took those stories from the Bible and used them to make up her own story."

"That's certainly what it sounds like. We call it syncretization, taking elements of older stories and putting them together in new ways, or combining them with other stories to make new and more useful myths."

Niki nodded, wondering if the psychologist actually believed anything himself, or only weighed religions and myths based on their utility. Outside, the fog swirled and made dim shapes that were there and then gone again, a mirage of silvery, ephemeral faces and bodies, and Niki looked away, looked at the clock, instead. She still had fifteen minutes until her time was up.

"Syncretization can be a very healthy thing," Dr. Dalby said. "It's often a normal part of cultural evolution."

"Spyder told them they were *descended* from those angels. The ones who stole the stone, the Nephilim. She told them it was still there inside of them, and they were being hunted, but *she* could protect them. She made a dream catcher from strands of their hair and told them that the things hunting them would try to get to them through bad dreams, but the dream catcher would keep them safe. Now, does that sound healthy to you, Dr. Dalby?"

The psychologist closed the Bible and shook his head, but didn't say anything.

"She told them that Robin had shown the angels where they were, during the peyote ceremony."

"Do you think she was trying to punish Robin, by telling them that?"

"She loved Robin," Niki said.

"Even so, she must have been very angry. Sometimes, we're much harder on people *because* we love them. You know that."

Niki stared at him and then looked at the floor.

"Spyder told them they'd be safe," she continued. "She

hid the dream catcher inside an old aquarium full of black widows that she kept in her bedroom. One night, Byron and Robin tried to steal it. That's how Robin died, that's how . . ." but then the knot in her throat hurt too much to keep talking, and she covered her face with her hands so he wouldn't see her cry.

"Nicolan, you can stop now if you need to. You've said more than enough for one session. I'm very proud of you."

And so she sat weeping on the sofa, and the clock on his desk slowly ticked off the seconds, and outside the fog struggled against nature to make something solid of itself, something from almost nothing, something more than shifting, insubstantial mist.

Around her, the city has begun to revolve, convulsing, turning itself inside out. Nothing here is even half solid anymore, nothing that she can't see through at a glance, and Niki stands outside the hotel on Steuart Street and is afraid that she's waited too long. Maybe if she hadn't wasted so much time trying to reach the airport, or if she hadn't gone into the restroom at the hospital, or lingered so long in the nightmare of Spyder's house, fooled by the grinning shadow with yellow eyes. She understands now, but now may be too late. Overhead, the sky flashes a million shades of blue and black and gray and orange, a million days superimposed one upon the other, a million flickering skies, worlds beyond existence and imagining. There is no still point remaining anywhere, no eye to this storm. Niki fights the dizziness and nausea, the pain in her hand; she grits her teeth and leans against a small tree growing outside the hotel. But the tree keeps becoming other trees, and things that aren't quite trees, and lampposts, and street signs, and stone pillars, and she thinks about sitting down on the sidewalk instead. If it's too late, if she's fucked it all up by dragging her feet, this is probably as good a place to die as any.

And then the small white bird at her feet, the bird which hadn't been there only a moment before, glares anxiously up at her with eyes like small red berries, and "You have to try," it says. "You're the Hierophant, and without you we're all doomed. Without you, the Dragon—"

"Shut up, bird," Niki whispers, trying not to vomit as the sky strobes and the earth beneath her feet twists and lurches. "Fuck off and let me die in peace. I want this to end now. I want it to be finished."

"No, you don't understand," it squawks indignantly. "I *can't* leave you." The white bird flaps its wings and flutters in the indecisive air a few feet above Niki's head. "The Weaver sent me to show you the way across. You can't stay here, Niki Ky. This place is rejecting you. Can't you feel it? It's trying to push you out."

Niki shuts her eyes, but that only makes the dizziness worse, and she immediately opens them again.

"You have to follow me *now*," the bird says frantically.

"Birds don't fucking talk," she tells it. "Even I know that," and she looks longingly back at the hotel, the shiny brass poles supporting a fancy red awning, tall doors leading into the brightly lit lobby. Ten minutes ago, she was still upstairs in the room with Marvin. She'd awakened from the nowhere place to the gentle salt-and-pepper light of the television. He'd left it on, the sound off, and fallen asleep in the chair beside the window. Marvin was snoring very softly, and his head lolled forward, his chin almost touching his chest. Outside, the sky was a wild, auroral thing, brilliant seizures of night and day, day and night, stars and sun and moons she didn't recognize. Niki got up, moving as quietly as she could, as quickly as she dared, praying to nothing in particular that she wouldn't wake him. She slipped on her blue Muppet-fur coat and her boots, not bothering with the yellow laces. The laces could wait. Niki took her backpack and whatever was already stuffed inside it and didn't leave a note because she was pretty sure there was nothing more to say that mattered.

She left the door to the room standing open, afraid shutting it might make too much noise, and she didn't want to

have to argue with Marvin anymore, didn't want him trying to stop her or following her.

"The Weaver said that we have to go south," the bird
squawks. "She said we have to reach the bridge while
there's still time."

"Time for what, and who the hell's the Weaver?" Niki
moans, steadying herself as the tree becomes a flagpole.
"Am I supposed to know what you're talking about, bird?"

"We have to hurry, Niki. We have to *fly*. Already, the
jackals are hunting you. The worlds have grown thin here,
and by now they'll have found a way in."

"You're not even a real bird, are you?"

"The Weaver will be waiting at the bridge, but we have
to go *now*."

"Why can't she come here?" Niki asks, and the flagpole
becomes a tree again, but its bark is soft and black, and she
pulls her hands away.

"The jackals are *coming*," the bird squawks.

"Then answer my question. Why can't the Weaver come
here? I'm sick, and I don't think I can walk all the way to
the goddamn bridge."

The white bird shrieks and dissolves into a spinning ball
of gray-violet light. It throws sparks that twinkle and whirl
madly about its equator.

"See, I knew you weren't a real bird."

And then there's a thunderclap so loud that windows up
and down Steuart Street shatter, and glass rains down to
the blacktop and concrete. Niki screams and covers her
ears as the sky turns a deep wine red and finally stops flickering.

"That's it," the ball of light murmurs, and it doesn't
sound anything at all like the white bird did. "They've
found the frequency. They're coming."

From the east, the direction of the Embarcadero and the
wharves lined up along the bay, there's a sound like howling wolves, if wolves grew half as large as elephants, wolves
so loud that Niki can hear them even through the ghost of
the thunderclap still ringing in her ears.

"The jackals," she says and then looks south, towards the interstate and the bridge.

"They run before the guard," the light whispers and glows a little brighter. "Go now, Niki Ky. Go if you ever mean to, or you'll die in this place, and two worlds will die with you."

"What if I just go back inside? What if I go back inside and wake Marvin—"

"You are dead to this city," the light replies. "You'd never find your way, and if you did, there would only be an empty room where you'd sit waiting alone for the jackals to sniff you out. It wouldn't take them long."

The light fades into a white bird, its feathers washed the color of funeral carnations by the bloody sky.

"Follow me, Hierophant. The Weaver is waiting."

Niki looks at the hotel one last time, at the dark window where Marvin sits asleep, and then she turns and follows the bird down the deserted black ribbon of Steuart towards the Bay Bridge and whatever's waiting for her there.

After the climb through the rubble of the Fremont off-ramp—over treacherous cement and asphalt boulders, broken roadway strata and rusted rebar teeth jutting crookedly from stone jaws—when she's finally standing on the buckled, sagging remains of I-80, Niki stops and looks back the way they've come. She still can't see the jackals, but she can hear them plainly enough, the terrible, frenzied noise of them searching for her through the ruins of San Francisco. Breathless and sore, she takes off the pack and sits down. Her heart is beating so hard, so fast, that it hurts, and she puts her good hand flat against her chest and tries to catch her breath.

"What happened?" Niki gasps. "What's happened to the city?"

"Nothing has happened," the white bird replies impatiently, lighting on the road beside her. "The city—*your* city—is still just the way you left it. But it has pushed you out."

Niki swallows, tasting bile. She's afraid she's going to puke and knows there isn't time for getting sick.

"Pushed me out *where*?"

"Where or when," the bird chirps, "is of no consequence. There's no time to rest here. They're not far behind us."

"If I don't rest, I'm going to have a fucking heart attack. Then it won't matter if they do catch me. I'll be just as dead, either way."

"They have your scent in their nostrils, your taste on their tongues," the bird frets and hops from one foot to the other. "I would not want to be in your shoes, Hierophant."

Niki gives the white bird the finger and then stares up at the red sky. There's no way to tell whether it's day or night, because there's no sun or stars, just the flat crimson light that seems to come from everywhere at once and nowhere in particular. She's never even dreamt a sky like this, so entirely empty, not even a scrap of cloud to break the endless, ruddy monotony of it.

If I were wearing a watch, she wonders, *would I know then? If I were wearing the watch Daria gave me . . . but maybe watches don't work in this place. Maybe there's not even time in this place.*

"There is always time," the bird says, "of one sort or another. Even the Dragon is a prisoner of time."

"You can read my mind?" she asks, and the bird pecks at the asphalt, but doesn't answer her.

"If you don't get moving," it says a moment later, "you'll die here. I hope you don't expect me to die with you. I'm loyal to the Weaver, but I won't die for some silly girl too stupid to run when the jackals are on her ass."

"Where are all the people?" she asks.

The bird sighs and glares up at her.

"What difference does it make?"

"Do you think they're dead? Maybe there was an earthquake, or an asteroid, or—"

"Maybe there never *were* any people in this city," the bird says.

"Then who the hell built it?"

The bird frowns at her and ruffles its feathers. "Maybe *no one* built it. Maybe it was always here. Maybe it's only a dream or a fancy or a possibility. You have to stop thinking like someone who only lives in one world, Niki Ky, if you mean to ever come out the other side in one piece."

The jackals begin to howl again, calling zealously back and forth to one another, their voices bouncing off the walls of empty buildings like sonar off the walls of submarine canyons, signals in the dark, guiding them closer.

"You'd think they'd be a little quieter," Niki says, reaching for her backpack. "I wouldn't be so hard to catch if I couldn't hear them coming."

"They would live for the chase," the bird says grimly, "if they were alive. They don't have to be silent. Nothing has ever escaped them."

"You're no end of cheer, you know that, bird?"

"There's no point in lying about the jackals, Niki."

She manages to get the backpack on again using only her left hand, and then she checks the bandages on her right. After the scramble up the collapsed off-ramp, they're dirty and beginning to unravel a little, but there's no sign of blood leaking through.

"I'm not asking you to lie," she says. "But I'm also pretty sure there are things I don't need to know."

The jackals have stopped howling again, and once more there's only the silence, the mute city pinned beneath that sprawling butcher sky, with not even an ocean breeze to spoil the desolate, unnatural calm.

"Bird, do you know how far it is to the other side?" she asks, and before it can answer, "Almost eight and a half *miles,*" she says. "That's how far it is. I can't walk that far, I don't care what's chasing me."

"We don't have to cross the whole bridge," the bird replies. "We only have to go a little ways more. The Weaver will meet us above the water, at the last tower before the island."

"And she can stop the jackals?"

"No. No one can stop the jackals. Not even the Dragon can stop them, once the hunt begins."

"Then what good is she?"

"She'll take you across and bear you safely to the Palisades. She'll set you on the Serpent's Road."

The Serpent's Road, and now Niki remembers the things that Spyder said before sending her across the Dog's Bridge. *You'll follow the road that Orc took, and Esau. You'll follow the road beneath the lake, the Serpent's Road, because He's watching all the other ways.*

"The Weaver," she says, and it's so obvious, so obvious she should have seen it right from the start. "The Weaver is Spyder, isn't she?"

For an answer, the bird squawks something incoherent and takes to the air, flaps its wings and soon it's wheeling far above Niki, circling the interstate. She shades her eyes, force of habit even though there's no sun to burn them, and watches the bird.

"I'm never going to see Daria again," she whispers. "I'm lost now, truly lost, and I'm never going to see anyone ever again." *Except Spyder,* she thinks, wishing that were the consolation it ought to be. Nearby, the jackals howl, and the bird stops circling and heads northeast towards the bay, its tiny shadow sweeping quickly along the wide, forsaken highway.

It takes Niki the better part of an hour to walk the two miles from the off-ramp to the last tower before the shaley cliffs of Yerba Buena Island. Almost an hour, and the only sounds are the steady tattoo of her footsteps against the pavement of the bridge's westbound upper tier and the occasional bellow and barking of the jackals, her own labored breathing and, from time to time, the white bird cries out overhead. Perhaps it's trying to warn her that the jackals are closing in, but when she stops and looks back there's never anything but the empty expanse of I-80 West leading towards the city. The bay stretches away on either side, bloodred and smooth as glass, not a wave or a ripple to break its mirror surface.

The last tower before the island, and in the light from

this alien sky, the steel beams seem to have been painted the color of pomegranates. Niki drops her backpack and sits down in the road, facing the entrance of the Yerba Beuna Tunnel. It might as well be the gates of Hell, "abandon all hope" spelled out by that black hole bored seventeen hundred feet through ancient metamorphic rocks. Maybe, she thinks, the jackals have circled round somehow, and now they're watching her from the conspiring darkness of the tunnel. When they've finally had their fill, when they've glutted themselves on her fear and dread and confusion, they'll come for her. She thinks about her meds, the prescription bottles tucked safely into her backpack, and wonders if a handful of Xanax would kill her quicker than the jackals.

"I'm sorry this has to be so hard," Spyder Baxter says, and when Niki looks over her left shoulder, Spyder's standing right behind her. "I thought we'd have a little more time before they figured out what's going on and came after you. I thought it would take them longer to break through."

"What is going on?" Niki asks her and gets up, turning to face the ghost of the girl with white dreadlocks and a cross carved into the flesh between her eyes. The mark her father gave her when she was only six years old, the mark so the angels he saw might forgive him and spare him the apocalypse of blood and fire that haunted his nightmares and waking dreams.

"A war," Spyder replies. "A war that was old a hundred billion years before there were men to fight on either side. A war that has scorched worlds beyond counting and stained the walls of Heaven."

"And what does *this* mean?" and Niki raises her aching, bandaged hand. "There's something inside me, Spyder."

"I tried to keep you out of this. If there had been any other way, you wouldn't be standing here now."

"But what *is* it? What the fuck's it doing to me? And why does everyone keep calling me the Hierophant?"

"A hierophant presides over certain ceremonies, and is a keeper of sacred mysteries."

"Yeah, I know what the word means. I don't know why people—why talking birds and fucking bridge trolls—keep calling me one. I'm not a hierophant, Spyder. I'm just crazy Niki. I'm just a goddamned schizophrenic."

"No, Niki. You aren't insane. You've never been insane. That's the very first thing that you have to understand. I tried to tell you that before."

"Why am I so angry, Spyder?" Niki asks, and she bites her lower lip because she doesn't want to start crying now. "I should be happy to see you, shouldn't I? I wanted to see you for so long. After you died, I thought that was the end of the fucking world. So why can't I believe that any of this shit is real?"

"I can't answer that question for you, Niki. Nobody can answer that question for you. That's something you have to figure out for yourself."

"Fuck you," Niki whispers, and wipes at her nose. "I don't want to hear any more of this. I don't want to *see* any more. I want to go home. I want to see Daria."

"I'm sorry. You can't do that," Spyder says and holds out a hand to Niki.

"Why the hell not?"

"You've been exiled by your world. It can't take you back. The Dragon—"

"Jesus, Spyder, there is no fucking dragon!"

And then the jackals howl again, so loud they must be very near, their voices to set all the suspender cables humming, and the bridge trembles slightly beneath her feet.

"Take my hand," Spyder says. "They're getting close. We're almost out of time."

Niki looks past Spyder, and she can see something impossibly vast rushing towards them across the bridge, something without shape or the faintest trace of color, only a single-minded purpose to define it. The jackals howl, and the Bay Bridge shudders and sways like a thing of string and twigs.

"The bird was telling you the truth, Niki. I can't stand against them. Now take my hand."

"What do they *want* with me?" Niki asks and takes a small step backwards, glancing from the formless, rolling mass of the jackals to Spyder's outstretched hand, then back to the jackals again. "I can't hurt them. I can't hurt anyone but myself."

"You can destroy them utterly," Spyder replies, "and they know it."

"But the bird said *nothing* can stop them."

"I can't force you to do this, Niki, and I can't do it for you."

"I want to go home, Spyder. I want to wake up."

"You're not dreaming, and you can't go home."

Niki Ky mutters a half-remembered prayer to the Catholic god of her mother, then accepts Spyder's hand, that milk-white palm, her skin as soft as silk, but she doesn't take her eyes off the jackals. They're no more than a hundred yards away now, a hundred yards at most, and the bridge is moving so much that she's having trouble staying on her feet. The steel groans and creaks beneath them, and Niki imagines the upper level collapsing, pancaking, crashing down on the lower, eastbound tier.

"It's a long way," Spyder says. "A lot farther than it looks."

"A long way to what?"

"The water," Spyder says, and she picks up Niki's back-pack with her free hand. "The water is our passage. The jackals can't follow us that way. They're things of earth."

"So all we need's a firehose."

"No, Niki. It doesn't work like that."

And Spyder leads her quickly to the edge of the heaving bridge, to the low concrete barriers, and tells her not to look at the jackals again. So Niki looks down at the bay instead, the flat and motionless waters like a mirror, like a polished crimson gem.

"I can't swim very well," Niki says.

"You won't have to swim, Niki. Trust me. You only have to fall."

"I'm going to die now, aren't I?"

"Everyone dies," and Spyder smiles for her, smiling as the jackals' paws hammer the bridge like artillery fire. "But it isn't what you think. You'll see."

And then she helps Niki over the concrete and squeezes her left hand tight as they step off into space, and gravity does

the

rest.

Tumbling towards amethyst light.

And the sound of falling water.

"Don't let go of my hand," and then she realizes that Spyder already has, and she's alone.

Falling

through

a hole

in

the bottom of

forever.

$+ \infty$

PART TWO

Wars in Heaven

Do you want to know that it doesn't hurt me?
Do you want to hear about the deal that I'm making?

—Kate Bush, "The Hounds of Love" (1985)

The day you died I lost my way.
The day you died I lost my mind.

—VNV Nation, "Forsaken" (1998)

CHAPTER SIX

Latitude and Longitude

The lines that hold the universe together, this universe and all others, elsewhere, elsewhen, closed strings and open strings, loops to break or strings held forever open, and the tension sings unfathomable chords along the lines of inconceivable instruments. Symmetry and supersymmetry, wool and water, looking-glass insects, and the space-time between a boson and its corresponding fermion.

These things happen.

These things happen.

These things happen.

And the mother Weaver at the blind soul of all creations dreams in her black-hole cocoon of trapped light and anti-matter, her legs drawn up tight about the infinitely vast, infinitely small shield of her pulsing cephalothorax. Her spinnerets spew quantum particle lines, opened or closed strings, depending on the dream. Explosions to spray a new cosmos across the common void, and "In *that* direction," the Cat said. The Weaver shivers in her sleep, twitches a fang, and stars die and are born in the gaseous furnaces of her vomit. All paths lead to her, and from her, beginnings and middles and ends, and the event horizons of her bottomless funnel webs leak only the finest, most distilled radiations.

"I don't much care where—" said Alice.

"Then it doesn't matter which way you go," said the Cat.

"—so long as I get *somewhere*."

Eternal spiderweb's dance of worldlines and world-sheets—*adagio, pirouette, pas de deux, pas de trois, pas de quatre*—and the particles that move through spacetime sweep out curves as strings will sweep out the invisible surfaces of worlds.

These things happen. And these.

And the Weaver in her hole opens one eye, sensing discord, shimmering disharmony as lines from *here* are drawn at last towards *there,* and for an instant two universes brush or grind or bleed, one against the other. She knows the great price of this contact and looks away.

Oh, you wicked wicked little thing.

But. These things happen.

And in a moment (as she counts moments), the strings will sing true again, in the age between an angel's heartbeats, and she has all the patience there will ever be. Patience drips like venom from her jaws.

But the wrinkle does not pass unnoticed.

At 2:38 A.M., a man crossing the Bay Bridge on his way to Alameda makes a 911 call from his cell phone. He describes a young Asian woman wearing a blue fur coat, standing at the edge of the bridge, staring down at the water. He tells the operator that he thinks she might be a jumper. When asked for his name, he hangs up, because the girl really isn't his problem and there's a nickel bag of pot and three tabs of ecstasy in his glove compartment. He turns up the radio, and his sleek yellow Jaguar roars eastward.

At 2:40 A.M., a security camera in the California Academy of Sciences' Hall of Insects records a bright flash and the sound of breaking glass. At 2:46, a guard finds three cases in the hall smashed and a fine gray powder covering the insect and arachnid specimens mounted inside. Days later, the gray powder will eventually be identified as a mixture of silica particles and industrial-grade graphite.

At 2:43 A.M., three teenagers walking past Alamo Square along Hayes Street experience what they will later report as a "downpour" of living spiders from the cloudless night sky. The three are forced to take refuge on the porch of a house facing the park and watch as the spiders blanket the ground. The rain of spiders lasts until about three A.M., when it ends as suddenly as it began. Spiders also fall from the sky at the eastern end of Bush Street and at several locations on the campus of the University of San Francisco. The spiders on Bush Street are all found to be dead and frozen solid. In the following days, zoologists will identify three distinct species present in samples collected from the spider falls—*Pityohyphantes costatus, Araniella displicata,* and *Tetragnatha laboriosa*—all native to the San Francisco area. The next morning, great quantities of a sticky white substance similar to, but not chemically identical with, spider silk will be discovered blanketing several acres of John McLaren Park.

Sometime before 2:45 A.M. a middle-aged woman named Eleanora Collins, living alone near Chinatown, awakens to a vision of five golden-winged angels standing around her bed. One of them smiles and speaks in a language she can't understand and then they disappear, one by one, leaving behind the scent of ammonia and roasting meat. Born in Birmingham, Alabama, Eleanora Collins was diagnosed as schizophrenic at the age of fourteen. Three weeks later, she will hang herself, leaving several apparent suicide notes written in a language no one can read.

According to the captain's log of the Japanese container ship *Hirata-Gumo Maru,* at precisely 2:57 A.M., as the vessel neared the Bay Bridge from the southeast, the captain and two crewmen watched from the compass deck as a "shallow, bowl-shaped depression with smooth sides" formed on the surface of the water directly ahead of them. The depression was estimated by Captain Takahashi to have been not less than twenty to thirty-five meters in diameter, and seemed to glow softly. Before orders could be given to reduce speed or alter course, all three sailors saw a body plummet from the bridge into the center of the depression, hitting the water without a splash. Within seconds, all evidence of the phenomenon vanished completely, and the *Hirata-Gumo Maru* passed beneath the bridge without further incident. Though the captain ordered a search for the body, no evidence of it was found. The duration of the anomaly was estimated to have been less than two minutes.

Ninety-eight years and seven months earlier, Mr. J. P. Anthony is awakened at 5:05 A.M. in his room at the Ramona Hotel on Ellis Street. He lies very still, silently watching a flickering, transparent apparition he will later describe to newspaper reporters in both Los Angeles and the town of Pacific Grove as "a coolie girl standing at the window, having a conversation with a white pigeon." He will be able to recall few details about the ghost, and almost nothing of what she said to the bird or what it said to her. He will clearly remember only one remark—"Not even the Dragon can stop them, once the hunt begins"—but will not remember which one of them said it, the girl or the bird. At 5:10, by the clock beside his bed, the ghost vanishes, and at 5:13 the city is hit by an earthquake that lifts the six-story Ramona Hotel off its foundations and collapses its roof. J. P. Anthony spends the rest of April 18, 1906, trying to escape the burning wreck of San Francisco on foot, one refugee among thousands, and, for a time, he will forget the strange sight immediately before the quake. In 1933, he describes the incident in a letter to Maurice Barbanell, editor of the spiritualist journal *Psychic News*. Barbanell will eventually connect Mr. Anthony's experience with similar reports immediately before other San Francisco earthquakes, including the massive shocks felt on October 8, 1865.

These things happen.

A few miles north of Lexington, Kentucky, at precisely 4:48 A.M. CST, a man driving a rusted purple Lincoln Continental with Illinois plates pulls off into the breakdown lane on I-65 South and stares through the windshield at the night sky above the interstate. He knows all the signs of Heaven, the secret tongue of stars and comets and meteors, and tonight he understands the things he sees happening above him. He wakes the woman sleeping in the front seat next to him, who calls herself Archer Day, and yes, she says, yes, she sees it, too.

They don't bother waking the girl sleeping in the backseat, the girl named Theda, the girl they found in Connecticut, because she still hasn't seen enough to understand what the lights signify, the bobbing blue and white lights that are neither stars nor airplanes nor only the man's exhausted, road-weary eyes. The man and the woman watch the lights for almost fifteen minutes, and when they finally vanish, he kisses her and wipes tears from her brown eyes. She makes notes in a leather-bound book she keeps beneath the front seat, and the man says a prayer before continuing their long drive.

Dreaming in the wide backseat of the Lincoln, the girl who calls herself Theda, because, arranged another way, the letters spell "death," remembers things that have happened and things that haven't and things that still might happen.

"You've *always* known," the white woman at the foot of her bed whispers, and smiles. "You knew you weren't like them. You were certain you were something more."

And yes, Theda tells her, she has always known these things, always, and she weeps, and tiny white spiders swarm across her bedspread, the crystal, snowflake spiders that have been dripping from the white woman's dreadlocks. She lets them climb across her skin, burrowing into her hair, slipping inside her nostrils and down her throat, filling her with the white woman's light.

"You will be me," she says, and Theda is starting to understand what she means.

In the dream, she wakes, still dreaming, and stares in wonder and secret satisfaction at the Dragon's fire outside her open bedroom window, inferno exhalations sweeping slowly across the sky to sear the rooftops of the Hartford suburb. Fire to burn everything clean, clean at last, and now she feels the crystal spiders growing inside her, spinning their webs, laying crystal eggs, and the smell of burning drifts across the windowsill into her room on a sizzling breeze.

"Freak," someone sneers and shoves her—every single humiliation reduced to this single word, this single moment, this one act—all the insults and countless embarrassments, and Theda turns to see all the hateful faces staring back at her.

"Freak."

"Fucking lesbo freak."

And then the cleansing fire falls down and takes them all at once, their perfect, normal faces melting together like wax and time, becoming indistinguishable, one from the next. But Theda knows she's the one it *really* wants, the reason it's here, and her tormentors are only fuel for the fire.

"Is it really that petty?" Archer Day asks and shakes her head disapprovingly. "Is that all you have inside you, little girl? *Revenge?* Is there nothing more?"

"Maybe it's enough for me," Theda replies. "Do you have something better?"

Archer coughs and lights another cigarette. "Go back to sleep. I'm tired of listening to you."

"A psychomaterial conduit," the white woman says, so maybe she hasn't awakened after all. "You are so powerful, so beautiful, you will bridge the void and draw the poison out."

"I don't want to die."

"It's not death. Only another kind of *being*, that's all. The things that you will see—"

Eleven of them waiting in the cemetery that night, and the tall man chose her. Ten chances to fail, to be passed over, but she was the one he'd been looking for all along.

"The truth is buried inside you," the white woman promises. "Ancient fragments, but the angels will find you too late, Theda. The angels will never find you at all."

And the big car rolls on through the Southern night, as the girl rolls from one dream current to the next, drowning in herself.

At 4:58 A.M. CST, Daria Parker opens her eyes somewhere above western Kansas and stares at the moonlight washing ice white across the tops of the clouds outside the cabin window of the 767. *They look like the tops of mountains,* she thinks. *They look like the tops of very high mountains covered with snow.* And then she remembers where she is and why, that she's on her way back to San Francisco and Niki, and that memory leads her immediately to all the other things she doesn't want to remember, and she closes her eyes again. The airplane hums reassuringly, the steady, everywhere rumble above and below and all around her, and *Maybe* that's *the dream,* she thinks. *Maybe I'm asleep in my hotel room in Atlanta, and Alex is holding me and this time Niki's okay.* Maybe she's never heard the strange message left in her voice mail, and Niki hasn't told her it's already too late, and maybe in the morning she'll be able to figure out a way to fix everything.

And then we all lived happily ever after.

"Wake up, Daria," Niki says, and she opens her eyes.

So, it really is a dream, and that ought to be another comfort, like the thrum of the jet's engines, but then she realizes that it isn't that sort of dream at all.

"I only have a second," Niki tells her. "I can't stay."

"I'm on my way, baby," Daria replies and touches Niki's

cheek, her skin so dark against the pale tips of Daria's fingers. "Just like I said. I'm racing the sun."

"I didn't want to ask you to do this. I wanted to let you go and never have to ask you for anything else ever again."

"I don't know what you're talking about."

And Niki Ky looks away, then, looks down at her hands folded in her lap and then up at the movie playing silently on the screen at the front of the cabin.

"We never saw that," she says. "I wanted to, but you didn't have time, and I didn't want to go with Marvin."

"When I get home, we'll rent the DVD."

"It wouldn't be the same, even if we could."

"Fuck it. I'll make the time," Daria says and puts both her arms around Niki, leans forward and holds her tight. Niki's wearing her blue fur coat, and it smells faintly of dust and jasmine, and Daria wants to bury her face in it and make this be a different dream.

"Listen, Dar. I have to be absolutely sure you understand me, because I can only do this once," and now Niki's speaking with an urgency that makes Daria want to shut her eyes and wake up. Back in the hotel or on the plane to San Francisco, either one, as long as it means she doesn't have to hear whatever Niki's about to say.

"When we left Birmingham, when we were on our way to Boulder—"

"That was a long time ago."

"—one morning, we had breakfast at a truck stop, the same day we made it to Denver, the first time we ever saw the mountains."

"We were always eating in truck stops," Daria protests and takes her arms from around Niki's shoulders. She turns back to the window and the moon and the clouds.

"This one had a jackalope."

"They all had fucking jackalopes, Niki."

"You're not listening. You have to listen and let me finish this."

"I'm not stopping you," she says, wanting a drink, wanting a cigarette, wanting to wake up.

"I gave Mort the rest of my waffles, and you asked me if I was feeling okay."

"Niki, how the hell do you expect me to remember breakfast in a truck stop ten years ago? I have enough trouble remembering breakfast yesterday morning."

"You *have* to remember this," Niki says quietly, just a little quieter and she'd be whispering, and Daria looks at her again. Niki's almond eyes sparkle wet in the dark cabin, in the reflected light from the movie screen. "You have to remember because I can't get back there myself. I thought I'd be able to, but there wasn't enough time. There's never enough goddamn time to do things the right way."

"Okay, so there was a jackalope," Daria says, because she doesn't want Niki to start crying, even if this is just a dream, doesn't want a scene and someone trying to help but only making things worse, one of the flight attendants or someone seated across the aisle or in the row in front of them. "We were having breakfast at a truck stop and you gave Mort the rest of your waffles."

"You asked if I was okay," Niki says, wipes at her eyes and blinks. "I said I was, even though I wasn't. I said I was going to the restroom, but I went outside instead, and you followed me."

"I don't remember any of this."

"Then just listen to me, and maybe you'll remember later. I didn't go to the restroom, I went outside instead. It was cold. It was really cold, but you followed me, anyway. I walked across the parking lot and through some grass and cactus to a place where there was just dirt. I buried something there."

"Wait," Daria says. "Oh, shit. Yeah," because now she *does* remember, all of it rushing back at her—the smell of greasy diner food and the freezing late December morning, the stunted cacti and strands of rusted barbed wire she stepped over to follow Niki.

"I took a ball bearing from my coat pocket. You asked me what it was."

"And you wouldn't tell me," Daria says, and then there's

a sharp pain in her chest, a red flower blooming suddenly behind her sternum, and she gasps and reaches for Niki. "Oh, God," she whispers. "Oh, Niki. You wouldn't tell me what it was. You just buried it there and never told me what it was."

"You never asked me after that. I never thought it would matter."

Daria gasps again and digs her fingers into the Play-Doh-blue fur of Niki's coat sleeve. In the secret, wet cavity of her rib cage, in the hollow of her heart, the pain flower doubles in size, triples, blood petals and ventricle sepals unfolding, tearing her apart, driving the breath from her lungs, and Niki only sighs and looks down at her folded hands.

"You have to find it for me, Daria. You have to find it and bring it to the basement of Spyder's house."

Daria opens her mouth to say something, something she has to say because she doesn't think she could ever find the ball bearing, not after a decade, but there's only the pain, eating her alive, picking her to pieces, and then Niki is gone, and a white bird is perched on the back of her seat, instead. It watches Daria with beady crimson eyes, and she wants to scream.

"Do not fail her," the bird says grimly. "The Hierophant will need you, at the end," and it dissolves in a small shower of yellow-orange sparks.

"Oh God," Daria wheezes. "Oh Jesus fucking god," and when she opens her eyes—when she opens them all the way and knows that the dream's finally over and done, that she's awake and *this* is real, as real as anything will ever be—there's a frightened stewardess beside her, loosening her clothes. And the pain in her chest, that's real too, the demon flower slipped out of the nightmare with her, and, in another second or two, it will burst from her chest and she'll die.

"Be still," the stewardess says. "There's a doctor in first class. He's coming."

And then Daria sees the blue strands of fake fur

clutched in the fingers of her right hand, and the single feather, white as snow at the top of the highest mountain peak, caught in the stewardess' hair, and she lets the pain have her.

"Either the well was very deep, or she fell very slowly, for she had plenty of time as she went down to look about her, and to wonder what was going to happen next."

"Open your eyes, Niki," Spyder Baxter says, and she does, even though she thought they were open all along. "You gotta watch that first step," and Spyder smiles. "It's a bitch."

And she's so beautiful that Niki doesn't know if she's breathless from the plunge or the sight of her. Not the Spyder she knew so many years ago, that sullen girl wrapped up in all her leather and bull-dyke defenses, and not the uncertain, unreal Spyder from her dreams and the fiery place before the Dog's Bridge. Maybe the most beautiful woman that she's ever seen, Spyder as some Pre-Raphaelite painter might have imagined her, Spyder reborn as something the gods would envy. She's still holding Niki's backpack.

"Are you okay?" she asks Niki Ky. "Say something."

"Daria's sick," Niki says, because she'd almost forgotten, seeing Spyder like this, and the roar of falling water is so loud in her ears. She wonders how they can hear themselves over the sound of it.

"Yes, Daria's sick. But that can't concern you now," Spyder says. "Maybe later on, but not now."

Niki starts to take a step towards Spyder and realizes that she's kneeling, on her knees on cold, mist-slicked stone. She blinks, then rubs her eyes, but it's all still there, radiant Spyder with her white hair—not Spyder's dark hair bleached white, but hair that grows as white as doves and milk and snowfall all on its own—Spyder in her gown that looks like something sewn from starlight, and the scar on her forehead has become a teardrop gem, the deepest ruby red, set into her skin. The water roars all around her, and overhead the sky is dusk and tempera sunset clouds in brilliant shades of tangerine and goldenrod and violet.

"Am I dead?" Niki asks, and Spyder smiles again and helps her to her feet. Niki's legs are weak, and her stomach rolls like she's just had three or four rides on a roller coaster, one right after the other.

"It's not exactly that simple."

"That's not an answer," Niki says. "I just jumped off a bridge for you, and now I want an answer."

"You didn't jump for me. You jumped for you."

"Whichever," Niki replies. "Am I dead or not?"

Spyder's smile fades, and she brushes Niki's long bangs from her eyes. "Yes, in the world where you were born, you died. They'll find your body. You'll have a funeral. You'll be buried."

"Cremated," Niki corrects her.

"Same difference."

"And I can't go back. Not ever."

"Not the way you mean," Spyder says, then turns and begins walking through the gathering mist, across the slippery gray-green rocks.

"So, is this Heaven?" Niki calls after her, trying to keep up and trying not to fall on her ass at the same time.

"Not even close," Spyder shouts back. "Anyway, I didn't think you believed in Heaven."

"Is it Hell, then?"

"Everywhere's Hell, Niki, if that's all you can manage to make of it."

"Goddamn it," Niki says and stops, almost slides on a patch of mossy-looking slime, and sits down. "No more fucking riddles, Spyder. Tell me the truth or—"

"Or what?" Spyder asks her, looking over her shoulder. "You'll go *back*?" And she points an index finger towards the Technicolor sky. "I'm afraid you're just going to have to be a little bit more patient. I've been here a long time, and I still don't understand the half of it."

"Can you at least tell me where the fuck I am? I don't

think that's asking too much. If I'm dead, and this isn't Heaven and it's not Hell, but I'm not on Earth anymore—"

"No, it's certainly not Earth," Spyder agrees and then turns to face Niki again. The mist swirls eagerly, nervously, around them both, like it wants answers, too, like it's hanging on every word they say. "This is another place."

"Another place? You mean another planet?"

"No, Niki. I mean another *place*."

"Like another universe?"

"Another place, Niki. I think we should just leave it at that for now."

"And right *here*?" Niki asks, and pats the rock with her left hand.

"We're at the Palisades," Spyder replies. "And we really shouldn't stay here much longer. There are safer places to be. You'll need dry clothes, and I need to look at your hand."

My hand, Niki thinks and holds it up. The bandage is still there, dirty and coming unwound, but she didn't lose it in the fall. It still hurts, now that Spyder's reminded her, still burns and aches and itches, and she glances up at Spyder.

"If I'm dead, then how come my hand still hurts?"

"I said that you died, Niki. That doesn't necessarily mean you're dead now."

"Christ." Niki sighs and laughs, laughing because she's scared and worried about Daria and so glad to see Spyder, everything pressing in at her in the same instant, and she doesn't know what else to do.

"What's funny?" Spyder asks and gives Niki the backpack. She unzips it and is surprised that everything's still inside, and that it's all still dry.

"Nothing," she replies. "Or lots and lots of things. I'm not sure yet. Ask me again later. So, what are the Palisades, anyway?"

Spyder peers through the mist and chews thoughtfully at her lower lip a moment before answering. And once again, Niki's struck by the perfect, simple beauty of her. *Have I changed, too?* she thinks. *Have I become that beautiful?*

"The Palisades," Spyder says. "You know back when most people still thought the world was flat, and that if you sailed too far in any direction you'd fall right off the edge? Well, if those people had been right about the world where we were born, then the Palisades is sort of like the place they were afraid of sailing over the edge."

"That figures," Niki mutters half to herself, zipping her backpack shut again, and she slips it on over her left shoulder. "The ends of the earth."

"More or less," Spyder says. "Now come on, Niki. I wasn't kidding when I said we shouldn't hang around here too long."

"The jackals?" Niki asks, but Spyder shakes her head, scattering light through the mist and across the rocks, her dreads like the phosphorescent tendrils of a deep-sea creature.

"Here," she says. "you're going to have a lot more things to worry about than the jackals. They might be the worst of it, but there are other things that can kill you just as fast."

"Is that supposed to be the good news?"

"Maybe," Spyder replies, and the tone in her voice to tell Niki she isn't joking, that the fall from the bridge was just the start, that she's tumbled out of the frying pan and into the fire.

"Before we leave, there's something I want you to see," Spyder says. "Just so you know it's not all monsters and wicked witches."

She helps Niki to her feet, and they walk together through the twilight mist, through the drowning roar of the Palisades, to a wide plaza carved directly from the stone. The plaza and the bottom landing of a staircase leading up a very steep cliff face. Niki looks at the wide steps, then the cliff itself, searching in vain for the place where the stairs end somewhere far overhead. "I just came from up there," she says and frowns. "I hope to God I'm not about to have to walk all the way back."

"You'll see," Spyder whispers. "You'll see."

*   *   *

By the time they finally reach the top of the winding granite staircase, Niki is out of breath and dizzy, and her left side hurts. Twice, she slipped on the wet stone and might have fallen, might have broken her neck or worse, if there's anything worse than breaking your neck. Harder things to fall on here than San Francisco Bay, harder things than the welcoming sea, and she leans against the low balustrade and waits for her heart to stop pounding. Above them, the last rays of the day have been smothered by the advancing night, and stars burn bright and cold in a sky that might have been stolen from a Van Gogh painting. And she knows it's real, because a whole boatload of crazy girls couldn't dream up a sky like that, those brilliant, glistening colors, the wild swirl of a billion distant suns.

"I never get tired of looking at it," Spyder says, not the least bit winded by the long climb, and she's leaning far out over the balustrade, the wind blowing through her white hair. "I never will, because it's always like the very first time."

The stairs have ended in a small balcony, rough-hewn half circle and a tall statue near the center that reminds Niki of a griffin, though it's really something altogether different. She stands next to Spyder and stares up at the Van Gogh sky, and then down at the abyss stretching away beyond the ragged edges of the Palisades.

"Some people say that's the way to Paradise," Spyder tells her. "And other people say it leads to an endless black sea filled with demons."

"What do you think?" Niki asks her, unable to look away, beginning to think she'll never be able to look away.

"I think I don't ever want to find out."

A mile or more beneath them, an ocean drains over the side of a world, a churning, roiling cataract as far as she can see to the left or the right, north and south perhaps, unless there aren't directions in this place. And she can also see that the balcony is perched near the top of one of the countless barren islands scattered out along the rim of the

Palisades, a spire of mist-cut rock rising like a crooked, skeletal finger.

That's enough, she thinks and shuts her eyes. *Don't look at it anymore, Niki.*

"What's wrong?" Spyder asks. "Did you see something?"

"I see that it's terrible," Niki replies between gritted teeth, and she wants to back away from the edge but is too afraid to let go of the balustrade. "At first, I thought it was beautiful, but it isn't beautiful at all. It's terrible."

"Can't it be both?"

"No, Spyder, it can't. It's like dying. It's *worse* than dying. It's like being alone and knowing that you'll never be anything else."

"Yes," Spyder says. "It is. It's exactly like that."

"Then how the hell can you stand there and say that it's beautiful, you of all people?"

"I'm not who I was, that's how. Now open your eyes, Niki. You look like a damned fool, standing there with them squeezed shut that way."

Niki shakes her head and doesn't open her eyes, wishing she could drive her fingers deep into the stone so there'd be no danger of the balcony shaking her loose. "I'm afraid I'll fall. It wants me to fall."

"That's silly. It doesn't want anything from you," but Spyder puts an arm around Niki and holds her close. "Turn loose, Niki. I wouldn't let you fall. You've fallen enough."

"Where does it *go*?" Niki asks, not releasing her hold on the balustrade. "All that water, and all the things that must live in it, all the fish and everything—"

"Over the side," Spyder tells her. "It all goes over the side," and Niki giggles and bites her tongue because it's better than screaming. But that's what she *wants* to do, wants to scream so loud and long and hard that she'll be hoarse for a week, and maybe then she can stop imagining what it would be like to be pulled over the Palisades. What it would be like to stare into endless night until her light-starved eyes finally surrendered and went blind. And even that would only be the beginning of it, because each and every second is the first in an eternity, and whatever's waiting past the Palisades, she knows that it must surely be eternal.

"Help me," she whispers, sinking very slowly down until she's crouching on the balcony, exchanging her grip on the top rail for one of the balusters. "I don't think I can do this, Spyder. It's too much for me. I thought I could, but it's just too much."

"Yes, you *can,*" and now Spyder's lips are pressed gently against her right ear, Spyder's breath as warm as the wind and mist are cold. "I know you can do it because you've come this far. If you couldn't do it, the jackals would have had you on the bridge."

"No," Niki whispers. "You're wrong. I want to go back. I want to go home."

"Well you *can't,*" Spyder snaps, her patience frayed in an instant and this anger so big, so certain of itself, it must have always been waiting there beneath the surface. "You can get up off your ass, and you can stop whining, or you can stay here and die. But you can't go back, Niki, so that's your choice. That's the only choice you have. And this time there's no fucking psychologist to give you pills and coddle you and pretend the world gives a shit what happens to you, and there's no fucking Marvin to do everything for you and make you think you can't even take care of yourself."

"Please stop," Niki begs, but Spyder shoves her, and she loses her balance, loses her grip on the baluster, and lands flat on her back, staring up at the mad and swirling stars. The night sky and Spyder Baxter standing over her, and the stone between Spyder's eyes has gone an ugly, vivid purple.

"This place was *born* hurting," she says, her lips throwing words like sparks to sear Niki's skin. "It was born insane and lost, and there's no room here for self-pity and weakness."

"I didn't *want* to come here," Niki whispers. "I was

scared, and you said you needed me, and I didn't know what else to do," and there are tears leaking from her eyes now, hot tears rolling down her cheeks. Spyder sneers and turns away.

"There's so much strength in you, Niki," she says. "But if you can't find it, if you can't *see* it, then I've made the wrong decision and we're all damned."

"I don't know what you think I can *do*."

"What I think doesn't matter. The only thing that matters now is what *you* think," and then Spyder starts back down the stairs alone, leaving Niki on the balcony with the statue that isn't a griffin and the stars and the unending, unequivocal roar of the Palisades.

In a little while, Niki Ky follows her.

Not far from the base of the stairs, there's a narrow catwalk leading up and then straight out across the swiftly flowing water and into the darkness and mist obscuring whatever lies beyond the Palisades. The wood creaks and groans underfoot and is almost as slippery as the stones were, weathered slats gone black with age and decay, sprouting small blue-gray mushrooms and moss and mold; in places, the wood has rotted completely through and Niki has to take very wide steps across the gaps. There are no handrails, just the noise of the draining ocean on either side, and she tries to keep to the center as much as possible. Spyder walks fast and stays always ten or twenty feet ahead; Niki imagines that the mist seems to part for her, seems to cringe as if it fears her touch and the clean white light that flows from her hair and gown to shine their way through the gloom.

"Are we going to walk all night?" Niki asks, finally, the first thing that she's said to Spyder since the balcony, not asking because she's too tired to keep going and her hand hurts, but because she can't stand the silence wedged in between them any longer.

"No," Spyder calls back, her voice warped and muffled by the fog so that she sounds even farther ahead of Niki than she is. "The nights are long this near the edge. You couldn't walk until sunrise. Not many living people could."

"I'm not sure I can walk another step," Niki says, then stops to catch her breath and glances back the way they've come. There's nothing there, at least nothing she can see, as though the catwalk has collapsed or disappeared in their wake. But the roar of the Palisades is growing more distant by slow degrees, each step carrying her away from the abyss. She doesn't have any idea how long they've been walking, or how far they've come, though it seems like hours and miles. In the mist, with even the star-choked sky hidden from her eyes, she has only the diminishing roar of the cataract and her exhaustion to gauge distance and the passage of time.

"Where are we going?" she asks. "I mean, where does this thing lead?" But if Spyder hears her, she doesn't respond. So Niki starts walking again, moving as quickly as she dares now, trying to close the space between them.

Somewhere to their right, there's a tremendous splash, as if a gigantic body has risen from and fallen back into the sea, and then there's laughter and a sound like thunder rolling across the water.

"You don't want to know," Spyder says, "so don't ask."

And the catwalk shudders slightly beneath their feet as the thunder fades away.

"Jesus," Niki whispers to herself, trying not to let her mind make too many pictures of the things that might be out there in the mist, floating or swimming just out of sight, watching their progress along the catwalk.

"Keep moving, Niki. There's a village up ahead. It's not much farther."

"Another island?" Niki asks hopefully, but Spyder shakes her head.

"Not exactly," she replies. "Just a little fishing village. But there will be men with boats there who can take us to land."

"Are you still pissed at me?"

"No. I'm still disappointed, that's all."

"Yeah, well," Niki says, keeping her eyes on her boots and the moldering boards of the catwalk. "Maybe that's because you expected too much."

"Maybe so. Or maybe it's because I know you've spent too many years looking for the answers you need in prescription bottles, listening to people who are too afraid of the truth or too stupid to even ask you the right questions."

"People tried to help me," Niki tells her, but she isn't sure she believes it, and she can hear the doubt in her voice. She starts to say something about Dr. Dalby, then thinks better of it. "Marvin tried to help," she says, instead.

"Did he?" Spyder asks, and leaps easily across a particularly wide gap in the slats. She stops and waits for Niki to cross it.

"Yes," Niki replies, gazing at mist filling the empty space left by the missing boards, wondering how far down it is to the water. "I think he did. Spyder, I don't know if I can get across this one."

"You have to. You can't stay here."

"If I fall—"

"—you'll drown," Spyder says. "Or something will eat you. Or both."

"Marvin tried to help me," she says again.

"Daria paid him to take care of you. You were his *job*, Niki, just like that other girl he told you about, the one who saw wolves."

"How do you know about her?" Niki asks, taking off her pack and handing it across the gap to Spyder.

"It's all about salvation," Spyder replies, and holds an arm out to Niki. "He couldn't save that girl, so he had to try to save you. When he lost her, he lost himself. You were supposed to be his redemption."

"I can't do it. I'll fall. It's too far across."

"Christ, girl. A little while ago, you were throwing yourself off fucking bridges. Now you're afraid to hop over a little bitty hole like that?"

"It's not the same," Niki says, and she looks up at Spyder, at her pale blue eyes and the glowing red gem between them. "There's nothing down there but water."

"How do you know that? You don't, do you? For all you know, there's another place waiting for you underneath this one. Hell, for all you know, next time it's Heaven."

"You just told me I'd drown, or get eaten—"

"Come *on,* Niki. Take a deep breath, and keep your eyes on me, and jump. I can help, but I can't do it for you."

"What makes you any better than Marvin?" Niki demands, looking back down at the hole. "You brought me here because you think I can save this place, because you can't."

"Yeah," Spyder says. *"Exactly,"* and when Niki looks up again, she's smiling. "Now you're thinking. Come on, Niki. You could make this jump in your sleep."

In my sleep, Niki thinks. *In my dreams,* and she takes a deep breath, filling her lungs with the damp and salty air, and jumps.

Just over the Tennessee-Alabama state line, the rusted purple Lincoln pulls into a BP station because the girl in the backseat is awake now, and she has to pee. The big car glides smoothly across the wide parking lot, past the double row of self-serve pumps and cases of canned Coca-Cola stacked up like Mayan ruins. Archer Day lights a cigarette and points at an empty parking space between an SUV and a pickup truck.

"Where the hell are we this time?" the girl asks from the backseat and rubs her eyes.

"Just about a hundred miles north of the asshole of the world," the driver replies and squints through his cheap truck-stop sunglasses at the sun glinting bright off the wide and tinted plate-glass windows of the convenience store.

"So we're almost there?"

"We'll be in Birmingham before noon," the man tells her and slips the Lincoln in snug between the SUV and the pickup, easy as you please. There's an NRA decal on the rear windshield of the truck and a bumper sticker that reads THOSE WHO LIVE BY THE SWORD GET SHOT BY THOSE WHO DON'T.

"Shit. It looks even worse than Kentucky," Theda says, and opens her door, letting in the cold.

"You ain't seen nothing yet," Walter Ayers says and removes his sunglasses. He glances at his aching, bloodshot eyes in the rearview mirror. Nothing a few drops of Visine and a couple more ephedrine tablets wouldn't fix, but he thinks maybe he'll let Archer drive the last leg. Maybe he'll get lucky and sleep an hour or so before the city. "From here on, it just keeps getting better."

"I'm sure it does," Theda sneers, and gets out of the car, slamming the door loudly behind her.

"I think she's having second thoughts," Archer says, whispering, watching the frowzy girl in her ratty black sweater and black-and-white striped leggings, her tall Doc Marten boots, the tangled poppy-red hair hiding her eyes. "Aren't you?"

"No," Archer Day tells him. "Not now. I know better now."

"Do you?" he asks, and slips his sunglasses on again. "Well, I gotta admit, that sure puts you one up on me."

"There's no time left for doubt."

"I'm not talking about doubt. I'm talking about finally having the good sense to look the other way. Maybe sit this shit out and let someone else pick up the pieces."

Archer turns her head and glares at him with her hard brown eyes. "After all you've seen?" she asks. "After all these years?"

He shrugs and turns the key in the ignition; the engine sputters once or twice and dies. "Sometimes I think you got a hard-on for Armageddon," he sighs.

"I know why I'm here, that's all. I know what I have to do."

Theda is standing in front of the car, talking to a short-ish, potbellied man in a John Deere baseball cap and a faded Lynyrd Skynyrd T-shirt. She points at the Lincoln, and the fat man nods and grins, showing off a mouthful of dingy, uneven teeth, then opens the door for her.

"You know, if we sit here much longer," Archer says and frowns, twirling a strand of her long yellow-brown hair around her right index finger, "there's no telling what sort of trouble she'll get into."

"She can take care of herself," he replies.

"Yeah, that's exactly what I'm afraid of, Walter. We're too *close*. We don't need any delays because Theda can take care of herself."

"Maybe we're not as close as you think, maybe we're not even halfway—" but she's already getting out of the car, already shutting the door, and *Never mind,* he thinks. Never mind, because this is all going to go down the way it has to, the way that Spyder always meant for it to go down, and, in the end, all he can do is read his lines on cue and go through the motions.

Because the story isn't complete without the villian.

Or the hero.

And these days he's forgotten exactly who is who and which is which, if he ever knew, if there's really any difference. Walter shuts his eyes, because he knows that Archer can handle Theda if she gets into any trouble, because they feel like he's rubbed them full of sand and cayenne pepper. No sleep since somewhere back in Pennsylvania, and that seems like at least a week ago.

And the dream is right there, waiting for him the way it always is, patient and unchanging, unconcerned about the drugs he takes to stay awake or the insomnia he's spent more than a decade nurturing. Some part of him, something small and ancient and driven more by simple instinct than intellect, tries to pull back from the slippery edge of consciousness. But it's too late, and he's already sliding down and back, across the years and memories, stumbling and lost in those hours or minutes or days after Robin's peyote ceremony, before Spyder comes down to the basement from the brilliant, burning hills to take him home, to lead him across the Dog's Bridge and back to the World.

The familiar, smothering aloneness, the severed cord,

the broken chain, knowing that Robin and Byron are free, that they've slipped away, escaped, and he's still cowering in the sulfur rubble on the crumbling edge of the Pit. The thing that Spyder called Preacher Man knows he's still there, knows that he's all alone now, and it roars so loud the heavens rumble and the Pit rips open wider, devouring more of this place that is no place at all. The powdered-glass ground beneath his feet tilts and is turning, accelerating counterclockwise spiral down and down, and the Pit yawns and belches, grinding its granite teeth.

Preacher Man fills up the entire roiling floor-joist sky, opens his scrawny, hard sermon arms as wide as *that,* and his ebony book has become a blazing red sun bleeding out his voice. Ugly black things cling to his hands and face, biting, burrowing things, and Walter is crawling on his skinned hands and knees now, clambering for a hold, crawling as the earth shivers and goes soft. He remembers his wings, beautiful charcoal wings for a mockingbird boy, and he knows that's why Preacher Man hates him. Walter tries to stand and spread his wings, but the fire and acid dripping from the clouds have scorched them raw and useless, and Preacher Man laughs and laughs and laughs.

"Come back with me," Spyder says, her hands tight around his wrists and Preacher Man filling up all creation behind her. "It's gonna be all right now, Walter," but the world turns, water going down a drain, down that mouth, and the earth is shaking so violently that he can't even stand up.

"Help me," he says, every time, and every time she smiles, soft and secret Spyder smile, nods and puts her arms around him. Preacher Man howls and claws the sagging sky belly, and the sour rain sticks to them like pine sap, turning the ground to tar. "He won't let me leave, Spyder. He knows what I've seen, what I *know.*"

And so she turns around and stares up into the demon's face, like there's nothing to fear in those eyes, nothing that can pick her apart, strew her flesh to the winds and singe the bones, and she says, "He's not part of this. You can't have him." The spiderweb tattoos on her arms writhe electric blue, loaded-gun threat, and now Preacher Man has stopped laughing. He retreats a single, vast step, putting the Pit between himself and Spyder.

"Lila," he roars. "What you've done to me, you'll burn in Hell forever." Voice of thunder and mountains splitting apart to spill molten bile. "What you've done to me, you'll burn until the end of time."

The holy blue fire flows from her arms, the crackling static cage that he won't dare touch, her magic to undo him utterly, and then she's pulling Walter from the muck, hauling him across the shattered plains. Days and days across the foothills with Preacher Man howling curses like lightning bolts, howling their damnation, but Spyder doesn't look at him again. She drags Walter over pustulant caleche and stones that shriek like dying rabbits, shields him from the rubbing alcohol wind that whips up dust phantoms and hurls burning tumbleweeds.

"Close your eyes, Walter," she says again and again, and at the end he does, because the long-legged things are so close, and he knows the climb's too steep, that he's too tired to do it, and she's too exhausted to fight anymore, and their jaws leak the shearing sound of harvest . . .

. . . and he wakes hard, like falling on ice, waking to the aching stiffness in his neck and shoulders and someone calling out his name over and over again. He reaches beneath the front seat for the Beretta automatic and is out of the Lincoln and through the front doors of the convenience store before the last terrible dream images have even begun to fade. His feet on black-and-white checkerboard linoleum and the fluorescent lights in his eyes, but his head still filled with red skies and the stink of brimstone.

"Well, it's about goddamn time," Archer says, and Walter sees the man behind the counter with the shotgun, and Theda on her knees, and the guy in the Lynyrd Skynyrd T-shirt backed up against a display of beef jerky, his eyes so wide it's almost funny. There are other people, but these are the only three who matter, and he aims the 9mm at the clerk.

"Stop pointing that thing at her right *now,*" he growls, and thumbs off the safety.

"Just look at her," Archer says, and shakes her head. "You gotta search long and hard to find someone that god-damn *stupid.*"

"He called me a freak," Theda croaks and coughs up an-other gout of the sticky white mess puddled on the tile in front of her. There are tiny black things wriggling in the vomit, trying to pull themselves free. She wipes her mouth on the back of her hand. "So . . . I thought I'd show him," she says and smiles up at the redneck.

"I *said* not to point the shotgun at the girl, mother-fucker," Walter tells the clerk, his voice as cold and calm as well water, and he takes a step closer to the counter.

"What the *fuck's* wrong with her?" the clerk asks and turns the gun on Walter, instead. "She got some sort of fuckin' disease or what?"

"Whatever it is, it ain't nothing that calls for a goddamn shotgun. You put that piece of shit down, and we'll be out of here before you can count to three."

"I can count to three pretty goddamn fast."

"Put it *down,* man. I know you don't want to die today, and I think you know it, too."

"Stupid fucking bitch," Archer hisses. "I'd shoot her my-self if I could."

The redneck in the Lynyrd Skynyrd shirt mutters some-thing unintelligible, and Theda snaps her teeth at him and laughs.

"She's puking up fuckin' *spiders,*" the clerk says, and Walter can see the greasy beads of sweat standing out on his forehead and cheeks, sweat soaked straight through the front of his green BP smock, can almost smell the fear coming off him like smoke off a fire. "You tell me what the fuck's wrong with her."

"Just put down the shotgun and none of this will be your problem anymore."

Theda laughs and vomits again.

"She's fucking disgusting," Archer whispers. "You know that, little girl? You're fucking *disgusting*."

"He called me a freak. I asked him . . . I asked if he wanted to see . . . just how freaky it can get—"

"So you showed him."

"Yeah . . . I showed him."

"If I put down my gun you'll shoot me," the clerk says and swallows, his eyes darting quickly from Walter to the girl on the floor to the bore of the Beretta, then right back to Walter.

"No, I won't. I've got business to take care of, and if I shoot you there'll be cops to deal with, and then I won't be *able* to do my business."

"Jesus," the redneck mutters. "Those are black widows. Those are goddamn black widows."

"Yeah," Theda coughs. "Aren't they pretty?"

"Get up off the floor," Archer tells her. "Get up, and go out to the car."

"I asked him. He said he wanted to—"

"I *mean* it, Theda. Right this fucking minute."

"Okay, *I'm* going to count to three," Walter says. "I'm going to count real slow, and whatever happens after that is entirely up to you."

"Who the hell are you people?" the redneck whimpers and tries to back away, knocking over the display of beef jerky and a life-sized cardboard cut-out of a grinning stock-car racer brandishing a bottle of Mountain Dew.

"Maybe we're witches," Theda snickers. "Maybe we're monsters. Maybe we're something *worse* than monsters. Maybe there isn't even a word for what *we* are."

"Little girl, there are a whole *lot* of words for what you are," Archer says.

"Archer, shut the hell up and get her out of here."

"Mister, if I put down this gun you're going to shoot me," the clerk says again. "You're all crazy, and if I put it down you'll kill me." His hands have started to tremble, and the barrel of the shotgun bobs and jerks.

"One," Walter says calmly, firmly, trying to figure out how everything could possibly have gone to hell so fast. How they could have gotten this close to Birmingham and not a detour or delay, and now he's about to have to put a bullet in this dumb son of a bitch's skull because Theda can't be trusted to piss without turning the morning into a horror show. He takes a deep breath and another step towards the counter. "Two," he says.

"Jesus, Frank, just put down the fucking shotgun before somebody gets killed," a man shouts from the back of the store. The redneck in the Lynyrd Skynyrd shirt is busy stomping at one of the black widows that's managed to free itself of Theda's stringy vomit and is crawling across the floor towards him.

"Hey, don't do that!" she yells. "You'll kill it."

"Damn straight, I'll fucking kill it," the redneck replies and squashes the black widow beneath the sole of his work boot.

"*Three*," Walter whispers, one word meant for no one but the clerk, one last word of warning and the look in his eyes to say that he isn't kidding.

"All right," the clerk says and sets the cocked Winchester down on the countertop, then holds both his hands up like a bank teller in an old Western movie. "There. I fucking put the gun down. Now get out of here, and take that goddamn freak bitch with you."

"You're a smart man, Frank," Walter whispers, so relieved that he wants to vomit, too, wants to get down on his knees next to Theda and barf up the hard, twisting knot that's settled into his belly. But Archer is already hauling the girl to her feet, and he reaches for his wallet instead, not lowering the Beretta.

The redneck stomps another black widow, and Theda moans and tries to pull free of Archer's grip. "I hope all your children are born without eyes," Theda snarls, spittle flying from her lips. "I hope your wife's titties rot off. I hope you never have another fucking night's sleep without dreaming about *me*."

"Don't be such a damned drama queen," Archer mutters, dragging her away towards the plate-glass doors. "If you hadn't put them there, he wouldn't be killing them, now would he?"

Walter fumbles his wallet open and pulls out a couple of folded bills. "Sorry about the mess. Take this and buy some bug spray and a mop. And you and your buddies here are gonna keep your mouths shut or all those things she just said," and he nods towards Theda, "that shit ain't *nothing* compared to what'll happen to you if I have to come back." He drops the money, a hundred and a fifty, on the counter, but the clerk just stares at it.

"All you guys gotta do is forget you ever saw us," Walter says, easing his finger off the pistol's trigger and reaching for the shotgun. "I hope you don't mind if I take this—"

"I don't give two shits what you do," the clerk replies. "Just take it, and get out of here."

Walter thinks about asking for the tape from the security camera mounted on the wall behind the counter, then decides not to press his luck. Archer's probably already seen to that, anyway, and there won't be anything for the cops but static and wavy lines.

"*Fuck* this," the redneck says. "They're fuckin' *everywhere,*" and he stomps another spider.

And Walter turns around, shoving the doors open with his right shoulder, and he follows Archer Day and Theda back out into the bright Alabama morning.

"They live in the deep places," Spyder says, "but when they die, their bones fill with gas, and the skeletons float to the surface. The fishermen bind the bones together and anchor them to the ocean floor."

"My God," Niki whispers, gazing up at the interlocking, jackstraw symmetry of the village ramparts rising from the fog-bound sea. "They must be bigger than whales. They must be bigger than *dinosaurs.*" And she's surprised by her own wonder, that she can still be amazed at anything after the Dog's Bridge, after the Palisades, after following the white bird through that other, ruined San Francisco.

"Yes," Spyder says. "They must."

Low waves surge and break against the high ramparts, against the pontoon bases of floating wharves and the hulls of the small wooden boats moored there. Hundreds or thousands of lanterns shine from hundreds or thousands of hooks, poles, and posts, flickering sentries against the night. There's a red buoy bobbing around in the water on Niki's left, not far from the edge of the walkway.

"There are many villages like this one—hundreds probably—scattered across the Outer Main," Spyder says. "But I've only seen a few of them."

"Where is everyone? It looks deserted."

"They're always wary of travelers approaching from the Palisades. Don't worry, Niki. It's not deserted."

"I *wasn't* worried," Niki says.

"We shouldn't linger here. Shake a leg," and Spyder starts walking again.

There can't be much more than a couple hundred yards or so remaining between them and the tall rope and bamboo gates where the catwalk finally ends and the village begins, but Niki's so tired she thinks it may as well be a mile, and her bandaged hand aches so badly it's starting to make her dizzy and sick to her stomach. She glances back up at the walls, steep, uneven barricades fashioned from the skeletons of leviathans, wire and wood and seamonster bone rising into the mist, the uppermost reaches almost entirely obscured by the fog. *Is everything in this place built out of fucking bones?* she thinks, and then realizes that Spyder's getting ahead of her and she runs to catch up, her footsteps echoing hollowly from the shadowed spaces beneath the punky gray boards.

Strings are drawn tight, or hang loose.

And clocks tick the spent moments away—third wheels, center wheels, brass pendulum shafts—as atoms trapped in the blazing hearts of stars decay, and suns spit prominences to arch forty thousand miles above photospheric hells.

In her trapdoor, black-hole nursery, nestled at the rotten heart of every universe, every bubble frozen in the forever-expanding matrix of chaotic eternal inflation, the Weaver spins in her uneasy sleep, casting new lines of space and time across the void. She dies and is reborn from her own restless thoughts. A trillion eggs hatch, and her daughters cloud the heavens.

Or drift down from night skies to swarm across rooftops and city parks.

Her heart beats, and *this* line is severed, or *that* line is secured.

A life is saved. A life is lost. Scales balance themselves or fall forever to one side or the other.

Twenty miles north of Birmingham, Alabama, a man who drives a rusty purple Lincoln Continental and knows how one world *might* end, sticks to the back roads and county highways, just in case. The ginger-haired woman sitting next to him chews a stick of spearmint gum and says her prayers to forgotten, jealous gods.

And at 10:37 A.M., a graduate student from Berkeley, searching for clams and mussel shells along a narrow stretch of beach below Treasure Island Road, pauses to admire the view of the Bay Bridge silhouetted against the cloudless morning sky. He spots something dark stranded among the rocks at the water's edge and thinks it's probably a dead sea lion, until he gets closer and can see the Asian girl's battered face, her skin gone blue and gray as slate, her hair like matted strands of kelp half buried in the sand. Her eyes are open wide, though they're as perfectly empty as the eyes of any dead thing. At first, he can only stand and stare at her, horror and awe become one and the same, beauty and revulsion, peace and death and the sound of hungry gulls wheeling overhead. After five or ten minutes, the noise of a passing helicopter brings him back to himself and he drags her nude and broken body to higher ground so maybe the tide won't carry it out into the bay again, then he scrambles up the crumbling cliffs to call the police.

A cell phone rings. And then another. And another.

News travels fast, and bad news travels faster still.

There is another shore, you know, upon the other side.

A syringe, a stethoscope, and electrocardiograph displays in a white room that smells of loss and antiseptic.

These things happen.

And then . . .

CHAPTER SEVEN

Snakes and Ladders

I'm going to fall forever, Daria thinks. *I'm never going to hit the water,* but then she does, and it's like hitting a brick wall. Not what she expected, but then few things ever are, and at least the pain only lasts an instant, less than an instant, as the cold waters of the bay close mercifully around her shattered bones and bruised flesh, accepting her, promising that there's nothing left to fear. Nothing ahead that's half so terrible as all the trials laid out behind her; she wants to believe that more than she's ever wanted to believe anything.

And she's certain this is real, because no one ever dies in dreams. If it were only a dream, she thinks, she'd have awakened in that final, irredeemable second before the long fall ended. That's what she's always heard, and she's never died in a dream. No one dies in dreams.

In another moment, you will not even feel the cold, the ocean whispers, as the southbound currents wrap kelp-slick tendrils about her broken legs and pull her down and down and down. Drawing her towards the black and silty bottom, away from the comfortless oyster light of the moon shining so bright that she can still see it through the shimmering, retreating surface of the bay. The light at the end of the tunnel, near-death or afterlife cliché, but she has no use for light anymore, and she's grateful that soon the moon and the sun and all light will be lost to her forever.

Was it like this for you? she asks, and the shadows swarming thick through the water around her sigh and murmur a thousand conflicting answers. So she takes her pick, choosing at random because she can't imagine that choices still matter. *No,* Niki whispers. *It's different for everyone.*

Daria stares up at the rippling moon growing small, hardly a decent saucer now when a moment ago it was a dinner plate, and she tries hard to remember if she's sinking or rising, if she's getting farther from the moon or it's getting farther away from her. *That doesn't matter, either,* the bay reassures her. *Don't even think about it,* and so she doesn't. She can see the inky cloud of blood leading back the way she's come, a blood road back to the moon, but Daria knows the bay will take care of that, as well, and soon there will be no evidence whatsoever of her passage.

A loose school of surfperch sweep hurriedly past, their mirror scales flashing the moonlight because they have no light of their own, and Daria knows exactly how that feels. Never any light but what she stole, never her own soul for a lantern, but only for cloudy days and shuttered rooms, closets and nights without stars.

That girl in Florida, the moon calls down to her with its silken, accusing voice. *Old Becky What's-her-name. You think that's the way she felt? You think that's what she heard when she listened to your songs?* And then it begins to whistle the melody of "Seldom Seen."

You leave me alone, Daria calls back at the moon. *I'm going down to Niki. It's not my problem anymore.*

The moon stops whistling, and *Ohhh,* it purrs, pretending to sound surprised. *Was it ever? Weren't you the lady that couldn't be bothered?*

Don't start listening to that old whore, the bay whispers. *She steals her light, too, just the same as you and those fish.*

And the water presses in on her, something that would hurt if she could still feel pain, an unfelt agony of pressure stacking up above, pounds and anamnesis per square inch, and maybe it will finally crush her so flat that the moon won't be able to see her, and she won't have to listen to it, won't have to think about all the questions she's never known the answers to. There's a final rush of air from her deflating lungs, and she watches indifferently as the bubbles rise (or fall) like the bells of escaping jellyfish.

You can't follow me, Niki says, her voice drifting up from some place so deep and black that Daria has never even dared imagine it, some endless, muddy plain where there's only night that runs on forever in all directions. A silent wilderness of fins and spines and the stinging tentacles of blind things, the rotting steel and wooden husks of drowned ships, and countless suicide ghosts mired in the ooze and labyrinths of their own condemning thoughts.

You can't stop me, Daria tells her.

It's all a dream, Daria. It's only a bad dream.

And now there's something floating towards her, a paler scrap of night dividing itself from the greater darkness, and at first she thinks it's only a curious seal or maybe, if she's very lucky, a shark come along to finish what she's started. But then she can make out Niki's face, the empty sockets that were her eyes before the hungry jaws of fish, her hair like seaweed strands swaying gently about her gray and swollen cheeks.

Not what you think, Niki mumbles, her clay-blue lips and a flat gleam of beach-glass teeth; where her tongue should be there are only the nervous coils of a tiny octopus nestled in her mouth. *You can't find me here. I didn't mean for you to follow.* Then the tattered girl holds out her right hand, and the ball bearing glimmers faintly in her ruined palm.

I'll never find it, Daria thinks. *Not after ten years. I'll never find it again.*

Not if you don't try, the octopus in Niki's mouth replies, and then her body comes apart like sugar in a cup of tea, dissolving back into the night and the bay, and Daria is alone again. She tries to remember a prayer she knew ages and ages ago, when she was a child and still thought someone might be listening, but suddenly her memories seem as insubstantial as the vision of Niki, and the fleeting, slippery words remain always just beyond her reach.

And the moon is growing larger again.

And has turned the color of a drowned girl's skin.

Daria opens her eyes and blinks at the warm late afternoon sunlight pouring in through the hospital room's window, a pale yellow-orange wash across the rumpled white sheets of her bed. The window frames a western sky that is broad and turning brilliant sunset shades of violet and apricot. And the dream is right there behind her, still close enough that she thinks it might continue if she'd only shut her eyes again and let it. Right there, so at least she's spared any sudden, startling disappointments when she remembers exactly where she is, and what's happened to Niki, and why Alex is sitting here watching her and trying too hard not to look worried.

"Hey you," he says, and there's the faintest suggestion of a smile to warp the corners of his mouth, but the smile gives up and becomes something else.

"Fuck," Daria whispers, and turns away from the window and Alex Singer and the setting sun.

"Would you like some water?"

"Unless you've got vodka," she replies, and licks at her chapped lips, her throat so dry it hurts, and she lies still and listens to the sound of him pouring water from a plastic pitcher into a paper cup.

"I talked to Marvin again," he says. "He rang, just before you woke up," and Alex holds the cup to her lips and supports her head. She only drinks a little, because it's warm and tastes like chlorine, then pushes his hand away, and he sets the cup down next to the blue pitcher on the table beside the bed. He presses one hand against her forehead like someone checking to see if she has a fever.

"I don't want to start crying again," she says.

"I know, love. I know you don't."

"I *told* her I was coming, didn't I? I fucking told her I was on my way," and Daria stares at the IV tube rising from the soft inside of her left elbow, a couple of strips of tape to hide the needle, to hold it in place, and she lets her eyes follow the tube up to the bag of clear fluid suspended from a metal hook beside the bed. "When are they going to stop pumping me full of that shit?" she asks Alex, and nods at the IV bag.

"I don't know. You were awfully dehydrated."

"Alex, you were sitting right there. You heard me tell her I was coming home. I know you heard me."

"Yeah," he says, "I did. I heard everything you said," and then he moves his hand from Daria's forehead to her right cheek. His skin feels cool and dry and familiar, his rough fingers to remind her of so many things at once, things that didn't die with Niki, and she turns away from the IV bag and looks up into his gray eyes, instead. Those eyes the first part of Alex Singer that she fell in love with, even before his music, eyes like smoke and steel, and she knows that she's going to start crying again, and there's nothing she can do to stop it.

"You can't start blaming yourself for this."

"Yes, I can," she says, and the tears cloud her vision and leak from the corners of her eyes. "I left her there. She begged me not to go and I went anyway."

"You did what you had to do. Niki was very sick, and you did everything you could to keep her safe. You pissed away the last ten years of your life trying to keep Niki safe, and it's almost killed you."

"No, that's not true. I *didn't* do everything. I was always too afraid to listen—"

"Stop it," Alex says, pulling his hand away, and he takes a quick step back from the edge of the bed. The anger in his voice like straight razors beneath worn velvet, and his gray irises spark with something that Daria doesn't want to see, not now or ever, so she closes her eyes. She tries to wish herself into the dream again, down to the freezing, silent wastes where no one will ever find her, that night without mornings or horizons and only the blind, indifferent fish and Niki's fraying ghost for company. But it's deserted her, left her stranded here in this white antiseptic place choked with sunlight and people determined to keep her alive.

"*You* almost died on that goddamn plane," Alex says. "You heard what the doctor said. Your fucking heart stopped beating, and you were real fucking lucky that they didn't have to take you straight from the bloody airport to the morgue."

"She's *dead,* Alex."

"Yeah, Daria, she's dead. She jumped off a fucking bridge, and if you'd been there *maybe* it wouldn't have happened, maybe she wouldn't have killed herself until next month, but you *weren't* there, and now she's dead, and that's something you're going to have to find a way to get through."

"You're a son of a bitch," she says, squeezing her eyes shut tighter, tasting her own hot tears leaking into her mouth, salt and snot and stingy drops of herself her body can't spare. Alex has started tapping his fingers hard against the side of the bed or the table with the blue pitcher, and she wants to scream at him to stop, to fuck off and let her be alone.

"Right. Maybe that's exactly what I am," and Daria thinks he doesn't sound half so angry as he did a moment before, that he sounds more like someone who only wishes he could stop talking before he makes things worse. "Maybe I'm a son of a bitch, and I'm sorry as hell about what happened to Niki. But you didn't kill her and I'm not going to let you lie there and convince yourself that you did."

"You don't know," she says. "You don't have any idea," and she opens her eyes, is about to tell him to please stop tapping his fucking fingers when she sees the white bird perched on the windowsill. It pecks at the glass with its beak, three times in quick succession, *tap-tap-tap,* then stares at her through the glass, its tiny, keen eyes the color of poisonous berries.

Do not fail her.

The Hierophant will need you, at the end.

"Oh God," she whispers. "Turn around. Turn around and tell me that you see it, too."

Alex doesn't turn around, but he glances over his left shoulder and then back at her, and she can tell from his expression that he doesn't see the white bird, that he doesn't see anything there at all.

"What is it?" he asks. "What do you see?" and *How am I supposed to pretend there's nothing there?* she thinks, unable to take her eyes off the white bird. *How can I pretend there's nothing, when it's right there, looking in at me?*

"Daria, tell me what's wrong."

"A bird," she says, "a white bird," and he glances at the window again.

"I don't see a bird. I don't see anything."

"I know," she whispers, and the bird pecks at the glass. *Tap-tap-tap. Tap-tap-tap.*

"I saw it on the plane, after Niki came to me, right after the pain started."

Alex rubs at his furrowed eyebrows and sighs. "That was a dream. You know that was a dream. I heard you tell the doctor—"

"Maybe I only thought it was a dream," she says and wipes her nose with the back of her hand, speaking as softly as she can because she's afraid of frightening the bird away. Or she's afraid it will hear her, and she's not sure which. "Maybe I was wrong."

"There's *nothing* out there, Daria," and he turns and walks across the room to the big windowpane, stands silhouetted against the garish Colorado sunset and raps hard on the glass with his knuckles. The white bird doesn't fly off, but it glares up at him and ruffles its feathers.

"What if you're not supposed to see it?" she asks, and the bird looks away from Alex and goes back to watching her. "Maybe it's only here for me, so I'm the only one who can see it."

Tap-tap-tap.

"Jesus, it's right *there*."

"Screw this," Alex mutters. "I'm going to get a nurse," and he starts for the door, but she yells at him to stop. On the windowsill, the bird blinks its red eyes and cocks its head to one side.

"You're sick, and you're very tired," he says, and she can hear the strained, brittle force in his voice, a thin disguise for exasperation and his own fatigue; he shakes his head and rubs at his eyebrows again. "You're hallucinating. It might be a reaction to the medication, or even DTs."

"I don't have the fucking DTs."

"How the bloody hell do you know that? You're an alcoholic, and you haven't been really sober since God wore diapers. How long's it been since you had a drink? Hell, must be coming up on at least ten or eleven hours now, right?"

"Alex, I'd know if it was DTs."

"No, you wouldn't. That's why they call it bleeding *delirium*."

Daria looks back at the window, and the white bird is still there, head cocked, its white feathers tinted ruddy by the fading day, its eyes so fiercely intent she knows that she'd go blind if she stared into them too long. And maybe, she thinks, she *has* gone crazy, and that's her punishment for all the years she spent denying the things she saw in Birmingham, that terrible, impossible night in Spyder Baxter's old house on Cullom Street. Her punishment for the lies she told Marvin and Dr. Dalby, for the way she treated Niki, and it would serve her right if she spends the rest of her life locked up somewhere, babbling about white birds and ghosts and the nightmares she's kept secret for almost a decade.

"If you get a nurse, I'll just say I didn't see it. I'll tell them I don't know what you're talking about."

"If it's a reaction to the medication—"

"Then I'll get better, or it'll kill me. Right now, I don't really care, either way."

The bird taps impatiently, insistently, at the glass, and

Daria shuts her eyes, trying to remember everything that Niki said to her on the plane. All the parts she's already told the doctors, because they wanted to know *everything* that happened to her, everything she felt, and all the parts she held back. Niki in her blue coat, asking her to make promises she couldn't keep, Niki frightened and desperate and rambling on and on about breakfast at a truck stop with jackalopes and something that she'd buried in the ground on a cold December morning ten years before.

"I don't care *what* you tell them," Alex says. "You can tell them the Pope's joined the bleeding C of E for all I care, but I'm going to get a nurse."

"Fine," Daria replies. "It's just as well," and she peels the two strips of tape off her skin and yanks the IV from her arm. There's only a little blood, not as much as she expected, and the trickle of saline from the hollow stainless-steel needle.

"What the fuck do you think you're doing now?" Alex demands, and the bird caws and taps approvingly at the thick glass.

"I'm getting out of here. So you go and find that nurse. Or a doctor. I'm sure there's going to be an assload of paperwork."

"Bollocks. You had a goddamn heart attack. You're not going *anywhere* until—"

"I don't believe that you or anyone else can stop me. Not unless the laws in Colorado are a hell of a lot different from the laws in California, and I don't think they are. Where did they put my clothes?" And Daria sits up, one hand covering the puncture in her left arm, and she swings her legs over the side of the bed. But then her stomach rolls and her head spins, and she has to sit still and wait for the dizziness and nausea to pass. From the window, the white bird spreads its wings wide, flaps them a few times, then starts pecking at the glass again.

"Look at you. You can hardly sit up straight, and you think you're well enough to leave."

"I don't know whether or not I'm well enough to leave.

I just know there's something I have to do, something for Niki, and I can't do it lying here."

"Niki is *dead*," Alex growls, and then he's standing directly in front of her, his strong hands on her shoulders like he means to hold her down if that's what it takes. "There's nothing else you can do for Niki. Right now, the only person you have any chance of helping is yourself."

"Take your hands off me," she says, blinking back the last of the dizziness, and when she looks him in the eyes it's easy to see how scared and confused he is, easy to see that he's only going through the motions because these are the words he thinks he should be saying. Something he heard in a movie or a television show, borrowed resolve, second-hand determination, and "Take your hands off me," she says again, and he does.

"Do you think you have to kill yourself now, because you couldn't save her? Is that it?"

"I need my clothes, Alex."

"Then you can bloody well find them yourself," he says and turns to leave, is halfway to the door when he pauses to look at the window again, and Daria looks, too. But the white bird is gone, if it was ever really there.

"I can't do what you did, Dar. Maybe that makes me an arsehole, but I can't waste my time trying to help someone who won't even *try* to help herself," and then he leaves the room and pulls the door shut behind him, and she's alone with the window and the setting sun and the not-so-distant mountains turning black and purple, stretched out like a barricade beneath the darkening sky.

After the bamboo gates are raised for them, and Spyder leads Niki from the ramparts of bone through narrow, serpentine streets, streets filled with shadows and lantern pools and nervous, suspicious whispers, they come, finally, to a tall door the color of butterscotch candy. It has a tarnished brass knocker and a symbol Niki doesn't recognize painted in red. Spyder knocks four times, waits a moment, and then knocks once more.

"So, when *will* the sun come up again?" Niki asks, craning her neck to glimpse the uneven sliver of night sky exposed above and between the steep walls and steeper rooftops of the closely packed houses. Those whirling, alien stars, writhing points of blue-white fire, and Niki wishes there were anything up there she recognized, anything sane, a dipper or a bear, Polaris or a zodiac lion.

"Later," Spyder replies and knocks again, and Niki isn't sure if she means that the sun will come up later or that Spyder will answer the question later, but she doesn't ask which. Her feet hurt almost as much as her bandaged hand, and she just wants a place to lie down, a place to sleep and not have to think about everything that has or hasn't happened since she left the hotel on Steuart Street. Maybe she can figure it all out later, or maybe she'll wake up in the room with Marvin and lie there staring at the ceiling, forgetting this dream and relieved that she never has to see those stars again.

"I need to sleep, and I need to take my meds," she says, and Spyder turns and glares at her, the gem between her eyes pulsing softly to some silent, secret rhythm.

"You can't take those pills anymore. Not here."

"I can't just stop like that. I'll get sick. You can't just stop taking Klonopin, Spyder. I might have seizures or convulsions or something."

"Not in this place. You don't need that shit here. I should have made you dump it all into the sea."

And before Niki can argue with her, the butterscotch door opens and candlelight spills across the threshold. The old woman clutching the candlestick is very thin, a stooped scarecrow of a woman in shabby gray robes, and she stares out at them from the matted salt-and-pepper hair that frames the angles of her pale face. Her eyes are open so wide that Niki can see the whites all the way around the irises, and she looks scared or surprised or both.

"Weaver," she whispers, her thin lips drawing the word out, stretching it so it becomes almost another word entirely. "We feared you were lost. We'd almost given you up for dead. There were signs—"

"There were complications," Spyder tells her. "The Dragon is closer than I thought."

And then the old woman seems to notice Niki for the first time; her eyes grow even wider, and she puts one bony hand over her mouth. "Is it truly her?" she asks, mumbling between her fingers. "Is *this* the Hierophant?"

"Are you going to make us stand out here on the doorstep all night long?" Spyder asks impatiently, but the old woman is still staring at Niki and doesn't answer her.

"By the spokes," she whispers, and a dank, salt-scented breeze causes the flame of her candle to gutter. "That I should ever have lived to see such a thing. Better I'd died a child."

"It's cold out here, Eponine Chattox," Spyder says. "We've walked all the way from the Palisades, and we're hungry and need to rest."

"Yes," the old woman says, and her hand slips slowly away from her mouth. "I imagine that you do."

"You should ask us inside."

"Should I? I'm not so sure. Perhaps I should strew myrrh and nettle across the groundsill and nail all the windows shut. Perhaps I should recite all the Points of Refutation backwards."

"Do you think your mistress would approve?"

"I think my mistress has no idea what she's letting into her house," the old woman named Eponine says, but she steps aside, anyway, and now Niki can see a long, dimly lit hallway beyond the cramped foyer. "I cannot keep you out," she says, speaking directly to Niki this time, instead of Spyder.

"Why are you afraid of me?" Niki asks her, and Eponine stares down at the flickering flame of her candle.

"You might as well ask me why the day fears night," she says. "Or why the living fear death."

"Don't listen to her," Spyder grumbles, taking Niki's good hand as she steps quickly past the old woman. "Sometimes I think Esme only keeps her around to scare away the peddlers and street preachers."

Niki looks back, and Eponine Chattox is busy tracing invisible signs in the air with a crooked thumb and index finger. Her lips move silently, and Niki thinks she must be praying.

"She doesn't want me here," Niki says.

"It's not her house," Spyder replies and pulls Niki along, past closed doors and a staircase and a noisy contraption of wood and metal that isn't exactly a grandfather clock, past walls hidden behind mustard-colored wallpaper and decorated with paintings of landscapes that seem almost as alien to Niki as the writhing Van Gogh stars.

"Then whose house is it?"

"It belongs to her niece, Esme, the fish augur who opened the passage beneath the bridge for you."

"Oh," Niki says and starts to ask what a fish augur is, but she's really too tired to care and half suspects that she wouldn't understand, anyhow. As long as there are beds here, or people who don't mind if she takes her boots off and falls asleep on the floor, fish augurs can wait until later.

"Esme is a great enemy of the Dragon," Spyder says, as the hallway turns left and ends abruptly at a door marked with the same red symbol as the entryway to the house. "Most of her family was taken by the jackals when she was still just a kid. Without Esme, I never would have found you."

"Spyder, I'm so tired. Can't we rest now, just for a little while?"

"We can rest after we speak with Esme."

"Right," Niki sighs. "Unless I drop dead from exhaustion first," and she touches the center of the symbol painted on the door—bright scarlet enamel on the dark, varnished wood. *It's like touching ice,* she thinks, *or Jell-0,* because now the door seems to quiver slightly beneath her fingertips, and then Spyder snatches her hand away.

"You have to be very careful what you touch in this house. It's best if you don't touch anything at all."

"But what does it mean? Is it some kind of magic?"

"It's a warning."

Niki inspects her fingers, checking to be sure they're all still there and that the door hasn't marked her somehow, hasn't left some incriminating stain or brand on her skin. "A warning to who?" she asks.

"A *warning*, Niki. And that's all you need to know."

"I think there's a hell of a lot I *need* to know," Niki mumbles, and wipes her hand on her jeans. "A lot of things you're not telling me."

"Sometimes knowledge is a luxury we can't afford," Spyder says, and knocks at the door. Niki watches as concentric ripples spread rapidly across the wood, shock waves beginning at the point where Spyder's knuckles rapped against the muntin, then spreading out and out and out until they vanish at sensible horizontal and vertical boundaries. Edges of the door, edges of the world, and *Back when most people still thought the world was flat,* Spyder told her at the Palisades.

I should probably be really freaked out by that, Niki thinks, still watching as the last of the ripples race themselves towards iron hinges and the ceiling and door frame boards. But perhaps she's seen too much, too fast, and nothing will ever amaze her again. The thought is vaguely comforting, and so she doesn't bother asking Spyder why the door doesn't know the difference between solids and liquids. And then it swings open, and there are rickety-looking steps leading down into darkness beneath the house, and the hallway fills suddenly with the moist stink of mildew and sea water and dead fish. Niki covers her mouth and tries not to gag.

"Follow me," Spyder tells her, as if she has any choice in the matter. "Stay close, and be careful. These stairs have seen better days."

"What's waiting for us down there?"

"Just Esme," Spyder replies, and then she's through the doorway and the old steps squeak like angry rats beneath her feet. Niki lingers a moment, looking back down the long mustard-colored hall, past the strange paintings, and

Eponine Chattox is standing next to the thing that isn't exactly a grandfather clock, staring back at her.

"Come on," Spyder calls, her voice echoing in the stairwell, and the old woman turns around and walks away, trailing candlelight and fear.

"Yeah," Niki says. "I'm coming," and she hurries to catch up with Spyder.

The cardiologist scowled and made grim predictions that she wouldn't be so lucky next time, warnings that there was only so much abuse a body could take, but in the end he let her go, because there was nothing else he could do. Daria signed everything they gave her to sign, release forms absolving Memorial Hospital of any and all responsibility, forms stating that she was acting against the advice of her doctor, and then they put her in a wheelchair and an orderly carted her down the hall to an elevator and back out into the world. Alex was waiting in the cranberry red Saturn he'd rented at the airport, and he helped her into the car and made her buckle her seat belt.

And now the wide night sky and the prairie land rush by outside her window, and Daria watches the rearview mirror as the lights of Colorado Springs shrink down to a fistful of fallen stars trapped in the lee of the Rockies. There's been hardly a word between them since the hospital, Alex keeping his mouth shut and both his eyes on the road, the asphalt belt of Highway 24 snaking north and east towards Falcon and Peyton and other places Daria's never heard of and never wants to see. There's a Tom Petty song on the radio, but the station is already beginning to break up, and soon there'll be nothing but country and gospel to choose from.

"I don't even know how to perform bloody CPR," Alex murmurs, and a passing semi flashes its high beams, so he slows down to the speed limit. "I had lessons once, in school, but I don't remember any of it."

"That's okay. I do. In a pinch, I can probably talk you through it."

"It's *not* fucking funny," he says, and she shrugs and nods her head, because it really isn't funny. But anything's better than thinking about Niki, or the white bird, or Birmingham, or a hundred other awful things that she can't stop thinking about.

"We should stop at the next exit," she says. "I need a pack of cigarettes."

"Over my dead body."

"Oh no, Alex, not you, too. One of us has to drive," and this time she laughs and then goes back to watching the night and the low, scrubby shapes huddled in the darkness at the side of the highway. Alex curses to himself and switches off the staticky radio, so the only sounds left are the hum of the tires on the road and the dry whir of the heater.

"I ought to have me fucking head bashed in," he says. "Going along with this crazy shite." And then they pass a Colorado state trooper parked in the median, waiting there with his lights off like some patient ambush predator, and Alex curses again and slows down just a little bit more.

"Did you call Marvin?" Daria asks. "Did you tell him I was leaving the hospital?"

"Yeah. I told him you were a goddamn lunatic."

"How'd he sound?"

"How the hell do you *think* he sounded?"

"I don't want to fight with you," she says, and rolls down her window an inch or so, letting in a blast of fresh, cold air. "I'm not going to talk anymore, not if you're going to keep trying to pick a fight."

"Just when the hell are you going to get around to telling me where we're going?" he asks, like he didn't hear a word she said.

"I'll tell you later."

"I think you need to tell me now."

"It's really a very long story," she says and chews at a thumbnail, wishing that she had a cigarette and anything alcoholic, a beer or a shot of Jack or anything at all to smooth out the jagged places behind her eyes.

"Yeah? Well, I think I can spare the time."

"Listen, Alex, if you're right, then it's nothing. All you gotta do is shut up and drive me to fucking Kansas and watch me make an ass of myself. If you're right—and you're *always* fucking right—where's the harm?"

"Why don't you try asking me that when you're having another heart attack," he says and checks the rearview mirror before speeding up again.

"Never mind," Daria says, and she rolls the window shut. She's about to close her eyes, because the thirst is getting worse by the minute, already so bad she's starting to sweat, and even bad dreams would be better than arguing, when something scrambles out of the blackness at her side of the road and into the headlights. Something on bandy, long legs that moves so fast it's hardly more than a blur of yellow fur and iridescent eyes.

"Motherfucker," Alex growls and swerves to miss the animal, stomps the break pedal, and the tires shriek as the car fishtails and bumps off the blacktop onto the uneven gravel shoulder of the highway. Daria feels herself moving towards the windshield, a long moment of weightlessness before the seat belt catches her, and she only whacks her knees against the dash. Half a second later and they're sitting in a cloud of dust, and the bitter smell of hot rubber is seeping in through the vents. Alex shifts into park and lets the engine idle, leans forward until his forehead is resting against the steering wheel.

"Bloody fucking fuck," he mutters and punches the seat between them.

"Did we hit it?" Daria asks, breathless, both her knees aching, and she's too afraid to turn her head and look behind them, afraid what she might see in the crimson glow of the taillights.

"Fucking goddamn deer," Alex says.

"But did we *hit* it?"

"No," he replies and punches the seat again. "I don't think so. Jesus Christ, it was big as a cow."

"It wasn't a deer. I think it was a dog."

"It was a fucking deer. I saw its horns."

"Deer don't have horns, they have antlers."

"You think I give a rat's fanny? It was a fucking deer."

"We might have hit it," Daria says, and unfastens her seat belt, opens her door, and an alarm buried somewhere in the guts of the car starts beeping loudly.

Alex raises his head and glares at her. "Where do you think you're going?"

"It might be hurt. We can't just leave it lying there in the road."

"Why the hell not?"

"Someone else will come along and run over it," Daria says, and she gets out of the car before he can tell her not to. The gravel shifts and crunches beneath the soles of her boots, and the night air's a lot colder than she expected; her breath turns to white steam and mingles with the settling dust. *Look quick, and get it over with,* and she does, turns around expecting blood and matted fur, twisted bone and muscle, but there's nothing at all in the road behind the car, no broken dog or deer or anything else that she can see. She takes a step towards the rear of the Saturn, and her left knee pops loudly.

"Where do you think you're going now?" Alex asks, and she doesn't answer him. She realizes that she's started shivering and hugs herself tightly. The car is still beeping, and Daria wishes that he would turn off the engine so it would stop. She walks around to the back of the car, and a night bird calls out somewhere in the distance. *It might be an owl,* she thinks, but she hasn't heard an owl in years and years, not since she was a little girl, so she can't be sure.

"We *didn't* hit it," she whispers, saying the words out loud to convince herself, saying them so she'll turn around and get back into the car. The bird calls out again, closer than before, and this time she's pretty sure that it isn't an owl.

And then there's movement from the darkness at the farthest limit of the taillights, a sudden, pale flutter and a twin flash like animal eyes. *Shit. We* did *hit it. We did hit it, but it's not dead,* and she takes a few cautious steps away from the car. Behind her, Alex blows the horn, and the eyes flash again, a brief red-gold glimmer, and now she's sure that they're eyes, watching her from the grass and scrub at the edge of the highway.

Go back. Go back, and get Alex. If it's hurt, it might be scared. It might even be dangerous, but Daria doesn't go back to the car. Instead, she takes another step towards the dim shape crouched at the side of the road.

When it speaks, it's a voice colder than the November wind blowing across the prairie, the voice of something that is neither hurt nor scared, a voice like frostbite and ice and starvation at the still heart of winter.

"Where are you going, Daria Parker?" it asks, the words pouring from it thick as syrup, and now the thing that she thought was a dog is standing up on its spindly hind legs, twice again as tall as she is, and its red eyes burn bright in the night. "We thought you were smarter than this. We thought *you* wouldn't be a problem. We told the Dragon he had worse things to worry about than the Hierophant's bitch."

Daria opens her mouth to scream, but only a soft puff of fog slips past her trembling lips. She can't look away from those hateful, noctilucent eyes gazing down at her, eyes that could pick her apart in an instant or burn her to a cinder, eyes to show the soul of something that has never even imagined mercy. Alex blows the horn again and the thing flares its nostrils and smiles, baring teeth that seem bloody in the gleam of the taillights.

"We have been wrong before," it says. "Though it would be much easier on you if we were not. It would be simpler for all concerned."

"Niki," Daria whispers, and she needs all the air in her lungs, all the strength in her body, to manage those two syllables.

"The Hierophant chose her path. Yours didn't have to be the same. What did you hope to find at the end of this road, anyway?"

And *that's* the question, the only question that really matters. Daria knows that, must have known that all along, and wants to ask the thing if it has the answer, but it won't let her talk, won't even let her move.

"There's only death, this way," it says, as the night curdles and shrinks down around her until there's almost nothing left but those eyes. The beast grins and opens its jaws wide to bay at the moonless sky, yawning like some hungry fairy-tale wolf before it gobbles up Red Riding Hood or blows down a house of straw. *Oh, what big eyes you have, what big teeth,* and when it howls the ground shudders, and Daria's bones hum painfully beneath her skin. It's coming for her, erasing the distance between them, and in another heartbeat it will grind her to jelly beneath its perfect, obsidian claws.

Death and sorrow.

Loss and waste and—

Alex's strong hands close roughly around her shoulders, and the beast dissolves in the deafening blast of an air horn, its eyes and teeth melting away to the blinding glare of headlights and a chrome radiator grill. He shoves her hard, and she stumbles, almost falls on the pavement, but he's still right there to catch her, and the truck passes so close that the wind off its trailer is a hurricane gale. And when it's gone, and there's only the beeping alarm from the rented cranberry Saturn, only its idling motor and the night bird Daria doesn't recognize, he holds her while she cries and shakes and tries to drive the memory of that voice from her head.

All the way down through the dark spread out below the house, round and round the tight, descending spiral, looking for the bottom of the rickety stairs, and the air grows closer and more fetid with every step. *If this were a story,* Niki thinks, and she's beginning to believe that's exactly what it is, and what it's been all along—a story—a story that she's been written into, or that she's written *herself* into, and now she's merely a character trapped in the obligatory, inevitable riptide of plot and subtext and metaphor.

If this is a story, and I'm walking through it, then these must be significant stairs, and surely some revelation is at hand.

Turning and turning in the widening gyre . . .

Round and round the foregone, snail's-shell path, and she knows there probably never was a center here to hold anything at all, only her exhaustion and the dim light from Spyder's hair and the gem between her eyes. *I could sleep for a month,* she thinks. *I could sleep for an age.*

I could sleep for a thousand years, easy.

She bites hard at her lower lip, the pain and a few drops of blood to keep her awake and walking, and Niki digs for other thoughts to push back the towering, satin-black wall of sleep. *We should be underwater,* she thinks, because there's no way that the house could possibly have a basement this deep, not even half this deep, not if the whole village is floating on a raft of bones and wire. They must have passed the waterline a long time ago—unless this is another sort of magic, like jumping off a bridge and never hitting San Francisco Bay. Maybe the second door with the red mark was more than an ordinary door, and this is another *place* entirely, and that thought sends icicle fingers down her spine and makes her want to turn and run all the way back up the stairs to the mustard-colored hallway and frightened, glowering Eponine Chattox. Spyder stops and glances warily back up at her, as if she's been eavesdropping on Niki's thoughts again.

"We're almost there," Spyder says in a tone that Niki knows is supposed to be encouraging, reassuring, but isn't. Her hand hurts like hell, and her feet hurt almost as badly, and she thinks maybe she's been dozing off while she walked, fading in and out of consciousness like a bad radio signal, and that's why it seems the stairs will never end.

Dead on my feet, she thinks and laughs out loud.

"What's funny, Niki?"

"Nothing. Nothing's funny. But I gotta sit down now."

"Not much farther, I promise."

And Niki realizes that it's getting easier to see, the stairwell brightening by slow degrees, and now there's a little light coming from somewhere below them, somewhere besides Spyder. A faint green luminescence like moonlight shining through the surface of an algae-covered pond, a muted absinthe light that seems the slightest bit brighter with every step she takes.

"I feel like I've walked a hundred miles," Niki says.

"No, not a hundred. Not quite that far."

"Well, far enough. These damned stairs better end soon, or I'm not going to make it."

"Look, Niki, we're here. We're at the bottom."

She blinks, squinting into the soft green light, and is surprised and startled to see that Spyder's telling her the truth, and they're standing together on a wide landing built of planks gone almost as gray and weathered as the decaying catwalk leading from the Palisades to the village. The landing at one corner of a vast chamber, and the stink of fish and mold is so strong here that her eyes water, and she has to breathe through her mouth. That way she only tastes it, rot-sweet aftertaste like the seas have all drained away, seven Chinese brothers swallowing the ocean; a million squirming things, dead and dying, lying trapped in the solidifying muck and seaweed beneath a blazing sun.

Past the landing is a sprawling, pick-up-sticks jumble of sagging piers and platforms, teetering shelves crowded with aquarium tanks—some clean and bubbling, others stagnant and choked with algae—books and scrolls and great glass jars filled with dark liquid and darker things floating inside. Here and there are places where wide openings in the wooden floor reveal inky pools of seawater, draped in mesh tents of fishing nets and lobster pots. There are long tables cluttered with medical instruments and microscopes and cruel-looking contraptions that Niki can't identify. And at the very center of it all, a stone dais rising from the seafloor, and then Niki notices the walls.

"My God. It's water. It's *all* water," and Spyder nods her head.

"Esme is a very skilled hydromancer," she says. "That's how she was able to open the portal to bring you across."

"A hydromancer," Niki whispers, and she stares up at the high and shimmering walls, a dome carved somehow from the sea itself, a gigantic bubble far below the floating village. And she guesses that explains the stairs as well, as much as it explains anything at all. The stone dais sits at the very center of the dome, beneath its highest point, and now Niki can see that the green light comes from a sort of chandelier or candelabrum hanging directly above the dais. Except there are no candles or electric lightbulbs, no gas jets, but, instead, light spilling from glass pots and bowls of living things hung from the rusted iron frame of the fixture. The walls of the dome glisten, revealing black and impenetrable depths, revealing nothing much at all.

"Well, I never thought we'd see *you* again," someone says, someone standing directly behind Niki, and she turns to find a young man. He's long-limbed and rail thin, a gaunt wraith of a man, his straight, mouse-colored hair pulled back in a tight ponytail.

"Is he talking to *me*?" she asks Spyder, and the man sits down on one of the bottom steps and winks at Niki. He's wearing a leather motorcycle jacket and blue jeans so worn and faded that they're hardly even blue anymore.

"She's a pretty one," he says, talking to Spyder but keeping his piercing, close-set eyes on Niki. "I've always said no one can question your taste in quim, Weaver."

"Or your manners," Spyder replies, and he laughs.

"Old Eponine said you'd come back to us, but I thought she was just having another one of her fits. We heard from Tirzah that the jackals caught up with you at—"

"Are you disappointed, Scarborough?" Spyder asks him, and the man grins and shakes his head.

"Are you kidding me? Hell, when we got the news, I cried for three days straight. I couldn't even eat or take a shit, I was so damn distraught."

"Is that a fact?"

"A fact or close enough. I mean, a man gets puking tired of moldy books and starfish, day in and fucking day out. I need a little variety, now and then," and he winks at Niki again. "And I know we can always count on you for variety, Weaver. Is she really supposed to be the Hierophant?"

"That's what everyone keeps telling me," Niki says and moves closer to Spyder.

"Well, you're not exactly what I expected," he says, and stands up, brushing at the seat of his jeans. "Vietnamese or Korean?"

"Vietnamese," Niki replies uncertainly.

"Yeah, that's what I thought. See, I spent a couple of months in Ho Chi Minh City before I—"

"Where's Esme?" Spyder asks impatiently, and the man named Scarborough frowns and motions past them, towards the labyrinth of shelves and netting and work tables.

"Oh, I'm sure she's around here somewhere, unless she's somewhere else," and he points at one of the open pools. "Lately, she's been spending an awful lot of time with a certain octopus. You ask me, she's got quite the unhealthy fixation on that old mollusk."

"But they *didn't* ask you, did they, Mr. Pentecost," a woman says with a voice like a frozen stream, and Niki turns to face the shimmering chamber again. And this must surely be the fish augur, Esme Chattox, a tall and willowy spectre standing on the dais, a thick leather-bound book tucked beneath her left arm and a large squid drooping lifelessly from her right hand. She wears flowing, layered robes that glimmer faintly beneath the living, phosphorescent chandelier, and Niki realizes that they're sewn from a crazy-quilt patchwork of fish hide. Her skin is a sickly green-gray color, like aged cheese or something drowned, and her stringy soot-black hair hangs down past her shoulders in sloppy corkscrew curls. She stands up straight and beckons Spyder and Niki to come closer.

"It's true, Weaver," she says. "We'd all given you up for

dead. Or worse. Tirzah and the ghouls down in Weir all scryed your fate. They aren't often wrong."

"It was kinda touch and go for a while," Spyder says, and then she leads Niki down a long, crooked aisle, between shelves that stink of formalin and dust, until they're standing at the edge of the dais. Esme carefully lays the thick book and the dead squid on a stone lectern and then stares down at Niki.

"The Hierophant," she says approvingly, her voice as ageless as any Niki has ever heard. "You've done well, Weaver. Please forgive me for ever doubting you."

This close, Niki can see how large and perfectly black Esme Chattox's eyes are, no distinction between iris and pupil and sclera, and when she smiles she reveals rows of razor-sharp teeth, a shark's teeth set in cyanotic gums. Her fingers end in long nails that may as well be claws, and there are thick webs between them.

"You don't look well, Hierophant."

"I don't feel very well, either," Niki replies. "And my name's Niki. Niki Ky."

"She's in a bad way," Spyder says. "She needs food and rest, and her hand—"

"Yes, her hand, indeed," Esme says and kneels down on the dais in front of them. "The ghouls saw that as well. A part of the Dragon has found its way into her. And that means it knows where she is, Weaver. That's not something we can afford to take lightly," and then to Niki, "Do you have the philtre, child?"

"The what?" Niki asks, trying not to wince or make a face or cover her nose, but the fish augur's breath is the worst thing Niki's smelled since she and Spyder started down the spiral staircase.

"The *philtre*," Esme says again, more emphatically than before. Her black eyes flash and grow a little wider as she leans nearer to Niki, bathing her in chilly waves of that brine and beach-rot breath, and this time Niki does cover her nose and mouth.

"I don't know what you're talking about."

"She means the ball bearing," Spyder says to Niki and then smiles nervously for Esme. "I'm afraid she doesn't. The jackals came too soon."

"Oh," Esme says and stands up, and now Niki notices the four bloodred slits on either side of her neck, beginning just beneath her chin, the feathery gill filaments exposed whenever the fish augur takes a deep breath. "Without the philtre we are lost," she says to Spyder. "You know that, Weaver. Without the philtre, *she's* just another useless . . ." and Esme hesitates, glaring at Niki while she searches for some particular word. "Just another worthless *pilgrim,*" she finishes.

"You know, I didn't *ask* to come here," Niki says, glaring back up at the tall woman in her scaly robes, meeting her empty eyes and those sharp white teeth.

Esme wrinkles her nose and turns back towards the lectern. "Hold your tongue, child, or someone else may soon be holding it for you."

"Don't threaten us, Esme," Spyder says and steps between Niki and the dais.

"But I wasn't threatening *you,* dear Weaver. No, you know that I'd never threaten *you.*"

"She's here because of me. You threaten her and it's the same thing as threatening me."

"This is tiresome." Esme moans. "Will you still protect her when the jackals find us because she could not perform such a simple task? Will you keep her safe then?"

"I don't remember asking *anyone* to protect me," Niki says, and her hand is hurting so much that she really doesn't care who or what she pisses off, who's threatening who or promising to keep her safe. "I asked Daria to find the ball bearing for me. When I was . . . when I was dying, I found her on an airplane and asked her to find it."

Esme Chattox cocks one thistleback eyebrow and looks down at them again. "What's she talking about? Who's this Daria?"

"Daria was my lover," Niki replies before Spyder can answer for her.

"And she'll do this for you? Find the philtre?"

"I think she'll try."

"You *think* she'll *try*. That's not terribly reassuring, Hierophant."

"I told her where to find it. I told her to take it to Spyder's old house in Birmingham."

"And what do *you* have to say about this, Weaver?" the fish augur asks and starts picking at the dead squid with her sharp nails. She pulls loose an eye and sets it aside.

"Esme," Spyder says, and she sounds tired and irritated, "we need to tend to her wound first. She needs rest. We can talk about these things later."

"You may soon find that there isn't very much *later* left us. The Dragon knows where she is, and without the philtre there's absolutely nothing to stop him from killing us all. That's what *I'd* do, were I him. I'd strike *now*," and Esme plucks the other eye from the squid. "Strike now and be done with it, once and for all."

"Then we hide her," Spyder says and quickly climbs the low stone stairs leading up onto the dais. The fish augur turns and frowns at the intrusion, the disembodied squid eye still hooked on the end of her left index finger. "I know enough spells without your help. When she's well enough to travel, I'll send her across to Auber and the Weir. Madame Tirzah—"

"Wants *nothing* of this girl," Esme Chattox growls. "She has to think of her people first. The Dragon has no quarrel with the *ghul*."

"The Dragon has a quarrel with everything *alive*," Spyder replies. "If Tirzah thinks it has any plans of sparing her or anyone else, then she's an even bigger fool than you, Esme."

"Daria's gonna find the ball bearing," Niki cuts in. "I mean the philtre. If it's still there, she'll find it. If she can," and then she sits down on the damp boards at the foot of the dais, because she can't stand up any longer. "Now *please*," she says, squeezing her eyes shut against the pain in her hand, the nausea and exhaustion crowding out her thoughts, "just stop fucking yelling at each other for five minutes."

Esme grunts and drops the second squid eye onto the lectern, then begins digging out the beak hidden among the limp white-pink tentacles. "I *know* you, Weaver," she says, pushing the words out between her gritted, serrate teeth. "I doubt you told this child half of what you've gotten her into."

"You can say that again," Niki murmurs and wishes that she weren't too tired to get her backpack off. "No one's told me jack shit."

"Then I suggest you remedy that," the fish augur says to Spyder. "As soon as she's rested and fed and a surgeon has seen to that hand. I suggest you tell her exactly where we stand and what's to be expected of her."

"I'd settle for a bed," Niki says and lies down on her side. With her ear pressed against the mildewed, fishy-smelling boards she can hear the sea sloshing gently against the timbers. It sounds like sleep, the soft rhythm of those waves hidden just beneath the wood.

"Eponine will show you to your room, and Scarborough will be back with a doctor within the hour. I have matters here that must be properly completed, or I'd attend to it myself."

Niki opens her eyes and sees that Spyder has come down off the dais and is standing over her. She looks worried, and the gem between her eyes has stopped glowing.

"I'm okay," Niki whispers, but Spyder doesn't look particularly convinced.

"We'll get you fixed up good as new," she says and helps Niki to her feet, puts one strong, tattooed arm around her waist to keep her from lying down again.

Esme stops picking at the mangled squid and stands with her head bowed, her hands gripping the corners of the lectern. Niki watches the red slits on her throat, opening and closing, opening and closing, red gashes that almost hurt to see.

"We have placed our lives in your hands," she says, and

Niki isn't sure if she's talking to Spyder or to her. "We have placed our *world* in your hands."

"It isn't over yet," Spyder says. "Not by a long shot. You're the one who told me never to give up as long as there's the smallest hope. You're the one who taught me never to despair."

"I have not yet despaired, Weaver. But I *am* afraid, as I've never been afraid before."

Spyder doesn't say anything else, as if there's nothing else left to say. She leaves Esme Chattox with her dissection and helps Niki back across the shimmering chamber, all but carrying her, and slowly, painfully, they make their way upstairs to the house again.

Almost all the way to the end of Highway 24 before Daria would let Alex stop somewhere, and every time the speedometer dropped below seventy-five or eighty she'd start drumming her fingers on the dashboard and looking nervously over her shoulder, out the rear windshield, at the night-shrouded road stretched out behind them. She talked and chewed aspirin and Tums while he drove, telling him all the things she'd sworn she'd never talk about with anyone, not friends or shrinks or even Niki. The secrets she's carried since Birmingham, what she saw in Spyder Baxter's house when she went in after Niki, all those years ago. And Alex listened, and drove, and didn't say a word.

Finally, a mile or so outside Limon, a mile or so left until 24 merges with I-70 West to Kansas, they pass a billboard— GAS-FIREWORKS-CIGARETTES-GEOLOGICAL MUSEUM-GAS— and Daria doesn't argue when Alex says that they're stopping. The tank is almost on empty anyway, the needle sitting on the red E for the last thirty miles or so, and it's a wonder they haven't wound up stranded somewhere.

"I need a drink," she says, as the Saturn bumps across the rutted, unpaved parking lot towards the pumps, raising dust and throwing gravel.

"Sure, fine by me," Alex replies, pulling up next to the self-serve regular, and he cuts the engine.

"I'm not going to get drunk. I just need a drink. Just a beer would do."

"Just a beer sounds bloody brilliant," he says and kisses her on the forehead before getting out to pump the gas. She sits in the car a moment, staring at the shabby, white-washed front of the gas station lit by halogen lights so bright they hurt her eyes after the long darkness of the highway. There are Halloween decorations and a large plywood sign propped near the door, an amethyst geode painted on it, purple and white and brown—WONDERS OF CREATION—and she silently prays to whatever gods might be listening that this isn't a dry county. The smell of gas is filling up the car, because Alex left his door standing open, the acrid, sour-sweet smell to make her stomach even worse, so she gets out and shuts her door.

"Go on ahead," he says. "I'll be in as soon as I'm done here."

"I can wait. I'm not sure I'm up to seeing people."

"You're fine. There's no sense you standing out here in the cold. I'll be right behind you."

"Cross your heart and hope to die?" and she smiles and wipes her runny nose.

"Whatever you say, love."

"I say what time is it?"

Alex glances from the digital display on the pump to his wristwatch. "Coming up on nine thirty," he says, and that's not nearly so late as she'd thought.

"You really ought to get something to eat, too," he tells her, and Daria looks back at the grimy windows half hidden beneath cigarette and beer ads and paper jack-o'-lanterns.

"There wouldn't be beer ads if this was a dry county," she says.

"No, there wouldn't," Alex agrees. "Now either get your ass inside or get back in the car before you freeze to death."

"Yeah," she says, and heads for the front door, buttoning her pink and gray cardigan sweater and imagining how good a beer will taste. Any beer at all. At this point, a fuck-ing PBR or Budweiser would be heaven, ambrosia sent down from Olympus to soothe her nerves and stomach, to take a little of the sting off the last few hours—the escape from the hospital in Colorado Springs, then almost getting her ass run over by a fucking semi because she was having a conversation with a monster, all the crazy, secret shit she's told Alex. Niki's suicide. *All* of it.

The door jingles loudly when she opens it, a cowbell rigged up just above her head, and the old man behind the counter, old man with long white hair and a beard to match, looks up from the biker magazine he's reading and nods at her. Kris Kringle on vacation from the North Pole and slumming as some desert-rat hippie, this old man.

"Good evening," he says in a voice as smooth as melted butter, but he doesn't smile.

"Hi," Daria replies and wipes her nose again. "Do you sell beer?"

"Yes, ma'am, we certainly do, just as long as you're old enough to buy it and can show me some ID," and he winks at her.

"Better watch yourself," she says and winks back, wishing that Alex would hurry up, because she isn't in the mood to be charming. "You really got a museum in here?" she asks.

"Now, I'll admit that sign exaggerates just a mite. But we do got a few things most folks don't see every day. You want a peek?"

Daria shrugs and glances through the grimy glass door, trying to see if Alex is finished with the gas, but there's a faded ad for Winston Lights in the way.

"I really just came in for the beer," she says.

"Ah, come on. It'll only take you a minute. Two minutes at the most. It ain't the goddamn Smithsonian Institution, but I got a couple of curiosities that'll make you look twice."

"I went to the Smithsonian once. But that was a long time ago."

"Well now, that makes one of us," the old man says, scratching at his beard as he steps out from behind the counter. "Back here," he says, "past the porno. You can grab your beer after we're done."

Daria glances longingly at the door again, but there's still no sign of Alex, just a glimpse of the Saturn around the edges of the Winston ad, and maybe whatever the old man has to show her will at least take her mind off everything for a few minutes. So she follows him deeper into the store, past a big display of *Hustler* and *Penthouse, Playboy* and at least a hundred other titty magazines.

"That stuff don't offend you, does it?" he asks and jabs a thumb at the magazine rack.

"Oh no," Daria says. "Not at all."

"You're a dyke, aren't you, girl?" he whispers and grins at her, showing off a dingy set of loose-fitting uppers. And before she's even quite sure that he actually said what's she just heard him say, the old man nods and shrugs his wide shoulders.

"Hey, it ain't no big whoop. My own goddamn granddaughter's a lesbo, and who the hell am I to start passing judgment? Way I see it, ain't none of it nobody's goddamn business if women don't want nothing to do with dick."

"Do you always talk to customers like this?" Daria asks, and he shakes his head.

"Not all of them. Just the ones look like they ain't got a mop handle shoved up their butts."

"I'll take that as a compliment."

"Well, I suppose you can take it however you want, miss. Ain't no skin off my snout," and he pushes open a brown door with a hand-painted sign that reads MUSEUM THIS WAY nailed to it. And then Daria sees the plaque hung above the door, an oblong disk of varnished pine and there's a jackalope head mounted on the plaque, glass-blind eyes and tall jackrabbit ears and a small set of antlers—the tiredest joke in the West—and she stops and stares at it.

"Ain't you never seen a jackalope?" the man asks, and Daria nods her head very slowly.

"Sure," she says. "Sure I've seen jackalopes."

"Well, that's not just any old jackalope, mind you. That there's Senior El Camino, the holy guardian jackalope of Big Sandy Creek. He does me a favor, watching over the place."

"You're a very strange man," Daria says, and he winks again and disappears through the brown door. She stands staring at the taxidermied hybrid a moment or two longer, remembering the dream that might not have been a dream at all. Niki on the plane, and a few strands of blue fur, a single white feather caught in the stewardess' hair.

You have to remember this. You have to remember because I can't get back there myself.

There's never enough time to do things the right way.

"So, when's it finally gonna start to sink in, that she's really gone?" Daria asks the jackalope's severed head, or she's only asking herself, or maybe she's asking no one at all. Maybe she only needs to *hear* the question. If Senior El Camino has an opinion, he keeps it to himself, and she steps through the doorway into a small, dimly lit room that smells like cobwebs and neglect.

"My youngest son, Joe, he started this thing, couple'a years before he moved out to Kansas to open his own place," the old man is saying, standing in front of a sturdy, homemade display case, and he wipes some of the dust off the glass with a red paisley handkerchief from his back pocket. "He went up to Denver when he was still in high school, to that natural history museum they got up there, and I guess it kinda, you know, inspired him."

Inside the case is a fossilized jawbone, almost as long as Daria's arm, studded with curved, two-inch teeth, gray bone and chocolate-black enamel, and she leans closer for a better look. The jawbone is laid out on green felt and surrounded by an assortment of fossil oysters and shark's teeth and tightly coiled ammonites. Some of the ammonites glint dully, despite the dust and dim lights, still wearing an iridescent covering of mother-of-pearl. There's a hand-lettered piece of cardboard near the jawbone, and she squints to read what's written there: PLATECARPUS, A MOSASAUR FROM THE CHALK SEA, 70 MILLION YEARS OLD, GOVE COUNTY, KANSAS.

"He's especially proud of that one there," the old man says, pointing at the case. "Dug it up and cleaned it off himself, showed it to some scientists in Denver, and they wanted it for their museum, but he told 'em no siree, no way. He found it, he was gonna keep it."

"What's a mosasaur?"

"That depends who you want to listen to, I guess. You ever read the Bible?" he asks, and she shakes her head no. "Well, see, it talks a good bit about this big ol' sea monster called Leviathan—'Who can open the doors of his face? His teeth are *terrible* round about. His scales are his pride, shut up together as with a close seal.' That's from the Book of Job."

"You don't exactly seem like the sort who quotes scripture," Daria says.

"Ain't you never heard that looks can be deceiving?"

"Never judge a book by its cover," she adds.

"Right you are, missy. Anyway, some damn Baptist preacher wrote all that down for me after I showed him this fossil. He said it was the remains of Leviathan. My son, on the other hand, says that Leviathan's just an old Hebrew name for crocodiles, and this mosasaur ain't no crocodile at all, but just a sorta big lizard."

"A *very* big lizard," Daria says. "So what do *you* think?"

"Well, now, I think it's a fine thing to find just laying there in the ground, either way you look at it. My son, Joe, says that way back when there was still dinosaurs alive, millions and millions of years ago, all these parts round here were at the bottom of the sea. That's where the mosasaurs lived, I reckon. And those shells, too," and he taps at the glass case. "That is, unless you listen to Baptist preachers, in which case it's all just junk from Noah's Flood. You want to see the rest?"

"There's more?"

"You bet there's more. I got a two-headed gopher snake

and a quartz crystal big around as my fist. I got Indian ar-
rowheads and a live Gila monster."

And then Daria sees something else in the case, just a
small, rusty metal sphere lying between the mosasaur jaw
and an especially large oyster shell, but suddenly there are
goose bumps beneath the sleeves of her sweater and a
pricking sensation along the back of her neck.

"What's that?" she asks, and the man stoops down for a
closer look.

You know what it is. You know exactly *what it is and
never mind how it got here, you know it anyway.*

"Oh, *that*," the old man says and taps on the glass again.
"Why, that's just a musket ball Joe found when he was picking up sharks' teeth by the side of the road. That ain't nothin',
but I figured I might as well put it in there with the rest."

"Can I see it? Will you take it out and let me see it,
please?"

"Wait a second now. That's not usually the way I do
things, letting customers handle the exhibits, I mean."

"Please," Daria says again, and the old man frowns and
rubs at his coarse gray-white beard.

"You make one exception," he mumbles, "you end up
havin' to make exceptions for everyone and his sister."

"Please, I won't tell *anybody*."

"But it's just an old musket ball, probably someone out
shootin' at deer or buffalo or—"

"All I want to do is see it."

He stares at her and rubs his beard indecisively, his eyebrows arched and furrowed like two albino caterpillars.
Daria's afraid to look away from the rusted ball, afraid it
might vanish, afraid it's just what he says, only dread and
wishful thinking making it anything more. *Which is worse?*
she wonders. *Which could possibly be worse?* and now the
old man has stopped staring at her and is busy looking
through dozens of mismatched keys attached to a big brass
ring.

"It ain't nothin' but a damned old musket ball," he
grumbles, and Daria nods her head.

"I know," she says. "I know it's just an old musket ball, but I need to see it, anyway."

"Well, I can tell you right now, the two-headed gopher snake's a hell of a lot more interestin'."

"I'm sure it is," she replies, and the old man's at the back of the case now, one of his keys to make tumblers roll and the hasp of a padlock pops open. "I'll see it later. I'll see it next time."

"Who you tryin' to kid? You ain't never gonna be coming back this way, missy. Hell, I been wondering what you're doing way out here in the first place, smelling like money and some big city by the sea."

"I was looking for something," Daria says, as the old man reaches past the dagger teeth of the mosasaur, and now she knows that's the *real* guardian, not Senior El Camino, but the jaws of this Leviathan.

"*Everybody's* out there looking for *something*. Sometimes, I think that's the only thing keeps the world spinnin' on her axis, all the goddamn people out there *looking* for something." He lifts the rusted metal ball from the red felt and holds it cradled in his palm for a moment.

Daria wants to reach for it, wants to snatch it from his hand before he changes his mind and puts it back and locks the case again.

"Lord, help the poor, damn fools that actually find what they're after," he says, then passes the musket ball across the top of the case to her. Only it's not a musket ball, just a rusty steel ball bearing with four letters written around its circumference. N-I-K-I in black ink so worn by time and rust and touch that she might never have seen them if she hadn't known there would be something there. Her knees buckle, and she grips the edge of the wooden case to keep from falling.

"She always said you'd be coming for it, Daria Parker," the old man says, "and I was to keep it safe, no matter what. She said the Hierophant would need it again one day."

"The Hierophant," Daria whispers, unable to look away from Niki's name, the faded work of a dead girl's hand, and when she looks back at the old man, he's holding one finger to his wrinkled lips.

"No questions, missy," he says. "You and that Englishman out there just get yourselves moving again before them others catch up with you. You can thank me when you come back to see that snake someday, like you said."

And then the cowbell jingles loudly in the next room, and Alex is calling her name. Daria holds the ball bearing tightly to her chest as the old man leads her back through the brown door and locks it behind them.

CHAPTER EIGHT

The White Road

Not the golden trumpets of Saint Michael's angels, but the demon wail of civil defense sirens to signal Armageddon, and what's the fucking difference? The last sound you'll hear before the fire comes down, and no, not *that*, either. Walter opens one eye and stares at the digital clock radio on the table beside the bed. Three thirty P.M. and it's only the alarm, because they were all so tired that Archer was afraid they'd never wake up on their own, might sleep straight through the night, so it's not angels *or* sirens, and he reaches over and punches the OFF button.

"I'm awake," Archer mumbles unconvincingly from her side of the bed, but she doesn't open her eyes. "What time is it?"

"Time to rise and shine, sweet pea," Walter says, rolling over onto his back to stare up at the low ceiling of the shabby motel room. There are brown water stains like the pressed blooms of some ancient flower, flower petals or bloodstains, and someone's written DIE YOU CRACKER COCKSUCKER in green Magic Marker directly above the bed. The room stinks of disinfectant and mildew, stale cigarette smoke and unwashed bodies, and he shuts his eyes again, just a moment's luxury before he has to fucking rise and fucking shine.

"It's *your* turn to deal with Theda," Archer Day says, her

face half-buried in her pillow and he can barely understand a word she's saying.

"Yeah, I know. My turn to deal with Theda," and behind his eyelids are the last fading, freeze-frame images of his dreams, hurricanes of blood and shattered glass, lightning the color of infection, the cities of the not-quite-dead finally become the cities of stumbling, undying corpses, plagues without names or reason or ends, plagues to rot away the molten core of the world.

Mount we unto the sky.
I am sick, I must die.
Lord, have mercy on us.

And Spyder—too pure to be real, too pure to believe— the only still point in the storm, and she made him the offer that she always makes. Sanctuary in her tattooed arms, in the silken snare folds of her soul, and all he has to do is stand beside her at the end. *And all this will be yours, all this and more.* Sleep without nightmares, forgetfulness and days without fear, a Heaven far from this wasted earth, and he only has to see that no one and nothing tries to interfere. She's never even asked him to face the Dragon, her Preacher Man, the idiot devil that she's dragged with her from one universe to another. Walter only has to take her hand and be there with Theda, in the basement on Cullom Street, when the moment comes.

The world shall burn, and from her ashes spring
New Heaven and Earth, wherein the just shall dwell . . .

No, not *this* earth. This earth shall only burn and then the ashes lie cold and undisturbed another five or six billion years, until a dying, supernova sun at last swallows the planet whole. She's never made a secret of that, has never tried to hide from him the destruction of *this* earth. *It's lost anyway,* she says. *It's never been anything else. You know I'm telling you the truth, Walter.*

And he *does* know, has known that all along, and some days it seems to matter, and other days it doesn't make any difference at all.

"I have to take a piss," Archer says.

"So, who's stopping you?" and she grumbles something about Theda, something he's heard so many times that the exact words don't matter anymore.

"I said I'll deal with Theda. It's my turn."

"Why does she always have to build her filthy little nests in the goddamn bathrooms," Archer says.

I can't do it without you, Spyder said, just like she's been saying all along, because of the three who went down and came back up again, he's the only one left alive, the only one who didn't die that long-ago November. Her crooked line back to *this* place, and for that reason alone he should have put a bullet through his skull. And maybe he would have, if Archer Day hadn't come along to show him that he wasn't insane, to show him that he still had a choice.

The first time I saw her, he thinks. *The very first time. Jesus, that's been almost four years,* and for a moment that's enough to drive back even the things that Spyder Baxter has let him see. A cheated dragon's wrath, the cities of gray ash, black skies and dead seas gone to pus and acid—*all* of it pale and insignificant against the moment Archer stepped out of the smoke and shadows of a North Hollywood bar. "I know your name," she said, her voice like honey and heroin and the morning after a stormy night. "I know everything you think no one else could ever know."

Never an easier or more immediate seduction, and he ordered her a whiskey, and then sat and listened while she told him about the coming of the Weaver and the prophesied arrival of the Hierophant, about the Dragon and its jackals, all her impossible, true tales of a flat land of vast granite spokes and basalt wheels where oceans drained off into an unfathomable abyss.

And he knew that it was true, all of it, because Spyder had already shown him every one of those things and more. But still he had to ask the question, how *she* could know, how these facts had come to her, and for a while Archer sat staring silently at the dirty barroom floor. When she finally answered him, there were tears in her eyes, and he didn't ask her anything else. They'd gone back to his room in an East L.A. flophouse, and she slept in his arms.

It was the first time in his life he hadn't slept alone.

"I have to piss *now*," she says, and Walter opens his eyes. They still sting and burn, no matter how much he sleeps or how many bottles of Visine and Murine he empties into them.

"I'm not stopping you," he says again.

"Just fucking take care of it, Walter."

And he marvels that this last day should be so much like all the others leading up to it, that it isn't marked by a merciful freedom from mundane annoyances and everyday crap. There should be something different, like a condemned man's final meal, whatever his heart desires, instead of the usual routine of bread and water, something to make this day special, *besides* the gas chamber or electric chair waiting at the end of that long, last walk. And then Walter gets up and goes to take care of it.

After the doctor—an apprehensive man with a black leather satchel and wire-rimmed spectacles—carefully removes the old dressing and lances the swelling on Niki's right palm, after a steaming cup of sweet black tea for the pain and an herbal poultice packed deep into the wound, then a fresh dressing, and after *all* this they finally let her rest. She lies beneath white cotton sheets and a quilt that only smells faintly musty and watches the orange-blue flame of an oil lamp sitting on a chest of drawers near the bed, the flame trapped safe inside its glass chimney, and she listens to Spyder and the doctor and the wind around the eaves of the house. *Maybe I'm so tired I won't be able to sleep,* she thinks, but then the room and the whispering voices and the wind slip away, and for a long time there's nothing else at all.

And she dreams of Esme Chattox, floating weightless in waters that will never see the sun, her crimson gills like living bellows, fish-skin robes become beautiful Japanese fans of spine and fin and fleshy membrane, and there are yellow-green rows of bioluminescent organs on her breasts and belly. She drifts down, past towering Atlantean ruins, past great stone doors sealed a hundred thousand years, shattered Corinthian columns and sunken temples to gods that have never been named. Esme's long legs become a sinuous tail, and she glides ever deeper, between the grotesque walls of yawning subterranean canyons, until there's no farther down left to go, only a perfectly level plain of gray-black ooze, a desolate landscape for urchins and sea cucumbers and brittle stars. And something else. Something that has lain here more ages than the minds of man can comprehend, tentacles and eyes the size of manhole covers, eyes that burn so brightly they slice the darkness and send even the blindest things scurrying for cover.

And the feverish, wordless prayers from Esme's hyacinth lips, *Mother Hydra, Father Kraken, awake and receive me, Sleeper in the Deep, Dreamer at the Bottom of the World.*

Esme embraces her lover, and it spreads her wide with a dozen suction-cupped arms, as the gray ooze floor of the ocean folds and collapses beneath their weight. And for a time Niki can't see anything through the tempest of silt thundering soundlessly across the boundless azoic wastelands.

And other things, an argument between an anglerfish and an eel, a heretic crustacean counting stars in a night it's never seen, and the silt settling kindly over Niki as the storm subsides and the wish that she could lie there forever, buried and unremembered, and still *other* things, before she begins to rise. Rushing towards the surface, falling towards the sky, as the gas in her bloodstream bubbles out of solution and her aching lungs expand until she's sure that she'll burst, but there's only the briefest, silver pain, and then she's standing on the Bay Bridge again, and the white bird is there, too, perched on the guardrail.

"She has found the philtre," it says, and it takes Niki a moment to remember, to realize that it means "philtre" and not "filter." "But there's so little time. It may already be too late."

"Then I died for nothing?"

"Everyone dies for nothing, Hierophant," the bird squawks. "Why should you be any different?"

"You *know* what I meant, bird."

"The jackals would have had her. They almost did, but they're weak in that world."

"So Daria isn't dead?" Niki asks and looks down at the water shimmering far, far below. The bird flaps its wings and shifts uneasily from foot to foot.

"Not yet," it replies. "But perhaps it's only a matter of time. She still has a long way to go. And there is another danger."

"Daria's strong," Niki says. "She's smart."

"You have no idea what's to come, do you?" the bird asks and hops a few inches farther away from her. "No one is smart enough or strong enough. We fight because we will not die in shame without a fight, but we *will* die, nonetheless."

"I've already jumped," Niki says, and the bird looks up at the low clouds sailing past overhead.

"That depends on when you mean. Some places you've already fallen. Others you haven't. Others you never will."

"Leave me alone, bird," she says, sick of anything it might have to say, and it vanishes in a burst of fire and mossy, sage-scented smoke.

And when Niki turns around—because *this* time she won't jump, this time she'll go back to the hotel on Steuart Street and wait for Daria—she's standing at the edge of a highway beneath a wide blue sky, hot asphalt on one side of her and the brown-green Kansas prairie stretching away on the other. She looks left, looks east, and the truck stop isn't far away, the one that Daria didn't remember, but then she did, she *did* remember, and Niki steps off the blacktop into dry weeds and cacti and over a tangle of rusted barbed wire. A few yards away, there's a young man in a straw cowboy hat and overalls, walking slowly across a place where rain and frost have worn away the soil to expose the chalky earth underneath. He walks with his eyes on the ground, and every now and then he bends down and picks something up, a fossil seashell or a bit of petrified bone, examines it closely before dropping it into the old Folgers coffee can that he's carrying.

And she understands that she's come here, to this when and where, because years later Daria won't have time to reach Kansas, because the jackals will be too close, and they may be weak, but not so weak that they can't kill, that they can't delay. The man stoops down and picks up something that looks a little like a large, wooden spool. He rolls it back and forth in his palm and then turns towards Niki. He smiles when he sees her.

"It's a fish vertebra," he says. "Paleontologists call this fish *Xiphactinus*. Big old fucker, fifteen feet long, if you'll excuse my French."

"What's that there?" Niki asks him, pointing at a metallic glint on the ground, picking her way along the chalk wash until she's standing beside him.

"Hi," he says. "My name's Joe."

"Right there, Joe," Niki says and picks the ball bearing up from the place where it's come to rest in the white-gray-yellow gully. "Look. There's writing on it."

"Damn," he says, taking the ball bearing from her and holding it up to the sun. "N-I-K-I," he says, reading out the letters. "Niki. Now what do you think that means?"

"You never can tell," she replies, and he smiles and puts the fish vertebra and ball bearing into his coffee can.

"Don't lose that, Joe. It's more important than you think," and then Kansas goes away, dissolves like frost on a summer day, and for a while she's nowhere and nowhen at all. It isn't dark, but there's no light, either, and she waits with the whispering ghosts of all the babies trapped in Limbo until she's finally somewhere else again.

Standing in Spyder's old house, almost dark outside and getting cold inside because Spyder never runs the gas heater, and Niki was asleep only a few minutes before. Asleep in Spyder's bed, until she woke up alone and the bedspread was missing. She called for Spyder but no one answered. The stub of a candle flickering on the floor, so it looked even darker outside than it really was, and there was the sound of hammering coming from somewhere in the house.

I got out of bed, Niki thinks, remembering a moment ten years or only a minute before. *I got up and walked from the bedroom to the living room, and I stood where I could see Spyder in the dining room, but she couldn't see me.*

There's the missing bedspread, a huge white crocheted thing stretched trampoline tight and hanging in the air in the next room, the old dining room where no one ever eats, because there's no table and it's full of Spyder's paperback books. Niki can see where two corners of the bedspread have been nailed directly to the wall, big nails driven through the peeling wallpaper, and a third corner stretched over to a leaning bookshelf and held in place with stacks of 1974 *World Book* encyclopedias. The fourth corner is somewhere out of sight, wherever Spyder is, Spyder and her hammer—*blam, blam, blam*—just around the corner, and Niki knows that if she steps out into the middle of the living room she'll be able to see Spyder in there, hammering it to the wall. But she doesn't, because she knows that if Spyder sees her she'll stop what she's doing, and then, then everything would happen differently.

"Oh," Spyder would say, "it's nothing," so Niki stays right where she is and watches and waits.

And then Spyder steps into view, wearing nothing but the black T-shirt she put on after they made love, the shirt she slept in a lot, but never washed, so it always smelled like sweat and patchouli. She's holding a bowling ball, a black bowling ball with scarlet swirls in it, and Niki remembers thinking that it looked like a strange little gas planet in Spyder's hand, the *first* time this happened, an ebony and scarlet Neptune or Uranus. Spyder holds it out over the center of the bedspread and sets it gently in the middle. And the bedspread sags with the weight of the bowling ball, drooping in the center until it's only about a foot or so above the floor, but it doesn't pull loose from the walls or the stack of encyclopedias.

She disappears, and there are toolbox sounds, and when Niki can see her again, Spyder has a fat black marker in her left hand and a yellow yardstick in her right; she leans over the bedspread, measuring distances, drawing carefully spaced dots, then measuring again, black on the white cotton here and there, beginning near the edge and working her way in, towards the sucking weight of the bowling ball. When there are thirty, forty, forty-three dots, she sets the yardstick and the Sharpie down on the floor.

Spyder vanishes again, and this time she comes back with a blue plastic margarine tub filled with ball bearings of different sizes, like steel marbles. She digs around in the tub and selects one, as if only *that* one will do, and places it on the first black mark she drew on the bedspread. The ball bearing makes its own small depression before it begins to roll downhill; Niki hears the distinct clack of steel against epoxy when it hits the bowling ball, a very loud sound in the still, quiet house.

"You're not supposed to be here again," the white bird says, standing on the hardwood floor near her bare feet.

"Shut up," Niki hisses, whispering so Spyder won't hear. "I'm the Hierophant, aren't I? I can go whenever I please."

"No you *can't*," the bird caws indignantly. "That's not the way it works."

"Shut up, bird, before she hears you."

In the dining room, Spyder selects another ball bearing and places it on the next mark—*clack*—and she repeats the action over and over again—*clack, clack, clack*—but never twice from the same mark, choosing each bearing and taking care to be sure that it starts its brief journey towards the center from the next mark in. Sometimes, she pauses between ball bearings, pauses and stares at the bedspread, then out the window, then back at the bedspread. Once or twice she stops long enough to measure the shrinking space between the floor and the bowling ball with her yellow yardstick. Spyder chews at her bottom lip, and there's something urgent, something terrible, in her blue eyes.

Niki's legs are getting tired, just like they did the first time, ten years ago, and she wants to sit down beside the white bird, but she's afraid to move. And she remembers wanting to say, "What the hell are you doing, Spyder?" What anyone else *would* have said right at the start, but then she would never have seen even this much, and so what if it doesn't make sense. That doesn't mean it isn't important, and if Spyder won't tell her what's going on—in her head, in the old house (if there was ever any difference between the two)—all she can do is be patient and watch and try to figure it all out for herself. Like a jigsaw puzzle, like a child's connect-the-dots book. Draw the lines, and there's the picture, Mickey Mouse or a bouquet of flowers or whatever drove Spyder insane.

"You need to leave," the bird says, and Niki wants to kick it.

There aren't many bearings left in the tub, and Spyder has to lean far out over the bedspread to set them on the marks now. There's hardly any time between the instant that she lets go and the clack of metal against hard plastic. The bedspread is almost touching the floor, straining with the weight, and Niki can see where the weave is beginning to unravel. Spyder works fast, as though she's running out of time, and now she holds the last ball bearing, and it reflects the pale November sun getting in through the dining-room window.

"Here," Niki whispers. "Right fucking *here*."

And there's a slow, ripping sound. Spyder grabs something off the floor, and it takes Niki a second to realize, to *remember*, that it's a roll of duct tape. Spyder uses her teeth to tear off a strip, and she's reaching for the rift opening up beneath the bowling ball when the bedspread gives way, spilling everything out the bottom. The bowling ball falls three or four inches to the floor, barely missing Spyder's fingers. Niki feels the vibration where she's standing beside the white bird, watching as the ball bearings spill out and roll away in every direction.

"Fuck me." Spyder sighs, and then she sits silently beneath the ruined bedspread and stares at the hole, the last ball bearing forgotten in her fingers.

One of the silver balls rolls into the living room and bumps to a stop against Niki's foot.

"Don't you *dare* touch that," the bird squawks, but she's already bending over, already picking it up. There's a single word printed on the curved surface of the ball bearing, one word that didn't mean anything at all to Niki then, and still doesn't mean anything now.

"When the Weaver learns what you've done—" the bird says, but before it can finish, she's somewhen else, somewhere the dead sleep, and it's almost Lafayette No. 1 Cemetery, almost New Orleans, except that the milky sky is the color of raw liver. The ancient trees bend low over the graves and mausoleums, and things that were angels lie twisted and broken in the shadows.

"We used to get stoned and sneak into the cemeteries," she says. "We hung out in Lafayette and St. Louis, praying that we'd see a ghost or a vampire. Just a *glimpse* would have been enough. We held séances and left flowers and bottles of wine."

Marvin is bending over one of the fallen angels, wiping blood from its lips, and he turns and looks at her with the white bird's red eyes.

"Did you ever think it would be like this?" he asks.

"No," she replies, "I didn't," and then he leaves the angels and walks with her through the cemetery, past broken headstones and plastic pots of plastic roses and carnations. And when the rain starts, fat drops drumming softly against oak leaves and weathered marble, Niki opens her eyes, and the man named Scarborough Pentecost is sitting in a wicker chair beside the bed, and the oil lantern is still burning brightly on the chest of drawers.

Walter stands in the narrow doorway of the motel bathroom and stares at the cocoon filling up most of the tub, cocoon or nest or fucking web. He has no idea what it really is, what it should be called, and he doesn't care. The thing that Theda makes whenever they've stopped to sleep, the thing she hides inside. There's a thin sheet of sticky silver-white strands leading up the wall to the ceiling, other strands stretching all the way over to the toilet and the sink. The thing in the tub, sheathed in spider silk, is the sickly color of buttermilk, and its sides rise and fall with the steady rhythm of Theda's sleeping breath. Walter looks back at Archer, sitting on the foot of the bed now, watching him as she lights a cigarette, and then he takes another step towards the vaguely girl-shaped thing in the tub. It looks unfinished, and Walter knows that's exactly what it is.

I could burn it now, he thinks. *I could burn it and be done with all this shit.* There are three full cans of kerosene in the trunk of the car—not the purple Ford, but the Chevy they stole before Birmingham, after the shitstorm at the convenience store—kerosene and the two thermite grenades he bought off a small-time arms dealer in Boston. Walter imagines the flames, Theda's chrysalis shell turning black, her body boiling inside there until the dying husk splits apart.

And then there would be no more indecision, no more waffling and deception, because the deed would be done, and Spyder Baxter and the fucking Dragon and Archer Day would know exactly what his intentions were. *He* would know what his intentions are, finally, and with the surrogate dead, the Hierophant could spend the rest of eternity trying to open the gate, and she might as well try putting out the fires of Hell with a two-liter bottle of soda water and a pail of sand.

"I'm not fucking kidding, Walter," Archer says. "I have to piss. Get her out of there."

"Why haven't we killed her?" he asks, standing at the very edge of the tub now, forcing himself not to look away from the pulsating mass of the cocoon. This close, he can see three or four female black widows, dangling from the silk like strange and deadly berries.

"She's going to hear you," Archer says.

"She can't hear me."

"You don't *know* what she can and can't hear when she's like that."

"But wouldn't that end it, killing her, I mean? Then there'd be no point in even going to the house," and Walter squats down beside the tub and presses the fingers of his right hand against the rough form of Theda's left breast. Like some half-formed waxwork, this abomination sleeping in its cold, porcelain bed, and it's never as soft to the touch as he expects it to be.

"We can't move too soon," Archer replies. "Everything has to be timed to the second. And you already fucking well know that, and I'm about to piss this bed, so please get her the hell *out of there*."

"Yeah," he says and pulls his hand back when one of the black widows crawls a little too close for comfort. "Get her out of there."

"It's not too late for you to screw this up," Archer says and exhales, smoke from her lips and nostrils, and maybe *she's* the only real dragon, he thinks. "You said you had the balls to see it through. All the way, that's what you said. I looked into your eyes and thought I saw that much courage in you."

Walter doesn't take the bait, far too little time left to bother squabbling with her. He presses his fingertips hard against the smooth place where Theda's face should be, and this time the cocoon splits, a vertical slit to reveal her right cheek, her mouth and chin, and suddenly the air in the bathroom stinks of rotting peaches.

"Come on, Sleeping Beauty," he says, peeling back enough of the gummy, fibrous material that he can see her right eye and most of her forehead. "Wake up, Theda. It's fucking showtime."

And then that single eye opens wide, almost all pupil at first, empty and hungry and glaring hatefully up at him. Walter jerks his hand away again as her lips part and a trickle of alabaster fluid leaks from the corners of her mouth. He stands up and steps back from the tub, because he knows that Theda can do the rest for herself. She coughs and more of the blue-white fluid drains from her lips.

"Come on, little girl. The old woman out there has to take a leak."

"Fuck you, asshole," Theda gurgles and shows him her teeth, so Walter kicks the side of the bathtub as hard as he dares; Theda's cocoon splits open a little more, and the rotten-peach smell grows even stronger than before.

"You better watch yourself, little girl," Walter warns her. "One day you might not be so goddamned indispensable anymore."

"Hey, fuck *both* of you," Archer growls, and she gets up off the bed, reaching for her jeans and sweater draped across the back of a chair. "There's a fucking gas station down the street. When I get back here, the two of you better have your shit together."

And he wishes that she wouldn't go, because he doesn't want to be alone with Theda, doesn't want to be alone in the motel room while the day winds down, and the shadows grow longer, and the girl they found in Stonington Cemetery slowly tears herself free of the tub. But he's not about to ask Archer to stay, because she knows too much about him already, too many soft underbellies revealed, and, besides, she wouldn't stay, anyway. He leaves the bathroom and sits on the bed, watching her dress and trying not to hear the sounds that Theda's making.

"We've only got about an hour and a half until sunset," Archer says, pulling her raveling cable-knit sweater on over her head, then fishing her long hair out of the collar. "After dark, we might not have a lot of time to spare."

"Take your gun," Walter tells her, and he reaches for the pack of cigarettes she's left lying on the bed.

"Yeah. Just get her out of there, okay?"

And then their eyes meet, not something that happens as often as it once did, and for a long moment all the secrets they've shared and the secrets they will always keep from each other hang heavy between them.

"I haven't come all this way to fail," she says and turns away. The first one to blink, and she steps into her jeans, left foot first, then right, trying to hide the doubt she wears like a murdered albatross around her neck, the misgiving he sees every time he looks at her. "I didn't choose exile just so I could watch the Weaver's handiwork from this side of the goddamned gate."

"Be careful."

"Clean her up, Walter. I'll be back in fifteen minutes," and she hands him the rest of her cigarette.

"Just be careful," he says again, and then Archer Day leaves the motel room without another word, shoes in one hand and her leather wallet in the other, her .38 hidden beneath the bulky sweater. And he sits on the bed while the monster dressed up in a girl's skin sits in the bathtub, talking to herself and picking spiders from her hair.

"Have yourself a good little nap, Vietnam?" Scarborough asks, and Niki looks up at him and the oil lamp on the chest of drawers, and then she rolls over so she can see the small stained-glass window on the other side of the bed. Shards of orchid and sapphire, cobalt and chartreuse, stitched together with lead solder to make some flower that she's never seen before. The glass is dark, the design difficult to discern, no sunlight to bleed through the window and set the colors ablaze, and so she knows that it must still be night, or night again, and she's slept through an entire day.

"How long have I been asleep?" she asks.

"Just a few hours," Scarborough replies, and the chair creaks when he shifts his weight.

"But it's still night—"

"You'll get used to that after a while. Long nights, longer days. You'll adjust."

"Where's Spyder?"

"So, how you feelin', Vietnam? The doc, he said the wooziness should pass."

"I asked you where Spyder is, and please stop calling me that."

Scarborough Pentecost leans back in his chair, lifts the front legs off the floor, and rubs at the side of his nose. "Stop calling you what?" he asks.

"Vietnam. My name's Niki."

"All I've heard anyone call you is Hierophant, and I figured just about anything would be better than that. And Vietnam isn't so bad. There was this great bar in Nah Trang, the Truc Linh—"

"I've never been to Vietnam," Niki says, lying down again because she's too dizzy to sit up any longer. "I'm from New Orleans."

"Is that so?" and Scarborough leans forward so that the front legs of his chair bump loudly against the floor. "I'm from Boston, myself. But I spent a little time in New Orleans, on business."

"So how did *you* get here?"

"Long story," he replies. "Wrong place, wrong time."

"Scarborough, where's Spyder?"

"The Weaver," he says and thoughtfully rubs at his nose again. "Right, well, she's with Esme, down on the rampart above the eastern docks. I wouldn't expect them back anytime soon. A warship showed up a couple of hours ago and dropped anchor in the harbor."

"A *war*ship," Niki says, and she looks fretfully back at the darkened stained-glass window again.

"I get the impression you don't really know what's what around here, Niki, or what sort of hornet's nest you've been plunked down in."

"I don't even know where *here* is."

"Are you hungry? Eponine always has a big pot of something on the fire. Her cooking's not half bad, most days, if you don't mind the taste."

"Thanks, but maybe later. I need to talk to Spyder."

Scarborough Pentecost stands, and now he's looking at the stained-glass window, too. His face is filled with a hundred thoughts that Niki can't read, things that she can only guess at, but she guesses that he's afraid and tired of being afraid.

"It's probably going to be a while before you see her again," he says. "She told me to tell you that."

"That figures," Niki whispers. "She just *left* me here?"

"You're to stay put, Vietnam, unless this thing with the ship gets too hairy, and then I have orders to take you and head for Auber and don't look back."

"And where's Auber?" Niki asks him. She vaguely remembers hearing the name passed between Spyder and the fish augur, Auber and a Madame Tirzah, but it's only a word without meaning, two syllables signifying nothing at all. She thinks about shutting her eyes and going back to sleep.

"It's a city, a city on dry land, mind you, about three hundred kilometers northeast of here."

"And how are we supposed to *get* there?"

"There's a boat waiting for us. With a little luck, we'll slip out of Padnée right under their noses."

"Padnée? Is that the name of this place?"

Scarborough walks over to the window and opens it, cranks a brass handle and the pane slides up a foot or so, letting in cool night air and the faint smell of saltwater. "You're starting to get that not-in-Kansas-anymore feeling, aren't you, Vietnam? Maybe Narnia or Earthsea or Oz, but definitely *not* Kansas."

"I told you, my name's Niki," she says and sits up, moving slowly because she doesn't have the strength to move fast; her head aches like she's been drunk for at least a week.

"Hell, you were lucky. I woke up at the Palisades all by my lonesome. Spent fucking *days* wandering through those rocks before I found the road to Padnée."

"Did you jump off a bridge, too?" Niki asks, and he shakes his head.

"No, some stupid son of a bitch who didn't know a gun from his dick put a bullet in my head," and Scarborough makes a pistol with thumb and index finger and thumps himself smartly between the eyes. "Like I said, it's a long story."

Niki puts her pillow behind her back, and when she

stops moving around the dizziness begins to subside again. "Are there a lot of us here?" she asks. "I mean, people who died *there* and wound up *here*."

"I don't think so," Scarborough says, kneels next to the open window and stares out across the rooftops towards the sea. "Just me and you, so far as I know, and the Weaver. But I'm not exactly sure she counts."

"Why not? Why wouldn't she?"

"She's some serious mojo, that one. Sometimes, I think she's almost as bad as the fucking Dragon, and we just haven't figured it out yet. And, what's more, Esme says she didn't have to die to get here."

"Why's that ship in the harbor?"

"Looking for your sweet little brown ass, Vietnam. Now maybe you should stop asking so many damn questions and get some more rest. If the word comes to move, you're going to need all the strength you've got. The doc said that hand of yours was pretty bad."

"Why would they be looking for me? What have I done?"

Scarborough turns away from the window and smiles at her. " 'Cause you're the goddamn Hierophant, that's why. And around here, that makes you one part Jesus Christ, one part hydrogen bomb. You and that philtre, you're the Dragon's worst nightmare."

Niki sighs and stares down at her hands, the right bandaged snugly in fresh white cloth. "I don't have the philtre, and even if I did, I wouldn't know what I'm supposed to do with it."

"You might know that, and I might know that, but the Dragon, all he knows is you've come to drive him out, send him packing."

"I have?" Niki asks, and she makes a tight, painful fist with her right hand.

"That seems to be the case," and then there's a rumble like thunder, and the whole house shudders around them. Scarborough curses and cranks the window shut again. "Well, Vietnam, that would be our cue. The fuckers just opened fire on the rampart, and I bet there's a landing party on the way. Do you think you can walk?"

"Yeah," she says, "sure," though it's a lie, and he brings her clean clothes and her boots, and helps her dress while the warship's cannons roar and pound the walls of bone.

Archer Day keeps her eyes on the sidewalk as she retraces the two blocks back to the motel, that squalid box for whores and junkies and drifters. Above her, the pale November sky is as bleak and unfamiliar as this whole goddamn city. Birmingham's no uglier than most of the cities she's seen here, but there's something different about it, something worse, like a fat green worm burrowing inside a shriveled apple, or a malignant tumor hiding beneath malformed flesh. Something past black and mean coiled at the soul of this city, and seeing it, *feeling* it, makes her more homesick than she's been since leaving the world where she was born. More weight to stand beside the knowledge that, no matter how the coming night plays out, whether she fails or succeeds, she can never go back; more weight that she might question the sacrifice she never thought to doubt until it was too late to change her mind. And maybe that's always the way with martyrs, she thinks. Everything noble and glorious until your head's on the block or the rope's drawing tight around your throat.

In the weathered concrete at her feet, there are faint impressions of leaves and pigeon tracks, frozen like the moment she let the red witches in Nesmia Shar lay their salt circles round her and mark her naked body with runes painted with the blood of innocents and beasts. It seems unthinkable that could be only four years past, her exit, the moment when the witches' chant of discharge reached its pounding crescendo and the priestess pressed the obsidian blade of a dagger against Archer's throat.

Only four short years, but it might as well have been her entire lifetime and all that *other* time, that other *world,* never anything more than a hazy, half-remembered dream.

On this day, in this haunted Southern city, she might only be a lunatic choking on false memories.

"Lose yourself, wanderer," the priestess whispered in her ear. "Forget everything but your quest, and your pain will be diminished."

And now, looking at the squalor spread out around her—cement walls and abandoned brick ruins, rusted, disused train tracks sprouting sickly weeds between their ties and the trash littering the streets—she knows that she *is* losing herself. The fabric of her being dissolved bit by bit in the acid dissolution of *this* place. *I am to die for this,* she thinks bitterly and kicks at a crumpled Taco Bell cup. *How many people* born *here would lift a finger to save it, and I'm supposed to die for it.*

"You are brave, daughter, and you will shame us all with your forfeiture," the priestess said, those words in the same instant that Archer felt the blade of cold volcanic glass break her skin, that first warm trickle down her neck. "Always, you will be remembered."

One meager life traded for an entire universe, that was the bargain, and, as Walter often says, it seemed like a good idea at the time. The wide-eyed acolyte of the red witches in their towers on the river Yärin and, in those days, she believed with a faith that she cannot now even imagine.

"Someone has to stop the Weaver, or a world and all its life and beauty will die," and Archer hadn't even thought twice before adding her name to the lottery that would determine who would make the passage. A child with a head full of holy duty and naivete dressed up as courage.

The trickle of blood pooling between her breasts, the seep before the hot flood. "The White Road lies before us all," the priestess said, "and the gods will know you by your deeds." And then she cut Archer's throat from ear to ear, and her life sprayed out onto the temple floor, and her loosed soul spilled out *into* something else.

And she was across.

She found the man named Walter exactly where they'd said she would, not sane, because no one touched by the

Weaver can remain sane, but not a lunatic, either, and she told him the things he'd been waiting so long to hear, and together they'd begun hunting for the surrogate. Walking the witches' White Road and even then, even after the rapture of death and the horrors of resurrection, even after her first appalling view of this wilting Earth, even *then*, she still believed. But as the short days and shorter nights rolled over her, as she saw deeper into consequence and desperation, and they finally found the abominable child who thought she'd been chosen by a protecting angel—the child she and Walter had both lied to so that Theda would *continue* to believe that deceit—as this place soaked in through her skin, Archer Day began to see. And that sight led her quickly to regret, and now there are mornings and nights when she thinks this world and the Dragon deserve one another, that maybe the cataclysm the witches have sent her here to forestall is only simple fate.

She has sat in motel rooms in Chicago and Manhattan, in Boston and Pittsburgh, and imagined city skylines set ablaze and the sun hidden behind black sulphurous clouds. *It would be a mercy,* she's thought, again and again. *It would only end their miseries.*

"You will be tempted to turn from the Road," the priestess in the high tower above the wide green waters of Yärin warned her. "Truth will seem as lies, and lies will take the place of truth."

Archer knows that either she's weak or the priestess was a pompous old fool.

She looks up from the sidewalk fossils, and there's a great fire-colored wolf crouched only a few yards ahead of her, blocking the way back to the motel. It curls its black lips to show her yellowed canines as long as her fingers. The hair along the massive hump of its shoulders stands on end, raised hackles to tell her not to move another inch, and a taunting growl begins somewhere deep in its throat. The wolf's eyes are as colorless as ice, and its breath steams in the late afternoon air.

"Harlot," it snarls, and Archer reaches for the .38 tucked into the waistband of her jeans, moving as slowly as she can, as quickly as she dares. "I *know* you, witchling whore. You have come all the way here to do my master's work. He will *smile* on you for your services."

"You don't know me, demon," Archer tells it. "And I am nothing of your master's."

"He will make you *his* whore, when the Weaver is undone. He may even show you the way home."

"Liar," she whispers, her hand closing tightly around the butt of the pistol.

"That's all you want, child. He *knows* that. I know that, too. I *smell* it on you, that longing," and the fire-colored wolf flares its nostrils.

"Liar," she says again. "All you are is lies."

"Soon, witchling, lies will be the only comfort left to you. You should learn to treasure them."

Archer draws the gun and aims it at the wolf's broad skull. It laughs at her and takes a step closer.

"What are you still fighting for, *apostate*? You've despaired. There's no quest left in *you*."

"Then I'm fighting for myself," Archer replies, and a delivery truck rumbles past, oblivious of the monster on the sidewalk. "If that's all I have left, then that's what I'm fighting for."

"An *admirable* purpose. Do your gods know this?"

Her index finger tightens on the trigger, and the wolf smiles and raises its enormous head, baring its throat to her.

"If you still *had* the courage, would I die, do you think?" it asks.

"Why don't we just find out, puppy dog," Archer says, trying too hard to sound brave, too hard to sound like fear's the very last thing she could even comprehend, when her hands are shaking and she can smell the piss running down the insides of her thighs.

"You're catching on, witchling," the wolf growls. "But don't catch on too *slowly*," and it lowers its head again.

"There's no shame in being a puppet. Not if the right person's pulling the strings."

And then the wolf is gone, and there's only the sidewalk and the crushed Taco Bell cup, the wind and a few dry brown leaves rustling hurriedly past. Archer Day sits down on the curb, the revolver cradled in her lap, and cries until her head hurts and she can't cry anymore.

After Niki has put on the clean, dry clothes laid out for her by Eponine Chattox—a pair of gray wool pants and a teal-green blouse and vest, a thick pair of wool socks, and her own boots, blue fur coat, and backpack—Scarborough Pentecost leads her quickly through the empty house, along the mustard hallway and past the thing that's almost a grandfather clock, and then back down the spiral staircase to the fish augur's chamber of nets and aquariums and pools of ink black seawater. Far overhead, cannon fire booms again and again, and the vaulted, liquid walls of the chamber ripple from the force of the blasts.

"Are they going to destroy the city?" Niki asks, looking worriedly back at the iron staircase dimly illuminated by the candelabrum.

"Certainly sounds that way, doesn't it?"

The next explosion seems much closer than any of those before it, and the concussion rattles the high shelves all around them. Several large jars tumble to the floor and burst, tainting the fish- and mold-scented air with the reek of alcohol.

"Either those assholes are getting lucky," Scarborough grimaces and steadies the nearest shelf, "or they've figured out where you are, Vietnam."

"I should be with Spyder," Niki says.

"That's exactly the last place you should be."

And there's another explosion, not so close as the last, but the candelabrum sways like a pendulum, throwing dizzying chartreuse shadows across the chamber.

"That old conjure eel's hocus-pocus can't hold this place

together for fucking ever," Scarborough says. "One more good hit and we'll be swimming with the fishies."

"If I tried to go back, to find my way to Spyder, would you stop me?" Niki asks and, for an answer, Scarborough grabs her roughly by the collar of her coat.

"Listen here. Odds are we'll both be dead in a little while, anyway, so why don't you just shut up about the Weaver and do as you're told."

"Let *go* of me," Niki snarls, and Scarborough brusquely exchanges his hold on her collar for an even firmer grip around the wrist of her good hand. He hauls her stumbling and cursing forward, between the aisles of teetering shelves and falling books, a thousand rattling, sloshing jars of pickled sea things, the rows of stoppered vials and flasks filled with powders and potions, great pyramid stacks of oyster, ammonite, and nautilus shells. They pass the stone dais and Esme's lectern, and then the next explosion throws them both to their hands and knees. The walls of the chamber bulge and roll as shelves collapse and come down, one after the next. The candelabrum groans under its own weight, a cacophony of creaking chains, rivets and welds strained beyond their limits, and finally tears free from the ceiling, plunging the chamber into near darkness.

"Jesus, Joseph, and Mary," Scarborough mutters to himself and coughs, as dust and the pungent, acrid stench of the contents of all the shattered jars and vials settles over them. "You dead over there, Vietnam?"

"I don't think so," Niki replies, mumbling through her fingers, through the mask she's made with her left hand, and then she starts coughing, too.

"Look, we have to get out of here. I think that last one got the house."

Niki squints through the haze and the gloom, the dust and noxious fumes stinging her eyes, and tries to imagine where there might possibly be left to run.

"What about Eponine?" she asks, and then Scarborough

has her by the collar of her coat again and drags her to her feet.

"Eponine Chattox *isn't* my problem," he says. "Right now, the only problem I've got is you," and he leads Niki through, around, and over the wreckage of metal and glass and splintered wood that the cannons have made of the fish augur's chamber. She glances up at the walls and ceiling, and even in the shifting half-light filtering down through the sea and up from the dying remains of the glowing things from the candelabrum, she can see that they're contracting, and the sea is closing in around them.

"It's getting smaller," she says.

"*What's* getting smaller?" Scarborough asks, pushing aside a heavy oak table obstructing their path, and she points at the ceiling.

"Yeah, I was wondering when you were going to notice that."

"We're going to drown down here, aren't we?"

"That depends on how well you can swim," Scarborough replies, and Niki nods her head and thinks about what Spyder said back on the catwalk leading from the Palisades to the gates of Padnée, that there might be other worlds waiting just beneath this one, and she wonders how many times she'll have to drown before she finds the bottom.

"Please, Vietnam, tell me you *can* swim."

"It's been a while. But that's not the sort of thing you forget, is it?"

"Let's hope not," Scarborough replies, and Niki can see that they've come to the edge of one of the open pools in the floor, not far from the shimmering, steadily advancing wall of the chamber. A large fishing net, studded with cork floats and steel hooks and lobster pots, has fallen across the pool, completely covering it. Scarborough curses, takes a long knife from his belt, and begins sawing at the heavy jute mesh.

"You mean we're going to try and *swim* out of here?" Niki asks him, incredulous, unable to look away from the vertical slab of ocean inching towards them like some sci-fi movie special effect, swallowing everything in its path.

"That's the general idea, unless you've got a better one you're not sharing."

"But . . . Jesus, we must be at least a hundred feet down. There's no way—"

"Two hundred and thirty-three feet," Scarborough says, correcting her as he slices cleanly through one thick, braided strand of the net and starts on another.

"Then why don't we just stand here and wait for *that*?" Niki asks and motions towards the chamber wall, no more than twenty or thirty yards away from them now and gathering speed. "Why even bother with the net?"

"Because things ain't always necessarily what they seem to be. It's all just doors in a hallway."

"What the hell's that supposed to mean?" but this time he doesn't answer her, just shakes his head and cuts through another strand of the net. Niki's ears have begun to ache and ring, and she can feel the pressure pushing painfully at her eyes and temples as Esme's bubble shrinks around them, compacting all the air trapped inside it. *So maybe we won't drown, after all,* she thinks. *Maybe we'll be crushed flat before the water ever reaches us, before we even get our feet wet.* And she can't be certain, but she's pretty sure that drowning would be preferable. She covers her ears with her hands and wants to close her eyes, too, wants to curl into a tight, fetal ball, leaving no weak spots for the air to force its way inside her. But Niki doesn't move, and she doesn't take her eyes off the towering, fluid wall of the chamber.

"Scarborough, it's *coming*. It's coming *now*!"

"Take a couple of deep breaths," he says. "Deep, *deep* fucking breaths," and he locks one arm tight about Niki's waist, pulling her down and through the hole he's hacked in the fishing net. The water that closes around her is so cold it instantly drives the air from her lungs, a sudden, silver rush across her trembling lips, as unseen icicle teeth stab her flesh and frost blooms sharp beneath her skin.

And either she's sinking to the bottom, or rising towards

the surface, but there's no way to tell which, down from up
or up from down. In the cold and the dark, in the pain and
the numbness waiting just behind the pain, it hardly seems
to matter.

*There's a hole in the bottom of the sea, there's a hole in the
bottom of the sea, there's a hole, there's a hole . . .*

Like the moment she and Spyder stepped off the bridge
above the bay and there was nothing there to catch her.

Dancing in the deepest oceans
Twisting in the water

Like the hollow place in her soul where Daria used to
be, and all her days alone in the big house on Alamo
Square, and Ophelia hung above her bed.

She's gone where the goblins go
Below—below—below

And Niki Ky lets go, letting go *again,* and it seems she's
always letting go; she opens her eyes on a blackness so absolute she's sure the sight of it has blinded her forever, and
she waits to die, or simply pierce the world hidden beneath
this one.

Hardly ten minutes from the motel on Fifth Avenue,
south and east to the old house at the end of Cullom
Street, but Walter had to down the better part of a pint of
George Dickel and three Valium just to make the drive.
Only ten minutes from *there* to *there,* but a ruined decade
as well, and what seems like a century of nightmares.

He keeps his eyes on the road—the white and yellow dividing lines, the stop signs and traffic lights and goose-
necked sodium-arc streetlamps that remind him of the
Martian invaders from *The War of the Worlds*—and he
tries not to listen to Theda babbling in the backseat about
Spyder Baxter and seraphim and fallen angels, or to the
brooding silence wrapped about Archer Day like an invisible caul. His palms sweat on the steering wheel, slick skin
against fake leather, as he steers the stolen Chevy through
the angular maze of South Side streets—past the stark
brick and concrete edifice of UAB, Eleventh Street South

to Sixteenth Avenue South, and finally he's turning onto Cullom, and the road rises up to meet the weathered limestone flanks of Red Mountain.

And Walter realizes that Archer's started mumbling something to herself in a language he doesn't understand. He guesses it's a prayer or incantation and hopes there's someone, some*thing,* somewhere, listening to whatever the hell she's saying.

"*Almost* time," Theda says, excited, eager, joyful, and Walter knows that she isn't speaking to him, and she isn't speaking to Archer, either. Lately, the girl spends most of her time talking to the spiders, the black widows and recluses and wolf spiders that grow in all the sticky, empty places inside her body. "We're so close now, babies, we're so very, very *close,*" she whispers to them.

"Tell me, Theda," Walter says and licks his dry lips, wishing he had the rest of the bottle of Dickel, "exactly what do you think you'll see when we get there?"

"*She'll* be there," Theda replies immediately, her voice become a jittery, bubbling tapestry of expectation and defiance. "The Weaver will be there, of course, to throw open the shuttered doors for us. And the *benad hasche,* Queen of Heaven, and Mordad, the Angel of Death, will stand beside her, and Shekinah will raise her flaming white sword, and the Grigori will rise from Hell to destroy the hunters of the Nephilim."

"Well, you just keep thinking those happy thoughts back there," Walter tells her, slowing down now because there's only a little way left to go, and he wants to make it last. The Chevrolet rolls through the blustery November night, past once-grand Victorian homes, their windows boarded up and roofs sagging with the weight of decay and neglect, flower gardens and front lawns lost to weeds and kudzu vines. He turns to Archer and nods towards the backseat.

"Our prodigy has it all figured out," he says, and a bead of sweat runs down his forehead into his left eye.

Archer shuts her eyes for a moment, then opens them and "Every world has gods and angels and demons," she says indifferently, staring vacantly out the window. "But their names mean nothing, Walter, nothing at all. Not if they cannot hear you, or have chosen not to listen. If their prophets are only fools and madmen."

"Which are we?"

"Which do you think?" she asks and starts chanting again.

And the truth is that he's spent years trying *not* to think about it. The three of them might be traveling in the same car through the same night, heading together towards some semblance of the same end, their fates interlocked like jigsaw fragments, but he has no doubt that they each have their own private motivations. Theda's worn right there on her sleeve, Archer's held close to her chest despite the things she's said and all that she's promised him. And his own not much more than a wish to finish something he never meant to start.

But I was the one who brought them the peyote, he thinks, *and none of this would ever have happened without me.* And that's true, Walter at twenty-two, the candyman for Spyder's fucked-up coterie of goths and outcasts, bringing them whatever he could score to win his way deeper and deeper into the group. A bag of weed, a few tabs of acid, a bottle of absinthe, a brick of hash, whatever came his way, but the peyote buttons had been something else, something special. Something that Robin had been wanting for a long, long time, and if she'd never gotten them, if he'd never *given* them to her, if he could take back that *one* simple exchange, the cash he handed over for a brown paper bag of dried cactus—change that one action and a different life would have been laid out before them all.

Change that one thing and Robin might still be alive.

"Did you love her?" Archer asked him once, not long after they met, at the end of a long night of sex and conversation.

"Does anybody really fall in love at twenty-one?" he replied, and she looked at him like she had no idea what he was talking about.

"In this place, you all seem determined to stay children

forever," she said, finally, and there was really no way he could disagree with that.

And then the road ends, and there's the house, waiting for him all this time, crouched beneath the limbs of the ancient live oaks and pecan trees, and Walter pulls to a stop at the edge of the driveway and shuts off the headlights.

"That's it?" Archer asks him, expectant and maybe disappointed, too, and he nods his head very slowly.

"Fuck," Theda whispers from the backseat. "It's fucking beautiful," and Walter wants to turn around and punch her in the face.

"It's just an ugly old house," he says instead, loading the words with as much hatred and anger as he dares, enough so there's no doubt in Theda's mind how he feels about the place. "It's an evil old house where terrible things have happened. There's nothing beautiful about it, and there never fucking was."

"Maybe you're not seeing the same house she is," Archer suggests unhelpfully, and "Yeah," Theda says. "Maybe you're not seeing the same house at all."

"I'm seeing the only house there is to see," he replies and cuts the motor. The Chevy sputters and in another second the night is silent, save the cold wind rattling the dry leaves in the trees. The house is in a lot better shape than he thought it would be, all but tumbledown the last time he was here, back when it was still just Spyder's house, the November that Robin died. Someone's painted it once or twice since then, and maybe there's a new roof, too, though it looks as if nobody's lived here in a while. All the windows are dark, and the wide front porch, which Spyder always kept heaped with all sorts of junk and garbage—a broken-down Norton motorcycle that she never could get running and an old washing machine, bits of bicycles and car parts and other rusting, unidentifiable machineries—is bare except for ankle-deep drifts of fallen leaves. It hardly looks worthy of the apocalypse brewing in its bowels.

"Are we just gonna sit here or what?" Theda asks, and Archer sighs and laughs softly to herself.

"There's plenty of time," she says. "Don't be so eager for what you can't avoid. It's coming."

It's coming, Walter thinks, and at least he knows that's absolutely fucking true. This last night when the scraps of his life will finally burn themselves out and, one way or another, *it's coming,* and that will be the end. The house, a squat and secret thing, bitter whitewashed walls and windows looking in on an insane soul, watches him, and he knows the house has been waiting for that end, as well. The white columns round the porch like the confining bars of a cell, or pine-lumber teeth sharpened by so much time and spite, and his end will also be the end of this rotten, cursed place.

Are we ready to die? he asks the house. *Are we ready to put it all to rest?*

Are we ready to dance?

"Okay. *Fuck* this shit," Theda grumbles, and then her door is open, and she's climbing out of the car, letting in the clean, spicy smells of the fall night, the fainter, sour undercurrent of disintegration. "You two can sit here all night long for all I care, but I didn't come all the way from fucking Connecticut to just sit in the goddamn dark and *look* at it."

"Should I stop her?" Walter asks Archer and reaches for his door handle, but Theda's already halfway to the porch.

"No. Let her go. It won't make any difference, and I'm tired of listening to her."

Walter takes a deep breath and lets it out very slowly, then leans back in his seat and stares at the ceiling of the car.

"It'll be over before you even know it," Archer says.

"And you really think this is going to work?"

Archer glances at him, her eyes distant and unreadable, and then she turns back towards the house. "Without the surrogate on this side, the Weaver can't effect the congruence. She has to stand on both sides of the gate simultaneously, which she can't do, so she has to have Theda here to act as her contralateral proxy. If Theda dies—"

"—the doors stay shut."

"Yes," Archer says and takes out a cigarette, but doesn't light it. "If Theda dies, the doors stay shut."

"And if we destroy the house, if we burn it to the ground, it won't do Spyder any good to find another surrogate. You're sure of that?"

"This house is the Weaver's nexus in your world. She can't create another. She can only reenter from the place she exited."

"Because this is where her father fucking raped her."

"Because that's the way it works. Walter, we've been over all this shit more times than I can remember," Archer says, and she stares at the cigarette a moment and then slips it behind her right ear. "Nothing's any different tonight than it was four years ago."

"Except we're actually *here*. I'd almost rather put a bullet in my head than go back down to that fucking basement."

"It'll be over before you even know it," Archer says again and opens her door. "Now pull yourself together. We don't know how much time we have. We don't even know whether or not the Hierophant has the philtre. We may only get one shot at this."

"I guess we're lucky no one's living here," he says.

"It wouldn't have made much difference. It wouldn't have changed what we have to do, or where we have to be to get it done."

"I'm right behind you," he says as she slips out of the Chevy and slams the door shut behind her. For a second or two, he's alone in the car, alone with his ghosts and visions and that house trying to stare him down or inviting him in, and he wonders how it might go if he started the car again and simply drove away. Drove straight to the interstate and kept on driving until he was somewhere so far away that she'd never find him again. There's nothing here that Archer can't do on her own. She's a big girl, after all, a big girl with secrets and powers he'll never begin to grasp, and he's nothing but a crazy man with a gun.

Run like I ran the first time, he thinks, and *Look where that got me.*

Just past the row of low, stunted shrubbery dividing the front yard from the street, Archer has stopped and is looking back at the car, looking straight back through the night and the windshield at Walter, her brown eyes poisoned arrows, and he knows his soul is naked to her. All his fears and doubts and second thoughts laid bare for her, as plain to see as the exposed and beating heart of a vivisection.

"I'm coming," he says, and she glares impatiently back at him with night-bird eyes, cat eyes, eyes much too intent for any human woman's face.

Walter checks the Beretta one last time, and the butterfly knife tucked into his boot, then takes the keys from the ignition and opens the driver's-side door. The night washes over him like memories and old blood, cheap white wine and pot smoke, and he would swear the house is laughing now.

"The sooner we get this over with, the better," Archer says. "There's no telling what she's up to in there."

"Hey, *you're* the one who said to let her go."

"That was almost five minutes ago. Stop stalling," and so he follows her down the narrow, overgrown walkway that leads to the porch, between oleander bushes and honeysuckle vines, and he has to walk fast to keep up with her. He climbs the stairs, and they stand together on the porch, standing inside the maw of the house now, and stare at the open door.

"She's a precocious cunt, isn't she," Walter says, and waves the barrel of his gun at the brass doorknob swathed in spider silk, silk clogging the keyhole, and here he's been planning to just break out a window.

"She'll be in the basement by now," Archer says, and Walter catches the faintest hint of anxiety in her voice, not quite panic, but something that might become panic in just a few more minutes.

"It's right back here," he says, stepping quickly past Archer and across the threshold, letting the house close around him before he can change his mind and run all the way back to the Chevy. But nothing happens, no haunted house clichés waiting for him in the tiny foyer, no disembodied, warning voices or wailing phantoms. Just an old house, a house made something monstrous by recollection and dread. It smells musty, shut away, and he wonders how long since anyone's been inside.

"The electric's off," Archer says, repeatedly flipping the switch on the wall at their left, the very same iron switch plate Walter remembers.

"You're not afraid of the dark, are you?" he asks and laughs, laughing from relief or nerves or both, not caring whether Archer thinks he's laughing at her or not. He pulls a Maglite from his back pocket and shines it across the dusty floor. Theda's footprints are easy to see, and the sticky, tangled trail of silk she's left behind.

"Goddamned stupid bitch," Archer mutters.

"Let's just get this shit over with and haul ass out of here," he says. "We can curse Theda later," and Archer mumbles something unintelligible and starts chanting again. He leads her from one empty room to the next, living room to dining room to the short hall past the kitchen. All of it repainted, white walls and floral-print wallpaper that can't be more than a couple of years old, and no hint whatsoever of the cluttered life Spyder Baxter once lived here.

In the hallway, the trapdoor leading to the basement is standing open, and Walter plays the flashlight back and forth across the gaping hole. There are sturdy wooden steps leading down to the earthen cellar beneath the house, and those are new, too, sensible replacements for the treacherous, dry-rot planks that were there ten years before. There are thick strands of spider silk clinging to the trapdoor, and the Maglite catches the glinting, smooth body of a black widow before it scuttles away into a crack.

"It's just a house," he says out loud. "Just an ugly, old house."

"You don't really believe that, do you?" Archer asks and takes the flashlight from him, is already descending the narrow steps before he can reply or try to stop her.

"Theda!" Archer calls out, her voice echoing beneath

the floor, directly beneath Walter's feet. "Where the fuck are you, you little bitch!"

"Just an old house," he says again, never mind what Archer might think, what Archer might *know,* and he starts down the stairs after her, following the bobbing white beam of the Maglite.

And then there's a gunshot, the sharp crack of Archer's .38 Colt, and Walter misses the next step and almost falls the rest of the way to the basement floor, would have fallen if there hadn't been a thick bundle of wires hanging from the underside of the floorboards, just a few inches above his head. But he comes down wrong on his right ankle, and there's bright pain and a wet snap like a handful of green branches broken across someone's knee, and he grits his teeth to keep from screaming. The Beretta slips from his fingers and clatters on the basement stairs.

Another shot from Archer's revolver, deafening in the close space, and Walter shuts his eyes and tries not to pass out or lose his balance. He can hear her talking somewhere not too far below, but it's impossible to make out the words through the roar of the Colt still reverberating inside his skull.

"Fuck," he moans, and he's leaning one shoulder against the hard-packed red-dirt wall now, just the wall and his left foot to hold him up, and slowly, he begins to lower himself into a sitting position on one of the steps.

"It's over," Archer says, or might have said, her voice muted by the noise in his head and then she turns and shines the flashlight up into his eyes. He squints, trying to find her through the glare.

"That *wasn't* the plan," he grunts and sits down; the wood squeaks loudly under him. "You *know* that wasn't the fucking plan. I fucking *told* you to wait until we were *both* in the fucking basement, and then I'd be the one to do her. *Christ . . .*"

"Their names mean nothing," Archer says, and she lowers the Maglite just enough that he can make out the rough outlines of her face, pale skin and those dark and gimlet eyes, the dull gleam off the muzzle of her gun. "Nothing at all. Not if they can't hear you, or have chosen not to listen. If their prophets are only fools and madmen."

Somewhere in the darkness below him, Theda giggles, and Walter swallows hard, swallowing so he won't puke, and stares back at the red witch watching him from the bottom of the stairs. "So . . . which does that make me?" he asks her, and she smiles, a sad and secretive smile, and then she squeezes the trigger again.

CHAPTER NINE

The Eighth Sphere

When there is finally nothing else left for him to do, Marvin goes upstairs and sits alone on the big bed in Niki and Daria's room. Nothing left to do, because all the necessary phone calls have been made, and all the necessary questions have been answered for policemen and relatives and friends, all the questions for now. He knows that there will be more later on. Reporters for the *Chronicle* and the *Guardian, Rolling Stone* and *The Advocate,* having failed to get their answers from Daria's management or the record label, have all been politely told that she's presently unavailable for comment and no, he has nothing to say himself. Which isn't the truth, of course. After the long hours searching for Niki and then the trip to the morgue to identify her body, he has a lot to say, but they're all words that will have to be saved for Daria and his therapist.

The Peruvian lilies in the Dresden-blue vase on the table beside the bed have begun to wilt, most of the coral-colored petals gone limp and starting to curl in on themselves, the heads of the flowers drooping, and he thinks that he should have replaced them two days ago. Back in that lost world where he worried about wilting flowers and groceries and whether or not Niki had taken her medication. Back in *that* world, there were never wilting flowers in the big house on Alamo Square.

Outside, the sun has set, and night lies heavy across the city; there's no light in the bedroom but the yellow-orange streetlight getting in through the window facing Steiner Street, and occasionally the glare of headlights from a passing car.

Marvin has taken down the Ophelia print from its hook above the bed, and now the heavy frame is leaning against the opposite wall. Millais' *Ophelia,* her eyes and arms spread submissively towards an unwelcoming Heaven, the painting like a sick and self-fulfilling prophecy, and he almost threw it out the window half an hour ago, imagined it hitting the sidewalk in a violent crash of breaking glass and splintering wood, a perfectly empty act of exorcism, expurgation come much too late to save anyone at all. So he set it against the wall, instead, and covered it with a clean sheet from the linen closet down the hall. Tomorrow, he thinks, he'll put it out for the garbage men to take away.

There's rosemary, that's for remembrance; pray you, love, remember. And there is pansies, that is for thoughts.

The antiseptic and dead people stink of the morgue still lingering thick in Marvin's sinuses, and there's no point trying not to see her lying there. Niki's broken body stretched out on a sliding, stainless-steel tray, the cold air spilling out of the refrigerated compartment set into a long wall of identical compartments. Neat rows of doors closed on other, waiting corpses, and nothing in the world could ever have prepared him for the sight of her. Not his fears nor the things that the white-coated coroner's assistant had told him. Her mottled gray skin and battered face and the damage that the fish and crabs had done, the black holes that had been her eyes, the cruel slashes left by the hooked beaks of scavenging gulls.

"But I *just* saw her, I mean, I saw her just last night," he said, confused and horrified that this pathetic thing was really all that remained of Niki, that a human body could be reduced to such a wreck of rotting meat so quickly. He turned away then, because there was nothing else he needed to see, nothing else he needed to be sure of, and in a moment he would be crying again.

"I'm very sorry," the man in the white lab coat said calmly, his voice wrapped with enough detachment and practiced sympathy to show that he'd seen this bad before, much worse than this, and he couldn't really afford to be very sorry every time.

And then there were forms to sign, and there would have to be an autopsy, Marvin was told, because she was a suicide. Niki always said that she didn't want an autopsy or embalming, that the thought of someone cutting up her dead body, draining all her blood and pumping her full of toxic chemicals was frightening and repulsive. But he didn't argue. If she hadn't wanted an autopsy, she shouldn't have jumped off the goddamn Bay Bridge. After the morgue was finally done with him, Marvin answered questions for a homicide detective who gave him lukewarm coffee in a paper cup, coffee with sugar and nondairy creamer that he only sipped once and then set aside.

Marvin stares for a few minutes at the sunflower-yellow sheet covering *Ophelia,* then turns his head and stares at the bedroom window. *Daria should be here,* he thinks for the hundredth or thousandth time that day. *Daria should be here, because this is where Niki would want her to be.*

Because this is where Niki needed *her to be.*

But Daria's on her way to Alabama, chasing Niki's ghosts.

The darkness outside the window makes him nervous, the night or something the night signifies, and Marvin goes back to staring at the draped Millais.

Her clothes spread wide, and mermaidlike awhile they bore her up . . .

"I didn't know it would be so bad," Marvin told the homicide detective, sitting in a hard, plastic chair in a tiny, cluttered office that smelled of cigarette smoke and bad coffee, speaking through the exhaustion and fog settling in around his head. "I've never seen anyone who drowned before."

"She didn't drown," the detective said, drumming on his desk with the eraser end of a pencil. "She fell more than two hundred feet before she hit the water. Do you have any idea how hard water *is* on the other end of a fall like that? She might as well have hit concrete."

And no, Marvin said, it wasn't anything he'd ever thought about before, nothing he'd ever had any reason to think about, and he wanted to ask the detective to please stop drumming with his pencil.

"You watched after Miss Ky for a long time, didn't you, Mr. Gale?"

And it took Marvin a moment or two to realize that the cop was talking to him, because no one ever calls him Mr. Gale. "Yeah," he replied, trying to remember just how long it had been since Daria had hired him. "A couple of years," he said finally. "They'd just bought the house."

"And before Miss Ky, you were taking care of a girl named . . ." and the detective paused to read something from a file lying open in front of him.

"Sylvia," Marvin volunteered. "I was taking care of a girl named Sylvia Thayer."

"That's right," the detective said, leaning far back in his chair, watching Marvin from beneath his thin gray eyebrows. "Sylvia Thayer. She killed herself, too, didn't she? Cut her throat with glass from a broken window."

"It was a broken mirror. Is it time for me to talk to my lawyer?" he asked, even though he didn't have a lawyer to talk to.

"No, I don't think that will be necessary," the detective said, "not yet, anyway," and he leaned forward again. He smiled, nothing at all sincere in that smile, but at least he'd quit drumming the pencil against his desk. "I just try to keep an eye out for coincidences like that. Sometimes it's all about noticing the coincidences."

Marvin thinks about going back downstairs and fixing himself a drink, gin or brandy or bourbon, something strong enough to put him down until morning, or at least until the next time the phone rings. Maybe, if he looks hard enough, he could find the same strength that Daria seems to find in a bottle. Maybe he could find enough strength to face the things he'll have to do tomorrow.

Maybe then he could stop thinking about Danny Boudreaux and Spyder Baxter and all the things that Niki told him about Birmingham. Maybe he could stop thinking about Sylvia Thayer and her wolves that no one else could see. And the spiders that fell from the sky to blanket Alamo Square while he was asleep in a hotel room on Steuart Street, while Niki was walking alone across the Bay Bridge, or as she fell, or after she hit the water like someone tumbling two hundred feet into a concrete wall.

Instead, he lies down on the bed, the comforter that still smells like her, wishing there were any tears left in him, because crying would be better than nothing at all. And in just a little while, he's asleep.

"*That's* right, birdeen," the fat man in a tattered justau-corps and a crimson brocade vest says. "Let it *all* out," and Niki obediently pukes up another gout of seawater and bile onto the listing deck of the little ship. She's on her hands and knees, like someone bowing to the wide mizzen-sail fluttering in the night wind.

"You'd think she done gone and swallowed the whole bless'd ocean," the man laughs, and Scarborough Pentecost coughs and wipes his mouth on the back of his hand. His ponytail has come down, and his hair hangs in wet tendrils about his face.

"It's not an easy trick," he replies hoarsely. "Takes prac-tice, and then it's *still* not an easy trick."

"Ah now, drowning's easy," the man in the red vest says and pats Niki on the back. "The sea, she makes it easy. I think it flatters her, mostly."

And Niki spits and stares up at the fat man dressed like a threadbare storybook pirate, lost in a tide of déjà vu so strong that she momentarily forgets about the pain in her throat and chest, until it passes, leaving her even more disoriented than before.

"Who the hell *are* you?" she croaks, and the man gnaws a yellowed thumbnail for a moment before he answers her.

"Me? Why, I'm the damn fool cabbagehead what ought to have better sense than to get hisself mixed up with the likes of you two, that's who *I* am," and he jabs himself in the chest with one finger.

Niki looks uncertainly at Scarborough, and then she vomits again. When she's done, she sits up on her knees, heels to ass, and "Did he just save our lives or something?" she asks.

"You might say that," Scarborough replies. "Esme paid him to be at the coordinates where the portal opened."

"Oh," Niki says, though she really has no idea what Scarborough's talking about. One moment they were in the fish augur's collapsing chamber and then he was pulling her down into icy black water. And there's nothing much after that, nothing but fading hints of dream, until she came to on the deck of the barque.

"You can call me Malim, if you're the sort what gotta go calling people by names," the man in the red vest says. "I suppose it's too much to be expectin' a *hierophant* to be callin' me Captain."

"He's a smuggler," Scarborough adds, and coughs again.

"Ah, now. Listen, boy. Don't make it sound like a shameful thing," Malim says and frowns dramatically.

"You mean the way you just said 'hierophant'?" Niki asks.

"Yeah, somethin' like that," Malim replies and scratches at the scraggly billy-goat beard perched on the end of his chin. He turns and looks towards the ship's stern and a red-orange glow staining the horizon. "Some words, there just ain't no way to get around the taint of 'em."

"You'll have to excuse him, Vietnam," Scarborough says and shakes his head. "Malim's a useful old fucker, and he won't stab you in the back—well, *most* of the time, he won't stab you in the back—but he's not much for prophecies and messiahs."

"Prophecies," Malim snorts and tugs at his beard. "Padnée's a blazin' inferno, thanks to that one there," and he points at Niki. "And I don't need no magics to tell me she's gonna get a lot of folks killed 'fore she's done. She's got that awful shine about her."

"Padnée's burning?" Niki whispers, wondering how long she was out, how long since the first cannonball hit the ramparts, how long since the cold and the dark.

"See for yourself, birdeen," Malim says and holds out a pudgy hand to her. Niki's stomach gurgles loudly and cramps, and she waits a moment before trying to stand, waiting to be sure that she isn't going to puke again.

"You go round talkin' revolution and uprisin', you start gettin' people killed, cities burnt down, all sorts of shit like that."

"I didn't do anything," Niki insists, taking his hand and letting him pull her to her feet, her knees so wobbly she wants to sit right back down again. "All I did was jump off a bridge."

"Now, is that so," Malim sneers and goes back to staring at the fiery glow where the sea meets the night sky. "Well, then maybe someone needs to be tellin' that to the Dragon, 'cause he seems to have gotten the wrong impression altogether."

"I didn't do that," Niki says very quietly, and she leans against the aftermast, because she's pretty sure her legs have gone too weak to hold her up. "Scarborough, please tell me I didn't do that."

Malim raises one beetling eyebrow and looks down at Scarborough. "It's sure a strange sort of savior you got yourself here, Mr. Pentecost. Me, I 'spected someone with a little more steel in her gut."

"How about *you* just stick a goddamn sock in it," Scarborough growls at Malim and stumbles slowly to his feet. "You didn't *do* it, Vietnam, but I'm afraid you're the reason it's been *done*."

"They're all dead?"

"Yeah," Scarborough says. "Well, most of them." Then the ship rolls to port, and he almost loses his balance and sits down quickly on a small barrel marked OIL: DO NOT DRINK. He covers his face with both hands and rubs at his temples. "Jesus, I fucking hate boats," he moans.

"Because of *me*. All those people, all of them are dead because of me."

"By Dagon's left testicle," Malim grunts, grinning a broad grin to show off a mouthful of teeth the color of walnut shells, and he puts an arm around Niki. "This is rich as sow's milk churned to butter, it is. I wouldn't 'ave missed this for the world. What in blue blazes did you *think*, missy? That maybe that old serpent was just gonna roll over, pretty as you please, and show you where to stick your shiv?"

"Leave her alone," Scarborough says and glares at Malim. The fat man in the red vest frowns and takes his arm from around Niki's shoulders.

"What about Spyder?" Niki asks. "Is she . . . is she dead, too?"

"The Weaver's been in worse spots than this," Scarborough says, then hides his face in his hands again. "I expect we haven't seen the last of her."

"And more's the bleedin' pity, if you asks me," Malim grumbles, "which, o'course, you 'aven't," and then he waddles away, leaving them alone on the barque's narrow poop deck. The sails rustle and flap loudly above them like the leathery wings of monsters, and the wind whistles through the rigging.

"I'm sorry," Scarborough says. "But it ain't some Disney movie, this mess you've gotten yourself into. It's a war, a *real* war, or at least it's the beginnings of a war, and it's going to be just as ugly as any war back home."

Niki rubs at her eyes, hoping that Scarborough hasn't noticed the tears, and she takes a deep breath of the warm, salty air. Maybe she catches a hint of smoke on the breeze, but she can't be sure.

"God, I fucking hate boats," Scarborough moans again; he gags, and a thick stream of spittle drips from his lips, but he doesn't vomit.

"Do you know that I'm insane," Niki says to him. "Psych wards, happy pills, the whole bit. Did Spyder even bother to tell any of you about that?"

"No," Scarborough says, "but it kinda fucking figures," and then he gags again.

"So, just where the hell is Captain Kidd smuggling us to?" Niki asks, and she takes one last, long look at the bright spot marking the flaming ruins of Padnée, before she turns her back on the western horizon. Maybe turning her back on Spyder, too, Spyder's deceitfully white ghost that's dragged her here, to this place, so that more people will die because of her. Spyder who couldn't be bothered to tell her what's going on or why or what the fuck she's supposed to do about any of it.

"Auber," Scarborough says. "He's taking us to Auber and the ghouls," and then he starts throwing up again.

"Right," Niki says, wondering what the ghouls are and what they'll do with her, and then she goes to Scarborough and holds his head until he stops vomiting.

Daria Parker is sitting alone in a mostly empty smoker's lounge in the Birmingham International Airport, impatiently waiting for Alex to finish taking a piss. The late morning sun shines too brightly through the curved Plexiglas wall that affords her a view of the runway, the big jets coming and going, taxiing or waiting to take on passengers via retractable, telescopic corridors, or just sitting there, idling on the tarmac. Even through her sunglasses, the day's too bright, and she turns away, facing the entrance to the lounge instead of the runway. She fishes another Marlboro from the pack in her leather jacket, and if Alex wants to give her shit for smoking so much he can go right on the hell ahead and do it. She's so very far past caring now, the last thirty-five or forty hours there to break apart whatever discretion she might have had left in her, whatever sense of self-preservation; all the racing time and pain and insanity since she sat in an Atlanta hotel room Monday night, checking her voice mail. The man who left his cryptic, threatful message and then her last, desperate conversation with Niki, the airplane and her heart attack—a fucking *heart attack* and she's only thirty-four years old—the dream of Niki and the white bird, the thing on a dark Colorado highway that tried to get her killed, the rusted ball bearing hidden in a case of Kansas fossils—

Dot to dot to dot to dot.

And now she's right here, here *again,* back in this wasteland, hellhole of a city where it all began ten years before, when she was only a barista in a Morris Avenue coffeehouse, when she was only a bass player and singer for a dead-end punk band, when Niki was just a lost girl passing through town, unlucky enough to break down before she reached the other side, unlucky enough to meet her, and Spyder Baxter.

Daria lights her cigarette and takes a deep drag, wondering how many of these stand between her and the next heart attack. But the smoke feels good, the nicotine seeping rapidly into her bloodstream, so maybe it won't be the cigarettes that get her. Maybe it'll be the alcohol, or the pills, or the news that the label's finally dumping her because she's just too big a flake, too big a risk. Maybe it'll be Niki's funeral, if she lives that long.

Daria exhales, watching the smoke and the sun shining through it, the sun getting past her silhouette and cutting shafts in the gray haze from her nostrils. And she thinks how strange it is that her head feels clearer than it's felt in days, more days or weeks than she can count. Alex made her sleep on the plane from Denver, and there were no dreams to wake her or undo whatever good the sleep may have done. She only woke when the plane touched down in Birmingham, the machine-beast roar of deceleration, the furious *bump* and rubber squeal when the 747's wheels touched asphalt, and "We're here," he said. "We're here."

"Excuse me, ma'am. Are you Daria Parker?" a woman asks, and Daria looks up, expecting a fan wanting an autograph and a handshake and conversation, and already she's trying to think of anything polite to say, anything to excuse her appearance.

There's a young black woman standing at the entrance to the lounge, and Daria guesses that she must be an employee from the food court because she's wearing a Chick-fil-A smock.

"Yeah," Daria says, and tries to smile for the girl. "That's me."

"Well, you got a call on one of the pay phones over there," the woman says, and points back at a bank of phones mounted along the wall outside and opposite the lounge.

"Thank you," Daria replies uncertainly, and the woman shrugs and walks away.

And at first there's only relief and surprise, that the girl didn't recognize her, and she doesn't have to play Daria Parker, Rock Star, at 10:30 A.M. in the goddamn Birmingham airport. But then the questions: Who the hell would be calling her on the pay phone? Who the hell knows she's here except Alex? And they've both turned off their cells. But maybe Jarod Parris has managed to track her down, maybe he put two and eight together and got Birmingham, or maybe it's someone from Sony, or maybe it's just all a big fucking mistake, and the phone call isn't even *for* her.

Daria takes another long drag off her Marlboro and squints at the phones, at the one with its handset dangling off the hook, wondering how long she'd have to sit here before the caller hangs up, and wondering if he or she would bother to try again. She touches the ball bearing through the fabric of her satiny jacket lining, the strangely reassuring weight and solidity of it still there, like all the things the old man at the gas station said to her the night before, words for insurance she doesn't yet understand. Words that might add up to something more than everything she's lost.

She said the Hierophant would need it again one day.

And Niki is the Hierophant, Daria thinks and almost laughs out loud.

She stubs out the half-smoked Marlboro in an ashtray filled with cigarette butts and sand and leaves the smoky sanctuary of the lounge, stepping into cleaner, less-welcoming air. She crosses the corridor and stands in front of the pay phones.

If Alex would come out now, she thinks and looks over her shoulder at the men's room a few feet farther down the corridor. *Right now, and then he could talk to whoever it is, or he could just hang up on them.*

And then she reaches down and picks up the black handset, because she knows no one's going to do it for her, not Alex Singer or anyone else. "Hello," she says, and at first Daria thinks that maybe they've hung up already, whoever it is, whoever it was, because nobody answers her. But there's no dial tone, just a slightly staticky quiet, so she says hello again.

And then a female voice, a voice that makes her think of the time in Boulder that Niki caught strep throat and had a hell of a time getting over it. A voice that weak and scratchy, that strained. A voice that hurts just to hear.

"Ms. Parker," the woman says. "You took your time. You act like you have all the time in the world."

"Who is this?" Daria demands and glances anxiously at the restroom again. *What the fuck are you doing in there, Alex? You could have drained fucking Lake Michigan by now.*

"My name is Archer," the woman says. "That's all you need to know. I'm waiting for you at the house on Cullom Street, and Niki's here."

"Niki . . ." Daria whispers, and suddenly her heart's beating too fast, too hard, hammering away at her chest like something that wants out. Her head is filled with the murmur of voices and the oily stench of jet fuel underlying everything, the frying, roasting smells from the food court, and some part of her mind that isn't busy trying to make sense of what the woman on the phone's just said thinks that maybe she's about to faint.

Or maybe *this* is the next heart attack.

The next one *and* the last one.

"Niki," she says again, "Nicolan Ky," and "Yes," the woman assures her.

"Niki's *dead*," Daria says, and she sits down on the carpeted floor, sits down before her legs give out and she falls. "I don't know who the fuck you are, or what you think you're doing—"

"You have the philtre," the woman says. "I have Niki. Bring me the talisman the old man gave you, and we'll call it even."

Daria shuts her eyes tightly and leans back against the wall. Nausea and panic and the pain in her chest, the terrible, labored ache in the woman's voice for counterbalance, and a cold sweat breaks out on Daria's face and arms.

"Don't do this to me," she whispers into the mouthpiece. "Please, don't do this to me."

"Don't *you* fuck around with me," the woman says. "There's still a chance that you can save her, if you do exactly as I say. All I want is the talisman. It's nothing that concerns you, anyway."

"No," Daria says. "No, it isn't, is it? Let me talk to Niki. If she's really there, please, just for a second."

"Don't you trust me?" the woman named Archer asks. "You know the way, Ms. Parker. You've been here before. If I were you, I wouldn't waste any more time." And then she hangs up, and there's only the shrill drone of the dial tone in Daria's ear.

"Dar, what the hell's going on?" Alex asks, and she opens her eyes, looks up and he's standing there above her. She can smell marijuana smoke coming off him, spicy and skunky and familiar, and *Well, that answers one question,* she thinks. And then she closes her eyes again and waits for the pain in her chest to stop.

*   *   *

Marvin opens his eyes, and there's sunlight streaming in through the bedroom window, sunlight to sting his pupils, and he winces and shuts them again. Kaleidoscope bits of a dream breaking apart in his head, dissolving in the twin solvents of consciousness and morning, and then he remembers what happened to Niki and Daria, remembering now like hearing the news for the first time the day before, and he only wants to crawl back down into sleep and hide in unknowing folds of dream.

Niki is dead, he thinks, the fact beyond all dispute or reason, Niki lying on that cold steel slab, and by now they've probably finished the autopsy, all their requisite, clinical violations of her violated flesh, and in a few more days, Niki will be nothing but ashes waiting to be scattered.

"I want my ashes scattered in the bay," she told him once, a year or two ago. "I want my ashes scattered in the bay so the currents will carry me far away, far out to sea. Some of me might make it as far as Hawaii, or even Malaysia, or I might go all the way around the world. I might even wash up on a shore in Vietnam someplace, and wouldn't *that* be ironic," she said.

So she threw herself into the bay, and the bay spit her out again, and now she'll have to be poured into the Pacific a second time. And that, he thinks, is irony.

Everything is irony.

All the things he *could* have done, while there was still time to act, the things that Daria might have done; could'a, would'a, should'a, and he ought to know better than to play that game. He ought to, but he doesn't, and *Maybe,* he thinks, *it's time to learn the rules.*

There's a noise from the foot of the bed, something falling to the hardwood floor, and Marvin opens his eyes again, this time taking care to shield them from the inconsiderate sun.

The thing standing in front of Niki's dressing table has its back to him, but he can see its face in the mirror. It's busy rummaging noisily through an open drawer, and

Marvin covers his mouth and grits his teeth against the scream building inside his chest.

No, I'm still dreaming, he promises himself, a frantic scramble for any way to make this sane, any way to make it something besides exactly what it is. *In a moment, it'll turn around, and I'll have to look directly in its eyes, but then I'll wake up. I'll wake up and have to remember that Niki's dead.*

The thing at the dressing table makes a disappointed, snorfling sound and drops a handful of lipsticks and eyeliners to the bedroom floor.

And then it sees him in the mirror, and its wet white eyes, like two halves of a boiled egg, grow very wide, and it jabs a long finger at the looking glass.

"*You,*" it growls, the guttural voice of a thousand horror-movie werewolves and demons. "Where did *you* come from?" And the thing taps the glass with the tip of a razor claw and then leans closer to the mirror. The muscles along its misshapen back ripple and twitch, and the thick auburn fur at the base of its bald skull bristles.

"The Weaver, *she* sent you here?" it asks and taps the glass again. "She sent you here to *stop* me?"

Only a dream, Marvin thinks again, wringing nothing like comfort from the possibility. *There's not a monster in Niki's bedroom, and it's not talking to me.*

"Whas' wrong? You got no tongue, blackie?" the thing asks, and now its wide, porcine nose is pressed smack against the mirror, steaming up the glass. "Did the Weaver take your tongue so you couldn't go telling me her *secrets*?"

"I don't know who the Weaver is," Marvin replies, because it's only a dream, and surely it's okay to talk to monsters in bad dreams. "I'm afraid I don't have any idea what you're talking about."

"You're *afraid*?" it grunts and cocks its head to one side, smearing its nostrils across the mirror. "If not the Weaver, then the red witches, those filthy *whores* in their *filthy* white towers."

"Strike two," Marvin says, and he laughs; the monster snorts and taps hard at the smudged glass again. "You're going to break that," Marvin says. "It's an antique."

"I bet it *is* the witches," the thing says, arching its right eyebrow in such a way that the dead-white eye on that side of its face bulges halfway from the socket. "I bet you my hide *and* eyeteeth it's the witches who sent you here."

"The only witch I ever knew ran a New Age bookshop down on Castro—"

"*Liar,*" the monster snarls, and specks of thick black saliva fly from its lips and add to the mess on the mirror. "They *sent* you here, just like the Dragon sent me, to find a piece of *her* and take it back. They want the same thing, the Dragon and the red witches, to stop the Weaver, only they want it for different *reasons.*"

"A *piece* of her?" Marvin asks the thing at the dressing table.

"The *Hi-ero-phant,* blackie. A smidgen of the darkling girl that the Weaver's called down upon us all, the one who holds the day and night in her dirty little bitch's fists. But one *hair* is all we need, one hair or a baby tooth or a snip of fingernail, and we'll send her back here *forever.*"

"Why don't you turn around and face me?" Marvin asks it, and he glances at the table beside the bed—the blue vase and the wilting Peruvian lilies, the alarm clock that reads 8:45 A.M.—and then he glances back at the monster. It's still watching him through the snot- and spit-smudged mirror, and Marvin thinks the expression on its long, angular face must be wariness.

"Ah, you would like that, wouldn't you," it growls. "But I know the law. And now I *know* you're from the witches, trying to trick me like that. Thas' how they operate," and the monster picks up Niki's hairbrush.

"Of course," Marvin says, looking from the brush clutched in the monster's hand to the vase and back to the brush again. "Yes, of course you do."

And it's only a dream, only the most ridiculous fucking nightmare that he's ever had, lying here in Niki's bed and talking with an ogre in broad daylight, but the way it's gazing at the brush, the way it's *smiling*—those obscene lips curled back to show uneven teeth like chunks of coal, the wicked triumph on its face—and then it begins to pick strands of hair from the bristles.

"One for the ravens, one for my wishes," it snickers to itself in a tuneless, nursery rhyme singsong. "One for the ladies, and one for the fishes."

"I've insulted you," Marvin says, thinking of Sylvia Thayer's wolves as he reaches for the vase on the nightstand. "You know the law."

"Turn from the mirror and lose your way," the monster mutters absently, inspecting a single strand of Niki's hair with the tip of its scabby pink tongue. "Turn away from the mirror, Mossrack, and you'll *never* come home again. Yes, I *know* the law, I do."

The vase feels very heavy in Marvin's hand, thick glass and at least half full of water, and he sits up very slowly, until the balls of his feet are touching the chilly floor, and the monster's so close that he could reach out and touch it, too.

"It's a lifeline, that mirror," he says, and the monster nods its massive head and pulls another hair from the brush.

"Five for the horses, and six for the foxes—"

"Without it we're lost," Marvin says, tightening his grip on the vase, "both of us."

"*You* know that," the monster grunts, and now it's beginning to sound exasperated. "You know that *perfectly* well. Without the mirror, there's only the void waiting to claim us. Even the red witches and their darky bastard lapdogs fear the void. Cold, cold, *cold* without ends, without even beginnings, either. No blackness in the void, 'cause there's never been so much as a spark of light to divide the one from the other."

"Sounds a lot like South Dakota," Marvin says. "I spent a whole week there one January. Sweet piece of ass, but he wasn't worth South Dakota."

The creature stops sniffing at the dark strands of Niki's

hair and glares at Marvin from the looking glass. A glare from those boiled-egg eyes so filled with contempt and confusion that he almost sets the blue vase down and waits for the nightmare to find another way to end.

"Your *skin* would look nice on the wall of my burrow," it says and grins again. "A sorry shame you're there, *behind* me. Perhaps, though, if you came closer."

"What comes after the foxes?" Marvin asks it and, before the monster can reply, he hurls the vase at the mirror. It sails past the thing's right ear and, for a moment, the entire world is lost in the sound of breaking glass.

And then Marvin is alone in the bedroom again, the sun shining in through the parted drapes, and he stares at the mess the monster's made of the dressing table, the hairbrush lying there, the reflecting shards of mirror and the Dresden blue vase, bent flower stems and water dripping from the cherry wood, the lipstick tubes scattered across the floor.

And he starts waiting to wake up.

In a narrow upper berth, somewhere far below the deck of the smuggler's four-masted barque, Niki lies wide awake by candlelight, staring at the planks only a few inches from her face. Scarborough is in the berth beneath her, trying to sleep off his seasickness. There's a tin pail on the floor beside his bed, half filled with vomit, but the air smells so bad down here that the odor from the pail is only a very minor nuisance. Air so redolent that she imagines she can see it passing before her eyes, almost as thick as the mist at the Palisades, the sour-sweet-spicy odors of mold and salt water and rot, the stench of fish and greasy tallow smoke and human filth. The hull is cold and damp to the touch, wood and pitch and the sea right there on the other side. From time to time, she hears the mournful calls of things that sound like whales, but she has a feeling there aren't any whales in this ocean. Maybe it's the enormous creatures that the walls and foundations of Padnée were built from, instead.

"Scarborough," she whispers, "are you awake down there?"

There's no reply, so maybe he isn't, and she should just leave him alone, let him sleep while he can, and she goes back to staring at the ceiling and listening to the timbers creak around her. It doesn't seem that long since she rested in the bed in Esme Chattox's house, that soft bed so much better than this hard, mildewed bunk, and there's really no point trying to sleep. She'd be up on the deck, but Malim came back and ushered them both below, for their "own good," he said. So she spent half an hour or so going through her backpack, emptying it, inventorying its contents, then neatly repacking everything before she zipped the nylon shut again. Her pills are in there, and she almost took them out of habit, went so far as opening the Klonopin bottle, but then she thought about what Spyder said and screwed the cap on again. Not so much because of Spyder's opinion that she didn't need her medication here, but because her head hasn't felt this clear in years. So long since she's thought clearly, thinking free of the haze of psychoactive drugs, that she can't be quite sure she's *ever* thought clearly before this very moment.

Her infected hand is itching beneath its latest dressing, the one the doctor in Padnée gave her. She wonders if he's dead now, too, and she wonders how bad the wound beneath the bandage looks. It hurts a lot less, so maybe that's a good sign.

"Scarborough," she calls out, louder than before. "Are you awake?"

"I'm dead," he moans. "Leave me alone."

"Did I wake you up?"

For an answer, she can hear him retching into the tin pail again and is surprised he could have anything left inside him to throw up. Malim ordered him to drink water from the brown ceramic jug on the floor beside the pail, so maybe he's just vomiting the water.

"I fucking hate boats," he groans.

"I think you pissed off the captain, calling his ship a boat."

"Fuck him," Scarborough says, and then she hears him moving around below her.

"I'm sorry if I woke you up."

"Don't be. I was only dreaming about being sick."

"I'm sorry," she says again, anyway, and rolls over, putting her back to the hull of the ship. She's using her pack as a pillow, because there wasn't one in the berth. "Which is worse?"

"I really don't think there's much fucking difference," Scarborough replies.

"Do you think he'll do right by us?" Niki asks.

"Who? Malim?"

"Yeah," she says. "I mean, who's to say he won't just dump us anywhere he pleases? Who's to say he won't cut our throats?"

"You're a trusting soul."

"I was just thinking about it, that's all."

"Don't worry. He only gets his money when he delivers us—*alive*—to Auber. And he only cares about his money, so that's where he's taking us."

Niki doesn't say anything else for a while, lies still, listening to the faintly booming, sometimes shrill not-whale songs bleeding in through the walls of the ship, considering Scarborough's logic as he climbs out of his berth and steadies himself against a beam. He uncorks the water jug, takes a mouthful, and spits it out onto the floor.

"Christ," he grimaces. "It's fucking brine."

"Salt water?" Niki asks, and he curses and throws the jug. It shatters loudly somewhere farther back in the hold.

"Maybe I gave him too much credit, after all," Scarborough says and spits again. "I'd give my left nut for a Coke."

"Yeah," Niki agrees. "A Coke and a Big Mac with fries and an apple pie," and that makes Scarborough throw up again.

When he's done, Niki apologizes, but he just sits on the

floor, the cramped aisle between the two rows of bunks, and shakes his head. "Just don't do that again," he croaks.

"I have questions, Scarborough," she says, because she does, and it seems like a good idea to change the subject. "Ever since this started, I've had questions, and no one's even *tried* to answer them."

"That's what happens when you fall in with all these mystical snoke-horns—the Weaver and Esme, the lot of them—they don't like answering questions. *None* of them do. Trust me on this."

"What's a 'snoke-horn'?"

"That's beside the point," Scarborough says and wipes the sweat from his face with the sleeve of his shirt. "You can't get a straight answer from them with a yardstick and a level and a double-barreled shotgun, *that's* the point."

"Can I get straight answers from you?"

Scarborough looks at her a moment, his face as pale as cheese, and then he sighs and looks up at the ceiling. "We're right beneath the foremast, I think," he says.

"Is that a 'no'?" Niki asks him.

"You've got this notion in your head that the answers are going to make it all better somehow," he replies. "You think, maybe if you know what's up, you might have some say in what comes next. Maybe you'll even have a choice. Am I right?"

"Something like that."

"You think it's that simple? I expound, give you a neat little infodump to shine some light into that pretty skull of yours, and at last you'll find yourself empowered against the forces of darkness and chaos?"

"But that's why I'm here, isn't it? I mean, that's what Spyder and that talking white bird kept saying to me, that without me everything was lost. But how am I supposed to save anything when I have no idea what's going on or what I'm expected to do about it?"

"It's just horse shit," Scarborough says and rubs at his temples. "The more I tell you, the less you'll know. That's how it always works."

"Is that some sort of riddle?"

"No, Vietnam, it's just the goddamn, sick-ass truth."

"What's the Dragon?" Niki asks, undaunted, and she leans over the edge of her bunk and looks down at him.

"You're not *listening* to me—"

"That's because you're not *saying* anything. Now, tell me, what's the Dragon, Scarborough?"

He pushes away the vomit pail and glares up at her, his bloodshot eyes and the sweat rolling down his face, bright beads in the candlelight. "I work for Esme Chattox. That's what I do. Before that, when I was alive, when I was home, I worked for something even worse."

"That's not an answer."

"What's the fucking Dragon?" he mutters and stares at the floor between his knees. "Jesus, you get straight to the point, don't you?"

"It's not a *real* dragon, is it? I mean, not some big scaly lizard thing with wings and fiery breath."

"Oh, you better believe it's got fire enough," he replies. "Don't you go forgetting Padnée so quickly. Before this shit's done, you're gonna wish it was just some big scaly lizard thing."

"But it's not?"

Scarborough stops rubbing his temples and peers up at her again. "The Dragon was always here. No one knows what the fuck the Dragon is. Maybe it's evil. Maybe it's God. Maybe it's just a goddamn force of nature or a bad joke the cosmos decided to play on this place, but when the Weaver came, she changed it somehow. Just her being here, or something she brought with her, and that's when everything started going to hell. But, hey, that was before my time."

"Spyder brought me here to stop the Dragon," Niki says. "She said it would destroy this place if I didn't stop it."

"Yeah, okay, whatever. But you gotta understand something. You gotta get it straight and *keep* it straight. This thing's complicated. We're not playing Dungeons and Dragons here. This isn't hobbits versus Sauron. If there's good and evil, black and white, it's just as hard to see here as it is back home."

"So, you're saying the Dragon isn't bad?"

"*No.* I'm not saying that at all," Scarborough replies wearily and wipes his face again. "The Dragon's a bad motherfucker, and you can bet your skinny Asian ass on that and come up flush every time. And he's got a lot of bad motherfuckers out there to do his dirty work. What I'm *saying* is that you need to see that the Weaver might not be so goddamn different her own self. On a good day, it's all just goddamn shades of gray, Vietnam. On a *good* day."

"Then what am I doing here?"

"Near as I can tell, making things worse," Scarborough tells her, and then he gags and doesn't say anything else for a while.

Niki lies in her bunk and thinks about the things he's said, the consequences of the things he's said, and watches the empty berth across the aisle from her. There are footsteps overhead, the inconstant tattoo of hobnailed boots and bare feet, and she tries to shut out all the sounds and smells of the ship. A runaway train since she stepped off the bridge, however long ago that might have been, no way of reckoning time when she doesn't have a watch, and the nights here seem to last forever. Back home, maybe Daria's dead, or maybe she went to Kansas and found the ball bearing, and she's on her way to Birmingham, or maybe she just went home with Alex Singer and they'll live happily ever after, freed from the inconvenience of having a crazy girl around.

"I wish you would stop thinking of yourself like that," Dr. Dalby said, more times than she can recall, but she does, anyway. Niki, the crazy girl hung about Daria's neck since Boulder, the stone to drag her down. Part of her can't blame Daria if she's glad to finally be rid of that weight.

And another part of her aches at the loss.

Maybe it's already been a month, or a year, or ten years back there, in the San Francisco where she started out.

Scarborough's remarks about Sauron and hobbits has her thinking about time and other books, Narnia and Oz and The Land, and how such a long time where she is could be a very short time in the "real" world. Maybe it's only been a moment back home, one tick of a second hand, and no one even knows she's dead yet.

Stop thinking of it as "home," she chides herself. *That's not home anymore, because I can never go back. Spyder said so.*

But what if Spyder lied, another voice inside her whispers. *What if Spyder's wrong?*

"They don't want me in Auber," she says. "I heard Esme say that to Spyder."

"Did you?" Scarborough replies, and he stands up again, propping himself against the edge of her bunk; she can smell him, sweat and sick and body odor, and wonders how she must smell. His lips are badly chapped, and there's a dab of blood at one corner of his mouth. "Well, I expect she was telling the truth. Anyone who takes you in is asking for what Padnée got, or worse."

"What if they turn me away? What if they won't pay Malim?"

"Why don't we worry about crossing that particular bridge when it pops up and smacks us in the face?"

"Chance favors the prepared."

"What the hell's that? Were you some sort of fucking Camp Fire girl or something?"

"I'm just really scared, that's all. And I wish Spyder had left me alone, like I was. I wish she'd left me *where* I was. At least there, only a few people didn't want me around."

"I think I liked you better without the self-pity, Vietnam."

"That puts you one up on me. I don't think I like me at all."

" 'My soul is crushed, my spirits sore; I do not like me any more.' "

"Dorothy Parker," Niki whispers, half to herself, and smiles, a familiar line or two of poetry almost enough to lift her spirits. "Daria always hated Dorothy Parker because sometimes the press would get her name wrong and print it 'Dorothy Parker.' Sometimes people writing fan letters even did it. I always told her she ought to be flattered."

"Who's Daria?" Scarborough asks.

"Never mind," she says, because she doesn't want to get started trying to explain Daria, what she did and didn't mean, and for all Niki knows, Scarborough Pentecost hates dykes. "I'll tell you about Daria some other time."

"Fair enough."

Overhead, there's a crackling thunder-and-lightning sort of noise, noise like the sky cracking open, so loud that Niki covers her ears.

"Just what I fucking need," Scarborough frowns, glaring up at the place where the sky would be, if all that wood weren't in the way. "A goddamn storm. The only thing worse than being on a boat is being on a boat in a goddamn storm. With my luck, it'll be a hurricane. It's that time of year."

"We used to have big storms in New Orleans," Niki says, thinking of the rain beating hard against her and Danny's windows in the French Quarter, remembering the night her mother came into her room and talked about fire falling from the sky. "I've been through a couple of hurricanes. Never on a boat, though."

"It's all kinds of fun, let me tell you."

"And you think Spyder's just as bad as the Dragon," Niki says, not asking, a statement to change the subject because even her doubts about herself and Spyder are better than imagining the little ship caught at sea in a hurricane.

"That's not what I said. I didn't say that because I don't know that. I just don't know otherwise."

"But you're trying to make me doubt her."

"I'm trying to make you *think*."

And then the thunder sound again, so loud that Niki can feel it passing through the ship, through the wood of her berth, through the fillings in her teeth.

"There are factions," Scarborough says, looking directly

at her now and speaking deliberately, parceling out his words like he's trying to ignore the thunder and what it means. "The Weaver isn't the only one who wants to get rid of the Dragon, but she's the only one cracked enough to actually try to fucking *do* it."

"Does that make her crazy, or does that make her brave?"

"You got spirit, Vietnam. I gotta give you that. Look, like I said, it's complicated. We've got this Madame Tirzah bitch and her ghouls over in Auber, right, and we've got the fucking red witches down in Nesmia and Sarvéynor, and *then,* like we need more troublemakers, we've got Esme and the Weaver. And it's not just that the right hand doesn't know what the left is up to. Most of the time, the right hand's just sitting around hoping and praying the left hand makes a wrong move and winds up on the Dragon's fuck-you-hard-right-now list, because every one of these bozos thinks they're the ones with the solution, and everyone else can go straight to hell."

"But the Dragon wasn't a problem before Spyder came?"

"I said she changed him. I didn't say he wasn't already a problem. Esme told me that when the Weaver came across, the Dragon took something from her, from inside her head," and Scarborough thumps himself smartly on the forehead. "Something that the Weaver believed, and it drove him insane, believing it, too."

And then the thunder again, and as it rolls away across and through the sea, one of Malim's crew pulls open the trapdoor to the hold and shouts down at them.

"The captain wants you both topside, and he don't mean tomorrow."

Niki glances upwards, towards the anxious, commanding voice, and there's clean white sunlight streaming in around the vague silhouette of the sailor's head and shoulders, illuminating the rungs of the tall ladder leading down to the floor.

"What the hell for?" Scarborough calls back.

"That weren't *my* business, and I ain't gonna go making it that way," and then the sailor's gone again, but he's left the trapdoor open, and Niki marvels at the light spilling into the squalid compartment with them.

"Thank goodness," she says, even though the light hurts her eyes. "I was beginning to think the night was never going to end."

Scarborough curses and spits on the floor again.

"Grab your gear," he tells her. "I got a feeling, whatever we've been hearing, it's not a storm after all."

"What else could it be?"

"I'm sorry to tell you this, but, as they say in the movies, you've got a lot to learn, kiddo," and then he rubs his stubbled cheeks and smoothes back his stringy brown hair with both hands before helping her out of the berth. Niki slips her pack and boots on, no time to bother with the laces, and lets Scarborough lead her up the ladder and into the warm maritime sun.

Daria sits alone on the hood of the rented Honda Accord, shiny new car the color of an eggplant, and watches the old house at the end of Cullom Street. Alex is still talking with the two Birmingham cops, the ones she begged him not to call, the ones he called anyway. They've been through the whole place, top to bottom, and didn't find anything but graffiti on the walls, trash and a few empty crack vials on the floor, a corner in one of the bedrooms that someone had been using as a toilet. Nothing much at all in the basement. No one's lived here for more than two years, they said, after a call to the owner, who said she was thinking about selling the dump and wanted to know if Daria was interested in buying it.

Only if I could burn it to the fucking ground, she thinks again. *Burn it down and sow the ground with salt and holy water.* She imagines herself marking the scorched and smoldering ground with a cross of white stones laid end to end, muttering prayers to a god she has no faith in.

One of the cops, a stocky, short woman with a mullet—and Daria clocked her right off—shakes Alex's hand again and then turns and waves enthusiastically at Daria, who pretends to smile and waves back. She asked for an autograph, when they were done with the house, and Daria gave it to her, scribbled on the back of an Alagasco envelope the cop had retrieved from her squad car.

"Just someone with nothing better to do, messing with your head," the other cop told Alex, even though whoever it was had obviously been trying to fuck with *her* head, not Alex's. All four of them standing out on the front porch because Daria wouldn't go inside, before she signed the back of the gas bill and then said good-bye and went to sit on the hood of the Honda.

"But how did she even know I was in the airport?" Daria asked him, the tall policeman with thick glasses and the beginnings of a pot belly, and he shrugged and shook his head.

"Who knows. The goddamn internet, maybe. Maybe someone hacked the airline's records and—"

"That's fucking ridiculous—" Daria began, but Alex was there to interrupt, there to say that they hadn't thought of that and shut her up.

She lights another cigarette and watches Alex watching the cops getting back into their car. She exhales, and her smoke hangs a moment in the late autumn air, withering smoke ghost slowly carried away by the cold breeze slipping silently between the tall trees. Daria shivers and pulls her leather jacket tighter, wishing that she had a coat, and as the police car pulls away from the house, Alex turns and walks towards her, crunching through the carpet of dead leaves.

"They're so full of shit," she says and taps ash to the ground. "Do you think she'd still have wanted my autograph if she'd known I was fucking you?"

"There's nothing in there," Alex replies. "*Nothing.* It was some sort of fucked-up prank, that's all. You're going to have to accept that."

"No one knew we were on that flight. No one knew I was sitting there across from that row of pay phones."

"Dar, you don't know what people know, not these days. Not when you're on bleedin' MTV and in all those goddamn magazines, you don't have any idea what people know."

Daria smokes her cigarette and stares at the house, trying not to remember the last time she was here and remembering it anyway. The night she and Mort and Theo came up here to find Niki, the night she went in there to bring Niki out. The white thing hanging head down from the ceiling of Spyder Baxter's bedroom.

"It might have been someone right there in the airport with us," Alex says, and then he takes the cigarette away from her, drops it to the ground and crushes it out with the toe of his shoe. "There's just no telling, not with something like this."

"You didn't hear her voice," Daria says, but she thinks she's past trying to convince anyone of anything. After the plane and the hospital, the white bird and the ball bearing and the old coot at the gas station with his fossils and Senior El Camino the jackalope.

"Daria, I'm sorry as hell about all this, but there's no one in the house. We need to get you home. You're sick, and we need to get you home—"

"So I can deal with Niki."

"Yes, so you can deal with Niki, and a whole lot of other shite you been trying to avoid ever since I met you. I followed you here because I knew if I didn't you'd never stop wishing you'd come."

Daria takes another cigarette from the pocket of her jacket and goes back to watching the house. "You followed me here," she says, slipping the unlit Marlboro between her lips, "because you were scared to let me come alone."

"Fine, but now we've seen all there is to see, and it's time for you to go home. I've got a room downtown for the night, and we can get a flight back—"

"Do you think I killed Niki?" Daria asks, mumbling

around the filter of the cigarette. Alex makes a disgusted, scoffing sound and kicks at the dead leaves.

"No, Dar, I don't think you, or anyone else, killed Niki," and it's easy to hear how hard he's working to stay calm, to be patient, to keep his voice down and steady. "Why do I even have to say this again? Niki was sick, and what happened to her wasn't your fault."

"That's what you think?"

"That's what I bloody well *know*. Now, let's get back in the goddamn car. I'm freezing my balls off."

"I know what you're thinking, Alex. All the things I told you last night, the things I saw in there. You think I'm insane."

"Is that why you never told Niki's shrink any of it?" he asks, and Daria glances at him and then back to the house. The front door's closed now, but the window to the right of it is broken, one of the windows looking in on the bedroom where she found Niki all those years ago, kneeling before the white thing. The afternoon sun glints off jagged glass fangs, and the cops said that was probably one of the ways the bums and crackheads had been getting into the place. The same window that she broke, once upon a time, because the house wouldn't let them out any other way. Not the same windowpane, but the same goddamn window.

"It's not good for you to be here, out in the cold like this," Alex says.

"It's not good for anyone to be here," Daria replies, the fingers of her left hand toying with the ball bearing through the lining of her leather jacket. The cloth, the steel beneath it, feels warm to the touch, but she knows that it's just heat stolen from her own shivering body.

"Come on," Alex says. "Let's go someplace warm. Let's find some coffee."

You have to find it for me, Daria, Niki said to her on the plane, Niki's ghost or her dream of Niki. *You have to find it and bring it to the basement of Spyder's house.* Daria shuts her eyes, listening to the wind and the traffic down on

Sixteenth, a few birds and a helicopter somewhere far away.

I saw it, she thinks. *I saw it all that night,* what Spyder had become at the last and all the evil secrets bubbling up from the belly of this house. And again she imagines burning it, setting cleansing flames to dance beneath the limbs of these trees, the smell of smoke to tell her it was all finally over.

"I fucking saw it," she says, letting the Marlboro fall from her lips to lie in the dead brown leaves. "I saw everything, Alex, just exactly like Niki always said, *more* than Niki said. But I never admitted it. I thought if I ever admitted it, that would make it true," and then she stops to wipe her dripping nose on the sleeve of her jacket and realizes that she's crying.

"But it was true anyway," she whispers. "It was true all along, and *that's* how I killed Niki." And the long shadows falling in dark and crooked streaks across the front porch of the house draw irrefutable lines of confirmation—lines leading her from then all the way to now, from that night ten years ago to this moment, from ghosts to daylight, from nightmares into wakefulness—and she knows its face, this house, and it knows hers.

"Dar, please, let's get the fuck out of here," Alex says, and, without another word, she slides off the hood and gets back into the car, because she doesn't want the house to see her cry.

This is someone else, not me, Niki thinks. Not, *This is not happening* or *This is not real,* because nothing in her life has ever felt half so real; all her doubt nested solidly in the infeasible reality of her *place* in this bright and undeniable moment: standing on the foredeck with Scarborough Pentecost and Malim and his first mate, a one-eared dwarf named Hobsen.

Around them the sea has gone almost as still as glass, and the ropes and canvas above them hang slack in air so still that Niki could believe no wind has ever blown in this place. And the bowsprit, like a wooden giant's finger, pointing up and out and at the heart of the maelstrom of light and thunder blocking their path. Niki keeps thinking it looks like a hurricane made from electricity instead of clouds, then turned on its side and half-submerged. A thousand feet across, she guesses, a thousand feet at least, and five hundred feet high. Its eye is the hard-candy color of a ruby, and at the edges of its counterclockwise rotation, the sea steams and bubbles and dead, boiled things swell and float to the surface.

"See that muck there, missy?" Malim growls, and he glares down at Niki. "That's a right proper demon, that is. That there's my greed finally come callin' for me." And Niki wonders that he can see her, that he would bother to talk to her, because she isn't here at all. She's somewhere else, surely, only *watching* this, and in a minute or two more she'll turn to Marvin and comment on the hokey special effects or ask him to change the channel, please. There must be something better on.

"What is it?" Niki asks Scarborough, and he shakes his head.

"Hell if I know. Maybe a portal," he says.

"*Maybe* a portal," Malim sneers. "Did ye hear that, Hobsen? This one 'ere, he thinks *maybe* it's a portal," and then, to Scarborough, "You know damn well what that thing is, just the same as me. It's the 'andiwork of the red witches, come to claim themselves a prize—" and Malim tugs hard at Niki's left ear. She slaps his hand away, but even the pain in her earlobe seems disconnected, distant, like something she remembers having felt a long time ago. *Dissociation,* Dr. Dalby would have said, peering at her through his spectacles, or perhaps *depersonalization,* one of those rambling, clinical words he trotted out whenever he wanted to say that her mind was trying to fashion a safe place for her to hide and only getting her into deeper trouble.

"I say we take the lifeboats and leave 'em here," the dwarf says and nervously wrings his small, grimy hands. "There weren't nothin' in our contract with the fish augur 'bout facin' down the Nesmidians, so I call it all null and void. If the red witches wants these two, fine, they can be my guest."

"I didn't steal this ship just so's a bunch of 'arlots and 'arpies could come along and wreck it," Malim says, and then he kicks Hobsen. "If anyone's going into a dinghy this day, it'll be the prophet and her seasick companion 'ere, not me nor mine."

Above them, the sky is turning from chalk white to an unhealthy, milky yellow, and Niki feels the fine hairs on the back of her neck and arms stand on end.

"The red witches don't want your leaking rat-tub of a boat," Scarborough says and scowls at Malim. "And they sure as hell don't want you."

"What if it's not the Nesmidians," the dwarf whispers fearfully. "What if maybe it's the Dragon hisself," and Malim tells him to shut up and kicks him again, harder than before.

"It only wants me," Niki says quietly, certain that she's right, and the detachment that's been clouding her head since she first saw the spinning disc rising from the sea vanishes.

Nicolan, we could sit here arguing reality all day long, Dr. Dalby tells her, speaking up from some afternoon that's already over and done with, or some afternoon that comes after she finally finds her way back to San Francisco, or, she thinks, some afternoon that has never been and never will be. *We could talk Descartes and Kant, metaphysics and epistemology, until bullfrogs grow wings and insects build rocket ships. But where's that gonna get us?*

The ruby eye at the motionless center of the vortex begins to pulse, one red flare after the next in quick succession, the breathless space between pulses growing shorter and shorter, and Niki steps forward, so she's sure that it sees her.

"I'm right here," she says, and the pulses stop as abruptly as they began.

Try to think of it this way, Dr. Dalby suggests, as he digs about in the bowl of his pipe, dislodging ash with a small silver scoop. *Imagine the universe is all of one essence, so that both consciousness and substance must be essentially identical.*

"Scarborough, I think you should all leave now," Niki says, and she motions towards the stern with her bandaged hand. "And I think you should probably hurry." In a heartbeat, the maelstrom has doubled in size and is beginning to turn clockwise.

Idealism, dualism, materialism, materio-dualism, it's all the same damn thing, in the end. These ideas are only minor variations on the same eternal chord, the same psychic resonance in the void.

"*Go*," Scarborough tells Malim and the dwarf, and then he steps forward to stand beside Niki.

"Wot's this?" Malim grunts indignantly. "What about me money, eh? I entered into an 'onest covenant wiv that old whore Chattox, and I expect *full* remuneration—" but Hobsen is already dragging the smuggler away towards the stairs leading steeply down from the foredeck.

"Do you know what's happening?" Scarborough asks her, and Niki shakes her head.

"Not exactly," she says. "But I know that thing's looking for me, and there's no way to run from it. And I know you should go, because it isn't looking for you."

"Sorry, Vietnam. But I made Esme a promise, and, unfortunately, I'm a man of my word. Most of the time." He takes her good hand, his sweaty palm slick against hers, his fingers so strong, and she's glad that whatever's coming, she doesn't have to face it alone.

I'm here, she thinks and keeps her eyes on the center of the vortex. *What are you waiting for?*

From the flickering, feathery edges of the maelstrom, lightning tendrils snake out across the water and crackle loudly through the masts and rigging.

Are you real, Nicolan? Dr. Dalby asks her as he stuffs fresh cherry-scented tobacco into his pipe. *Am I? Are all the things that Spyder showed you? Is* any *of this real? If you can answer that one question, to your* own *satisfaction, I think you'll find all the courage that you're ever going to need.*

"Hang on tight," Niki says, and then the lightning sweeps down from the foremast, and they fall into the ruby eye of the storm.

CHAPTER TEN

At the Crossroads

In the basement beneath the old house, the red witch sits on earth packed almost as solid as cement, dry clay gone the color of cayenne or weathered bricks, and she watches the thing growing from the low ceiling. She's been watching it for hours, by the bobbing globe of blue-white light she summoned with a murmur, amazed and horrified at Theda's determined metamorphosis. It started only a few minutes after Walter died, a few minutes after the red witch put a bullet in his head. She dragged his body, *bump-bump-bump*, down the wooden stairs and left it lying in a heap in the center of the basement floor, because she figured Theda might get hungry later on.

Hours and hours watching the swollen, dripping thing, night and day and then night again, and she's recited every prayer and blessing that she learned before she died and the towers on the banks of the Yärin were lost to her forever. Words and almost-words that were at least enough to hide them from the police that the Hierophant's lover brought with her, and also enough to grant her the patience to wait. Because she knows that Daria Parker will return, and next time she'll come alone.

The floorboards and sagging joists creak and pop from the increasing weight of the thing suspended in its black chrysalis, and Archer Day aims her pistol at it again. Staring down the barrel of the .38 and reminding herself that she *still* has choices, maybe not so many as she had the night before, but that's the price of decision, the price of action. The ebony membrane holding the thing together shudders, and Archer puts as much pressure on the trigger as she dares. Only a *little* more, and the hammer would fall, and the gun would fire, and then the future would change again.

"Can you hear me in there, little girl?" she asks Theda, and the chrysalis shudders again, straining at hardened secretions and the countless riblike cremasters holding it in place. "Yeah, that's what I thought," and she wonders if Theda knows that they brought her down here to murder her, that Walter took the bullet meant for the Weaver's surrogate. The bullet inscribed with the secret names of two goddesses, the ravenous ladies of flame and ice, the bullet Archer anointed with melissa and arsenic and dandelions.

"What the hell's this rotting world to me?" Archer whispers to herself as she lowers the gun again. "Let the Dragon have it *all*," but she knows that she doesn't sound half so confident as she did the night before. She doesn't *feel* half so confident, either, and curses herself for being weak after all she's seen, for falling to the temptations of the great red wolf, but also for ever having bought into the childish faith and suicidal altruism of the Sect in the first place.

The basement smells dry, like dust and cobwebs and the spores of a dozen different fungi, but Archer can't smell the chrysalis, as if it has no scent.

"This was never *my* war, little girl. Four years ago, I was still a goddamn child. Of course, it had to be a child they sent, didn't it? No one else would have gone through with such madness."

The chrysalis skin ripples, and more of the green-black fluid leaks from the thumb-sized spiracles spaced unevenly along its sides, dripping to the dirt floor and onto Walter's corpse.

"Oh, you *are* hungry aren't you? I bet you're starving to

death in there, poor thing," and Archer watches as the thick fluid slowly breaks down flesh and bone and cartilage, turning it into something soft, something gelatinous, something that the thing growing inside the chrysalis can use when the time comes.

"Soon, little girl," Archer promises, looking away from the dead man to glance down at her wristwatch, the one she bought in Manhattan years ago, cheap watch from a Chinatown kiosk, gold hands gliding endlessly across a field of white. "Not much longer, and then I bet you'll never be hungry again."

She used her bare hands to trace a perfect circle an inch deep into the hard dirt below the chrysalis, a holding circle to enclose Walter's body safely within its circumference and serve as the Hierophant's focal point. All the numbers in her head to guide her raw and bleeding hands—mathematics, alchemy, geometry—and the forbidden language of the singing rocks along the Serpent's Road slipping easily from her lips. All the things the fire-colored wolf has taught her in the dreams she spent so long trying not to acknowledge.

And now all she needs is the philtre, a single silver orb, and she might have been little more than a child when her blood spilled out hot across the temple floor, but she knows enough to scry that Daria Parker has the talisman, that she's found it and has brought it here. A surrogate for a surrogate, obscene relay from one hand to another, the passing of the monstrous key that is all keys, heart key, soul key, key of Diamond and Lost Faith. The key that will throw open the door the Weaver left ajar.

The chrysalis shudders again, more violently than before, and the spines where Theda's shoulder blades were begin to twitch and quiver in the musty basement air, humming softly like the mating call of some great insect.

"No, no, no. Not just yet," Archer Day cautions the thing, and she raises the pistol again. The steel glints dully in the sizzling blue light she's made. *Could I kill it if I tried?* she wonders. *Are there enough bullets in this gun, enough bul-*

lets in this world, *to put down the abomination gestating in that black husk?*

And then she shuts her eyes and tries to think of nothing but the Hierophant's lover, sleeping somewhere in the city, sleeping with a man she loves more than the Hierophant, and the red witch searches until she finds a tiny breach along the outermost rim of Daria Parker's uneasy dreams, and slides herself in. And for a time, she forgets about the flame-colored wolf and the dragon and the thing hanging from the basement ceiling.

Four miles away, northeast across autumn-silent streets and the creosote cross-tie and iron-rail stitchery of railroad tracks, Daria Parker sleeps on the sixth floor of the Tutwiler Hotel. Held tight in Alex Singer's arms and surrounded by sturdy plaster and masonry laid and mortar set the better part of a century before, she dreams.

Her father, wounded, heartsick man who died of cancer years before, and he's trying to explain to her why he and her mother could never work things out. Mistakes and transgressions, apologies for the divorce and the drama, the day he took his daughter and ran away to Mississippi. Daria listens disinterestedly (she's heard it all before) while a waiter with tattoos and the spiraling, narwhal horns of an African antelope serves them hot tea and fresh-baked biscuits with apple jelly and melted butter. The morning sun through the cafe windows is warm, and the little tables are surrounded by terra-cotta pots of philodendrons and ferns.

"Charles Lindbergh once held a press conference here, you know," the waiter says and winks at her, quoting the hotel brochure and interrupting her dead father. "And Tallulah Bankhead held parties here. The Jewel of Birmingham, that's what they called the place—"

"Excuse me," Daria says and frowns at the waiter, "but we're trying to have a conversation."

"I hadn't noticed," he snips, and she realizes that the chair across the table from her is empty.

"You have a telegram from a Miss Nicolan Ky," the waiter continues, nonplussed by her father's disappearance. The waiter has become a very large macaw, its feathers painted the deepest tropical reds and blues, and Daria can smell licorice on his breath. The bird holds out a silver tray, tarnished but ornate silver serving tray, and there's nothing but a slip of yellow paper on it.

"It's not *over* till it's *over*," the macaw squawks rudely, but when Daria reaches for the telegram it becomes the rusty ball bearing with N-I-K-I written on it. "Turn away no more, why wilt thou turn away?" says the macaw.

Daria takes the ball bearing from the platter and tries to remember how she got all the way from the hotel downtown to the house on Cullom Street. How day became night and she didn't even notice, but the answer is obvious, and it comes to her on the cold wind blowing across the mountain. *Another dream, another goddamn, stinking dream.* Her whole life seems to have come to little else, a clamoring parade of nightmares strung together with twine and guitar string and baling wire, and she's always waking in unfamiliar, unwelcoming rooms or the rumbling bellies of jet planes. Always waking to disorientation or loss, fear or pain, all those supposedly different things that are exactly the same, the slippery facets of a whole too vast and terrible to glimpse in a single moment. Even *this* dream, the one that binds them all in the gray-matter wrinkles of its infinite variations, even it permits only incomplete disclosure, stingy bits and pieces at a time, mean impressions, like blind men feeling their way around an elephant.

Daria Parker climbs the five cement steps to the porch, and then she stops, glancing back over her left shoulder at the dusky shapes moving quickly between the flickering, plywood trees, the long-legged, skittering beasts, Spyder's defenders or prison guards, and maybe there's no difference.

"Would you like the check now," the macaw waiter asks, though she can't see him anywhere, "or should I charge it to your room?"

She stands shivering on the long, cluttered porch, her hand wrapped tightly around the brass doorknob. She looks over her shoulder again, half expecting Mort and Theo in the driveway, waiting for her in the idling red Ford Econoline, Stiff Kitten's junk-heap set of wheels, but there's only the shoddy, back-lot trees, the narrow, bound-less spaces left between them, and the matte-painting dis-tance rising up to the cloudy charcoal edges of the November sky.

Is this the way it was? Did I really come up here alone? Did I already love her that much?

Have I ever loved her at all?

"I always loved your mother," her father mumbles, his words like lead shot falling into a deep pool.

And she turns very slowly back towards the front door that's no longer there, anticlockwise minute and hour hands of bone and corrosion sweeping her backwards, sweeping her back to the night before *that* night, and she's standing in a freezing alley behind the dump where Keith Barry lived. This is the night of his wake, the night before she went to Spyder's house to find Niki. Everyone else has gone, all the motley, drunken mourners, the sin-eaters, and left her to lock up. Daria hugs herself and notices the tall boy in a black Bauhaus T-shirt watching her from the other side of the alley, and she wonders how long he's been standing there. One of Spyder's gothedy loser friends, she thinks, someone she's seen skulking around Dr. Jekyll's, but if she's ever known his name, she doesn't remember it now.

"The dining room closes in five minutes," the macaw an-nounces, pointing one wing at a clock on the wall behind her, and then he becomes the ruby-eyed white bird from the plane, from the window ledge of her hospital room.

"Time is beside the point," the white bird insists. "There is only *one* moment, which moves endlessly, and you stand there always."

"What the hell do *you* want," she barks at the boy in the Bauhaus shirt, ignoring the white bird and sounding at least as drunk as she is, sounding like a drunken old whore, and the boy looks nervously up and down the narrow alleyway before he crosses it to stand beside her.

"Do you have a *name*?" she asks, trying not to slur and failing and deciding that she really doesn't care.

"Walter. My name's Walter Ayers. I used to be a friend of Spyder Baxter's."

You'll remember me, later on. You'll remember the night I tried to warn you about Spyder, the night in Birmingham when I told you Niki was in danger.

"One moment," the white bird says again, "that's all," and it stares up at her from the spotless linen table cloth. Margarine sun pours across its feathers, and its eyes sparkle resolutely. "That's all any of us ever get."

"Did Spyder send you?" she asks the bird, and it blinks and pecks at the scraps of her biscuit.

"I used to be a friend of Spyder Baxter's," the boy says again, like he thinks she didn't hear him the first time, and Daria tries to forget about the white bird and her unanswered question.

"But you're not anymore," Daria says to the boy named Walter, "not her friend, I mean," and she's started walking, because it's too cold to stand still any longer. He follows close behind, their footsteps loud in the long empty alleyway. The mute hulks of abandoned warehouses rise up around them, cinder block and brick and corrugated aluminum to brace the unreliable sky.

"Well, I think that's what *she'd* say, if you asked her," he replies, walking faster to catch up. "I'm pretty sure that's what she'd say. She thinks that I had something to do with what happened to Robin."

"You mean Spyder's girlfriend?" Daria asks, and she stops, and the boy named Walter stops walking, too, and stands there trying not to let his teeth chatter.

"Yeah," he says, "I mean Spyder's girlfriend," and then he looks back the way they've come, his anxious eyes trapped in an anxious, exhausted face.

"Well, did you?"

Walter doesn't answer the question, just keeps staring back down the northside alley like he's afraid they're being followed.

See into the dark

Just follow your eyes

"Who was the girl that left with Spyder tonight?" he asks her, changing the subject. "The Japanese girl."

"Her name's Niki Ky, and she's not Japanese. She's Vietnamese, and she's Spyder's *new* girl. Haven't you heard? She moved in with Spyder a couple of weeks ago."

It really doesn't matter if you don't believe or understand what I'm saying. You will. *Niki's on her way back to Cullom Street. She's received the mark. You've seen it, on her hand. Niki Ky is becoming the Hierophant, and she'll open the gates. She'll unleash the Dragon.*

"Is she a friend of yours?" he asks, and "Yeah, she's a friend of mine," Daria replies.

"Then you should know she's in danger. Spyder's not right."

"Spyder's a goddamn basket case," Daria says and starts walking again. "Spyder's the fucking poster girl for schizos."

"No. I don't mean because she's crazy. I mean, she's not *right.*"

We have to be there to stop her. All of us have to be there to stop her. All the worlds are winding down. All the worlds are spinning to a stop. Find her, Daria, before the jackals do. Before I do. If I find her first, I have to kill her, and I've killed too many people already.

"Spyder's not right," he says again, as if she'll understand him if only he keeps repeating the words over and over. "If you care about your friend, you'll keep her away from that house. Robin knew about Spyder. She tried to tell us, and now she's dead."

"Yeah, well, now Niki's dead, too, spooky boy, so I guess you're a day late and a dollar short, and we're both shit out of luck."

And then the moments and seconds are collapsing

around her, playing-card houses and sand-castle dissolution, a sudden and furious implosion of time with her standing somewhere much too near ground zero. She sits on the hotel bed in Atlanta, holding her cell phone, and at the sunlit table with the white bird. She stands in the alley with Walter, and grips the brass knob to the front door of Spyder's house.

Only one moment . . .

And she opens the door.

And the house is full of light.

Silver-white light draped in shimmering, Christmas garland strands and floating lazily on the bright air, lying in tangled drifts upon the floor. Daria shields her eyes, opens her mouth to call for Niki, or only to stand there slackjawed and stupid at the sight. But then she hears the hurried, scuttling noises at her back, something big coming up the steps, coming fast, and there's a crash as a piece of the porch trash tumbles over, and she doesn't look, steps quickly across the threshold and slams the door shut behind her.

And she stands very still, remembering how the threads burned her, stands listening as they settle gently across the floor and furniture, the sound of them like falling snow. And she also remembers finding the open hole leading down to the basement. Remembers the warmer air rising up from that pit and the incongruous scents: mold and earth, jasmine and the sweeter smell of rotting meat. And the imperfect blackness pooled at the foot of the stairs, the dim red-orange glow at the center of that pool, blood-orange glow, and there was laughter from the hole, insane and hateful laughter.

"You don't have to do this again," the white bird informs her, preening itself now that it's finished with the biscuit. "You saved Niki Ky *that* night. Some mistakes we only have to make once."

"Mistakes? You think it was a mistake, saving Niki?"

"Did I say that?" the white bird squawks and peers suspiciously up at Daria, squinting its red eyes in the glare of the sun. "I don't think that's what I said at all. I think your head's stuffed full of cotton, old woman."

"I just fucking *heard* you. You said, 'Some mistakes we only have to make once.' "

"Why would I have said a thing like that? The Hierophant is our savior. Without her, all is lost."

"Liar," Daria hisses, and she turns from the bird to watch the traffic outside the cafe's window. She wonders if Alex is ever coming down to breakfast, and if the cafe really closes in five minutes. If the white bird's a liar, the macaw might have been lying, too.

"We're wasting time we don't have to waste," a woman says, and when Daria turns back to the table, the white bird is gone, and there's a pale woman dressed in scarlet robes sitting across from her, sitting in her father's chair. The woman is very young, younger than herself, probably younger even than Niki. Her hair is neither blond nor brown, some color in between that Daria can't recall the word for, and her brown eyes are desperate, but not unkind, and seem to lead away somewhere safely beyond the borders of this dream.

"While there's still time, you have to listen to me, Daria Parker. I'm Archer Day. I called you at the airport—"

"I came to the house."

"You brought policemen with you. That was stupid."

"What do you want?" Daria asks, and suddenly the dream doesn't feel like a dream at all, as though the flowing, undecided fabric of her unconscious mind has congealed, and now she's trapped here and will never be able to wake up again.

"It's not too late," the woman says. "But this time you have to come alone. This time you come alone, or you never see Niki again."

Something taps on the cafe window, and Daria sees that it's the white bird, stranded on the other side of the glass. Its beak is striking the windowpane so violently that there are tiny sparks.

"The bird can't bring her back to you," Archer Day says.

"Nor can the Weaver. I'm the only chance you've got. Come before morning. After that, it may be too late. Theda won't sleep forever."

"Who's Theda?"

"Bring the philtre," Archer says, and when she stands to leave, the window shatters, spraying diamond bits of glass across the table, across Daria's lap, and the white bird is torn apart in the flood of darkness pouring in to wash the brown-haired woman away.

And it all feels like a dream again.

Daria holds the dead and broken bird in both hands, its blood oozing thickly from the spaces between her fingers and dripping to the ground charred black as soot. There is no cafe now, and no sunlight, and no potted philodendrons. She stands alone on a high and rocky place, beneath a night sky choked with smoke, and jagged lightning tongues lick greedily at the ruined and burning world below.

"I'm sorry," she says to the bird, and it seems as though there are other things she ought to say, but she can't think of any of them.

"It's no fault of yours," Spyder says, and Daria turns to find her standing only a few feet away. But this woman is not the Spyder Baxter she remembers; there's a glowing red gem set into the skin between Spyder's eyes that's the same color as the dead bird's eyes.

"She was my courier. She never expected to live through this."

"Where are we, Spyder?"

"A place. A time the Dragon is preparing for us all. The red witch is insane, you know, but you have to do what she asks. Niki needs you."

"The red witch," Daria murmurs, repeating the three words as she turns to face the blasted landscape stretched out below her, as she stoops down and lays the dead bird's limp body on the heat-cracked stones.

"She told you her name was Archer Day. It's not, but that isn't important. She was sent to stop me, but she's fallen now. She's renounced her vows—"

"And she has Niki?"

"Niki needs you, Daria."

"You didn't answer my question," but now there's something stirring in the depths of the flames, something enormous made of scales and teeth and leathery wings, and a rain of ash and embers has begun to fall from the scorched clouds.

"You didn't die that night," Daria says. "You only found another place to hide, didn't you? And you're still trying to use Niki—"

"Shut up," Spyder snarls, and the ground rumbles beneath Daria's feet. "I'm here because I tried to *protect* Niki. I gave my life, I loved her so."

"Is that why she's dead?"

"That's" why she's dead," Spyder says, "and *that's* what you have to save her from," and as if it's heard her and knows the cue, the Dragon rises from a smoldering jungle of twisted steel and strides across molten asphalt highways, its tireless, searchlight eyes hunting, hunting, hunting, and now Daria knows exactly who it's looking for.

"My father was a serpent," Spyder whispers in her ear, Spyder standing so close that Niki can smell her, vanilla and patchouli and Old Spice cologne, hate and spite and bitterness. "My father opened his eyes one day and saw angels following him, and *this* is what they made of him. And, in return, *this* is what he made of me."

Daria looks down, and there's a horde of white spiders, a billion pinprick dots swarming ankle-deep around her feet and flowing over the edge of the cliff to meet the Dragon's gaze. She wants to scream, wants to open her mouth wide and never *stop* screaming, but she doesn't, stands absolutely still and silent instead, while all their scurrying, jointed legs brush across her bare skin. And when they've gone, there are only bones and feathers where the white bird was.

Niki opens her eyes, blinks, and the first thing she notices is that she's still holding Scarborough's hand. Or he's still holding hers. And the deck of Malim's ship and the becalmed ocean and the devouring vortex with its crimson heart, so much like the gem between Spyder's brows, have all been replaced by wavering firelight and shadows and a rough stone floor. The source of the firelight is a wide, triangular pit set into the floor at the center of the chamber; the air is close and reeks of unfamiliar spices and musky incense. Above them, wide strips of some fine cloth hang suspended from the ceiling, an elaborate confusion of vertical and horizontal lines, zigzags and multispirals, the strips of a vast, discontinuous tapestry. The firelight plays yellow and orange ghosts across the fabric.

"Hell, I should have fucking run," Scarborough laughs, a hard and humorless laugh, and he cracks his knuckles. Niki nods and looks around her at the great chamber, this one a far grander thing than the fish augur's magic bubble. The walls are constructed of massive blocks of the same gray stone as the floor, slate gray shot through with glittering silver-white streaks, like veins of mica or pyrite crystals. On the other side of the fire is an altar—there's no mistaking it for anything else—a long stone table set at the clawed feet of a statue or idol so tall that its head almost brushes the roof of the chamber, fifty feet or more above them. There's a rusty iron trough that leads from the table down to the fire pit, and Niki doesn't want to think about what that means, or whether or not all those stains are really rust, so she looks back up at the statue.

"Where are we, Scarborough?"

"If I had to hazard a guess, I'd say we're somewhere in the Melán Veld."

"And that means—?"

"Bad shit, Vietnam. It means some real bad shit. Melán Veld is the sacrificial temple of the red witches of Nesmia Shar."

"Yeah, well, I figured it had to be something like that. The way things have been going, I really wasn't expecting happy pixies."

And Niki stares up through the tapestry strips at the idol

staring down at her with its faceted, maroon eyes, eyes that might be garnets, if there were ever garnets as big as basketballs. And she knows that she's seen this thing somewhere before, this thing or something very much like it, and a moment later she remembers where. Those same powerful, feline haunches, the same four wings like ragged sails of skin and bone, the hooked beak, and she's pretty sure it's meant to be the same creature as the statue she saw at the Palisades, the thing that was almost a griffin.

"*They* brought us here, these red witches?"

"Like you said, it wasn't happy pixies."

"There isn't much time left for questions," someone says, a voice that streams like water over polished glass, that clear and easy, and a woman in long red robes and a sage green skullcap steps out of the shadows at the base of the statue. Niki can tell that she was very beautiful once, but she's grown old, and there's a terrible scar running across the bridge of her nose and both cheeks. Her hair is almost the same drab gray as the stone floor.

"You know, I'm so sick of hearing that I could fucking puke," Niki says, and now there are other women stepping out of the shadows that lie along the edges of the chamber, dozens of women in identical, flowing cerise robes. A few of them wear skullcaps the same shade of gray-green as the woman standing near the statue, but most of them have simple white bandanas tied tightly around their heads. All of the women are barefoot, and the callused pads of their feet rustle softly against the rough stone.

"*Look* at her, sisters and daughters," the woman on the altar commands, and now her glass-and-water voice is clouded with contempt and disgust. "Look at her very closely. This *girl* is the Hierophant, the chosen and willing tool of the Weaver, the one who has come among us, to *our* world, to set the Dragon and all of its agents free. Because of this girl, we have given up one of our own."

In response, the red women standing around the walls of the chamber begin to talk among themselves, speaking in nervous, hushed tones, a flurry of shocked and angry half whispers. Niki releases Scarborough's hand and takes a step nearer the fire pit and the altar and the woman in the sage skullcap.

"So, is this supposed to be some sort of trial?" she asks. "Is that why you brought us here? Are we on trial?"

"No," the woman replies. "You're already condemned, by your own selfish actions and by the actions of the Weaver. There's no need for a trial, Hierophant."

Niki glances back at Scarborough, but he's staring at his feet or the floor and doesn't seem to notice.

"I am named Pikabo Kenzia," the woman says, and Niki gives up on Scarborough and reluctantly turns to face her again. "Here, I am Mother and Voice—in this hall, in this tower, and throughout the protectorate of Nesmia. I know well that the Weaver has kept many things from you, girl. She has never trusted the truth of matters to get her work done."

"I didn't *want* to come here," Niki says, and she wonders how many times she's said that since San Francisco. She holds her head up and tries not to flinch at Pikabo Kenzia's cold eyes almost as impervious, as impenetrable, as the eyes of the idol towering over them all. "Spyder told me I had to come, that I had to come or two worlds would die, mine and yours. That's what she said. That's why I jumped off the bridge. That's why I *died*."

"And you believed her? Do you even believe yourself?"

"I *saw* things. She showed me things—"

"Listen, it's really not what you think," Scarborough interrupts, and the murmuring crowd grows suddenly and ominously silent. "She's not a hierophant," he continues. "I don't even think that she knows what a hierophant is."

"You," Pikabo Kenzia roars, "you do *not* speak here!"

But Scarborough Pentecost continues, as though he hasn't heard her, "The Weaver *lied* to her. You just said as much yourself. The bitch has lied to everyone—"

"Another word, another *sound,* and I will personally cut the tongue from out your mouth."

"You're enemies of the Dragon," Niki says quickly, before Scarborough can say anything else. "That part's true, isn't it?"

"Yes, Hierophant, that much of what she told you is the truth. We have opposed the Dragon for more than a hundred centuries."

"But whatever Spyder's trying to do to destroy it, you don't think that it'll work."

Pikabo Kenzia steps down from the altar and walks past the killing table with its scabby iron trough, the hem of her robes and her bare feet almost silent as she strides across the floor to stand on the other side of the fire pit from Niki. The flames between them, the flames and so many other things that Niki knows she could never comprehend, and now she can see that the witch's eyes are the softest shade of violet.

"You're going to kill me," Niki says and looks away from Pikabo's eyes, into the depths of fire and cinder-black logs.

"No, Hierophant. I'm not going to kill you, nor will I allow any other here to raise her hand against you."

Niki doesn't take her eyes off the burning logs, determined not to let the red witch see her surprise or relief or confusion. "You said I was condemned."

"Yes, you are condemned. You are, I suspect, damned. But that's not my doing. It's the Weaver's, and it's not my role to pass sentence upon you."

"Spyder . . ." Niki begins, and then she realizes that there are human bones mixed in with the logs in the fire pit, the cracked shafts of long bones and ribs and a jaw going slowly to ash, and she wishes that she were home in her room, and today she and Marvin might go to a movie or to Fisherman's Wharf and have boiled crabs at McCormick's and Kuleto's. If only she knew the way back to the Palisades, and then some trick to turn Spyder's magic inside out, and she'd never tell Daria or Dr. Dalby a word of what she's seen. They wouldn't listen anyway.

"You were about to speak?" Pikabo Kenzia asks her, and Niki shrugs and forces herself to look up, looking away from the scorched bones, and she meets the red witch's gaze through the dancing curtain of fire.

"The Weaver," she says. "I loved her very much, a long time ago, and then I lost her. But I thought that I still loved her. I thought I could trust her with my soul."

"And she used your love to her own ends."

"Did she? Or is that just the easiest thing for you to believe?"

The red witch doesn't reply; she sighs and tosses a pinch of something powdered into the fire pit, and it begins to burn more brightly and the flames take on an unhealthy greenish tint.

"I may not sentence you," Pikabo Kenzia says. "You are a being more powerful than all but the Dragon and the Weaver herself. As I said, I may not pass sentence, but"—and she pauses for a moment and peers deep into the flames, adds another pinch of powder, and the fire gutters, then burns almost as green as leaves on a summer's day—"I do have a role in all of this. That much was written at the beginning, even before Dezyin came down from the stars and set the spokes to spinning, *that* much was certain. Now I can only follow the course of my life."

"Why did you bring me here?"

"*We* brought you here to show you what we know, what we believe is the Weaver's design for you, in hopes that you will listen and believe in turn." And then, in an instant, the fire is extinguished, and there are creaking, mechanical noises rising from beneath the floor—gears and pistons and unseen engines—and Pikabo Kenzia takes a step back from the pit. Niki follows her example.

"When the Weaver came, she came to destroy the Dragon, which she mistook for something else, something malignant from her world. There are those of us who believe that she thought the Dragon to be the ghost of her father, and some others say she thought the Dragon was a powerful demon. She went out among the people and worked miracles and eventually raised an army against Kearvan Weal, the Dragon's hall at the world's hub. She was not entirely unsuccessful."

"But the Dragon was stronger?"

"No, not stronger. They're like darkness and light, the Weaver and the Dragon, like life and death, equal and inseparable. In the end, what little remained of the Weaver's armies fled across the spokes, returning to their homes or hiding in the wilderness. And that's when we learned what had happened to the Dragon, that it had been changed somehow by its contact with the Weaver. Her beliefs had infected it, as though her mind were a disease," and Pikabo Kenzia presses the tip of her left index finger to the point between her violet eyes. "A disease to which even eternal creatures like the Dragon are not immune."

Niki glances back at Scarborough again, and this time he's watching her, and their eyes make contact for an instant, long enough that she can see that he believes what the red witch is saying, and then he looks quickly away.

"The Dragon saw something in the Weaver that shattered its very soul, Hierophant. What this thing was, I cannot even begin to imagine, nor do I ever want to. But the inner wheels fell dark following the war, and there was talk that the Dragon had sent forth newly conceived lieutenants to find and kill the Weaver. She calls these beings *angels,* and she fears them above all else."

"Yeah," Niki whispers, more to herself than the red witch. "This part's starting to sound familiar."

"But now, all these things are history," Pikabo Kenzia says, gazing intently at Niki from the other side of the fire pit. A few wisps of greenish smoke are still rising from the ashes, and the smell reminds Niki of fresh basil. "What concerns us *this* day is that you understand the choice that you have been condemned to make."

"Spyder said I was to travel the Serpent's Road, and cross the Dog's Bridge—"

"That would take you to the ruins of Kearvan Weal, where we believe she's opening a portal."

"A portal to where?"

"A passageway between this world and the one you have come from, a portal through which the Dragon will be driven before the passage is closed again, exiling it there forever. She convinces her followers that she's doing this to *save* our world, but we suspect her motives have more to do with revenge than salvation. And regardless, we can't stand by and watch while another world is ravaged that we might finally be free of the Dragon."

Niki listens to the mechanical sounds coming from beneath the floor and thinks about her final night in San Francisco, standing at the window of the hotel room talking to Daria for the last time, and then her vision of blue fire and a dragon rising from the bay to devour first one city and then a planet, and eventually, an entire universe.

"And the philtre," Niki says, "Spyder needs the philtre to open this portal."

"Yes. The philtre and the Hierophant and a surrogate whom she has chosen to stand on the other side in her stead."

"But I don't *have* the philtre," Niki tells the red witch, and a cautious glimmer of something like hope washes quickly across Pikabo Kenzia's scarred face and is gone.

"The Weaver can open the portal without the philtre," she says. "There are other ways, if she has been successful in finding a surrogate. Without you and that talisman she would never be able to shut it again, but she's mad, and driven, and so that alone might not stop her from *trying*."

"She was in Padnée," Scarborough says, still looking at the floor. "Do you know what happened to Padnée? Maybe she died there."

"Your friend has a sort of thoughtless courage, Hierophant. But it won't save him, if he speaks again."

Niki turns to Scarborough and holds a finger across her lips, shushing him, and he looks up long enough to roll his eyes at her.

"The Weaver can't die, not so long as she's here," the red witch says. "Only in the world where her existence began may it be undone. Would that it were otherwise. Our assassins would have killed her years ago."

"But if I don't have this philtre, then I can't do what she wants me to do. I'm useless to her."

"No, you are *still* part of her key, and you still have a choice to make," and the women in the temple begin to talk among themselves again, louder than before. Niki looks to Scarborough, but he's turned his back on her.

"You must understand what lies before you," the red witch says, and when Niki looks again, the triangular fire pit has vanished completely, and in its place is a circular table made from the same gray stone as the rest of the temple. The top of it is a sort of three-dimensional map, rugged mountain ranges and deep river valleys and oceans chiseled from the rock and painted so realistically she almost believes that if she reached out and touched an ocean her hand would come back salty and wet.

"*This* is our world, Hierophant," Pikabo Kenzia says, and Niki realizes that the table's much more than just a map, that it's a globe, a globe for an impossible hemispherical world. She listens while the witch points out the craggy rim of the Palisades stretching the entire circumference of the globe and shows Niki the catwalk road through the mists to Padnée. At intervals, the globe is divided into bands, each one narrower than the one before it, bands which make Niki think of the nested circles of Dante's *Inferno*. And she understands that, unlike the equator or the Tropic of Capricorn, these divisions are not imaginary.

"The wheels turn," Pikabo Kenzia says, and the globe seems to respond to her voice, so that each circle begins moving to the raw scraping of stone ground against stone. The outermost band, which includes the Palisades and the wide blue ocean called the Outer Main, turns clockwise, and the next band in turns counterclockwise, and the next clockwise, and so on to the still center of the globe. *The hub,* Niki thinks, recalling what the red witch has said, and she recognizes the Dog's Bridge spanning a blistering sea of molten lava.

"Nesmia, where we are, is here," Pikabo tells her and points at the globe, "well inside the third wheel, beside the river Yärin. Even by the Serpent's Road, it's a long journey to the halls of the Dragon."

"It doesn't matter how *far* it is," Niki replies. "I'm not going there, not if what you've told me about Spyder is true—"

"You're still not listening to me, Hierophant. Whether you go or not, she will open the portal."

"How can you *know* that?"

"Because I have *seen* the things she's done. We have nursed the victims of her war—" and Pikabo Kenzia's eyes flash with some cold, inner fire, and she spreads her arms wide to include all the women in the chamber. "But first she will come looking for you. And we can't stand against her."

"And you think I can," Niki says doubtfully, looking at the tortured maze of canyons and volcanoes at the center of the globe.

"I'm saying that you have a *choice*. There is a way that you can defeat her, Nicolan Ky," and the sound of her name from the red witch's lips makes Niki look up from the table's lunatic geography. All the women along the walls have fallen silent again, and there are dark and bloody tears streaking Pikabo Kenzia's cheeks.

Daria stands alone in the night filling up the house and listens to the wind whistling through the trees, across tar-paper shingles, and around the eaves and sagging, leaf-gorged gutters.

She left the rental car in the Tutwiler's parking lot and took a taxi back to Cullom Street. An old Ford station wagon painted lemon yellow for a taxi, and the burly Mexican behind the wheel mumbled things in Spanish that she couldn't understand. After the dream, after she awakened in the dark hotel room and sat for almost an hour, smoking and listening to the comforting rhythm of Alex sleeping beside her, she got dressed as quietly as she could and managed to slip out without waking him. She left a note on her pillow, hastily scribbled on a sheet of hotel stationary. "I love you," she wrote, "and I will come back, if I can." There wasn't anything else she could think of to say, or at least nothing she had the time to write down, and so she decided that would have to do.

She had the Mexican drive her to an all-night Western Supermarket on Highland Avenue, where she bought another pack of Marlboro Reds, a bottle of cheap Merlot, and a small flashlight. The flashlight was an afterthought, and she finished half the bottle of wine before they reached the abandoned house at the end of the street. Standing at the edge of the driveway, she paid the driver and tipped him ten bucks; he grunted something grateful in Spanish and then drove away. It didn't surprise her when she found the front door standing open.

The wind sounds like voices, a lot more like voices than it sounds like wind, dozens of lost children muttering to themselves all at once. And she wonders again if coming here was suicide, if she's come here to die and maybe she's not so different from Niki after all.

All these empty, dusty rooms, without a single stick of furniture, devoid of life or even the trappings of life: a foyer and living room, the dining room and kitchen, a short hallway connecting the bathroom and two bedrooms, the one that had been Spyder's when she lived alone, and the one that she and Niki shared after Niki had moved in. And the trapdoor concealing the basement stairs. For a long time, Daria has stood watching that varnished rectangle of pine, a brass handle bolted at one end, wondering what, if anything, is waiting for her down there.

She switches on the flashlight and plays it slowly across the trapdoor. There are handprints in the thick dust, and she supposes some of them must belong to the two cops. She finishes the bottle of Merlot and sets it on the floor near the wall. The wine has left a gentle, welcomed buzz inside her, and a scrap of courage, though she knows it's only the smallest fraction of what she'll need.

If anyone's around, she thinks, *they can hear me. If anyone's here, they must know I'm here, too.*

But she doesn't call out, because she isn't that brave, not

half that drunk. She eyes the empty bottle, wishing she'd bought two.

When the bitch is ready for me, when she wants this game to end, the bitch can come find me, and Daria goes to the smaller bedroom, the one that had been Spyder's before Niki came to live with her, and she sits in a corner, facing the door. She switches off the flashlight, because she isn't sure how long the batteries will last, and she'd rather not have to confront the basement without it. Outside, the sky is cloudy, so no moon through the bare windows, and only a little streetlight reaches her through the backyard gone wild and choked with kudzu vines.

She wonders if Alex is still asleep, or if he awoke, needing to take a piss, and found himself alone. If he found her note, and maybe he's on his way right now, speeding through the deserted Birmingham streets in the rented Honda. She switches on the flashlight long enough to read her wristwatch and then switches it off again. Almost four A.M., and she's starting to think the dream was only a dream, that the call in the airport was only a prank, and there's no one named Archer Day. In a few hours, the sun will rise, and that will be the end of it, and she can go home.

Her ass is beginning to go to sleep, the floor's so cold, so goddamned hard, and so she shifts her weight, lifting herself up with both hands just long enough to restore blood flow. A floorboard beneath her left hand pops loudly, and she almost loses her balance and topples over.

Outside, there's a sound like a dog rooting about in the bushes, a dog snuffling along the edge of the house, and Daria sits very still listening to it and looking at the loose board and wondering why her heart is beating so fast. Something Niki told her on the way to Boulder, before they stopped talking about Spyder Baxter, something that she'd almost forgotten. That Spyder sealed off this room after Robin broke in to steal the dream catcher.

There were things in there, Niki said, *secrets, parts of herself no one else was ever meant to see.*

Outside, the snuffling sounds stop, and Daria hears something trotting away through the tall brown weeds.

She nailed sheets of plywood over the door and filled the cracks with epoxy. She didn't ever want anyone going in that room again.

Daria pries away the loose board, tearing spiderweb veils and disturbing a large black beetle that makes an angry, clicking noise and races away across the floor. She turns on her flashlight again and shines it into the narrow space the slat concealed.

She even boarded up all the windows. And then she hung that fucking dream catcher on the door, like a warning, and Daria remembers the way that Niki said "dream catcher," like someone uttering the name of a devil or the single most potent word in a curse. And the beam of the flashlight shows her more spiderwebs and dust, another black beetle with sharp, pinching jaws, and the warped and mildewed wedge of an old spiral-bound notebook.

Parts of herself no one else was ever meant to see, Daria thinks in Niki's voice, as she takes the notebook from the hole in the floor. The cover's in bad shape, but she can tell that there was once a picture of the Pink Panther printed on it. She lays it on the floor and opens it carefully, but a lot of the pages are stuck together, and mold and insects have eaten away most of whatever was once written there. A child's handwriting, gray words printed neatly between blue lines, and at the top of the first page Daria can make out "My Stories by Lila Baxter" and in the upper right-hand corner, "August 7, 1976."

"My God," Daria whispers and slowly turns another page, imagining all the summers and winters this notebook has lain here in the darkness, how many years must have passed since the last time Spyder put it back into the hole and covered her hiding place with that loose board. Maybe not since she was a child, and Daria does the math in her head, trying to guess how old Spyder might have been in 1976. There's page after page after page of her handwriting, the paper filled from top to bottom. Most of it's too far gone to read, just bits and pieces of fairy tales, from what Daria can see, a hash of make-believe names, magical amulets and trolls and witches.

She turns another page, then has to set the flashlight down so she can tease it free from the page before it, and the two separate with a dry crackling and a puff of dust and mold spores. There's very little writing on this page, but there's a drawing made in colored pencils. Daria picks the flashlight up again, revealing a sketch of a beautiful, dark-skinned woman holding some sort of glowing sphere in her hands. On her shoulder is a white bird with scarlet eyes, and behind her are the forms of other women, all dressed in long red robes. Over it all, a fearsome dragon hovers, its bat-wings spread wide against a blazing sky. At the very bottom of the page is a single line of text: *The Hierophant Leading the Red Witches into Battle.*

"Oh Jesus," Daria whispers, "Jesus fucking Christ," sudden understanding like fire behind her eyes, and she reaches into the pocket of her leather jacket, and her fingertips brush the ball bearing from the truck stop.

And then there are footsteps in the hallway, and when Daria looks up from the notebook, a lean and haggard woman is standing in the doorway, pointing a pistol at her. The woman's face and clothes are streaked with dirt and what appears to be dried blood.

"The wheels do turn," she says and smiles a weary, sleepy smile. "They sure as hell got that part right."

CHAPTER ELEVEN

Wishfire

Niki bends over the globe, studying the sculpted forests and marshes and ancient battlegrounds, the hills and lakes, the varicose network of roads and rivers; rotating circles held within rotating circles, like the vision of Ezekiel. She's counted the circles several times and is certain that there are only twelve, beginning at the Palisades and moving inward to the Dragon's hub. And maybe twelve means something, something that she should understand, and if she *did*, then everything could go another way. But she doesn't understand, if there's even anything there beyond the random languages of this cosmos.

All the red witches have gone now, except Pikabo Kenzia. She wanted Scarborough sent away, because men are not permitted in the towers, but Niki insisted that he stay. "He stays, or I go *with* him," she said, and Pikabo didn't argue. "And I'll need to ask him questions," Niki added, "so you'll have to let him speak."

"Our rules are old," Pikabo Kenzia protested. "They were handed down to us by the thralls of Dezyin before the first stones were laid at Yärin."

"Is that thing there supposed to be Dezyin?" Niki asked her and pointed at the idol, and the red witch nodded her head. "Well, no disrespect, but unless Dezyin's going to come to life and deal with this crap himself, Scarborough stays, *and* he gets to talk whenever I need him to. No, whenever he *feels* like it."

And once again, Pikabo Kenzia relented, but Niki could see there was a limit to her ability to make concessions and perhaps it had been reached.

Niki traces the Serpent's Road with the index finger of her good hand and tries not to notice the way the wound in her right has begun to throb again. The road starts at the edge of a line of steep, wooded hills not far from Nesmia Shar, but that would still leave nine bands she'd have to cross before reaching the hub.

"It would take you months," Pikabo Kenzia said when Niki asked, "*if* the bridges were all with you. If they were against you, it might require years, and do not forget, Hierophant, the jackals are abroad, and the *angels,* who hold their reins. You'd never make it."

Niki looks over at Scarborough, who's sitting on the floor a few feet away. "What do you know about numbers?" she asks him.

"You mean like mathematics?"

"No, I mean like numerology."

"A little. More than you might think."

"Then impress me. Tell what twelve means."

Scarborough frowns and makes a derisive, snorting noise. "Vietnam, the lady's already told you, there's only one way to get your ass from here to there quickly and in one piece. You're grasping at straws—"

"Does twelve *mean* anything?"

Scarborough Pentecost shrugs and stares up at the strips of fabric suspended overhead. "Twelve means lots of things, in *our* world. It's the zodiac, twelve signs on the house cusps. There are twelve members of the Dalai Lama's council, and Jesus and Mithra both had twelve apostles. The Hebrews say there are twelve fruits growing on the Tree of Life and twelve gates into the Heavenly City. Herodotus wrote that there were twelve gods and goddesses on Olympus. Do you want me to keep going, or are you starting to get the picture? And anyway, you've got thirteen levels there, not twelve. You have to count the hub."

"Then what does thirteen mean?"

But this time Scarborough only laughs at her and shakes his head.

"I have shown you the only way," Pikabo Kenzia says firmly. "Soon, the Weaver will have discovered where you are, and once she arrives—"

"There *has* to be another way," Niki mutters and goes back to the map, as if she could somehow close the distance between the third band and the hub by force of will alone. "I won't accept that someone has to die to get me there. You've already killed one woman, to get me *here*."

"There is no other way," the red witch replies, "not in the time remaining. And if the Weaver finds you, if the portal is opened, the number of people who will die because of you is beyond reckoning."

"Why don't you just fucking *do* it?" Scarborough asks the red witch, but she doesn't respond, stands glaring down at him, and the look on her face like she would kill him this very minute if she could. "You didn't need her permission when you snatched us off that ship, so why the hell do you think you need it now?"

"Shut up, Scarborough," Niki tells him, wishing she'd never insisted that he be allowed to speak, and then she walks around to the opposite side of the globe, turning her back on Pikabo Kenzia.

"Twelve," she whispers. "Thirteen. Twelve and thirteen. There *has* to be something here that I'm missing."

"Yeah," Scarborough says, "the obvious."

Pikabo Kenzia goes to Niki's side and rests a hand on the shoulder of her blue fur coat. "We're almost out of time, Hierophant. The Weaver *must* be very near."

"What about twelve *and* thirteen," Niki asks Scarborough, ignoring the red witch. "What do they mean *together*?"

"Twenty-five," Scarborough replies unhelpfully.

"There's no other way," Pikabo Kenzia says again, and

now she grasps Niki firmly by both shoulders and turns her away from the stone globe until they're standing eye to eye. "We're reaching the end, and we must accept the costs of taking the one option which has been left to us."

"You *said* that it's my choice," Niki snarls and pulls free of the red witch's grip, surprised at the woman's strength. "That's what you said. That it had to be *my* choice."

"How you face the Dragon and the Weaver, that's where your choice lies. Perhaps you misunderstood—"

"*No.* You will *not* force me to let some woman be sacrificed to this Dezyin bastard just so I get an express ticket to Hell. I'm not fucking worth another life."

"No," the red witch agrees, "you're not." There are thick blood-tears gathering at the corners of her eyes again, and Niki watches as the frustration drains swiftly from Pikabo Kenzia's purple irises and realizes too late that what has replaced it is decision.

"You're just gonna have to forgive me for this, Vietnam," Scarborough says, and then his hand comes down hard across the base of her skull, and there's an instant of pain, and then, for a while, only the unacknowledged peace of oblivion.

In some silly horror movie, Daria thinks, she might have fought Archer Day for the gun. Or they could have struggled on the basement stairs, and maybe Daria would have pushed her, or she might have fallen on her own. In a horror movie, she might not have handed over the ball bearing the first time the woman asked for it. And in a horror movie, Alex would be pulling into the weedy driveway at the end of Cullom Street with the police right behind him.

But she knows this isn't a movie, and this time it isn't a dream, either, and she stands in the unreal blue light filling the space below the house, the pistol's barrel pressed to her spine, and watches as the wet and mewling thing tears itself free from the black cocoon on the ceiling.

"Daria Parker, meet Theda," the woman says. "Theda, *this* is the Hierophant's bitch-dyke whore, Miss Daria

Parker, who came here—all the way from California—just to save the world. Hell, you know what? I bet Theda here has all your records," and she pushes Daria nearer the circle drawn on the cellar floor.

"Where's Niki?" she asks, trying not to look at what's inside the circle.

"Oh, so far away from *here*, my lady," Archer Day chuckles and jabs Daria in the ribs with the gun. Then she begins to sing in a high and hitching voice, " '*Far, far away is my love of yesterday, She's gone, gone, gone, gone, from me, from me—*' "

"I fucking *gave* you what you wanted. I gave you what you fucking *asked* for."

"Yeah, you did, and just look at how well that's working out for you," and then she starts singing again, an old Roy Orbison song that Niki used to ask Daria to play when she was still just doing bars and nightclubs. *Far, far away is my love of yesterday,* and something, or everything, about Archer Day's voice makes her sorry that she ever believed Niki was insane.

"You're not telling me because you don't know."

And Archer Day tangles her fingers in Daria's short hair and jerks her head back sharply so that she's staring directly into the eight, unblinking ebony eyes of the thing writhing on the ceiling. Daria feels cold metal behind her right ear, the pistol pressed to the soft flesh of her neck, and *Close your eyes,* she thinks. *Close your eyes so you won't have to see it.*

"Personally, I think poor Theda's getting a lot more than she bargained for."

"Is Niki dead?"

"Well, I know there's at least one coroner in San Francisco that'll swear to it. But then you people seem to have an awfully narrow view of life and death. Now, open your eyes."

But Daria keeps them shut tight, too far past even the desire to simply survive, because she'd always have the memory of the black thing on the ceiling and the mess inside the circle. Because she'd never be able to forget the sound of this madwoman's voice, and whatever Archer Day intends to do to her, Daria knows that she's going to do it, regardless.

"I said to open your fucking eyes, *bitch*. Don't you *want* to see this? Imagine, two universes touching across the void—"

"The man who called me in Atlanta," Daria interrupts, wishing there were some way to shut out the sounds of it all, as well as the sights, "the man who wanted me to find Niki, so he wouldn't have to hurt her—"

"—is dead. Plans changed, and he was never very flexible. Why won't you open your eyes? You're going to die, anyway."

"I *know* that."

"Then wouldn't it be better to witness such wondrous events first—the birth of a goddess, the Dragon's coming, the beginning of the end? A few marvels to keep you company through infinity?"

"Thanks," Daria hisses between gritted teeth, "but I think I'll pass," and Archer Day curses and shoves her; she stumbles and falls hard near the edge of the circle.

"Don't you *dare* fucking presume to judge me," the woman snaps and pulls the trigger. Trapped inside the basement, the gunshot is earsplitting, thunder in a bottle, and the dirt floor a few inches from Daria's left knee explodes. She begins scrambling backwards, away from the circle and the thing on the ceiling and the crazy woman with the gun.

"Daria Parker, you cannot begin to imagine the sacrifice, what this has cost me, what I've given up—"

There's a sound then from the thing hanging above the circle, and even through the ringing in her ears the sound makes Daria think of a watermelon splitting slowly open, and suddenly the basement air smells like shit and ammonia. And now she looks, following an instinct stronger than the knowledge that she doesn't *want* to see, some undeniable, primal twinge, and for this moment, she's only a very

small and frightened creature huddled in the trees while
hungry reptilian giants stride past.

"My life, my calling, *everything* which I'd ever believed
and held sacred, I let them take it *all* from me," but now
Archer Day and her gun seem far away, small concerns, at
most, and there's no room left in Daria for anything more
terrible than the burst cocoon and what's crawled out of it.
It crouches over the puddle of meat and bone inside the
circle and begins to feed.

"For *you,* I did that, so don't you dare fucking judge me,
whore!" and she pulls the trigger again. This time the bullet grazes Daria's left shoulder before it buries itself deep
in the basement wall.

She screams and covers her ears with both hands.

And the black thing stops eating and raises its head.
Eight eyes deeper than the sea, more secret than eternity,
watch her briefly before it turns towards Archer Day. What
Daria sees in its face, all it has told her without uttering a
single word, is enough to wipe away the faintest hope that
she might somehow survive this, that she would ever *want*
to survive this.

"That's enough," she whispers to herself or whatever's
listening, no more room left inside her for revelation or
horror or the damning perspective that follows either. And
she crawls to the basement wall and stops because there's
nowhere left to go.

"What the fuck are *you* looking at?" Archer Day asks
the thing crouched inside the circle. "Isn't this exactly what
you wanted? Isn't this Heaven, little girl?" and the ball
bearing clutched in her left hand has begun to glow, a hot
light like melting iron, light that might be red or orange,
but everything's the wrong color down here. There's steam
rising from her hand, but she doesn't seem to notice, all her
attention focused on the black thing staring out at her from
the circle.

"You're the *lucky* one, Theda. You're the lucky, lucky little goth girl who went looking for transcendence, and now
you've found it in spades, wouldn't you say?"

I won't see this, Daria thinks. *I won't look,* but her eyes are open wide, and she doesn't turn away, doesn't hide her face in the sanctuary of her own shadow.

Inside the circle, the black thing makes a strangled, gurgling sound, and the cat's cradle of its jaws opens wide.

Light has begun to seep from the empty cocoon or chrysalis; a liquid light like careless drops of mercury, yet no color that Daria has ever seen before, some shade a little or a lot too far beyond one side or the other of the visible spectrum. But she's *seeing* it now, anyway. It splashes across the high spines on the back of the black thing and trickles down its emaciated xylophone sides, though the creature doesn't seem to notice. It doesn't turn away from Archer Day, who suddenly looks more frightened than insane. She's raised her gun again and is pointing it at the thing's open mouth.

"Oh no, you little cunt. *I* get to go home. *That's* the goddamn deal, and we're playing by the rules."

Daria silently begs herself to shut her eyes, shut them quick while there's still time not to see what's coming next, but she doesn't close them, as though she's forgotten how to work her lids.

The thing from the cocoon opens its spindle jaws wider still and sprays Archer Day with some viscous, oily fluid, a living stream like the purest, darkest night, like the aching, barren distance between stars, erupting from its throat. Her body shudders once before she sinks slowly to her knees, and the ball bearing rolls out of her hand towards the edge of the circle drawn in the earth. And the creature turns back towards Daria, cold night dribbling from its skull. Beyond it, the ball bearing glows, a tiny sun dropped in the dust.

Archer Day slumps back against the basement wall and lies still.

Daria manages to keep her eyes on the ball bearing, surely the lesser of three evils. The earth around it has begun to burn the same indescribable color as the stuff oozing out of the cocoon, and the fire spreads quickly.

* * *

Niki wonders how long there have been slivers shining through the soothing nothingness, how long there has been *something* to mar the exquisite absence of anything. The singularly when-where consciousness began again, and all these intruding thoughts take longer than she expected them to; before they're done, the slivers have become radiant gashes and ugly strands and clots of existence are spilling through. If she had a needle and thread, or knew a little of the red witches' magic, perhaps she could seal them up again. Then she could float nowhere for a trillion billion years until there are no universes left that want any part of her. But she doesn't, never mind that she's the Hierophant, she doubts she could pull a rabbit out of a hat, even if she'd put it there first. She clutches in vain at the shreds of nothing coming apart all around her.

"Time to get on with it," Danny Boudreaux whispers from one of the clots or strands, and this is not the cruel spectre of Danny that haunted her in San Francisco. This is simply Danny, the boy who might have become the girl she could have spent her life with, if she hadn't been so afraid. "If we could lie in bed all day," he says, "if we could lie in bed all day listening to the people in the street. Remember that guy who used to wander up and down Ursulines shouting, 'The monkeys are coming! Repent! The monkeys are coming!'?"

And she does, as the variegated waves of being wash over her, like frothy ocean waves around her knees. But she doesn't answer him, and she doesn't know why.

"You were always the strong one, Niki," he says, and she imagines his smile. She wants to tell him that's not true, that she isn't strong, and she's never *been* strong, no matter what's happened or what people have expected of her. But there are strings now, as if she's tumbled into a black room crisscrossed wall to wall and ceiling to floor with countless lengths of kite string dipped in glow-in-the-dark tempera paint or, no, *not* string, but fiber optic filaments in all the hues that roses grow—deep reds and pale pinks, snow and cream and vivid yellow fringed with vermeil—and if she moves, if she so much as *breathes*, she might sever a strand and bring it all down on her head.

"Mind you, this is only a representation," Dr. Dalby tells her. "A rude cartoon, if you will."

The filaments begin trading their colors, a game of musical chairs or a Halloween masquerade for the cast of the chaotic eternal inflation, carnival bulbs flashing first one delirious color and then another, and this is better than any acid or mushroom trip or schizoid hallucination, she thinks, even if it is only a representation.

Beyond the event horizon, the gashes have become gaping holes, drawing her ever nearer their rotting ivory teeth. The flashing strings part to let her pass, though she wishes that they wouldn't.

"Wait," Spyder calls out, and Niki looks back, and her heart breaks again, and again, and again, at the beauty of the white, white woman who had once been someone she loved. The filaments are winding themselves into Spyder's gown and dreadlocks, and the red gem between her eyes devours them alive.

"You go so far with a thing, Niki, there's no turning back. Do you know what I mean?"

"I think so. But maybe there *is* a turning back. I just turned my head to see you, didn't I?"

"There's no *direction* here," Spyder mutters, annoyed, like Niki should have known that.

"But you know what I *mean*," Niki insists. "I know you know. What they've told me, is it true? Is that why you brought me here?"

"My father was a serpent. My father was an old snake in a tree with apples and candy and razor-blade Bible pages to cut my hands."

"He was only your father. And he's dead now. He isn't the Dragon. Not *this* dragon."

"You've been listening to old Pikabo. I knew you had."

And Niki realizes that she's feeling *pulled*, caught in the competing, evenly matched gravities of Spyder and the reality holes. *They'll rip me in half like a theater ticket,* she thinks and wonders if it will hurt as much as she imagines.

"With the Nesmidians, we could have killed him. We could have killed him here, and none of this would have been necessary. She sees nothing but balance, Niki, balance at any cost."

"You would set the Dragon loose in our world?"

"*This* is our world. What is there back there worth saving? Tell me that, why don't you? Name just one thing."

And Niki doesn't have to think. "Daria," she says immediately, and there are other things, more than she could list in a lifetime, but she can see from Spyder's expression and the way the strings are winking out around her that there's no point in continuing.

"She has betrayed you. You know she has. You know she doesn't want you around anymore."

"But that doesn't mean that I don't still love her," Niki says, words that cut her tongue, her lips, the deepest parts of her soul, but they're true words, and she clings to them. "It doesn't matter if she doesn't love me."

"Then you're a fool."

"Let me go, Spyder. I won't do this for you. I won't fight the Dragon for you."

Galaxies swirl in the irises of Spyder's angry, pale eyes, supernovae and blue giants, and Niki knows that the holes, which have now become

a single
hole,

 {horizon} (tidal gravity)

are winning the tug-of-war. And she wishes that Scarborough had hit her just a little harder.

"Without the Dragon, this world would be perfect," Spyder says.

"There's no dragon where we came from, and it's not

perfect," Niki replies, and now the things in Spyder's eyes are unrecognizable.

"There are dragons everywhere. There are serpents and dragons and devils."

"I won't do it," Niki tells her again, and then she's falling, which means there must be direction, after all, maybe direction that's only just come into being. Not so very different than

the
fall
from
the bridge

and she watches Spyder

d
     i
         m
           i
              n
                 i
                   s
                     h

falling the *other* way, until she's become only a bright

speck,

a particularly white star all but lost among the infinity of twinkling worldlines.

I'm near
the edge
now.

she thinks, but isn't at all sure what she means.

And then Niki slips through the breach, dropped back

into her body so hard that her teeth clack together and she bites her tongue. The salty, metallic taste of blood, iron molecules torn from hemoglobin and dissolving like Communion wafers on her tongue.

My mother was Catholic, my father was an old serpent, but no, that last part was Spyder, not her, and she has to remember that if she's to do this one last thing.

The temple at Nesmia Shar, that enormous, somber room of gray stone, flashes before her eyes like an epileptic slideshow. Images flickering lightspeed across her retinas, engulfed by her shrinking-swelling-shrinking-swelling pupils, and now oblivion seems very, very distant.

The red witches, assembled before the towering, graven image of Dezyin, their glowering griffin, gryphon, *gryphus, grypgryps* that isn't, neither half lion nor half eagle. The air of the chamber clouded with incense and the vocal press of chanting. The idol's eyes blaze almost as bright as Spyder's did.

Pikabo Kenzia, solemn and fearful and beautiful in her sage-colored skullcap, and all her sisters and daughters spread out around her like fallen autumn leaves set afire, smoldering, bleeding the smothering fumes of herbs and dung and amber.

And there I am, Niki thinks, spotting her naked self stretched out on the stone table set at Dezyin's taloned feet. One of the women with a white bandana tied around her hair stands on the table near her, and the sight fills Niki with something worse than helplessness or sorrow. She would slither right back into the place of strings, if she knew the way.

"We ask nothing of you, daughter, that you have not already pledged," Pikabo Kenzia says, and the woman standing beside Niki takes off her crimson robes, and they fall to the floor, revealing skin as white as bone. "You are brave, and you will shame us all with your forfeiture. By your sacrifice might worlds be saved."

No! Niki screams, but her lips are as still as the lips of the dead. *Not for me, goddamn it! Don't let her die for me!*

The flicker across her eyes, and she raises a hand to cover them, the hand that the Dragon opened and curled up inside so long ago now that it seems like lifetimes passed and passed again, and now she can see that there are things *growing* in there. Not maggots, but the things that maggots worship, and they are eating her, one tiny mouthful at a time.

And she can see *through* her hand, as well, as though it were only glass or plastic that no maggot-god would ever want to taste. The flat-world globe has been replaced by the fire pit, and the naked woman in the white bandana stands at the top of the long iron trough. An old woman is painting Niki's skin with elaborate runes or ideograms, blood to ink, and for just a second, Niki thinks the characters might be Vietnamese.

Pikabo Kenzia draws a great, curved knife from her own robes, and the firelight glints brightly off its blade.

"The body of woman is like a flash of lightning," she chants, "existing only to return to nothingness. Like the summer growth that shrivels in winter. Waste thee no thought on the process, for it has no purpose, coming and going like dew."

Fuck this! Niki screams at the red witch. *Fuck you all!* but even she can't hear herself. The old woman has finished dabbing the runes across her breasts and stomach and thighs, and she lays the dried corpse of a small turquoise lizard across Niki's forehead.

"Like a wall, a woman's body constantly stands on the verge of collapse," Pikabo continues, "and still, the world buzzes on like angry bees. Let it come and go, appear and vanish, for what have we to lose?"

Neither awake nor dreaming, Niki Ky stands before Dezyin, and blood drips from its sickle, raptor beak. Its wings give birth to typhoons. "I am *not* your daughter," she screams, "and you don't get *anything* in my name!" but the god ignores her, as gods do, and leers hungrily down at the offering standing at its feet.

And Pikabo Kenzia's arm swings round in an arc, drawing a vicious quarter circle, as her silver blade cuts the thick and smoky air.

And the god thing smiles, satisfied, ready to grant Pikabo's wish.

Obsidian against skin, and the woman's belly opens wide, spraying blood and releasing her intestines. And her scream wriggles up through the miasma of holy scents and the smoke and the swooping tapestry shreds suspended overhead. Not mute like Niki, this woman, and she screams again as the red witch's knife continues to take her apart.

Her blood rushes down the trough and sizzles loudly in the fire pit.

And Niki feels herself

slipping

again.

Her mind anchored nowhere firm, no tether to her sleeping body, and this time it's Dezyin, the old grifter whom the witches *call* Dezyin, who moves her like a wooden marionette.

The fish augur's spells, and Spyder's angels.

Dr. Dalby's pills and books.

The Dragon's jackals.

The witches' flimflam man.

And the strings pull taut again as the dying girl crumples to the stone table, her eyes glazed with shock, eyes gone blank as any slaughter's, and Pikabo Kenzia raises her knife again.

The blood, and the meaty smell of boiling blood, the chanting women and the drying lines traced on Niki's body, all these and a thousand other things for strings. *Will you, won't you, will you, won't you, won't you join the dance?*

And the temple dissolves around her and, rising into that alien night, those Van Gogh stars, Niki looks down at moonlight rippling over the waters of the Yärin and falling on the ruins of the temple a thousand years from this moment, as the forest reclaims the stubs of shattered towers.

Will you, won't you, will you, won't you

dance the ghost with me
And the wheels turn.

Daria lies on the dirt floor of the basement, curled fetus-small and round, watching as the flames from the ball bearing spread, consuming earth and wood and anything else they touch, and there is no smoke or burning sounds, and there is no heat.

Do not fail her. The Hierophant will need you, at the end, and the black thing trapped inside the circle turns towards her and gurgles, as though her thoughts have grown so loud she may as well be screaming them through a bullhorn. When Archer Day fell, the blue glow illuminating the cellar flickered out, and now there's only the strange light from the cocoon and the fire. It shimmers across the creature's glossy hide, skin like living latex, across eight eyes that are all pupil. She recognizes the fear in those eyes, the fear she *ought* to feel, but doesn't, because she knows she won't live through this.

She thinks the ball bearing was meant to go *inside* the circle, but that can't be helped now.

A few feet away, Archer Day's body convulses inside its contracting, hardening shell, the midnight gout from the thing's throat quickly setting around her like a polymer built somehow from the absence of matter and energy and sanity. Something from nothing, and *Yes,* Daria thinks, *something from nothing exactly,* and watches the creature's face as it tries to catch her thoughts.

She's pissed herself, and maybe that's the very worst of it.

The fire spreads to the basement ceiling, and soon it's eating away at the empty cocoon. There's a sickening smell like burning hair, but still no smoke. This fire too complete for smoke, too intent upon consuming everything.

"I don't know what to do next," she whispers. "I don't know what I'm supposed to do, Niki."

The black thing gurgles pathetically once or twice and then turns away to watch the advancing fire.

"I found it for you, Niki, and I brought it here, but now I don't know what to do. I don't know what to do but die."

Now the black thing has reared clumsily up on its splayed hind legs, and Daria realizes that it's trying to crawl back inside the flaming chrysalis. The fire accepts it like an oblation, enveloping it in a heartbeat, and the thing begins to scream with the terrified, hurting voice of a teenage girl.

"You can't even hear me, can you?" Daria asks Niki, as though she were sitting right there to answer the question. The creature stops screaming and collapses in a shriveling heap, and the fire begins to swirl around it, like a tornado trapped within the borders of the circle. Daria squints into the blazing whirlwind, the color that is no color, and wonders how long until it blinds her, how long until it devours her, too. When she closes her eyes, that alien light leaves no afterimages, and she opens them again.

And notices the child near the bottom of the basement steps. For a while, the child just stands there, indecisive, looking at Daria, and Daria thinks maybe she should tell her to run. Run for help, or just run, but she doesn't. The girl turns her head and glances up the stairs, so Daria thinks she'll run after all, until she turns back and warily descends the last few steps to the basement floor. She walks past what's left of Archer Day, staying clear of the flames, and a few seconds later, she's kneeling between Daria and the whirlwind. A silhouette against Hell, mouse-hair and eyes so blue they're almost a bruised sort of white. Her overalls are ragged and threadbare, and she's wearing nothing under them.

"You're the lady that found my book, ain't you?" she asks, and Daria feels the wet heat of the tears beginning to leak from her eyes.

"Yeah, that was me. I found your book."

"No one was ever supposed to find my book."

"I know that. It was an accident. I didn't mean to find it."

The child glances over her shoulder at the fire and then back at Daria. "I know that," she says. "Did you read it?"

"Just a little bit," and the girl reaches out and brushes Daria's wet cheek with her fingertips.

"Are you going to die here, too?" she asks.

"I don't know. What do you think I should do?"

The girl's eyes seem to spark with some inner light of their own, some suspicion or misgiving, and then she leans close and whispers in Daria's right ear.

"I'm only a moment. I can't answer questions like that," and then she sits up again.

"A moment," Daria whispers, and looks past the child at the fire, still held within the circle, but straining at its circumference.

"If you stay, I'll show you the rest," the girl says. "I have it all in here," and she touches an index finger to an angry pink-red scar between her eyebrows, a coarse sort of cross carved into her skin. "Where the angels can't ever find it."

"If I stay, will I be a moment, too?" Daria asks, wiping her eyes, sitting up, and she can see that the fire has swept over Archer Day's body, and there's no path left back to the stairs.

"You're *already* a moment," the child says, as though it's the silliest question in the world, something everyone should know without having to ask.

"And you'll stay here with me?"

"Yes," the girl says. "I'll stay here and tell you stories. I know so many. I didn't write them all down. There wasn't time."

Daria puts her arms around the child and holds her close, holds her tightly as she dares. The girl doesn't protest or struggle, only returns the embrace, and they hold each other as the silent inferno gorges itself, burning its way through the basement ceiling to the house overhead.

"Don't you be afraid," the girl tells her and rests her head on Daria's shoulder. "Niki knows what to do now, I think, even if Spyder doesn't. But don't look up, please."

And then the old house at the end of Cullom Street begins to come apart, collapsing in on itself, drawn down by the fire, and Daria does as the child's told her to do and doesn't look up.

Niki Ky stands alone near the center of the bone and wire span of the Dog's Bridge. She stares into a blistering, acid wind, trying to glimpse the other side through spiraling veils of smoke and ash and brimstone, and waits for the nausea to pass. The clothes she was given in Padnée are all gone now, and her blue fur coat and backpack, too. Instead, her body is protected, head to toe, in what she first thinks is a suit of armor, part sci-fi animé and part Hollywood Joan of Arc, but then she realizes that it isn't something that she's *wearing*. It's her own skin, changed somehow by the red witches, her skin grown smooth and shiny and jointed, a hard exoskeleton tinted the somber color of winter storm clouds—the bluest gray or grayest blue. Only her wounded right hand is unchanged; she's lost the bandage and the Dragon's bite shines red and swollen with infection. She knows now that there's a poison festering in that hand that will kill her, that will make her no more than food for the maggot-god, if something else doesn't kill her first. In her left hand is a broadsword, its tip resting on the bridge, the hilt clutched in her jointed, gauntlet fingers.

She knows that Daria's dead, because she saw that much in the shimmering, lantern-show passage from Nesmia Shar to the Dog's Bridge. And she also knows that the portal Spyder would have opened has been sealed shut at the other end. Maybe that means it's all over and done with, and now she can lie down and *really* die. Or maybe it only means that everything will be worse somehow.

Niki stares down at the sword in her hand, certain that she doesn't have even half the strength to lift such a ridiculous thing, but when she tries, it seems to weigh almost nothing at all. It might as well be a child's sword of cardboard and aluminum foil, and she holds it up so that the broiling light of this place gleams hot across the blade.

"A sword," she says incredulously, and the greedy wind

snatches at her voice. "A goddamned sword." Behind her lies the interior limit of the final counterclockwise turning band, and ahead of her are the scabby hills and igneous wastes of the hublands, and the Dragon, too, waiting for her deep inside the ruins of Melán Veld. But Niki knows that the red witches haven't given her the sword and this armored skin for fighting the Dragon. When she looks to the far side of the bridge again, she sees Spyder walking slowly across the bones towards her, and Niki bends over and lays the sword down in front of her, because she isn't going to use it against Spyder, either.

"It's over!" Niki shouts, shouting to be heard above the roaring wind, and Spyder stops and gazes up at the low, sulphurous clouds. Niki follows her gaze and notices the Weaver's portal for the first time, a point not very far above the bridge where the clouds have begun to swirl, a nascent, inverted cyclone, and she looks back at Spyder.

"It is fucking *over*!" she screams, but Spyder only shrugs and starts walking again; in another minute or two, she's standing in front of Niki.

"Did the witches do that to you?" she asks and points at the shiny new skin. "Not half bad."

"Listen to me, Spyder. Something's happened. The portal's been sealed shut from the other side. Can't you feel it?"

"Yeah. Daria's failed you again," Spyder Baxter says and looks down at the sword lying on the bridge between them. "I'd hoped, when the Nesmidian's mole got cold feet and jumped sides like that, that *she* might see that the philtre reached its nexus. But no, she was a fuck-up, too." And when Spyder raises her head again, Niki sees that her pale blue eyes have gone a luminous, opalescent ultramarine, a blue so bright and piercing that Niki can hardly stand to face it.

"It doesn't matter anymore," she says. "Even if you could lure the Dragon into that thing, and even if I'd help, or even if you don't *need* me, there's nowhere for it to go."

"As long as the fire burns and a single stick of that house

remains, there's time, Niki. As long as the surrogate's ashes are caught up in the tempest, there's time. So, no, it's *not* over, not just yet."

"Spyder—"

"Is that thing meant for me?" Spyder asks and kicks at the sword. "Is that the best they could come up with? A sword? Do you think it's at least magical?"

"I'm *not* going to fight you. I don't care how many women died to send me here."

Spyder's blue eyes flare, bleeding so much color that Niki has to look away. "Well, you can't sit on the sidelines this time. And I can't let you go on thinking that you can. It's like Bob Dylan said, you know? You gotta serve somebody, and it might be the devil or—"

"Then I serve *me*," Niki says and reaches for the sword. But Spyder kicks it, and the weapon goes spinning end over end and comes to a stop mere inches from the edge of the Dog's Bridge.

"Nope. Sorry. That's not one of the options. It's either me or the Dragon. And that old cunt Pikabo can't help you this time."

"You *used* me," Niki growls and hits Spyder hard, slaps her, and Niki can feel bone and teeth breaking beneath the blow, beneath the hammer that the exoskeleton has made of her hand. Blood spurts from Spyder's nostrils, pours from her lips, and she staggers backwards a step or two and shakes her head like a stunned animal. Her blood spatters across the cracked, bleached bones at their feet, thick drops that quickly turn to glittering beads of crimson glass. She spits out part of a tooth, and it lands near Niki's right foot.

"Nice piece of work, Pikabo," Spyder mumbles and spits again, more blood and so, in only a moment, more red glass. "But it doesn't make any difference."

"The Dragon *belongs* here," Niki says. "You're the one who doesn't. You and me both."

"Nothing belongs *anywhere*. Nothing's ever anything but what we *choose* to make it, what we have the *resolve* to make it."

The bridge lurches and shudders beneath them, a million bones all set to rattling at once, and a geyser of flame a thousand feet high rises from the molten sea off to Niki's right.

"He's coming," Spyder says, and she laughs. "And he won't be alone, Niki. Oh, no, my father is a serpent, and he'll bring his lieutenants, Michael and Gabriel, Raphael and Uriel and the rest of the mangy lot, and their jackals that hunt the Nephilim, and he'll bring other things, beings you can't even begin to imagine."

"No, Spyder. The Dragon isn't your father. And there are no angels here. Maybe *it* thinks these things are true, but that's only because you taught it to believe them," and Niki glances quickly at the sword lying near the edge of the rattling, swaying bridge. Spyder catches her looking at it and smiles.

"*So* . . . maybe you want to fight after all," she whispers, and wipes blood and flecks of glass from her face. "Go on ahead. Get it, if that's what you want. I'm not going to try to stop you. But you better hurry. There's not much time."

"I loved you. I don't think you have any idea how much I loved you."

"You think I don't love you? I fucking left, I came *here*, because it was the only place I could be and not hurt you. I'd already hurt so many people, Niki. After Robin—"

The bridge shudders again, and the geyser of fire falls back into the sea, only to be replaced by another.

"Listen to me, Spyder—"

"—I wasn't going to let him have you, too. I wasn't going to let anyone else die just so he could keep hurting *me*."

"You didn't kill Robin. She tried to get to the dream catcher. She broke into the house, and the black widows in the tank killed her, or they made her so sick she froze to death."

"I *put* it there," Spyder snarls, and her lips are pulled back to show her broken, bloodstained teeth, and her face has become a vicious mask of fury and loss.

"You put it there to keep them all safe from him, from your father."

"No, Niki. I put it there because I was scared that they would all leave. My father was a serpent—"

"Your father was only a *man*, Spyder. A very sick man who thought he saw angels, who hurt you because he was crazy and thought you wouldn't let him go to Heaven. You told me that yourself."

Far away, somewhere in the hublands, in the stony bowels of Melán Veld, something gargantuan stirs, awakening from endless nightmares, and the horizon burns white as the heart of a kiln, the fissioning heart of a nuclear explosion, and the sky is filled with the blare of trumpets.

And suddenly the pain in Niki's hand has become almost unbearable, and she bites her lip to keep from screaming. As if answering the Dragon's call, her wounded hand has begun to change as something cancerous bubbles from the hole in her palm. A blackness to reshape her bones and flesh and skin, and in only another moment it's reached the place where the blue-gray exoskeleton ends at her wrist and has begun to melt through her armor.

"There's no more time," Spyder says. "You have to make your choice now."

Niki gasps, struggling against the pain to drag enough breath into her lungs that she can speak, but her voice is only a hoarse whisper. "I've already made my choice, Spyder."

And as a third fountain of lava rises from the magma sea that divides the hub from the wheels, the Dog's Bridge shakes so violently that cables snap and sections of the high piers begin to crumble and fall. Niki falls too, and lies staring up into the widening portal that Spyder's opened above the bridge. It's a sort of mouth. She can see that now. A toothless mouth of clouds and wind, and its throat runs across hyperspace infinities to a collapsed dead end. It has begun to pull at her, the same irresistible tug she felt in the place of colored strings, the pull that dragged her back into the temple by the Yärin. That pull or something close enough. She looks away from the portal and watches as Spyder walks across the swaying bridge and picks up the sword.

"I'm no good with scripture," she says. "But I think you've heard that line about plucking out the eye that offends you, or cutting off the hand, or whatever it says. At least, I think that's in the Bible. Maybe it's Shakespeare."

"Please, Spyder," Niki croaks, and glances back at the widening gyre above them. "Close it."

"You need to pay attention, Niki, because this is going to hurt. Even now, he's trying to take you away from me, and I have to stop that from happening," and Spyder kneels down beside her, the sword gripped in both her hands. "Someone really should have done this days ago."

Niki wants to ask what she's talking about, but her throat has gone too dry, her head too full of pain, and the white light approaching from the hublands, too filled with the trumpets and the portal's nagging pull on her soul.

"He wants to make you like him, because then I'll have to hate you."

Oh, Niki thinks, understanding come too late for her to do anything but turn her head to one side, her cheek pressed against the bones, and watch as Spyder struggles with the broadsword. She's using both arms, and it's still all she can do to lift it. And then Niki sees the fingerless, palpitating thing that her right hand has become, a tumor of scales and spines, and there's a single bloodred eye staring back at her as its corrosive secretions eat away at her wrist.

"I'm sorry," Spyder says and brings the sword down, severing Niki's hand at the wrist and burying the blade deep in the deck of the Dog's Bridge. The one-eyed thing squeals and tries to wriggle away, but Spyder catches it and flings it over the side, into the flames.

And the pain is gone.

Niki turns her head to face the yawning, rotating maw of the portal again.

"It had to be done," Spyder says. "You'll be stronger now. You'll *see.*"

"Yes," Niki murmurs, tasting blood and bile, and *This is what I do now,* she thinks clearly. *This is what happens next, and then it will end.*

And the absolute gravity of the portal pulls her from herself, tears her from the dying shell of her body, and she doesn't try to fight.

This is how the story ends, and she only regrets that Spyder will never grasp *why* this is how the story ends, and that Daria is dead, and those women sacrificed in the temple of the red witches, and Marvin will have to find another girl to save from the wolves. The portal draws her in like a lover, the last and most perfect lover that she'll ever know. Niki can hear Spyder screaming down on the bridge, Spyder shaking her limp body, and she can also hear the trumpets of the angels, and the armies of the Dragon pushing their way towards the Dog's Bridge.

And then the portal closes, sealing itself shut around her.

You are brave, Niki thinks, remembering Pikabo's Kenzia's chant, *and you will shame us all with your forfeiture. By your sacrifice might worlds be saved.*

But the red witch never would have understood this either; Niki knows that. She can feel the cloud walls of the portal beginning to close in about her as she ends the storm that Spyder began, and knows that the portal is sealed at both ends. And without her, or the philtre, or the house on Cullom Street, Spyder will never build another. Niki opens her arms wide as galaxies swirl about her, *through* her, colliding and reforming, one star system cannibalizing another, and in the silent death and birth of universes, in the most infinitesimal sliver of a second, the collapsing star named Niki Ky winks out, and winks in, the pulsar rhythm of her being, and eternity rolls on.

And the mother Weaver at the blind soul of all creations *still* dreams in her black-hole cocoon of trapped light and antimatter, her legs drawn up tight about the infinitely vast, infinitely small shield of her pulsing cephalothorax.

Satisfied, she draws tight a single silken thread, one world-line held taut between her jaws, and snips it free to drift in the void. And then she collects a second, and sets it free, as well.

These things happen.

These things happen.

Her black matter spinnerets work endlessly in her sleep, dividing time from space and stitching the two together again.

And her daughters, grown to fat, long-legged spiderlings in electrostatic egg sacs laid in the spaces between worlds, emerge at last from the squeezing, oscillating tidal forces of their mother's singularity to scramble across the swirl of the hole's vast accretion disk.

And to drift free across the sky.

EPILOGUE

Land's End

Marvin flips open the rusted snaps on the battered black guitar case, flipping them up one after the next, and then he opens it. The morning sun glints unevenly off the twelve-string cradled in worn crimson velvet, shining off wood and varnish scuffed and scratched by all the years that this was the only guitar Daria Parker owned. The one she found cheap in a pawnshop and played for spare change on Pearl Street in Boulder. But she put it away in the attic when they bought the house on Alamo Square, putting away that part of her life, though sometimes Niki would sit up there alone and pick at the strings, pretending she knew how to play, or only pretending Daria was there to play for her.

He looks up at the wide sky stretched out above Horseshoe Cove, only a few shades lighter than the surging blue of the sea. The waves slam themselves against the granite edge of the continent, spraying foam and stranding fleshy stalks of kelp, and above him, the white gulls wheel and dip and cry out to one another.

The sun was barely up when Marvin left the city, locking the front door of the house on Alamo Square for the last time before he drove across the Golden Gate Bridge and then north along Highway 1, the decrepit Volkswagen sputtering and complaining all the way to Bodega Bay.

And then he turned west, towards the sea, driving until the roads finally ended, and he hiked the rest of the way, carrying the guitar case in his right hand and the brass urn with Niki's ashes tucked securely into the crook of his left arm, a small backpack strapped across his shoulders. The November sun was warmer than he'd expected, even with the northerly wind, and by the time he found the trail leading down to the water, he was tired and hot and sweaty.

He came here once before, with Niki, almost a year ago now, and they watched birds together and hunted sea urchins and anemones among the tidal pools. He likes to think that Daria would have been happy here, too, if she'd ever had the time to see it.

Marvin opens the urn and carefully transfers Niki's fine gray ashes into the hollow body of the twelve string. Then he sets the empty container down among the slippery rocks and opens his pack. There are flowers in there, only a little worse for wear; four yellow roses for Niki, yellow roses with petals fringed in red, because those were her favorites, and for Daria, a single white rose. He threads the thorny stalks of the flowers in between the guitar strings.

For days, he tried to think of something appropriate to read or say. There was a memorial service in the city, no bodies but a lot of people there who said a lot of things, mostly things about Daria and her music, and how they wished they could have gotten to know Niki better. So maybe everything's been said that needs saying.

He lifts the guitar, holding it up and out to the sun and sky and the screeching gulls, and wishes there were more of Daria here. But they found nothing in the hole burned by the fire in Birmingham, nothing at all. A fire that made CNN and MSNBC because no one had ever seen anything like it before, or anything like the hole it left in the melted limestone bedrock of the mountain. So the old Fender will have to do, and he knows that's the heart of her, anyway. Marvin stands up and casts it out into the Pacific; it lands in the water a few feet from shore, only a soft splash, and the twelve-string has become a funeral ship, its long neck for the bowsprit. He can hear the strings singing softly above the noise of the surf.

"No more wolves," he says, "for either of you."

About the Author

Caitlín R. Kiernan is the author of *Silk, Threshold, Low Red Moon, Murder of Angels,* and *Daughter of Hounds.* Her award-winning short fiction has been collected in four volumes—*Tales of Pain and Wonder; From Weird and Distant Shores; To Charles Fort, With Love;* and *Alabaster.* She lives in Atlanta, Georgia with her partner, doll maker Kathryn Pollnac.

www.caitlinrkiernan.com
greygirlbeast.livejournal.com
www.myspace.com/greygirlbeast